O'Halloran; or, *The Insurgent Chief*

An Irish Historical Tale of 1798

James McHenry

Copyright

To the memory of all those who fell in the
conflict that was intended to,

*'unite all classes of Irishmen,
without regard to religious distinction'.*

and to all on our island
who are now united for peace and reconciliation

Contents

Volume II

Publisher's Note

The original manuscript for *O'Halloran* was written over 200 years ago and first published in 1824. This edition follows that text with the addition of new forewords and supplemental reference material.

All spellings of towns, other place names, characters and odd peculiarities of the language of that time (Tygers and monied as examples) have been left as per the original text and readers may find these at odds with current usage. The prolific use of semi-colons has also been left, for the most part, and if nothing else is an insight into the editing style of the early 19th century.

Misspellings of other words within the prose that are still in common use have been amended to follow modern-day conventions, in case the reader thinks I have been remiss in my editing. However, I am also sure some may have been missed and for that I offer my apologies, whilst being harangued by the author himself, who wrote this admonishment some two centuries ago:

> *"… to deceive thee into the belief that they have been guilty only of the fact of publishing, and consequently, are not answerable for any imperfections in either the design or execution of the performances. O! sons of disingenuity and fraud, how vain are your efforts to impose on the wise people of this sagacious age? Your shallow artifices are easily seen through, and not one novel-reader in ten thousand believeth your foolish statements on this subject."*

Everyone's a critic…

I am indebted to Stephen Dornan, David Hume, Angeline King, Stephen McCracken and Claire Mitchell for their generosity in providing such insightful forewords and to Guy Beiner for his kind endorsement on the back cover. Thanks also to Marian Kelso of the Larne Museum and Arts Centre for her unstinting support of projects such as this. Lastly, to the author, Dr James McHenry, I trust you would be pleased with our efforts.

Ian Hooper

Here, by the bonds of nature feebly held,
Minds combat minds, repelling and repelled;
Ferments arise, imprison'd factions roar,
Represt ambition struggles round the shore;
Till overwrought, the general system feels
Its motions stop, or frenzy fire the wheels.
Goldsmith.

Ulster united

Ian Hooper

It is an intriguing thing to come from the North of Ireland.

For over 850 years many terms, including British, Irish and more recently, Northern Irish, have been applied to anyone who calls that piece of land home. For most of that time, and to most of those terms, someone or other has objected. The constantly contentious nature of naming 'what you are' has been joined in the last century by the troublesome matter of naming 'where you are'. Is it Northern Ireland or the North of Ireland, is it both, neither?

And yet, there is another constant that reverberates down the centuries. To be from **Ulster** seems to be a term that all, regardless of heritage or belief (spiritual or otherwise) can settle on.

I am from Ulster, is a statement that anyone from the province can claim, even if the idea of Ulster differs from one to another, not least about whether the entity they are referring to comprises six or nine counties, but let's not get dragged down another rabbit hole of difference; instead, let's concentrate on what we and history can agree on.

For it does indeed seem to be a common theme from the ancient annuals of the *Táin Bó Cúailnge* through to today, that those of us who come from Ulster are somewhat different to the rest of the peoples on this island, and it would seem that it was ever so.

Dr James McHenry was an Ulsterman. Born and bred. He was to leave Ulster's shores for America, but would return at length and subsequently die and be buried in his home town of Larne. When a boy in that town, he was witness to the events of the 1798 Rebellion and its aftermath. Like most Irish attempts at rebellion, *The '98* was a 'glorious failure' or less romantically, a disastrous calamity of violence that led to old schisms not just being reopened, but deepened, widened and having caustic poured into them.

It was not meant to be. It was meant to be a glorious uniting of the peoples, regardless of religious belief or societal caste, an affirming of the rights of 'man' as so recently established in the American Colonies and the new French Republic. It was meant to be the beginning of a New Ireland. It was meant to be different. And it arguably could have been. Especially in the province of Ulster, where almost 200,000 United Irishmen (a society founded in Belfast) were prepared for revolution. They, with pike upon their shoulder, made ready to stake their claim to a new social order, but they were undermined by various government measures in the months preceding the rebellion and, critically, by reports of religious massacres being carried out in the other provinces during the rising itself. The accuracy of the reports, the provocations, the reprisals and any other actual truth of what occurred were (and even with the distance of hindsight, still are) confused. As the adage says, the first casualty in war is the truth. In Irish History, it seems that particular casualty doesn't revive after the conflict is over. As the historian, Guy Beiner, made clear, 'For two centuries, the Turn-Out in Ulster was purposely shrouded in obscurity and buried in silence.' (2018: 42).

But of course, not completely. James McHenry, Larne-born novelist, poet and doctor, wrote about it and included details of the actions that occurred in Larne on the night of the 6th/7th June which were to be later, 'confirmed by local testimony' (LLAJ, 1839:1 in Beiner, 2018:248). And it is rather a good job that he did, for most histories of the time omit any mention of Larne. But, to be fair, most histories omit any mention of McHenry as well. Which is a shame, as James was fêted in his day, recognised as a talent and referred to on more than one occasion as the 'Bard of Larne'. Yet, when I was studying literature at my Larne school, I knew nothing of him. I was told of Thomas Hardy, Trollope, Shakespeare and Longfellow (the latter of these was well known to James) but there was no mention of McHenry.

Now, decades after my schooldays and as a Larne-born author and publisher myself, when fellow Larne author, Angeline King, drew my attention to James and the *O'Halloran*, encouraging me to re-publish the novel, I leapt at the opportunity. It may not restore Dr McHenry to a central place in the town's lore, but it may allow him to peek from the side, reminding us that he was seen as an authority on the Ulster he knew so intimately and that he so evidently loved. And if you too are from Ulster, I am sure that love for the *auld place* is something on which we can all be united.

Ian Hooper is an author, ghost-writer and the Executive Director of Latharna Press.

For references and bibliography, please refer to rear of book.

O'Halloran, McHenry and a neglected street

Angeline King

In 2020, I began working on a PhD in Creative Writing at Ulster University, with the objective of writing a diary novel.

I was researching female novelists who write in Ulster Scots or Scots when I took a little diversion to read *O'Halloran*. Although I had often seen James McHenry's name in the graveyard at St Cedma's, I wasn't quite sure what to expect from his work. After wading through a mammoth adventure novel on screen, I sent an email to my friend and publisher, Ian Hooper, to say, "I think you should publish this."

I knew that Larne people would want to read it and I knew that historians and enthusiasts of 1798 would also appreciate it. Ian, himself a Larne man, agreed with me.

O'Halloran contains an impressive record of early 1800s' Ulster Scots speech, with long passages of dialogue that might not have survived the scrutiny of a twenty-first century editor. Although my work-in-progress and *O'Halloran* are dramatically different novels, there are parallels of place and language — and perhaps even a desire to tell an alternative history. While McHenry was dissatisfied with the absence of Ulster people in Irish novels of his time, I was concerned with the female voice.

McHenry was born and raised in Larne town centre, just off Dunluce Street, an historic street that has sadly been torn asunder by neglect over the last few decades. Republishing this novel is a positive step in remembering James McHenry, the man who knew President Andrew Jackson, published Longfellow's poems and was respected in his time for his literary endeavours. Perhaps his memory and the fortunes of Dunluce Street could be revived in tandem.

Angeline King, currently Writer in Residence at Ulster University, is a novelist from Larne. Her latest novel, Dusty Bluebells, is available in both English and Ulster Scots.

Discovery, disorientation and debunking

Stephen Dornan

Not many people these days have heard of the novels of James McHenry: he is hardly a household name and even academic specialists often gloss over, or ignore, him in surveys of Irish and Scottish novels of the nineteenth century. Certainly when I first encountered his books, it seemed astonishing that they even existed.

There's something incongruous, something disorientating, something unlikely about these novels. They seemed to go against the grain and, consequently, to complicate some prevalent assumptions about modern Northern Ireland.

For example, they debunk the depressingly persistent, though slightly bizarre, myth that Ulster Protestants don't write, and the not unconnected tendency to look down on certain market towns of east Ulster as cultural backwaters. McHenry's novels also challenge the peculiar notion that Ulster Scots is a recent phenomenon: the Ulster Scots dialogue of his characters is rich, realist and authentic. Furthermore, an explicit purpose of McHenry's writing is to celebrate the cultural, linguistic and religious diversity of the island of Ireland, by conveying the distinctiveness of the north of the island. This notion of northern distinctiveness a century before 'partition' is interesting in a modern context in which many seem to believe that particular political arrangement was arbitrarily imposed out of nothing in the 1920s. Finally, McHenry's novels challenge one of modern Northern Ireland's most cherished, and structurally ingrained, assumptions: that its dynamics are the product of an intractable binary between 'two traditions'. McHenry depicts a more complex, triangular, situation with the Scottish influenced Ulster Presbyterians constituting a third, distinct cultural group.

Although the layers and combinations in James McHenry's cultural and political makeup weren't uncommon amongst his own milieu, they can be disorientating to those familiar with the dynamics of Northern Ireland's modern identity politics. McHenry was born in Larne, and died and was buried in the same town, but his life took him well beyond the parameters of east Antrim.

He trod the well-worn route of many Ulster students of his day when he studied medicine in Dublin, before completing his studies in Glasgow. This was necessary due to penal restrictions against Presbyterians graduating at Trinity College Dublin. He practised medicine in Belfast for a number of years before emigrating to America with his family. He lived in several American cities before settling in Philadelphia.

In Philadelphia he enthusiastically involved himself in various political, literary and religious controversies. For a while, he championed President Jackson, who is considered to be founder of the modern Democratic Party. He kept up a keen interest in Irish affairs as is demonstrated by his enthusiasm for the campaign for Catholic Emancipation, the consummation of which he celebrated with an effusive poem in 1830. But his interests were international and he took partisan positions on many of the key controversies of the day. He also seemed to enjoy the rough and tumble of literary controversies and took aim at English Romantic poets and Irish Romantic novelists alike. His literary career, and specifically his interest in the theatre, also clashed with conservative religious authorities and actually resulted in him being barred from taking communion in the Presbyterian church to which he belonged. Overall, McHenry's politics were rooted in a belief in democracy and popular participation in politics, in the contractarian theories of the Scottish enlightenment, in the dissenting tradition of Ulster Presbyterianism and in the idealistic belief in the expansion of liberty.

So McHenry's Ulster Presbyterianism sat alongside an international outlook, a critical view of government and a steadfast belief in the importance of religious tolerance. His Presbyterianism also co-existed with his strong Irish cultural nationalism: an open form of nationalism that rejected narrow definitions based on Gaelic ethnicity or Catholicism. His precise opinion on the brand of Irish republicanism created by people of his milieu a generation earlier, is more tricky. Certainly, in *O'Halloran* he expresses sympathy for the injustices suffered by the insurgents and admiration for their high ideals, though he stops short of uncritical outright endorsement, opting instead to emphasise the obligations both of governments and the governed.

It was in America that McHenry set about pursuing his literary ambitions. He wrote a number of novels set in Ulster, and several set in America. Besides his novels, he wrote several collections of poetry and an epic poem based on the book of Genesis. He authored a popular play which was staged in Philadelphia. He also established a literary and current affairs journal in the city. Eventually he returned to Ulster as an American citizen, in the formal capacity of American consul in Derry.

As for the novels themselves, they too can be disorientating. There are clearly aspects of the stories and descriptions that are realist. The places are familiar and many of the minor characters were real people or historical figures. And, of course, it was McHenry's intention to represent accurately the manners, character, language and politics of the Ulster communities he describes. However, he counterbalances these realist elements with novelistic devices of the period: a fictional hero with a sentimental love interest, unlikely plot coincidences and melodramatic scenarios. This mixture of elements can be disorientating for modern audiences.

When categorising James McHenry and his novels it's difficult to avoid resorting to composites: he has been read as both an Ulster Scots and an Irish American writer. This problem of categorisation, as well as tendency to defy the expectations of modern readers and critics alike, are arguably contributing factors in the neglect of his novels today. But there is much in these novels, and in *O'Halloran* in particular, that is worthy of our attention: it stands as a great story and provides a fascinating glimpse into the culture and history of Ulster as it came to terms with the intense trauma of the 1798 rebellion.

Stephen Dornan is a poet and writer with a particular interest in the Ulster Scots literary tradition.

An outstanding literary ambassador for Larne: Dr. James McHenry

David Hume MBE

Dr. James McHenry has been all but forgotten in his native town. The re-publication of his work *O'Halloran* should be a positive step in addressing this somewhat sorry state of affairs. McHenry was a writer, poet and playwright as well as a medical doctor. He introduced the first Ulster family – the Frasers – into American literature. His historical novels preserved stories of a bygone era in County Antrim. He is seen as a pioneer in what has been called 'American Frontier Gothic' literature.

How true in McHenry's context is that well-known Biblical phrase that, "A prophet is not without honour, except in his own country, among his own relatives and in his own house." His family are the exception to this; they were extremely proud of him, and his gravestone in St. Cedma's cemetery does, in fairness, refer to him as an author. In 1904 a portrait of the author was presented by Sir Hugh Smiley, on behalf of McHenry's daughter in Philadelphia, to the Larne Urban Council, but this was perhaps the last gesture that brought him to the fading attention of the wider public.

His direct family had no connection to Larne by that time, and the Smiley connection would also fade as Sir Hugh and then Lady Janet Smiley passed on. The twentieth century dimmed his memory in his native town.

But he is due a revival.

And rightly so, for there is no doubt that this was a man who loved his native soil. In September 1839 Stewart's Hotel on Larne's Main Street was the venue for a complementary supper in honour of Dr. James McHenry, when 40 gentlemen assembled to pay tribute to him and bid him farewell as he prepared to leave for the United States.

In his remarks McHenry, accompanied by his son, majored on his love of his native town: "…what native of Larne, when in foreign lands, has ever forgot to cast a long and lingering look of fond fancy on the Curran Castle, that venerable memorial of feudal times…For myself, often have I, in youthful days, lain at the foot of those interesting ruins and resigned myself to the contemplation of past ages," he told those gathered that night.

It is possible to imagine a different time, when the young McHenry walked the Curran shore, as you absorb those words. From the point of view of local history, the author and poet has much to say to us, and his reference to Curran Castle (which we can take to allude to Olderfleet as the castle ruins are known today) is a reminder of the rich history that the town holds. There were two castles in the area, Curran and Olderfleet, but the latter name has eclipsed the former in more modern generations. This is a mere footnote in comparison to the anecdotes and history which McHenry preserved in his novels.

O'Halloran and *The Hearts of Steel* are historical novels set in an extremely formative period in Ulster history; both involve the activities of radical Presbyterians who, as 'Steelboys', attacked landlord's property but more significantly threatened social revolution, and as 'United Men' attempted to turn the political world upside down in Ireland as their cousins had done in America during the Revolution. These novels bring us characters, many if not most of them, actual people, who kept their names or were given new ones by the author. But the stories are the same and they take us back to a radical time in history. The overall historical accuracy of what is presented to the reader is without question. In the context of *O'Halloran*, it is fascinating to think of the young McHenry witnessing the events around the political tensions of the 1790s and the United Irish Rising (referred to by the canny Presbyterians as the 'Turn oot') in Larne itself. Of course he builds a dramatic plot around these – he is, after all, a novelist – but the essence of the event has been distilled and bottled for us within the pages of his work.

In this alone, there is much to be thankful to James McHenry for.

The fact that he published his 'Soloman Secondsight' novel less than 30 years after the events of the Rising means that it must surely have been eagerly sought out in Larne, to ascertain who had appeared and what had been said about them. Coming from Ballycarry, I noted in my early research that the incident of the hanging of William Nelson, the 16 year-old Ballycarry martyr, had seen one name change, that of Sir Geoffrey Carebrow, who plays a leading part in condemning young Nelson to his fate. With the benefit of local knowledge, this was actually Richard Gervas Ker, who as magistrate, was said to have had the final say that June 30th of 1798 and who later referred to his tenants as a 'lawless banditti' in the weeks after the defeat of the rebels at Antrim town and Ballynahinch.

McHenry did not tax himself too much in changing the name – Ker became Carebrow, the author telling us that, "The real name of this personage is but little disguised by that given him in the novel; and in consideration of the respectable connexions shall not be more precisely expressed here."

As an Ulster Scot historian, I enjoy the author's forays into the language and speech of the people whom he obviously knew in the Larne of old. There is Peg Dornan's, "Fare fa' ye" greeting for one instance, and another good example is the line, "Come in awee, an' tak' a dram," said Jemmy, "an' I'll gang wi' you directly." In *The Wilderness*, Gilbert Fraser has a dialogue with a young Philadelphian whose grandparents were from Londonderry:

"Then ye hae been in Ireland, sir?"

"Yes: within these last six months I sailed from Londonderry."

"Frae Derry! Frae Derry! – An' hoo did the auld country an' the aul city look? An were ye at Maugherygowan too, dootless?"

"Yes, I spent part of the last winter there."

"An' was every thing the same? Ah! I doot na, there are mony changes there syne I saw it. But I need na ask sae fool a question frae you, that was na then in the lan' o' the leevin."

There are other scattered uses of the Ulster Scots of McHenry's native area;

"I think Miss O'Halloran will noo be tired waitin'; I maun see her hame."

"Why, she's gane lang since," said the sentinel.

"Maybe sae, an' maybe no'. I'll see wha's within, however," replied Hunter. There is also the use of words such as Ken, Oot, Rin, Stap, Brocht, Wad na, and Sae. Like the Ballycarry Bard, James Orr before him, McHenry is reflecting what he hears around him and the language that the people were speaking, a hybrid Ulster Scots which had been eroded over generations by the much more dominant English language, the linguistic cousin of Ulster Scots. One does wonder how readers not familiar with the dialect managed to cope with some of the dialogue of McHenry's characters.

James McHenry provides many elements in his writing which continue to be of interest almost 200 years after his death. The landscape of McHenry extends from Livingstone's Court in Larne to the American frontier of the 1820s – both of which are gone - and his work takes us back to a time and landscape barely recognisable in the modern world. He is a major literary figure who, most certainly in the case of *O'Halloran*, has provided us with a time capsule of the past. He is long overdue recognition and respect in his native town; the town he loved so well and came home to at the end of it all.

David Hume is an author, historian and broadcaster with a special interest in Ulster Scots language, history and culture. He is a member of the Ulster History Circle and works in local government.

A previously unknown source

Stephen McCracken

I was first introduced to *O'Halloran* by Larne writer, Angeline King, after she attended one of my 1798 tours of the Battle of Antrim sites.

Previously ignorant to the 1798 events in Larne, the book set me on a course to delve deep into what actually happened and compare that to what is recorded within McHenry's work.

James was encouraged, perhaps compelled, to weave his Ulster Scots writing within the United Irishmen story by his (possibly fictional) Aunt Nancy, who considered herself somewhat of an expert in the world of conspiracies concerning Larne and *The '98*. I feel, if she was indeed real, that she may have been involved herself as she would have been about 40-years old at the time of the rebellion. Many of the book's characters do represent real people who took part in the wider rising, although there are a few I have not been able to identify.

Since first reading *O'Halloran*, I have however, discovered the court martial records and many witness depositions which have aided me in building up as complete a picture as possible on the United Irishmen activities in Larne on the 6/7th of June 1798. Given what I have uncovered within my research, the rising in Larne has become one of my favourite battles which took place in Ulster. Yet it is, for the most part, unknown in wider historical records.

The common narrative that United Irishmen events surrounded Antrim and Ballynahinch has been captured by McHenry. The Government brought out its own publication on the events of '98 and comprehensively played down events in the North; Larne doesn't even get a mention and today not one memorial or commemoration board stands to those who fought in the town.

The book opens in 1797, when William Orr had been languishing in Carrickfergus Gaol for being a United Irishmen. The account in the book, as with much that relates to the real events, is accurate, if differing in dates a little. That follows consistently throughout, but I don't think detracts. It is, after all, a work of fiction based on historic events, not a history book. For example,

McHenry correctly states that the Acts of Parliament passed in 1792/3 destroyed the very popular Volunteers movement. As those volunteers were now forbidden to hold arms and meet, half went underground into a movement organised by Wolf Tone and other leaders. The fictional O'Halloran, by way of explaining this, was one of the Officers of the Volunteers and now became an officer in this new society, the United Irishmen.

What is worth noting is the extent to which McHenry, a native of Larne, recounts the actions within the town. This has to be one of the earliest accounts of the Battle of Larne and the subsequent Battle of Antrim. It is to McHenry's great credit that he has correctly represented many of the important details and included many of the main leaders by name, although I was surprised that the actual leader of Larne's UI, James O'Rourke, had been omitted. It is, of course, reasonable to think he was the inspiration for the title character, although Beiner concludes that, 'O'Halloran's character was loosely based on the county Antrim landowner James Agnew Farrell of Magheramorne' (2018:194).

The United Irishmen movement was started in the north or Ireland. Belfast at the time was described as the 'Athens of the North'. The town (it wouldn't gain city status until 1888) was a melting pot of radical ideas originating from the many enlightenment writings and revolutions in both America and France. The movement was a successful attempt to eradicate the barriers of sectarian division and aimed to unite the people to *fend of the shackles of British unfair and unjust policy in Ireland which favoured members of the Established Church*. This soon led to the Society getting banned and moving underground. In turn this led to the movement seeking a rebellious solution. This was accompanied by the rise of the popular weaver poets, (a term coined by John Hewitt) which is an underlying strand throughout the book, taking writing inspiration from the Ard's poet, Rev Porter and many others.

Over 100,000 people had joined the United Irishmen by the spring of 1797 in Ulster alone, and many Larne men swelled their ranks. However, for the common Ulsterman the society had one shot at rebellion and later attempts would fail spectacularly in the province, gaining little to no support. The failure of the rising tore apart the radical Presbyterian leadership in Ulster and many of the more high-profile persons were exiled to America or further afield. For the rank and file United Irishmen, they were executed, sent to serve in the British forces in the West Indies or dispatched to serve the King of Prussia and never heard of again. Retributions were too much for the general populous to take and they wouldn't rise again, instead making a home within the newly prosperous Union with the rest of Britain. That Union, formed with the passing of the 1801 Act of Union, and in-fighting within the Presbyterian community over Arianism in the early 1800s, veered the new Presbyterian leadership's attention away from the radical ideas of the United Irishmen and turned them into arguably the strongest supporters of the United Kingdom of Britain and Ireland.

Stephen McCracken has, since coming to Antrim in 2010, immersed himself in the history of the area, focusing on the United Irishmen for his guided tours and subsequent publications.

O'Halloran and the dis/remembrance of 1798

Claire Mitchell

While *O'Halloran; or, The Insurgent Chief: An Irish Historical Tale of 1798* was a new discovery for me, the ideas I found within it were wonderfully familiar. I was thrilled to find a book about 1798 set in Larne, a most unexpected hotbed of revolutionary activity. I was rooting for James McHenry and his (possibly fictional) Aunt Nancy's stated hope, of lovingly restoring the reputation of the Antrim Presbyterians, who, he says, were often treated as "beneath the notice" of outsiders.

Steve Dornan, in a 2009 essay, offers some explanation for this dismissal. He argues that McHenry's work has been largely ignored because it has been difficult to categorise in a politically polarised setting. Dornan thinks there was too much of the particularity of Ulster in McHenry's writing – Ulster Scots and Presbyterianism in the case of *O'Halloran* – to be included in surveys of 19th century Irish fiction.

I have written about a similar misfitting type of Ulster Protestantism. A modern tribe which in many ways has grown out of the 'disremembrance' of 1798 – a term, of course, borrowed from Guy Beiner. My own book, *The Ghost Limb*, tries to trace the lineage of 1798 through to the current politics of some northern Protestants.

The ghost limb is a metaphor for a feeling of absence within my own Protestant identity. A sense of awkward Irishness and United Irish style of civic republicanism which is – like McHenry's work – sometimes difficult to categorise in a politically polarised setting. A sense of belonging which stretches across both sides of a communal divide. In *The Ghost Limb*, I talk to nearly twenty other northern Protestants, many of whom feel a similar sense of dislocation. Others gift me ideas for the ghost limb's healing. Our conversations give me the insight and courage to understand myself as part of this long, often disremembered, tradition of Protestant dissent.

Reading *O'Halloran*, I am struck anew at the looping nature of political thought and social relationships in this part of Ireland. The ideas expressed by the characters in *O'Halloran* are traceable through to the present. The book gives voice to ardent Protestant Irish nationalists, like O'Halloran himself and many of his United Irish colleagues. To loyalists, Establishment and gentry. To cynical economic profiteers. And in the central characters of the Recluse, Edward Barrymore and Ellen O'Halloran, there is great internal nuance. These characters have family relationships and friendships that straddle political divides, so they cannot succumb to black and white thinking. They inhabit the grey.

I find this nuance so resonant today. In the pages of *O'Halloran*, we read frank and respectful exchanges between people with hearts set on democracy and justice, who differ on the pace, methods and urgency of change. Who struggle with ideas of violence and non-violence. Who are capable – on all sides of the argument – of deep self-reflection.

The nuanced characters in *O'Halloran* underline that Protestants in Ulster have always been various. They, and we, are fully capable of imagining our lives in the context of the island of Ireland. They, and we, are often to be found deeply engaged in civic republican thought. They, and we, have a textured, multi-layered sense of Irishness, often heavily laced with Scots. They, and we, are capable of nuanced loyalism and unionism. They, and we – in most cases – are fully capable of loving our neighbours, protecting our friends and being sensitive in one another's company. Relationships in *O'Halloran* manifest in all these ways. And in this sense, I think McHenry did a good job restoring the reputation of the people of Larne, and the surrounding area, as being honourable and decent.

McHenry can certainly be criticised for wearing rose-tinted spectacles though. The ending scenes of *O'Halloran* are an overly sanitised resolution. The events of subsequent Irish history defy McHenry's conclusion that, "rebellion was converted into submission, and disaffection into loyalty". For many, this was the case. But it was not universally so. The trauma of rebellion, and the brutality of its suppression, cascaded down through generations. The pardon and comfortable lifestyle afforded to O'Halloran, the fictional United Irish leader, was not representative of the gruesome fate of most of the actual rebellion leaders. McHenry's conclusion that benign patriarchal elites were best placed to offer solutions to the kind of citizens' democracy that the United Irishmen wanted, is extremely problematic. As such, Guy Beiner concludes that the happy ending has more to do with the author's political outlook than with reality (2018:195).

Perhaps a deeper truth is revealed in the final scenes of *O'Halloran*. The book's resolution after the rebellion is an all-Protestant marriage between an Anglican and a Presbyterian. Catholics, who are sometimes portrayed in the book as the most zealous of the United Irishmen, are not included in the solution. That said, the book often identifies Catholics' oppressions and rights, and I am left with a lingering feeling that McHenry was somewhat sympathetic to the United Irish cause. Others like Clarke-Robinson (1908) have formed this impression too. Whatever the truth of it, it is useful to be aware of the push and pull between these dynamics, and readers will no doubt have their own interpretations.

There are many fascinating threads of social history running through *O'Halloran*. Larne hitting the booze at the yarn fair. The intriguing, floorboarded and plastered out, secret caves. The role of choice for women – O'Halloran's attempt to force Ellen to marry Carebrow is portrayed as a deep injustice (although there is much female swooning and patriarchy too). The importance of poets, minstrels and bards. The weaving of verse and song throughout the book. The inclusion of thoughts from Thuanus the Druid. The ghostly apparitions after visits to shebeens. Itinerant characters like Peg Dornan who crouch in long grass gathering information which they use to help their friends, who in turn treat them with respect. The solidarity of the community potato pick for imprisoned United Irish comrades, so their crop did not spoil. I particularly enjoyed the description of clothes. Green velvet hooded cloaks and long-hanging, ornately patched waistcoats. It is not possible to read *O'Halloran* and conclude that it is a book about dour Ulster Protestants. It is vibrant, soulful and bursting with colour.

Whether McHenry's *O'Halloran* stands up to contemporary standards of literary criticism or historical fact is for others to judge. But it is not something that preoccupies me. Instead, what I take from *O'Halloran* is a reflection on disremembrance. The book's relative absence from the canon of historical fiction – literary or popular – might tell us something about stories that do not fit into easy categories. It gives us an insight into Protestant disremembrance of 1798. McHenry's desire to 'solve' the conflict by ironing out continuing divisions is a fascinating example of the (attempted) social construction of reality through fiction.

Even more interestingly, I have enjoyed thinking about what it could mean to restore these works to our modern consciousness. This book stubbornly refuses stereotype. It shows the Ulster Protestant community in 1798 in all their tangled beauty. Radical and conservative. Humane and zealous. Serious and fun. Industrious and idle. I hope that seeing all this nuance laid bare might encourage contemporary northerners to be braver and more expansive in the ways that we choose to view not only our history, but also our 21st century selves.

Claire Mitchell is a writer and researcher, focusing on identity, memory, religion and politics. She is the author of three books and a wide range of journalism, essays and prose.

For references and bibliography, please refer to rear of book.

Preface (To the original 1824 publication).

THE conspiracy and insurrection of the United Irishmen, were undeniably of the most interesting, and, perhaps, of the most important character of any that ever agitated a country. Its leaders exhibited a combination of talents, courage, and disinterested patriotism, which has but seldom been equalled, and which, in conjunction with the generous nature of the principles for which they contended, could not, and did not fail to attract towards them the admiration and sympathy of all classes of men in Christendom, without excepting even those against whose authority their arms were wielded. Their enterprise failed, whether fortunately or unfortunately for mankind, it is not the business of the novelist to inquire, but had it succeeded, and the designs they had formed for the advantage of their country been realized, what epithets of praise would have been considered too high for their deserts? Their cause would have been called holy, and their efforts glorious. Even as it is, all parties admit that they were zealous for their country's good. The purity of their motives is not denied; it is only the accuracy of their views, and the soundness of their principles that are called in question.

Whatever our own judgment on this subject may be, we have refrained from expressing it; and in writing the following narrative, which, we seriously assert, contains numerous facts that have never yet appeared in print, the course we prescribed for ourselves was that of strict impartiality not only in relating the events, but in detailing the opinions, and delineating the characters of the different parties. The United Irishmen and the loyalists, are permitted to express their sentiments with equal force and freedom. The fanatical and the fierce on either side, are painted as such, while the moderate and lenient, we hope, have ample justice done to the rationality of their views.

We have thought it necessary to say this much in behalf of the neutrality of our plan, because many of the actors in the scenes we have described, are yet living, whose prejudices either for, or against the principles which occasioned the contest, may induce them to expect either a defence or reprehension of their doctrines and conduct. These men, whether republicans or royalists, must expect no such thing, and we caution politicians of every creed, against identifying our private sentiments with those of any of the characters we have drawn. These characters are drawn nearly as we knew them in life; and with respect to the events, it was our lot, although then in our childhood, personally to witness many of them; of many others of the class, that assume to be historical, we have obtained our information from sources of unquestionable authenticity. As to these events, however, we will not deny that we have exercised the privilege of our calling, by giving to many of them the colouring of romance, but during the singular period that has supplied our subject, numberless exploits and transactions took place highly enough coloured of themselves, and requiring no embellishment from fancy to suit them to the appetite of the most choice admirer of extraordinary facts that ever derived gratification from novel-reading. These it was not thought necessary to array in any other garb than that of the simple truth.

For any further information that may be wanted relative to the writing of these volumes, the reader is respectfully referred to the following *Introductory Address* to himself, in which he will find that he is spoken to plainly and familiarly, as one friend should speak to another.

Judicious Reader,

Having the enjoyment of thy good opinion very much at heart, I cannot but feel extremely anxious respecting the impression which my hardihood in submitting the following history to thy perusal, will cause thee to imbibe concerning me. There may be innumerable errors in the work, which I cannot discover, but which may be very apparent to thy superior discernment.

While therefore, the great object of my ambition is to appear in thy sight a very wise man, thou mayest be inclined to look upon me as a very great fool, for expecting to acquire thy esteem by such a trifling — or as thou mayest, peradventure, say, silly performance.

It hath, in these latter times, been the custom with some authors, who, like me, have approached the awful tribunal of thy judgment with trembling steps and palpitating hearts, to attempt evading at least a portion of thy censure, by ascribing the authorship of their productions to persons altogether innocent thereof; and falsely assuring thee that the manuscripts fell accidentally into their hands, and that they are only the editors. By this means they expect to deceive thee into the belief that they have been guilty only of the fact of publishing, and consequently, are not answerable for any imperfections in either the design or execution of the performances.

Oh sons of disingenuity and fraud, how vain are your efforts to impose on the wise people of this sagacious age? Your shallow artifices are easily seen through, and not one novel-reader in ten thousand believeth your foolish statements on this subject.

In vain doth the pathetic author of the "Man of Feeling" assure us that he rescued the manuscript of that affecting work, from the unfeeling fowling-piece of a fat, sporting curate; or that the amiable Mrs. Wistanly made him a present of the original of "Annesly's Sorrows." It is equally vain for the authoress of "The Modern Philosophers," to declare, that she found a chambermaid's brush about to consign the papers containing that cleverly told tale, into a kennel, along with the dirt and rubbish swept from a lodging house. A respectable Dutchman of the name of Knickerbocker, hath also been accused, by Mr. Washington Irving, formerly of New York, of having written an amusing history of that ancient and venerable city: but nobody, now-a-days, believeth him. Fruitless also hath been the attempt of the most prolific of all novelmakers, to deceive the children of this generation, by fathering a number of his own multitudinous offspring, upon a schoolmaster's usher.

But it would be tedious, benevolent reader, to go over the catalogue of these writers, who have had recourse to this method of screening themselves from thy condemnation.

It will be sufficient to observe that not one of them hath succeeded, but that in consequence of thy great penetration, they have always been detected; and thou hast, as became thy great and inflexible justice, uniformly acquitted the accused, and condemned the accusers.

With such warning before my eyes, I would be guilty of something far worse than folly if I should imitate these writers in their detected falsehoods. I shall, therefore, boldly and unreservedly avow myself to be the bona fide author of the following history, and must, consequently, submit to whatever doom thou shalt assign me; as such, humbly requesting, however, that in consideration of my candour in pleading guilty, thou wilt, in pronouncing my sentence, mingle mercy with justice.

But, although, my dear reader, I cannot, with a safe conscience, deny being guilty of having both written and published this history, yet I will make a statement to thee, which, I trust, thou wilt consider as, in a great degree, apologizing for my fault. By this statement thou wilt perceive that I had either to commit that fault, or lose one hundred and fifty pounds a year, which, as I am like too many other authors, but a poor man, I hope thou wilt think that I acted wisely in securing.

The facts are these:

My Aunt Nancy, who died about two years ago, bequeathed me her whole property, amounting to the before mentioned annual sum, well secured in real estate for ever, on condition that I should, within three years after her demise, write and publish such a narrative of the rise, progress, and termination of the conspiracy and insurrection of the United Irishmen, interweaving therewith such an account of the views and feelings, manners and customs of the people of Ulster, at the conclusion of the last century, as would meet with the approbation of her executors. In default of my performing this condition, she ordered her property to be distributed, in equal proportions, between nearly three-score and ten nephews and nieces; to prevent whom from enjoying their several pittances, I hope thou wilt, indulgent reader, think that I was in prudence bound to make an effort; especially, as I found that the greater number of them were not much inclined to thank their deceased relative for her bequest.

Thou wilt, no doubt, wish to know what could induce my Aunt Nancy to make such an odd disposal of her property; and, as I am desirous to gratify all thy reasonable wishes, I shall, with pleasure, inform thee.

My aunt, as thou already perceivest, was a curious woman. She was sixty-one years in this world, and lived all that time in a state of single blessedness; and, what is as true as some may think it strange, she did so from an actual preference of that state to the more popular one of connubial felicity.

When I first remember to have known her, she was on the upper side of forty; of a tall, slim figure, with small, keen, hazel eyes, a nose tolerably well sized, but somewhat sharp pointed, and a chin of more than ordinary longitude. In fact, the contour, (pardon a French word, dear reader, I shall not often offend in that way) of not only her countenance, but her whole person, was remarkable for the length, thinness and keenness of its aspect. The effect of this natural conformation upon the beholder, was very much increased by the fashion of her dress, which was that which prevailed during the earlier half of George III's reign. Its most prominent parts were a long-bodied gown, closely fitted to a pair of tightly-laced stays, which reached from the arm-pits to the haunches, and compressed the whole body into the smallest possible dimensions; a huge head-dress, called a "mob," which towered half a foot higher than a grenadier's cap above the crown; and shoes, the tapering heels of which elevated their wearer several inches from the ground. When my aunt stood upright in this uniform, she was no bad representation of what may be seen in several of our large cities, a tall slender iron bar stuck into a thick stone pillar, and supporting a large globular lamp at its top.

So much for my aunt's person.

As to her manners, she was rather precise and serious in her deportment, and perhaps, possessed a little too much affected gentility, and was too solicitous about the minute forms of politeness, to be quite agreeable; besides, she had contracted a filthy habit of using snuff immoderately. But as she was, upon the whole, tolerably good natured for an old maid, and, as she always made an excellent cup of tea, and was somewhat of an epicure in good toast, those who were familiar with her could occasionally contrive to spend a comfortable evening at her table.

With respect to her mind, she had, in her youth, improved it much, by reading a multitude of the most exquisite and wonderful plays, novels, and romances in the language. For the last ten years of her life, however, she had devoted her faculties to the graver studies of the history, antiquities, geography and statistics of her native island; and, as a natural consequence, she had latterly permitted politics also to engross a great share of her attention.

Amidst the immense multitude of volumes which she had perused on these subjects, she was surprised to find none that gave anything like an accurate account of the people among whom she had spent her whole existence; and whom her local partialities induced her to consider the most interesting, if not the most important people on the earth. She was much chagrined with the carelessness with which even professed travellers through Ireland have uniformly mentioned its northern province.

Some, she would say, seem to treat the people of Ulster as altogether beneath their notice; others take delight in making them the objects of misrepresentation and slander, while none manifest for them that sympathy and respect, to which, from their spirit of enterprise and industry, they are assuredly entitled.

The authoress of the "Wild Irish Girl" particularly provoked her indignation, by the invidious and unfair comparison she hath drawn, in that work, between the Southern and Northern inhabitants of the Island; for she thought that an Irishwoman at least, ought not to have been so wilfully and unjustly abusive of any portion of her countrymen, even if they did not happen to be descended from Milesian ancestors, and were unable to speak the original language of the country. She ought, especially, to have spared her attacks upon that portion, to whose activity and intelligence the nation is chiefly indebted for whatever it possesseth of either prosperity or importance.

My aunt was also much displeased at the very partial and inaccurate accounts which have been given to the world of the motives, designs, and transactions of the Northern United Irishmen; and, as she conceived that her opportunities of knowing the facts entitled her to be a tolerably good judge of these matters, she took the greater liberties in condemning the writers of such accounts.

During the last two or three years of her life, she had, by constantly meditating, conversing, and writing on this subject, excited herself to such a pitch of enthusiasm concerning it, that she declared that she would not die contented unless she would meet with something approaching, at least, to a fair statement of the manners of the people of Ulster, and of the part they had taken in the late rebellion. But all her inquiries after such a work were in vain; and, it is said that the vexation, occasioned by this disappointment, greatly contributed to bring on her last illness.

However that may be, the tenor of her will proves that she had laid the matter much to heart. I hope, therefore, that if, where she now is, she still feels the same interest concerning it, the work which I now submit to thee, dear reader, will yield her gratification, and remove her uneasiness. It has already been approved of by her executors, and has consequently procured me her property; and it now only wanteth thy approbation to procure me that reputation, which I would esteem a far more valuable reward for my humble efforts in its production.

Having told thee what caused me to become an author, I may now mention how I became capable of being one. My father who was far from being abundantly supplied with any other possession except a numerous family of sons and daughters, could not afford to expend much worldly substance upon my education. But on account of the studious disposition which I had manifested from my infancy, I had early become a great favourite with my aunt. She, therefore, generously took the charge of this matter upon herself. It was the wish and intention, of both her and my father, to prepare me for the pulpit, and I have accordingly been, for many years, a probationer, belonging to that learned and reverend body, the Synod of Ulster. But not being gifted with sufficient effrontery to make a good preacher, I believe, now that I have come into the undisputed possession of my aunt's income, I shall give up the employment, for which I had never any great predilection, and shall follow a life of literature, if thou, kind reader, by thy patronage of my present work, wilt give me any encouragement thereto. If not, I must content myself with creeping indolently and uselessly through this weary world; and, if the withholding of thy patronage hath been owing to the evil counsel of any ill-minded critic, upon the head of such critic be all the blame of my indolence and uselessness, for my own conscience will acquit me thereof.

Benevolent reader, thou wilt see, by the following pages, that I had, in writing them, another object in view besides gaining my aunt's money. I also wished to give all the great men of the earth, of whom peradventure thou art one, a good advice, not to be too rigid and harsh with those in subjection to them, but to treat them with kindness and good nature, and leniently overlook their faults, as, I hope, thou wilt overlook mine.

Solomon Second-sight.

Volume I

CHAP. I.

A gallant youth, just fresh from college halls, With love of nature glowing in his breast, Roams venturously amidst her wildest scenes, With fervid and romantic admiration —
Thaunus the Druid.

Perhaps nowhere in the British Islands, will the admirer of the grand and sublime, in the works of nature, find more gratification than along the northern shores of the county of Antrim. From the Gabbon precipices, near the entrance of Larne Harbour, to Port Rush, near Colerain, a long range of rocky coast, extending upwards of fifty miles, exhibits, in some places, the boldest promontories jutting into the sea, and perforated with numerous caverns, into many of which the raging waters pour with reverberating noise. In other places, small bays, occasioned by the mouths of the rivers and rivulets that there seek a junction with the ocean, interrupt the continuity of the rocky chain, and by affording to the visitor the view of towns and villages, surrounded by the fertility of nature, and the conveniences of art, produce a striking and pleasing contrast to the prevailing wildness of the coast, and make its grandeur still more grand. The Giant's Causeway, which forms a part of this wonderful coast, has long been an object of astonishment, both to the philosopher and the peasant. It is annually visited by travellers from all countries, where science excites curiosity, and the wonders of nature inspire admiration.

Edward Barrymore was in his twenty-second year, and had just finished his education at Trinity College, when he resolved to visit this interesting coast, and examine with his own eyes, those immense structures, of which he had heard so much, and which, both as a man of science and of taste, he was so well calculated to enjoy. It was in the afternoon of a very fine day, in the month of May 1797, when he arrived at the promontory of Ballygally.

He alighted and sent forward his servant with the horses to the next town, which was about three miles distant, intending after he had explored the cliffs, to follow along the beach on foot.

He descended the crags, and got to the beach, when turning round a huge rock, he perceived an elderly gentleman, with a young lady, advancing along a sandy portion of the shore towards him. Not wishing to be seen, and, at the same time, struck with the appearance of the lady, he concealed himself in such a manner, that he had a fair view of them, without being himself noticed. They advanced slowly until they came to the bottom of the rock where he was stationed, when all at once they disappeared, but not until they were so near, that he heard the lady utter the following exclamation: "Oh father, what miseries are in store for thousands!" and, immediately he was startled with a sound, as if part of the cliff on which he reclined had broken off. Full of astonishment, he got down to the bottom of the rock, but could perceive no traces of the persons, who had just the moment before excited so much of his attention. Their sudden disappearance was to him quite unaccountable, unless he should suppose, that they had found admission into some cavity within the rock. He viewed it at every accessible point, and minutely examined every fracture and crevice, in the hope of discovering some concealed entrance, but in vain. He imagined, however, that he heard, as from a distance, the sounds of footsteps and voices, but they soon died away, and left nothing audible, but the screaming of the sea-fowl, and the dashing of the waves upon the shore.

Edward, however, determined to remain near the spot until night, in hopes that something might take place that would lead to an explanation of the mystery. For this purpose, he chose a recess on a level with the beach, under an over-arching ledge of the precipice, by which he conceived the fair vision, and her companion, if they were really mortal, must return, as he knew that there was no passing by the way he came, unless by clambering up the rocks, a task which would be almost impracticable for the lady.

Having a small volume of Dryden's Virgil in his pocket, the loves of Æneas and Dido, soon engrossed his attention, and the time unheedingly stole away, until the shades of twilight aroused him from his situation. The tide, which had been advancing all the time, now rolled at his feet, and rendered it impossible for him to retreat from his recess without the greatest danger. He was a good swimmer, but the shore was unknown to him, so that he could not tell how far he might be from any spot, where it would be possible to land. To stay where he was, was evident destruction. The tide encroached rapidly upon him, and he had no alternative but to encounter the wave. He, accordingly, plunged in, and endeavoured to gain the mysterious rock, for the purpose of escaping by the way he came. A current of water, however, that issued, now that the tide was so far advanced, between that and another rock farther out in the sea, rendered his efforts unavailing, and becoming exhausted, he expected nothing but immediate dissolution.

In this situation, he heard a scream, and immediately a loud voice calling, "Swim a little more to the right, and out to sea — I shall help you!"

He obeyed, and got out of the influence of the current that had baffled him, but was on the point of sinking with fatigue, when a powerful arm seized him, and dragged him to the shore in a state of insensibility.

When Edward recovered, he found himself in bed, in a small apartment belonging to a respectable farm house. The mysterious gentleman was employed rubbing his breast with warm spirits, while his fair companion sprinkled hartshorn drops over his brows and temples, and occasionally applied them to his nostrils. An elderly peasant woman was also busy rubbing his feet and legs with warm flannels.

"Oh, father! thank heaven! he breathes," were the first sounds heard by Edward, on his recovery.

"God be praised! then all is well," was the reply.

He lifted his head to look at his preservers, and to thank them, but his voice faltered, and he could only press the hand of the young lady, in token of gratitude. A lovely blush suffused her countenance, but she spoke not; while her father exhorted Edward to remain silent, as perhaps exertion, in his present exhausted state, might be attended with bad consequences. Edward obeyed, for his mind was so distracted with the hurry and variety of his reflections, and the strangeness and intensity of his emotions, that he knew not what remarks to make, or if he knew them, he could not find suitable expressions to convey them. He was glad, therefore, to conceal his confusion in silence.

He was not long in this confused state of agitation, approaching almost to delirium, until a doctor, for whom the old gentleman had sent immediately on getting him ashore, arrived from Larne, the adjoining town. After extracting some blood, and administering a composing draught, he ordered the room to be kept quiet, so that the patient might have an opportunity in silence and repose, to recover from his fatigue and agitation; then giving a few other necessary directions, and assuring the by-standers, that all danger was over, he took his leave, promising to return the next morning. The old gentleman and his daughter, then wished Edward a good night, and retired.

Left to himself, he gave a range to his imagination, on the strange occurrences of the day. His fair attendant still seemed to bend over him, as she did when he first opened his eyes from his trance; and the fervour of her joyful exclamation, at his recovery, still seemed to reverberate in his ears. His exhaustion, however, and the influence of the medicine he had taken, soon interfered with these waking dreams, and he fell into a refreshing sleep, which continued till midnight. When he awoke he found that he had been attended by two decent-looking elderly people, a man and woman, who appeared to have been reading a newspaper.

Not perceiving when he awoke, they continued the conversation which had been excited by the newspaper. "An' they are raising a subscription for the benefit of Orr's family, an' I this day put my name down for half a guinea, for you know, my dear, that what is gi'en to the persecuted, in a guid cause, is never lost; besides, I would not let it be said, that William Caldwell, refused to help a man who was suffering for his country."

"Ah, my dear, you did well to gie the money, but I wish these things may come to a good end. There's sea mony sodgers in the country, and sea mony informers, and sae mony kingsmen, that I'm feared the poor United Irishmen will never do ony guid. Not but I wish God may bless the cause, for if they get leave to gae on, they will persecute and kill a great mony more of us, for no crime at all, as they did poor Murphy, an' the four militia men at Blarismoor. But though I love Mr. O'Halloran, I wish he could not have persuaded you to join the United Irishmen, for I fear this work will bring trouble on us all."

"I could not help it. He argued that it was my duty; told me how poor Ireland was enslaved — an' when he mentioned the sufferings of Orr, an' the killing of Murphy and the militia men, I felt my blood get warm, and I tauld him, I would tak' the oath, let what like come o't!"

Here Edward not wishing longer to act the mean character of a listener, especially to such discourse, made a noise, as if he had just awoke from sleep. He asked what hour of the night it was. The woman told him; when having enquired how he felt, she requested permission to bring him some wine and toast, which she said the doctor had allowed him to take, as soon as he wished for refreshment. "The wine," she remarked, "must be very good, for it was sent from the castle by Mr. O'Halloran, God bless him, just of the kind he kept for his own use. Oh! Sir! how fortunate it was, that he and Miss Ellen were at the Point, when you were a drowning, otherwise you would hae been drowned altogether, for he jumped into the sea, and saved you, just when you were sinking the third and last time? And then, Miss Ellen, how she attended to you till you recovered! God bless her every day she rises, for she's as good as an angel, and as beautiful too. But I was forbidden to speak owre muckle to you, for fear I should disturb you, but you look sae weel, that I'm thinking my talk doesn't hurt you."

Edward assured her that he was delighted with her communications, and begged to know whether Mr. O'Halloran lived far off, and whether he might not have an opportunity of thanking him the next day in person, for the important service he had rendered him?

"Oh! that you will," she replied, "for he lives only about a mile off, and I'm sure he will be here in the mornin', for he will not be easy till he sees himsel' that you are gaun to lieve an' be weel."

"And the young lady," said Edward, "does she live with him? Is she his daughter?"

"She is his grand-daughter, but he still calls her his own child, for since that jewel o' a woman, her mother, died she is now all that he has."

"Jenet!" cried the husband, "you disturb the gentleman owre much wi' your cracks. You had better let him sleep. The doctor said sleep would be good for him. Come awa', we'll send Peggy to tend him."

"Aye, aye," said the wife, "Peggy is a tidy lass, an' winna mak' sitch a clatter as I hae done. Poor thing! she's amaist owre shy, to speak much. Guid night! or, rather guid mornin', sir; sleep sound, an' whatever you want just ask it frae Peggy, an' you'll get it at yince."

They both left the room, and Edward had just begun a train of reflections on the strange incidents of the preceding day, when the door gently opened, and a pretty modest-looking peasant girl, apparently about seventeen years of age, entered the apartment without noise. As Edward lay quiet, treading on tip-toe, she slowly approached the bed in order to ascertain if he were asleep. Presuming that he was, for he purposely feigned to be so, she was about retiring in the same slow and noiseless manner, when wishing to detain her, that he might get some more information concerning O'Halloran and his lovely grand-daughter, he asked, in a tone as if he had just awoke, if any one was there?

"Yes, sir," was the reply, "my mother sent me to see if you wanted ony thing."

"My pretty girl, I want nothing but to enquire in whose house I am, and by what strange accident I have been brought here?"

"The house is my father's, William Caldwell's, and you were brought here carried by Mr. O'Halloran, our landlord at the castle, quite dead, for he found you drowning, in the sea, at the Point Rock."

"And are you acquainted, Miss Caldwell, with the young lady his grand-daughter?"

"With Miss Ellen? yes, I am sir, right well, for she has no pride at all. She sends for me often to walk with her from one house to another, when she visits the poor sick people of the neighbourhood, and carries things for their use; and, we often go together to the top of the hill, when it is a clear day, where we can see Scotland and the ships passing back and forwards. For, she says, it is a beautiful sight, and takes great delight in looking at it."

"And, my dear girl, does she ever speak of her parents? Do you know anything of them?"

"I remember her mother. She died about seven or eight years ago, when I was a very little girl. Miss Ellen was then very little also; for she is not quite two years older than myself. She often talks about her parents, and laments their misfortunes so much, that it makes her rather pensive in her disposition, though she is generally one of the merriest and liveliest young ladies you ever knew. Her father, it is said, fled the country for fear of being punished for killing some lieutenant in the army, in a duel, when she was but an infant."

"Have they never heard of him since?"

"Not that we poor country folk know of."

"Did you ever hear his name?"

"Yes; his name was Hamilton, and she should be called Miss Hamilton, but her grandfather will let her be called nothing but Miss O'Halloran."

"Has she any brothers or sisters?"

"No; her father and mother did not live long together. They never had any children but herself. But, sir, the doctor told us not to fatigue you by talking to you, too much. Would it not be better to leave you to your sleep? for you must be very weak and distressed after being drowned. If you want anything, tell me, for I ought not to stay longer with you, unless to attend you."

This impatience in Peggy, arose from the manner in which Edward had almost unconsciously caught her hand, and pressed it rather warmly, as he listened to her account of Ellen's parentage. Peggy's cheeks displayed a blush, which plainly discovered that she felt the indelicacy of her situation with a young man, who in place of being as she expected, half dead with drowning, seemed quite alive to all the impulses of gallantry and feeling. He checked himself, however, and bade her good-bye, thanked her for the information she had given him, and the attention she had manifested to his comforts.

The alarm that Peggy felt was quite natural, and, to handsome young women who have been in similar situations with handsome young men, any explanation of it would be unnecessary. Even Edward felt that her withdrawing had relieved him from an impending danger. For whether it was occasioned by the sweetness of her looks, or the interest he took in her communications, he felt, as he pressed her hand, a warmer tide of blood than usual, flowing from his heart, which was not cooled for some minutes after her leaving the room, when the idea of the fair Ellen, excited a flow of affections, more congenial to his principles, and more agreeable to his feelings, because more capable of being approved of by his reason.

The various agitations of his mind, together with the still fatigued state of his body, however, soon again found relief in sleep, from which he did not awake until the arrival of the doctor, accompanied by O'Halloran and his granddaughter in the morning. The doctor found him rather exhausted, with a slight degree of fever, which, although chiefly caused by the state of his mind, was readily enough accounted for by the preceding day's accident. He was assured, however, that the only inconvenience that could result, would be a few days confinement. O'Halloran was desirous that he should be conveyed to the castle until his recovery; which, after the adjusting of some preliminaries, such as apologies and expressions of gratitude on the part of Edward, and assurances that he considered it nothing but his duty, on the part of his deliverer, was at last effected. The doctor then having given some directions for his management, took his leave, carrying a letter to Tom Mullins, Edward's servant, whom it was expected he should find at the Antrim Arms, in the town of Larne. In this letter he informed Tom of the accident he had met with, and instructed him to continue at the inn until further orders, without communicating to anyone his master's real name or quality, as he had important reasons for wishing to remain unknown in this part of the country for some time.

Edward Barrymore, was of a very conspicuous family, distinguished alike for its rank, wealth, and devoted attachment to those political principles, which had set the family of Brunswick upon the British throne. With respect to England, their politics were exactly those professed and acted upon by the Whigs of the country. Hence they were in favour of extending every kind of indulgence to the dissenters, and had opposed the American war, and lord North's administration. In Ireland, however, where their principal property and influence lay, they supported every high-handed measure of the government, and were rigid sticklers for the protestant ascendancy. Whatever were their motives for such difference in their political conduct with respect to the two countries, it is certain that they acted only as many other great Irish families at that time did. Their avowed reasons were, that it would not be safe to allow the mass of the Irish community the same political privileges, that might with advantage be allowed the English, because the former were chiefly Catholics, professors of a religion which, they insisted, inculcated direct hostility to the establishments of both church and state, in either country. Those sentiments, while they made the family of Barrymore high in favour with the ruling powers, caused them to be looked upon as no better than Tories, by those Protestants, whose views with respect to their Catholic fellow-subjects were more liberal. By the Catholics, they were held in utter detestation, as their natural enemies, and as the supporters of a tyrannic system of government, which had deprived their ancestors and themselves of some of the most valuable privileges of the constitution.

At the period at which our history commences, Edward's paternal uncle, the earl of Barrymore, was a member of the Irish privy council; and, his father, who was a member of the House of Commons, had distinguished himself by his strenuous opposition to some measures, which had recently been introduced into parliament for the relief of the Catholics.

In consequence of these circumstances, Edward supposed, that if he made himself known, he should be no welcome guest in the house of O'Halloran, whose political principles, he had reason to believe, were in direct opposition to those of his family; and, as he could not venture to incur the dislike of the lovely Ellen, or her venerable grandfather who had saved his life, he determined on concealment.

CHAP. II.

One evening as I wandered forth,
Along the banks of Ayr,
I spied a man whose aged step
Seemed weary worn with care;
His face was furrowed o'er with years,
And hoary was his hair.

Burns.

On the fourth evening after his arrival at O'Halloran Castle, our hero (for the reader will, by this time, have perceived that Edward Barrymore is that important personage) being considerably recovered, took a walk in company with his host and Ellen, along the beach, in order once more to view the spot that had likely to have been so fatal to him. Returning homewards, they took a path along the edge of a rivulet, that led to a small glen, not more than the fourth part of a mile from the Castle. The ground was overspread with primroses, violets and daisies; and the ash, elm, and beech trees that skirted the banks of the stream, were intermingled with abundance of willows, sweetbriars, and honeysuckles, which had opened their blossoms, and yielded a delightful fragrance; while a thousand warblers from amidst their branches, produced a melody, the sweetness of which can only be known by those who are acquainted with the music of the Irish groves, in the spring and summer seasons of the year.

Struck with the beauty and romance of the scene, Edward paused. "This, indeed, Mr. O'Halloran," exclaimed he, "is a delightful place."

"Yes, Mr. Middleton," (which was the name Edward had assumed, being that of his maternal relations) "our country is, indeed, a pleasant one. Her soil is fertile, her sons are brave, her daughters fair, but she is an oppressed country — she is a betrayed country. Thousands of her sons have sold themselves to strangers, whose delight is to rule her, not with a sceptre of justice, but with a rod of cruelty; and a country that has been blessed by Heaven, is accursed by man."

"My friend," replied Edward, "I will not, I cannot, altogether differ with you, in those sentiments; for, I believe that the authorities of the country, have not done as much as they could to promote its prosperity. They have not attended sufficiently to the encouragement of industry among the poor, by directing their attention to internal resources, and facilitating that spirit of enterprise among the wealthy, which would not only discover and establish sources of employment at home, but greatly contribute to extend our commerce abroad."

Edward had scarcely finished this remark, when the attention of the party was drawn to a man of peculiar appearance, who advanced slowly towards them. On coming forward, he took off a gray cap, made of rabbits' skins, which had covered a head the hair of which was as white as snow, and making a respectful bow, asked God to bless them, and was passing on, when Edward, who wished to avoid renewing the political conversation, and whose curiosity was really excited by the appearance of the stranger, thanked him for his civility, adding, "My good sir, perhaps you are like myself, a stranger in this part of the country, and not having the good fortune to meet such friends as I have met with, may require some assistance from those who may be willing to afford it." So saying, he held out a handful of silver to the stranger, which, to his astonishment, he refused, but without any air of offended pride.

"Although I am a forsaken old man," said he, "I cannot take your money. In this glen it would do me no good. Mr. O'Halloran and my other neighbours supply me with food, I get water from that brook, and very little more clothing than I have on me, will be sufficient to cover my carcass, until the grave covers it."

Edward was in the act of putting up his money, when a coarse unhesitating voice called out briskly, "Giff auld Saunders dinna tak' yere money, my bonny young gentleman, ye need na' be at the pains to pit it up; Peg Dornan winna refuse it."

Edward turned round, and beheld a stout weather-beaten woman, in the habit of a beggar, apparently between forty and fifty years of age. She made a low, unceremonious courtesy, and held out her hand for the money. Edward hesitated, but in the most unabashed manner, she continued, "Giff ye dinna like to gie't, I'll no' be affronted, but his honour there can tell you I'll no' drink it."

"I cannot answer for that, Peg," said O'Halloran, "and you should be ashamed to ask any gentleman's money in so rude a manner."

"It's likely you may be richt," said Peg, "ye ken them things better than I do, but gin the gentleman likes, he may either keep it or gie't; I'll no' insist."

Edward now saw something so amusingly independent about Peg, that he immediately handed her the money, enjoining her not to make a bad use of it. She made another courtesy, and told him, she would buy herself a new bonnet, and wear it on Sundays, for his sake, though he might never see her again.

"But gin ye should na," she continued, "bonny Ellen will, an' surely that will gie you pleasure." She then stalked away, with such a solidity of step, and length of stride, as gave Edward the idea of a female Hercules.

"This Peg Dornan," said O'Halloran, "is one of the most forward beggars in this part of the country, whereas our friend Saunders here, is one of the most modest pensioners that ever lived on the public bounty."

The old man's face seemed to redden a little at this remark; and again wishing God to bless them, he bade them good evening, and ascending the glen a little further, disappeared among the bushes.

Old Saunders, as he was called in the neighbourhood of O'Halloran Castle, appeared to Edward to be about sixty years of age. His beard was of a flaxen white, and about an inch in length. His eyes were of a dark blue colour, possessing a greater degree of liveliness than might have been expected from his advanced age. His height in the prime of life, might have been nearly six feet, but as he now bent forward very much when he walked, it did not seem more than about five feet eight inches. His gait, bent as he was, was evidently firmer and indicated more strength than could have been expected from his age. He wore a dark brown great coat, which looked as if it had done the service of half a century. His cap of rabbit skins we have already noticed. His waistcoat had nothing peculiar, except its being made in the old fashion, with the pockets inserted into large lappets, that hung half way down his thighs. It was variegated in its appearance, owing to some heterogeneous patches with which it was here and there ornamented, but the ground work seemed to have been gray cloth, similar to that which formed the great coat. His breeches were of dark velvet, but were now pretty much party-coloured, in the same manner, and from the same cause, as the waistcoat. They were bound at the knees by a huge pair of buckles, that might have belonged to some cavalier in the days of Charles the Second.

As to his boots, they exhibited nothing singular, except their uncommon strength and size, and the sameness of colour which existed between the tops and the legs. There only remains to be mentioned, a belt which he wore round his waist, and which, at a distance, resembled a military sash, with a sheath at each side for a dirk or a pistol, but which, on a nearer approach, discovered itself to be a more harmless appendage — it being nothing more than a common horse girth, with a buckle and a large loose-hanging strap at the one side, and containing at the other, a pouch for holding any little donation that the country people forced upon him. For it was remarkable of old Saunders, that he never carried a bag on his shoulder like another beggar. As he was a good scholar, he was fond of voluntarily teaching the children of those who were charitable to him; so that there was scarcely a family in the parish to which he did not, in this way, give value for what he received from it.

When he left our party, as before stated, to an inquiry of Edward, O'Halloran replied, that the old man's habitation was in the side of a hill, at the upper extremity of the glen, and only a short distance off. "It is about five years," he continued, "since he came to this part of the country. As I found him to be a sensible man, and even somewhat of a literary disposition, I, at one time, prevailed on him to open a regular school, but being rather of a melancholy temper, and fond of solitude, he in a few months, gave up that employment, and retired to this glen, where he now leads altogether the life of a hermit. He has become much esteemed in the neighbourhood, having rendered himself very useful to the people, by occasionally teaching their children, and advising them in their perplexities. So that a number of them are as punctual in sending to his habitation their weekly donations, as if he had a legal claim upon them. I have myself wished to enjoy more of his society than he appears inclined to permit; and when curiosity has at any time, prompted me to make any inquiries into the history of his life, I have been always checked by the reserve he has ever shown on that subject, although he is communicative enough on every other. After sunset he never admits any one into his dwelling, otherwise we might visit him, and you would be sure of a kindly reception."

"Mr. Middleton," said Ellen, "must not think that it is from any surly humour, that our Recluse keeps his cell sacred from visitors after sunset. Although we have found him often pensive, I believe surliness forms no part of his character; much less can he be suspected of any superstitious whim in this part of his conduct, as I have found him more liberal than most men in such matters. I believe that it is from a mere wish to enjoy his own meditations uninterrupted, that he has adopted this rule; for without it, such an enjoyment would be impossible, on account of the social temper of his neighbours, and the esteem in which they hold him. Indeed, it is my opinion, that, if he would permit it, his cell would every night be made the scene of boisterous conviviality."

Conversing in this manner, they had nearly reached the outer gate of the castle, when a horseman overtook them at full speed, and delivering a packet to O'Halloran, rode off again without saying a word. As soon as they entered, O'Halloran hastily broke the seal, and evidently with some emotion, glanced over the contents. He then suddenly told Ellen that he must be absent for a few hours, and desiring that a light and some refreshments should be left in his library to await his return, he bade Edward good night, and hastily withdrew.

On finding himself alone, with a lovely young woman, of whose influence over his heart, Edward was, by this time, fully aware, he felt embarrassed; and although he had abundance to say, he found himself utterly destitute of expression. Silence for a few moments ensued. At length he made an effort, and approaching Ellen, remarked, "It is a remarkable circumstance, Miss O'Halloran, that when the emotions of the heart are most acute, the capability of expressing them, is the most difficult."

"Sir," said Ellen, hesitatingly, "your observation, I believe, is just. Moderate emotions may be expressed without effort, but strong and extraordinary feelings, require language correspondently strong to do them justice."

"And, therefore," resumed Edward, "not at all times to be commanded. How well Miss O'Halloran, have you accounted for the difficulty of speech, under which I now labour? My sensations since I first saw you, have been of that extraordinary character, of which common language can convey but a feeble idea."

"Mr. Middleton," she replied, "the extraordinary and almost fatal circumstances, under which your acquaintance with my grandfather commenced, being still recent, may very well account for the extraordinary feelings you mention. You are still feeble from your late accident. Neither your strength of body, nor tone of mind, is yet recovered; and, consequently, occurrences seem strange, and make an impression on you, that, in other circumstances, you would have scarcely noticed."

"I cannot, Miss O'Halloran, attribute my present agitation, in the slightest degree, to this cause. I scarcely feel the worse for the accident, and am persuaded that I should in a short time forget it altogether, were it not for the feelings of gratitude and admiration for your grandfather and yourself, that it has excited, and, which, believe me, it shall be the study of my life never to forget. Oh! how happy I should be, if I only enjoyed the confidence, the favourable opinion of persons, to whom I am so much indebted, and who shall be for ever so dear to me!"

"That favourable opinion," she observed, "we are never in the habit of withholding from those we think deserving of it. Hitherto our impressions concerning you, are, I believe, as much in your favour as you could wish, and until you do something to forfeit our esteem, of which I am not afraid, I can almost assure you, that you shall enjoy it."

Edward was about thanking her for her kind sentiments, and vowing never to forfeit them, by any voluntary thought, word, or action of his life, when he was prevented by a servant entering with the tea equipage. During the time they sat at table, although not an expression was uttered by either of them in the presence of the servant, that might not have been dictated by mere politeness, yet, if any disinterested person of discernment could have seen them, he would have been convinced that their thoughts ran more upon each other, than upon the whole world besides. Many a stolen glance they mutually detected, and many a tender thought was only half expressed, lest it should be expressed with all the tenderness with which it was conceived. On the part of Edward this embarrassment only occasioned a few blunders, which he got over pretty well, as there was no one present who laughed at them, but on the part of Ellen, the detected glances, and little slips of the tongue, occasioned blushes, which were only rendered more apparently lovely and interesting, by her attempts to conceal them.

CHAP. III.

In varying cadence, soft or strong,
    He swept the sounding chords along;
The present scene, the future lot,
    His toils, his wants, were all forgot,
Cold diffidence, and age's frost,
    In the full tide of song were lost;
And, while his harp responsive rung,
    'Twas thus the latest minstrel sung.

Scott.

After tea, Ellen, afraid of a renewal of the love conversation, proposed to call up Mr. Arthur O'Neil, the harper, who had, for several months past, generally attended two evenings in the week, for the purpose of instructing her on that instrument. Although at that moment, perhaps, Edward would have preferred an arrangement which would have given him her company alone, he acceded to the proposal. He was rejoiced at the opportunity of seeing the only individual then living of that venerable race, whose profession had once been so respectable in Ireland; and he seized the occasion to enlarge on a subject dear to the heart of Ellen, and gratifying to his own, the praise of the bards of their native country.

He was observing that no country had ever possessed a race of men who so much excelled in all the tenderness and pathos of music, or who had produced strains of sentiment so much calculated to affect the heart, when the old, blind musician appeared, led by a boy whom he kept to attend him.

He was struck with his appearance. He looked upon him as a remnant of antiquity; and was ready not only to pay him respectful attention, but to yield him all that veneration and homage which was once yielded to the bards of Tara.

Indeed, the appearance of Arthur O'Neil, detached from any consideration of his profession, was sufficient to command an uncommon degree of respect.

He was nearly sixty years of age, and in height about five feet ten inches, ro-
bust, but not unwieldy in his person. His head was gray, and somewhat bald
towards the front, displaying the wrinkles, but not the debility, of age, upon
his high and arching forehead. His nose was of the most dignified Roman
make; while his whole countenance, which was oval, although somewhat
weather-beaten, exhibited a freshness, which indicated that the possessor had
long enjoyed a healthy and active frame of body. His coat was of dark brown
cloth, made in the old fashion, wide in the skirts, and without breasts. His
waistcoat was a little longer than usual, but had no affectation of singularity in
its construction. In short, the whole of his apparel was characterized, not by
its peculiarity, but by its comfort, decency, and durability.

After an introduction to Edward, in which the usual Irish salutation of
'God bless you' was not forgotten by the venerable minstrel, he adjusted himself to his harp, and began the beautifully sweet air of the *Blackbird*. When he
had done, he asked Ellen if she had committed to memory the verses to that
air, which he left with her on his last visit. On her replying that she had fulfilled
his desire in this instance, he expressed a wish that she should sing them, while
he accompanied her voice on the harp. She, at first, hesitated, but on Edward
joining in the request, she complied; and with a voice sweet as a seraph's, at
least so it sounded in her lover's ears, she sung as follows:

On Ballygally's summits wild,
The slowly-setting sun delay'd, The dewy lips of evening smil'd,
In nature's vernal charms array'd; Soft fragrance scented every shade,
From every tree soft music fell, While zephyrs wanton'd o'er the mead,
Fraught with the sweets of Tobergell.
As musing here I chanc'd to stray,
A lovely maiden caught my view, To whom creation seeM'd to say,
All these my beauties are for you!
The fragrant gale, the pearly dew,
The wild-bird notes with love that swell, Each night their off'rings here renew,
To you, sweet maid of Tobergell!
She slowly trod the flow'ry lea,
Soft, modest beauty in her mien; Oh! who could stand unmov'd to see,
So fair a nymph, and fair a scene!
My quick'ning pulse, and rapture keen,
Confess'd the charms that did impel My very soul to tread the green,

With the sweet maid of Tobergell.

Not in the palace of the great,
The diamond blaze of lab'ring art, Must we expect the happy seat,
Of scenes whose beauties reach the heart: But feelings pure, spontaneous start,
That raise the soul with mystic spell, To taste what nature's sweets impart,
In scenes like these at Tobergell.
Give me a home midst bow'rs like these,
With such a maid as this to gain, And health, and just enough of ease,
Sometimes to weave the rural strain: Then bustling pomp, and grandeur vain,
Away! with me, ye ne'er shall dwell, For happy here I'll still remain,
With the sweet maid of Tobergell.

"Ah! poor M'Nelwin," exclaimed O'Neil when she had finished, "how gratified he would be to hear that sweet voice sing his verses! The poor lad was afraid you would be displeased at his presumption in sending them to you, but I knew you were too good for that. He said you might think that he wished to flatter you, but he declared every sentiment of the piece to be the genuine dictate of his heart, when he wrote it."

"Mr. O'Neil," she replied, "you may return the young man my thanks for the compliment he has paid me. Tell him that I respect his poetical talents, and that I am proud of his favourable opinion, but that I hope he will, for the future, select a more worthy subject for his complimentary effusions, than he has done on this occasion."

"That, I believe, is impossible," said O'Neil.

"It is — it is absolutely impossible," thought Edward.

Then starting suddenly, as if he had just awoke from a trance, "Miss O'Halloran! Mr. O'Neil," said he, scarcely knowing what he said, "I beg pardon for not expressing my admiration sooner of your performance. Either the musician, or the poet, or the singer, or perhaps the combination of the merits of the whole three, produced such an ecstatic impression on my feelings, that I found it impossible for some moments to collect my thoughts sufficiently to thank you in a rational manner; and, believe me, I can, with your poet, sincerely say, I do not flatter."

"Mr. Middleton," said O'Neil, "your enthusiasm of compliment is highly gratifying, but I make no doubt that the sweet voice of the singer has had the greatest share in exciting it."

"You, too, can compliment as well as Mr. Middleton," said Ellen, "but if I may give an opinion, I must ascribe a great deal of our friend's present enthusiasm, to his patriotic delight in listening to the strains of his country's favourite and venerated instrument."

"In our inquiry into the causes of our friend's delight, we must not forget the poet," replied O'Neil in a lively manner. "If not the verses themselves, at least their subject must have been in unison with his feelings."

"I believe you will allow me the right to settle this controversy," said Edward, willing to relieve Ellen from the embarrassment into which the harper's last observation had thrown her. "It would be ungallant, as well as untrue, to deny the share which the sweet songstress has had in administering to the pleasure afforded me this evening. You must, however, take to yourself, Mr. O'Neil, a due portion of the merit. What Irish heart that reveres the ancient music of his country, and is proud of her former excellence in this most delightful of all arts, but must feel an unusual glow of satisfaction, on seeing for the first time, the only remaining branch of that illustrious stock of bards to whom her musical eminence is to be ascribed; and on hearing for the first time, the inspiring tones of that instrument, on which they awoke those soul-moving numbers, that, at once, constituted the delight of our ancestors, and their own immortality. The recollections thus produced must, indeed, be thrilling!"

Edward made a pause. O'Neil sighed, and appeared to be too much affected to reply. He, however, poured forth the fervour of his soul upon his harp; and pathetically swept the chords, accompanying their tones with the following words of a song written by his friend M'Nelvin.

Oh! the days are long past since the music of Erin,
Delighted her sons in the mansions of kings,
Since her chiefs in the joys of the festive board sharing,
Were rous'd by the magic that flow'd from the strings!
O! 'tis long since the patriot heart was affected,
By strains that the deeds of our forefathers told;
And long since the bard and the harp were respected,
By Irishmen free, independent and bold!

Our island long flourish'd the pride of the ocean,
As the olive of Europe, she blooM'd in the west,
And learning when chas'd by war's barb'rous commotion,
In her shamrock-clad vales found protection and rest.

When he had finished, he exclaimed with energy, "Do not fear — I shall no more be the last of Irish harpers, than M'Nelvin shall be the last of Irish poets. Yes; gloomy as our present prospects now are, a day shall yet dawn in which the bard and the harp shall flourish together, and be cherished in the hearts of Irishmen." He then requested Ellen to come forward, and receive a lesson.

She had scarcely seated herself to the harp, when a servant entered with the following note, which he delivered to Edward.

"The old man whom Mr. Middleton met in the glen this evening, and to whom his benevolence prompted him to offer charity, solicits the favour of an interview. He shall wait for him at the place where the late rencontre happened until 10 o'clock."

Edward immediately obeyed the summons, telling Ellen that he had occasion to go but a short distance, and did not expect to be long absent.

On arriving at the place mentioned he found the Recluse true to his appointment. "Follow me," said he to Edward; and he led the way up the glen until they came to a place altogether overgrown with trees, shrubs, and brambles, and various other kinds of undergrowth. They then turned to the left, and keeping close along the margin of the stream, in a few minutes came to the bottom of a precipice between thirty and forty feet high, which formed one bank of the rivulet, a corresponding precipice banking it on the other side. These banks approached almost close to each other at the upper termination of the glen, which was formed by their gradually widening and diverging from each side of the brook until they were lost in gentle swellings on the sea shore. A small distance farther up the brook than where these banks began to leave it, a beautiful and romantic cascade was formed by the water rushing over a breast of rock nearly as high as the banks themselves, and which formed their junction. But before coming to this cascade, Edward and his conductor reached the mouth of a cavern which the latter said was the entrance of his abode.

When they entered a few yards, they were stopped by what Edward supposed to be the solid rock at the farthest extent of the cavern, but the recluse taking a key from his pocket, soon opened a door which the darkness had prevented him from seeing.

They now entered a large clean apartment with a well baked earthen floor, at one side of which blazed a large turf fire. It also contained several chairs, a table, a large lumber chest, a few working utensils, a large old fashioned bureau, and several mats of straw heaped on each other for a bed, and covered with bed clothes looking extremely clean and comfortable.

"You are welcome to my habitation," said the old man.

"Why really" replied Edward, "you have a more comfortable dwelling beneath the surface of the earth than many I have seen above it."

"As to that, you have as yet only seen one portion of my abode. I shall now introduce you to another, and you will be aware of the progress you have already made in my estimation, and the confidence I repose in you, when I tell you that you are the second individual living to whom I have ever opened its door."

He then approached what Edward supposed to be the large bureau, and touching a concealed spring in one side of it, it flew open and displayed to view a handsome parlour, lighted with two wax candles, having a boarded floor, and plastered and ceiled in the neatest manner. Edward's astonishment was still more increased, when advancing, he perceived at the farther end a large and elegant assortment of books, arranged along shelves which seemed to have been erected in a temporary manner for the purpose of containing them.

"The surprise I perceive in your countenance," said the old man, "is natural. But sit down, and I shall, in part, account for what you see, by stating that I am not the person which to the world I appear to be. I have met with misfortunes, Mr. Barrymore! Do not startle. I know your name, and about five years ago received some civilities from you at Trinity College. You were then, to be sure, less firmly made than at present, but I think I cannot be mistaken as to your identity with the individual to whom I allude."

Edward acknowledged the identity, and confided to the old man his motives for concealing his real name from O'Halloran's family. The old man approved of them.

"You have entrusted me with a secret which I shall keep," said he. "I shall now entrust you with one of more importance. Indeed it was for this purpose I requested this interview. Yours is one only of a temporary nature, mine involves very serious interests. It is calculated to affect no less than the life of a man whom we both highly esteem. But it is from a regard to that life, that I entrust you with it. By enlisting your family influence in favour of this person, I foresee that it will be one day in your power to contribute to his safety. To him you owe the preservation of your life. To him you are therefore bound by gratitude. I shall commit the secret of his offences to your bosom, honour will, therefore, bind you not to betray him, and I know you possess honour. But there is, as I before suspected, and as you have just now confessed, another circumstance, a tie which binds you to his interests, if not of a stronger, at least of a more endearing nature than either gratitude or honour — I mean love; for the filial affection of his granddaughter, I am convinced, is so strong that she would never survive his public execution. Ah! sir, I tremble for that young lady, when I think of the danger into which the ardent but mistaken patriotism of O'Halloran is likely to involve him. I have endeavoured for several months past, to prepare her mind for whatever calamities may overtake her, by lessons of fortitude. But I still dread the consequences of her grandfather's imprudence. I wanted a coadjutor to assist in delivering him, if possible, when the day of calamity shall come. For I clearly perceive that such a day is fast approaching — how far it is distant I cannot tell — but come it will. On such a day I shall have a recourse to you. I know your power is great and your heart is willing. I thank that Providence which threw you in my way before the cloud had burst; and I look upon it as a favourable omen, which bids me hope that Ellen Hamilton and Henry O'Halloran, the two dearest objects I have on the earth, shall survive the fury of that storm under which thousands are doomed to fall."

Edward was affected with the Recluse's fervency. He assured him that he would, at any time, be ready to undertake any thing that should contribute to the safety of O'Halloran, and the happiness of Ellen. He hoped, however, that whatever were the circumstances which occasioned such an alarm in his mind, they would not entail the misfortunes he apprehended. That if he would inform him of the particulars he should be the better prepared to act on any emergency, and he might rely upon his honour, without taking into view the high interest he felt and ever must feel for the welfare of O'Halloran and his granddaughter, as a sufficient pledge of secrecy, so long as secrecy should be attended with any advantage to either of them."

"I am satisfied on that head," said the Recluse, "your political principles, opposed, as I know them to be, to those of O'Halloran, will not, I am persuaded, prevail with you to break through the various ties of honour, gratitude, and love, which bind you to the interests of this worthy but mistaken old man. Yet I cannot but think that your conscience will scruple at enlisting your services on behalf of a man, whom, when you are informed of the whole of his conduct, (and of the whole of it you must be informed before you can be sensible of the extent of his danger) you will be inclined to look upon as a traitor to his country, and to that constitution of government, which, from your youth, you have been taught to venerate and consider as the most excellent that ever was framed for the benefit of society."

"I indeed acknowledge my admiration of the excellencies of the British constitution," replied Edward. "At the same time, I am sensible that it contains a great many imperfections; and, in various minor points, should be an advocate for its amendment. But, whatever may be my opinions on this subject, depend upon it they never can alter my affection for the interesting family to whom I owe so much. Still, I hope, that Mr. O'Halloran has not acted so as to deserve the severe epithet of traitor, which you have applied to him."

"Would to God!" said the Recluse, "that I were unjust in applying that epithet to him. But, I greatly fear, that when you hear the particulars, you will be but too much convinced that the laws of this country would make the same application. Against that statute which defines treason to be the abetting and encouraging the enemies of the country, it is but too true that with many others of the society with which he is connected, he has offended. That it does not amount to treason to be a United Irishman, I am aware; and if my friend were only such, I should neither feel the uneasiness, nor give you trouble concerning him, which I now do."

"I am ignorant," said Edward, "of the designs of the United Irishmen. But I am aware that their association has occasioned a great deal of disturbance in the country; although I am also aware that the severe measures resorted to by the present administration to suppress this association, may have provoked many of the atrocities that have been committed. As, however, you are better acquainted with their proceedings and intentions, I shall be glad of your information, but of this you may be satisfied, that nothing you can tell me of a mere political nature, shall lessen my esteem for our friend, or alter my resolution to serve him, if ever Providence shall so order it that I may have the power."

"This," said the Recluse, "is the point I wished to gain. I shall not, therefore, hesitate to communicate all I know concerning O'Halloran's connexion with this association. Among the United Irishmen there are numbers of virtuous characters, and, at the commencement of the society, it was joined by men of the purest patriotic and constitutional principles. The avowed object of its founders, was only to unite all classes of Irishmen, without regard to religious distinction, in exertions to obtain those rights, and the redress of those grievances which the volunteers had failed to obtain.

The three leading objects with them, are the same for which many of our best and most enlightened statesmen, both in and out of parliament, have long contended; namely, a reform in the representation of the commons, emancipation of the Catholics, and a melioration of the tythe system. These are just and constitutional demands for the people to make; and had the government granted them to the solicitations of the volunteers, we should never have heard of United Irishmen. But the administration became jealous of that gallant army of patriots; and as soon as they no longer needed their aid, not only stopped short in their reluctant concessions to their just demands, but in defiance of the wishes of the nation, occasioned their disorganization.

"Some of the leaders of the volunteers, and other men of restless and active dispositions, and many, no doubt, from the purest motives, determined to persist in urging their claims; and, since they were forbidden to arm as a public body, they resolved to arm as a secret society. The plan they adopted was originally suggested by Theobald Wolfe Tone, whom I have frequently seen in this part of the country, on his visits to ascertain the progress of the association, and to give instructions respecting the management and regulation of its concerns. Mr. O'Halloran, who had been a leader among the volunteers, became active in recruiting for the new establishment, which, at its origin, was hardly considered in any other light than as a substitute for that which had been so arbitrarily and unwisely suppressed.

"Unfortunately the French revolutionists began at this time successfully to propagate their disorganizing doctrines throughout all Europe. Numbers of their emissaries were scattered over Ireland, and, in consequence of their exertions, a spirit of innovation upon every kind of ancient establishment spread itself rapidly among the people. This was, however, somewhat checked by the seeming spirit of conciliation which the ministry of Britain manifested in sending the Earl Fitzwilliam, a man who was known to be friendly to the popular wishes, as viceroy to the country. Happy it would have been for the people, and happy also for the government, had he been permitted to remain at the head of our affairs. The United Irish Association would, of itself, have dissolved by being gratified in the principal of its wishes. But, unfortunately, it was not the design of Mr. Pitt and his colleagues that the people should be gratified. Accordingly the popular viceroy was withdrawn. He left Ireland in tears, which I am afraid will never be dried until they be changed for blood. His successor, Lord Camden, you are aware, has adopted a different system of government. Instead of a redress of grievances being granted, oppression is increased, under the plea of suppressing treason, until numbers have actually been irritated into treason, who would otherwise have remained peaceable and loyal; and the red arm of vengeance has been bared to inflict punishment for crimes that would never have been committed, had not the same arm been previously employed in oppression. To Camden's ill-fated and ill-managed administration, the whole of the evils that now overspread the land are to be attributed. By passing the impolitic law of the last session, called the Insurrection Act, which has for a season, surrendered the liberties of the people into the hands of an executive that has shown itself so ill disposed to make a proper use of such a trust, the parliament has sharpened the sword of oppression, and given a cruel sanction to the military outrages that are now committing throughout the country. That act has permitted the ordinary forms of judicature to be superseded by tribunals, unknown to the constitution, and military courts are now busied, in many places, in hurling the vengeance of power wherever disaffection is suspected, or even wherever it is convenient for interested malice that it should be suspected.

"The captivity and sufferings of William Orr, a respectable man of this county, who, under the operation of that unfortunate act, has been, since September last, immured in prison, among many other instances of misgovernment, have contributed much to excite the present incalculable and fearful degree of irritation which has seized the minds of the people of this province. Immense numbers of every class view the present state of things with horror, and the legislature having legalized the oppression under their labour, they also view them without any hope of deliverance, except by an exertion of their own strength. Hence thousands who before the existence of the Insurrection Act resisted every solicitation to join the united ranks, are now voluntarily coming forward to enrol themselves upon their lists, and to take the oaths of fidelity to their cause. Ambitious men, in the interests of France, have taken advantage of this enthusiasm among the people, and have, of late, been too successful in infusing principles absolutely treasonable into the minds of many.

"Among the most zealous for revenge upon the oppressors of the country, we may consider our friend, Mr. O'Halloran. Excited by the integrity of his nature to a hatred of every species of injustice, and being fearless and persevering in whatever cause he embarks, he has taken a lead in the existing

conspiracy, not, like many others, from selfish views, but from the purest motives — from his ideas of duty, and from his feelings of benevolence and
patriotism.

"Many, however, on the contrary, of the ablest men who were conspicuous
at the commencement of the confederacy, have become dissatisfied at the
lengths to which matters have latterly been driven, and are now either altogether inactive, or have thrown their weight into the scale of government. But
encouraged by the great accession they have received in point of numbers
from the lower orders, the more zealous leaders, instead of being discouraged
by this defection of the more moderate from their cause, have become bolder
in their measures, and have not stopped short of treason in their views. They
avow, unreservedly, their intention, with the assistance of France, to establish
a republican form of government in this country, altogether unconnected with
Britain; and these imprudent men now regulate the whole concerns of the
united confederacy. The lower orders look up to them as the only true patriots,
and brand those who wish to restrain them in their mad career, with the name
of apostates; and it has unfortunately happened in this, as in all other cases of
national excitement, that the most violent have become the most popular."

"Is there any system of insurrection yet organized?" enquired Edward.

"There is no time, I believe, yet fixed upon for taking the field, but they
have given up all idea of again applying to government for a redress of grievances, and appear resolved to trust to arms alone for the success of their cause.
Still I am of opinion that conciliatory measures on the part of the government,
and granting them their just and constitutional demands, would so separate
the members of the confederacy, as to check the progress of the threatened
rebellion, and render the machinations of the more violent and fanatical abor-
tive. But I have so little faith in the government adopting these healing
measures, that I expect nothing else than a state of things to take place, more
disastrous and unfortunate for the country, than any she has ever yet experienced. The government is obstinate, it is oppressive; the people are inflamed,
and imprudent, and under the management of ambitious, rash, and desperate
men. Oh my friend, what misery awaits our unfortunate country?"

Edward felt the full force of the old man's sorrow. His heart bled at the
prospect thus opened before him of the calamities that were about to overspread the land of his nativity; the land of his affections; the abode of all that
was dear to his feelings and pleasing to his hopes, and he heaved a sigh as he
confessed that he could see no means by which the threatened misfortunes
might be averted.

The Recluse now gave him an account of numerous instances of misrule and oppression committed by the government, and of the violent measures frequently resorted to by the United Irishmen in retaliation throughout the northern parts of the country. At length Edward took leave of the old man, with a promise not to depart from the neighbourhood until he should have another interview with him on the subject.

On his way to the castle, his heart, distracted with sorrow and with love, became overpowered with his emotions, and before he knocked for admittance at the gate, which, at that hour of the night, was always closed, he retired into a little arbour behind the porter's lodge, to give vent to his feelings.

He had scarcely entered, when a coarse voice called out, "Wha comes there?" which he immediately conjectured to be the voice of Peg Dornan.

"Is this you, Peg?" was the reply.

She started to her feet, muttering, "In the name o' Gude! what brings you here at this hoor of the nicht? Surely you ha' na been out exercising wi' the crappies. Poor lads! they maun aye tak' the dark covering o' the nicht to be drilled, for fear o' the blackguard informers, or the king's red-coats, that would shoot them or hang them without mercy. The deil tak' them!"

"Is this where you make your bed at nights, Peg?" said Edward.

"Sometimes, sir; ony place does Peg Dornan." At this moment they heard the sound of voices approaching. "It's his honour," said Peg, looking out at the entrance of the arbour, "an' anither I dinna ken, gaun to the castle. Na doubt they're talking politics. I ne'er fash my head wi' sic things, except to sing a crappy sang noo an' then, an' to wish Gude to bless the cause, be it richt or wrang."

The speakers were now so near that Edward could distinctly hear O'Halloran saying to his companion, "We have now upwards of a hundred thousand men sworn to us in this province, and, I think, we might have things prepared for a general rising as soon as your government can effect the landing of ten thousand troops on any part of the coast. My last letters from the Dublin Directory inform me, that in the various part of the kingdom there are upwards of three hundred thousand United Irishmen and Defenders ready to take the field at the first signal!"

To this the other answered, "Our government has the interests of your country much at heart, and if our transports can only escape the fleets of Britain, the number of troops promised you may rely on receiving at the stipulated time." The sounds now died away, and the increasing distance of the speakers prevented Edward from hearing more. The fact that French aid in order to assist in separating Ireland from England, was negotiated for by the leaders of the United Association, was now to him no longer questionable; and that the only parent of his Ellen, the preserver of his life, was deeply implicated in this traitorous and dangerous measure, sunk heavily to his heart, and impressed him with such a degree of vexation and sorrow, as he had never before experienced.

"I will not disturb you longer, Peg," said he, "when I stumbled in here, I did not expect that the place was previously occupied."

"Guid nicht!" she cried, "and Gude be wi' you; an' thank ye for the money — I had na' sae muckle this twal month before."

CHAP. IV.

Who has e'er had the luck to see Donnybrook fair,
An Irishman all in his glory is there,
> *With his sprig of shillelah and shamrock so green.*
His clothes spic and span new without e'er a speck,
A new Barcelona tied round his neat neck;
He comes into a tent and he spends half a crown,
Comes out, meets his friend, and for love knocks him down,
> *With his sprig of shillelah and shamrock so green.*
Popular Song.

When Edward had retired to bed and begun to ruminate on the distracted and dangerous state of the country, he found sleep to be utterly out of the question. So many images of the distress and misery about to take place, crowded on his imagination, that when he, at length, fell into a slumber, the state of his mind excited the most frightful dreams. At one time, he thought that his old friend was seized by a party of dragoons, and hanged at the gate of his own castle, which was fired by the military; and, before he could fly to prevent it, he thought he saw his beloved Ellen consumed in the flames. Here the horror of his feelings increased to such agony that he awoke.

The day was dawning, and as it was in vain for him to seek again for repose, he wandered to the garden, which was situated at a small distance from the castle. It was a lovely May morning. A thousand warblers saluted the rising sun from the trees and hedges around him.

"How happy are you!" thought he, "ye little songsters, when compared with man, that lord of the creation! No vicious, turbulent passions agitate your contented bosoms. You do not, like us, enter into combinations to bring upon each other misery and ruin. Ambition never swells your breasts, nor does revenge goad you on to mutual hatred and destruction. The sweeter and more amiable passions alone find admission into your bosoms, and the enjoyments of love, friendship and innocence seem to be the only occupation of your lives. Your lot is, indeed, that of innocence and joy."

Absorbed in these contemplations, he moved slowly along the garden walks, amidst a profusion of cowslips, daisies, hyacinths, tulips, and numerous other flowers that scented the air all around, and from the leaves and petals of which were suspended myriads of pearly globules, glittering in the early beams of the eastern sun. "But there is one of our race," thought he, "as lovely as these, whose breast to me is fragrance, and whose voice is music. Oh! may heaven grant her protection amidst the dangers that surround her; for her bosom is the seat of innocence, and her soul too pure for the vengeful feelings of the times!" This soothing walk, and the contemplation of Ellen's charms, calmed the perturbation of his spirits, and he was enabled to meet O'Halloran in a more unembarrassed manner than he expected.

After breakfast he signified his intention of going to town, in order to give some directions to his servant, observing at the same time, that, as he wished to remain a few weeks in the neighbourhood, he should take lodgings at the inn where his horses were kept. O'Halloran invited him to make the castle his home so long as he remained in that part of the country. He declined the invitation, but mentioned that he should frequently obtrude upon them as a visitor. O'Halloran then expressed his intention of going to town with him, on condition that he would accompany him back to the castle in the evening, a stipulation with which he complied.

On the road, O'Halloran introduced the subject of politics. "You are a young man," said he, "I believe, of generous sentiments and a liberal mind, and such I have ever found to be possessed of that first of virtues, patriotism. You cannot, therefore, but feel the injustice, cruelty, and despotism, with which the government of Britain has always treated this country. It has been the policy of our haughty, domineering neighbour, ever since we have been so unfortunate as to be connected with her, to treat us as a conquered people. She has taken advantage of our religious dissentions, and made them the means of fomenting divisions amongst us, that she might the more easily oppress us, and incur no danger from her tyranny. We are, however, Mr. Middleton, resolved no longer to be her dupes. The minds of all classes of our people are enlightened, and whether Protestants, Presbyterians, or Catholics, a cordial brotherhood has taken place. We feel oppression, and are resolved to endure it no longer. We know the natural rights of men, and shall assert them in the face of our enemies. They have made us slaves, but we are determined to be free. It is the duty of every true Irishman to assist in such a cause,

a cause which cannot but obtain the approbation of heaven, and be successful."

"My friend," replied Edward, "of all accusations, I should wish to avoid
that of being indifferent to the welfare of my country. I feel that Ireland has
not a son who more fervently desires her prosperity than I do. I have seen her
distresses, and I have grieved for them. I have contemplated the calamities
that seem hovering over her, and if a sacrifice of my life, or any other sacrifice
in my power to make, could preserve her from them, it should be joyfully
offered. Oh, sir! while we were a quiet people, living in obedience to the laws
of the land, without embroiling ourselves in impracticable schemes for the
attainment of merely abstract and controverted rights, were we not a happy
people? Were we not in possession of every practical good that could arise
from the enjoyment of known laws, and a firm and well-regulated government? Our lives and our properties were secure from violence; and no earthly
power, except the power of offended laws, could injure us with impunity. I
grant that our government has often been wrong. Everything human is liable
to error, and our government is human. We should have been content with
applying, in a legal manner, for redress. Ah! my heart is sore to think of the
state to which matters have been carried. The administration has been unwise,
and the people imprudent. The one is obstinate, and the other rash; and, in all
probability, it will require a deluge of blood to extinguish their mutual animosity."

They had now arrived at Larne. It happened to be the monthly yarn mar-
ket-day, and the market for May in that town, is always the largest in the year.
Edward was astonished at the multitude of people of all ages, sexes, and ranks
that filled the streets; some for amusement, and some for business, making a
confused mixture of sounds, loud and discordant indeed, but at the same time
cheerful, lively and diverting. After making their way, with some difficulty
through the crowd, they, at length, arrived at the inn where Edward's servant
had stopped. They entered a small room where two decent looking countrymen were adjusting the payment of some linen cloth which the one had
purchased from the other. After an interchange of civilities with Edward and
O'Halloran, he that received the money, insisted on calling for something to
treat his companion; and immediately rapping aloud on the table with a small
wooden mallet called a bruiser, an instrument used in mixing punch throughout the North of Ireland, a young girl quickly appeared.

"Were you calling gentlemen?" said she.

"Bring us half a pint of Innishown, with some sugar and water," was the
reply of the linen-seller.

Edward wondered at the quantity ordered at once for only two individuals. But as soon as the materials arrived, he found that although O'Halloran and he had not been formally asked to accept a share, they had been provided for in the countryman's calculation. The linen dealers immediately applied themselves to their glasses; and O'Halloran without hesitation followed their example. But Edward declined until he saw that it was necessary for the sake of civility to comply, which he did, however, sparingly.

The conversation now turned upon politics; and Edward soon perceived that his two new companions were United Irishmen; for seeing him in the company of O'Halloran, they took no pains to conceal their sentiments in his presence. After commenting on the usual topics of the Insurrection Law, and Orr's sufferings, they adverted to the punishment that had been recently inflicted upon one William Murphy, a soldier belonging to the king's artillery, who had become a United Irishman, and deserted. It appeared that he had been apprehended in the house of the man who had bought the linen, and who told them the whole story with as many exaggerations as he thought necessary to ornament the narrative, and blacken the conduct of the military.

"Murphy's a damned clever fellow," said he, "for when the soldiers threatened to burn the house over us if we did not give him up, he jumped out of his hiding place and went out to them, in spite of us all. You are a fool, said I, you might escape out of the back window, and up the loanin, and behind the stack-yard, an' it's ten to one if they would see you, until you would be so far off that they could neither catch you nor shoot you. 'And don't you know,' said he, 'that they would punish you for letting me escape?' Never fear that, said I, they have nothing against me. 'They would soon find something against you,' said he, 'your letting me off would be enough. But I'll be damned if they shall injure you on my account.' He then called to the officer not to burn the house for he would surrender, and he resolutely walked out to them. 'Damn you Murphy,' said the officer, 'what a pretty scrape you have brought yourself into with these cursed croppies — you will get a sore back for it, I'll warrant you. But we must see whether the good codger within, has any hospitality for honest soldiers, as well as for deserters. Good morrow, Mr. Clements,' said he to me, coming into the house with a dozen of soldiers after him, 'you have acted wisely. What a devil of a sin it would have been for you to have let the house be burned about these pretty chubby cheeked daughters of yours! What are you crying for,' said he to Nancy. 'Ah sir!' said she, 'I am afraid you will flog poor Murphy.' 'He shall only be used as every cowardly deserter should be used, my pretty girl! But I am damned hungry. Come, Clements, let's have something to eat, for curse the morsel either I or my men have tasted since we left Carrickfergus. Come, my tender hearted little damsel! Quit sobbing, and take pity on starving soldiers. Prepare us some of this bacon, with a few eggs and some bread and cheese, and a bottle or two of whiskey, to warm our stomachs, or, by G—d, we shall save you the trouble and do it ourselves.' Weel, Nancy, to gain their favour for poor Murphy, treated them as well as she could. At parting we all shook hands with him, but our hearts were heavy. He kissed Nancy, she wept like a child. 'May God protect you,' said he, 'it is likely we shall never meet again in this world!' And heaven knows they never did, nor never will. Even the officer himself was somewhat affected; and to do him justice, he treated us civilly enough, though he was a hard-hearted rascal in the main, for when they had left the house, as I followed them a little way, I heard him tell Murphy to prepare, for he had no mercy to expect!"

"Perhaps," said Edward, "the admonition might have been given to induce Murphy to a timely preparation for death. Under such circumstances, I think, I should wish at once to know my doom."

"By heaven! you are right," cried the linen-seller, "I should like to know the worst that I might prepare for it. Death is bad enough, but it is soon over, but suspense is — is — confound me, if I know what to call it! It is worse than death."

"It is lingering torment," said Edward.

"By George, you have it," returned the linen-seller, "just what I wanted to call it. We must have another round for the gentleman's 'cuteness." But before he could get once more applying the bruiser to the table, a woman entered the room with a face of inquiry.

"Wull ony o' ye, gentlemen," said she, "tell me how much six spinal and a half o' yarn comes to, at eleven pence ha'penny a hank?"

"Wha gets your yarn? Nanny," asked Clements.

"Billy Boyd, sir."

"Has Billy ony wabs to sell the day, ken ye?"

"I doubt na, sir, he has; though I canna tell for certain."

By this time the other linen dealer, who had suspended his attack upon the table, to calculate the amount of Nanny's yarn, told her that it came to one pound, four shillings and eleven pence; and handed her the figures, marked with his pencil upon a piece of paper, with an air of conscious superiority in scholarship, that might have become any pedagogue philosopher in the country. He then invited her to take a dram; and asked her if she had any more yarn to sell.

"No," she replied, "but, I believe, my sin Jemmy's wife has twa or three spinal o' six hank yarn."

During this dialogue, Edward who wished to avoid the second bacchanalian attack which he saw contemplated, withdrew. He was soon followed by O'Halloran, who invited him to take a ramble through the streets in order to witness the humours of a Northern Irish yarn market.

"The market," said he, "in this town, is held once a month, and is generally attended by people from all parts of the country who wish to buy linen cloth or yarn, although, besides these articles, there are exposed for sale great numbers of cows and horses, and generally all kinds of merchandise, either the growth or manufacture of the country."

They had not gone far until Edward perceived the scene diversified by the tents of hawkers, erected on the sides of the streets, in which were vended a great variety of haberdashery, cutlery, &c. Not far from these were stationed the humbler stalls of a species of travelling huxters called ginger-bread women, constructed either of old doors supported on the ends of barrels, or of two-wheeled cars leaning on supports of a similar description.

Turning a corner near the market-house, he perceived to the left, a man elevated on a table selling waistcoat patterns and shawls by auction, and bawling lustily in order to attract customers. On the other side of the street, an old female ballad-singer exerted her lungs at a most powerful rate, in successful opposition to the auctioneer. The course jests of the one, and the ludicrous gestures of the other, were in complete rivalry. The ballad-singer, however, seemed to attract the greater attention, perhaps owing to her subject, which was of a political nature, giving an account of the trial, death, and heroism of the four militia men before noticed, who had been lately shot for treasonable practices, at Blarris-Moor, near Belfast. Of this elegiac composition of some of the rustic political bards, whose numerous effusions were then so prevalent and so eagerly sought after in the country, it may not be amiss to give the reader a few stanzas, as a specimen of those lyrical productions, which, although utterly destitute of the graces of fine writing, yet being adapted to popular airs, being in unison with the popular feelings, and containing sometimes a great deal of simplicity and nature, were altogether suited to the taste of the lower orders, and produced in their minds a wonderful degree of political enthusiasm. It has been asserted that the prevalence of those songs did more to increase the numbers of the conspirators than all the efforts of the French emissaries, or the writings and harangues of all the political philosophers, and age-of-reason men of the times. Some of the stanzas that now attracted the attention of Edward were as follows:

Ye Muse, grant me direction, To sing that foul transaction, Which causes sad reflection,

Late done at Blarris-Moor,
By wicked Colonel Barber;
Should I proceed much further, And call his conduct murder,

        'Twere treason, I am sure!
Belfast may well remember, When tyrants in their splendour, In all their power and

        grandeur,

They hois'd them on a car;
While infantry advancing,
And cavalry were prancing, And glittering armour glancing, All in the pomp of war!
They were of good behaviour, No heroes e'er were braver, But a perjured base deceiver,
Betray'd their lives away.
For the sake of golden store; The villain falsely swore; And the crime we now deplore,

        In sorrow and dismay.

Amidst a hollow square, Well guarded front and rear, With guns and bayonets there,
Their constancy to move.
When they receiv'd their sentence,
Their hearts felt no relentings; They bow'd to each acquaintance, And kneel'd to God

        above!

Then their foes held consultation, To find out combination, And thus in exhortation,
Curs'd Barber did propose:
Arise from your devotion,
Take pardon and promotion, Or death will be your portion, Unless you now disclose.

Some moments then they mused, For their senses were confused, Then smiling they

        refused,

And made him this reply:
We own we are united,
Of death we're not affrighted, And hope to be requited, By him who rules on high.

The guns were then presented, The balls their bosoms entered, While multitudes lamented
The shocking sight to see
Those youthful martyrs four,
Lying weltering in their gore, And the plains besprinkled o'er, With the blood of cruelty.
In coffins they were hurried, From Blarris-Moor were carried, And hastily were buried,
While thousands, sunk in grief,
Cried, "Granu! we much wonder,
You rise not from your slumber, With voice as loud as thunder, To grant us some relief!"

When Edward had listened to a few stanzas of this song, he perceived Dr. Farrel, his physician, approaching, who saluted him with great cordiality. Edward, who really esteemed this gentleman for his good sense and urbanity of manners, returned his salutation with unfeigned pleasure. The three gentlemen had not walked far together, until O'Halloran was taken aside by a square built, stout-looking man, in the habit of a traveller, who desired to converse with him in private. Edward and the doctor therefore walked on, while O'Halloran and the stranger went off in a different direction. Edward found in his new companion an inexhaustible mine of intelligence concerning the manners of the people of the North.

"You see," said he, "how open every man's countenance is; how ready every individual is to be civil. No matter how much he may be jostled in the crowd, he is willing to submit to the inconvenience, and to yield the way to his neighbour. This state of things, however, will only last for a few hours. Whiskey will soon overcome discretion, and you will then see this prudent, cautious people, who now seem so anxious to avoid giving offence, that they will not resent even real annoyances, taking fire at a look, and becoming ready to knock down every man who comes in their way!"

A recruiting party of soldiers now passed them, for whom the crowd made way without seeming to pay them the slightest attention in any other respect. Far different was their deportment to a party of rope-dancers and equestrian performers, who next advanced, mounted on their well-taught steeds with trumpets sounding, and preceded by a Pickle Herring, whose antic grimaces and low jests excited frequent peals of laughter among the assembled multitude. It was with some difficulty that Edward and his companion kept their ground until this splendid and noisy procession had gone past; when, proceeding onwards, they came to the tent of an itinerant dealer in haberdashery, at the one end of which sat a group of well-dressed country girls. Edward immediately knew one of them to be his acquaintance, Peggy Caldwell; and while the doctor's attention was drawn to a fine, noble looking horse which a jockey was putting through his paces at some distance, he approached her.

"Miss Caldwell," said he, "I am glad to meet with you here. Is there anything within this tent I can have the pleasure of bestowing upon you, in token of my gratitude for your attention to me during my confinement in your father's house?"

"I believe, sir," she replied, somewhat abashed, "it would be wrong in me to take any present from you."

"You will gratify me," said Edward, in a persevering manner, "by receiving some gift — a new gown, or a new shawl, or anything else you choose, as a testimony of my regard for you."

"Hold!" cried a loud determined voice behind him. "Gentle or simple, by G—d, you shant affront Miss Caldwell in my presence."

"Who are you?" demanded Edward, as he turned round, and beheld an active looking young fellow whose countenance indicated that he felt an offence, and was determined to resent it. "Who are you, who dares address me so rudely in the public street?"

"As to that," said the other, "I will let you feel wha I am, gin you dare to affront that young woman again in my hearin. She's no o' the kind you tak her to be."

"I am as incapable of insulting that young woman as you, or any other of her friends can be," returned Edward, "but I am capable and determined to punish any unprovoked rudeness that may be offered to myself."

Peggy here interfered, and explained to the young man that the gentleman had not offended her; that he was the person whom Mr. O'Halloran had saved from drowning, and on whom she had attended when he was confined in her father's house. The doctor now advanced, for he had overheard part of the altercation.

"What is the matter? Jemmy," said he to the young man.

"Naething," replied Jemmy, "I see I mistook the thing; and I beg the gentleman's pardon. I was owre hasty. But I hope his honour an' you will oblige me, by comin' wi' Peggy and these ither lasses, to tak share o' half a pint, an mak' up the matter."

"Since your acknowledgment is as candid as your attack was unprovoked," said Edward, "I shall drink to our reconciliation, but it shall be only on condition that Peggy previously receives from me some donation, as I before proposed, and you yourself may choose it for her."

A silk shawl, alternately striped with green, white, and red, an arrangement of colours then much affected by the United Irishmen, was accordingly purchased for Peggy, and the party immediately retired into the next public house, every room of which was so completely filled with people, that they could scarcely find seats.

"What a terrible consumption of ardent spirits," thought Edward as he seated himself, "must take place in the markets and fairs of this part of the country! No bargain, it appears, can be concluded, nor any offence atoned for, without the interference of this enemy to human happiness."

While he thus meditated, Jemmy Hunter seated himself beside him, and in a low whisper, said, "Ye maun ken, sir, that Peggy an' me are sweet-hearts. I like her sae weel that I canna see ony body else lookin' at her, without taking it amiss. Besides, ye maun grant that it was na very creditable for a poor bonny lass, like her, to be ta'en notice to by a rich lookin' gentleman sa far abune her, in the market. I hope ye wanna be offended at me, as I did na ken that you only wanted to pay a debt o' frien'ship."

"Your motive, I perceive," replied Edward, "was good; and not being acquainted with the etiquette of this part of the country on such occasions, I may have done wrong. On these accounts, I assure you, I entirely forgive the harshness of your conduct, but, could this explanation not have taken place, without accompanying it with such a useless ceremony as whiskey drinking?"

"Na, na, sir, by my troth, we'll ha' nae dry reconcilements. Besides ye maun ken (whispering close into Edward's ear) I wanted to treat the lassie hersel to a dram. It mak's courtin' sweet on market days."

Edward having no argument to oppose to this last remark, gave a smile, and nodded in acquiescence to the propriety of Jemmy's method of courting.

When the company in various parts of the room began to grow noisy, which, as the country people had now commenced setting themselves thoroughly to their cups, was soon the case, Edward and the doctor thought proper to withdraw. On reaching the street, they perceived a great commotion among the crowd; the people running all in one direction. They soon understood that a quarrel had taken place between two drunken fellows; and observed that the men were running pell-mell either to gratify curiosity, or to see fair play, while the women were hurrying fearlessly forward to separate and pacify the combatants. The combatants, at length, were seen belabouring each other heartily with large sticks, whenever the crowd permitted them to approach near enough. Their immediate friends, at last, coming upon the scene, they were carried away in different directions, streaming with blood, and each uttering the most terrible imprecations, not so much against his antagonist as against those who had interfered to prevent a longer continuance of the affray.

Edward was persuaded that the assistance of his medical friend would have been immediately required by some one of the parties, but the doctor assured him that he expected no such thing. "Such quarrels," said he, "generally produce only black eyes, or a few bruises about the head, for which the people who engage in them care so little that they scarcely ever drink a single gill the less on account of them. Formerly these fights occasioned considerable animosity between the families related to the parties. At present this is not the case. As soon as sobriety returns, the combatants forget their rage, shake hands, drink a few gills more in token of friendship, and in the height of their conviviality, perhaps again dispute, and try the strength of each other's sculls with renewed fierceness and animosity. If, indeed, the dispute be of a religious or political nature, it often assumes a more malignant character, and involves numbers in its consequences. Often pitched battles are appointed, and actually fought by the contending factions, when the civil power has to interfere for their suppression. In these threatening times, the military are frequently called out in aid of the constables, in order to preserve the peace, which otherwise it would be impossible to effect."

At this moment, a guard of soldiers was seen approaching, commanded by their lieutenant, but under the direction of the high constable of the town. Having dispersed the crowd, which the late fight had collected, they entered every public house to ascertain if all was quiet, while the constable left strict injunctions upon each landlord to entertain no company later than nine o'clock that evening, on pain of being subjected to the penalty for keeping an irregular house, which the late law, adapted to the troublesome nature of the times rendered very severe upon publicans.

CHAP. V.

Light care had he for life, and less for fame. But not less fitted for the desperate game;
He deemed himself marked out for others hate, And mocked at ruin so they shared his
fate.

What car'd he for the freedom of the crowd, He raised the humble but to bend the proud.
Inured to hunters, he was found at bay, And they must kill, they cannot spare the prey.
In voice, mein, gesture, savage nature spoke, And from his eye the gladiator broke.
Byron.

The doctor being called away on some business, Edward returned to the inn where his servant staid. Here he found O'Halloran and the stranger who had some hours before taken him aside on the street. They were sitting, one at each end of a table, in an angle of a tolerably large room, which, like every other in the house at that juncture, was quite full of people enjoying the convivial cup with great noise and good humour. Edward observed that his friend and the stranger were the two most silent people in the room, and he was surprised to find that O'Halloran, although he was evidently on an intimate footing with the stranger, never named him.

The latter was wrapped in a great coat, booted and spurred, and held in his hand a huge horseman's whip, heavily loaded with lead. He appeared to be about forty years of age, slightly pockpitted, very muscular, and broad shouldered, fully five feet ten inches high, with small gray eyes and heavy eyebrows. There was something very daring and at the same time very gloomy in his countenance. He sat with his back to the wall seemingly abstracted in deep meditation, with his hat drawn forward over his face, so as partly to conceal it. O'Halloran appeared also to be rather in a thoughtful mood, although there was something of satisfaction visible in his countenance. He was proposing to Edward to return home, when the attention of the company was attracted by the arrival of two dragoons at the door of the inn, with intelligence of an alarming nature from Belfast.

They gave an account of the assassination of one M'Bride, an informer, which had taken place in that town, the preceding evening, by means, it was conjectured, of an air-gun, no report having been heard, although the deceased was shot dead on the spot. They produced some printed handbills describing the persons of the supposed perpetrators, and offering a reward of five hundred pounds, for the apprehension of each. They said, that parties of the military had been dispatched in all directions, in search of them, and that they had come on the northern route for that purpose.

The whole Inn now became a scene of confusion, occasioned by the multitude rushing in to obtain particular information of the affair. This confusion continued until the arrival of George M'Claverty, Esq. the principal acting magistrate of the neighbourhood.

He stationed some soldiers to guard the doors, until he should examine every suspicious person in the house, and compare him with the descriptions in the hand-bills.

The stranger had disappeared on the first arrival of the horsemen. Edward, therefore, was almost the only person in the house totally unknown to the magistrate. He was accordingly very particular in scrutinizing him. The first description was read.

'Five feet ten inches' — that was nearly Edward's height — 'Firm made and very muscular,' he was the former but not the latter. Still so far it might do — 'Slightly pock-pitted' — Edward had only one or two traces of the small-pox. — 'Full-chested' — he was portly enough in his appearance. All this might answer. — 'Forty years of age' — Here the description was totally out. Edward did not appear to be much above twenty. — 'Reddish, straight hair' — Here the application altogether failed. Edward's hair was black, and somewhat curled.

"Well!" said the magistrate, "let us see the other description. Five feet high — That won't do — Stoop shouldered — That won't do either. Young man, what is your name?"

"Middleton, sir."

"Where do you come from?"

"From the neighbourhood of Dublin."

"A damned seditious neighbourhood! What is your business in the North?"

"Curiosity, sir."

"A damned suspicious employment! Is there any one here who knows you?"

"Mr. O'Halloran, sir."

"A damned suspicious — I was going to say seditious acquaintance — Mr. O'Halloran, I beg your pardon. Although as yet we have no information against you sufficient to warrant your committal, we have heard enough to render you suspected. I am sorry for it, as I know you are, in other respects, a worthy enough character."

"I thank you," said O'Halloran, "for your favourable opinion. As to this gentleman, if my report in his behalf will not be taken, perhaps that of Doctor Farrell will."

"If Doctor Farrell says that he is a true man," replied the magistrate, "I will immediately crack a bottle of wine with him to His Majesty's health, and you will join us, I hope, Mr. O'Halloran. The King has not a better subject in his dominions than the Doctor."

The Doctor soon made his appearance, and having declared his opinion in favour of Edward's loyalty, the wine was introduced by the magistrate's order. Edward immediately filled a glass to the King's health, and drinking it started to his feet. "Mr. M'Claverty," said he, "you are an entire stranger to me, and I now find you on important official duty, enquiring after the perpetrators of a shocking murder. These circumstances amply excuse if they do not quite justify the manner in which you have accosted me. Were it otherwise, no man with impunity should have made insinuations of my being either an assassin or a rebel. I will not obstruct you in the doing of your duty, nor take offence at being exposed to an examination to which my being a stranger under the present circumstances, rendered me sufficiently liable. If you have done with your interrogatories, however, I shall now, if Mr. O'Halloran accompanies me, withdraw. Should you want me at any time within the space of eight days, you shall find me either at this inn or at my friend's castle."

He then retired with O'Halloran, and immediately ordered out their horses. While they were getting ready, Tom Mullins took Edward aside, with a face of great importance.

"Master," said he, "I want to ask your honour, would it be right to be made a croppy? Here is a very good friend of mine, they call Tom Darragh, who says it will make a man of me; and that every true Irishman ought to be united. By Jasus, said I, I am an Irishman, every drop of my blood, but if my master, who knows everything better than I do — which you know you do, your honour — says I shouldn't, then I think I may still belong to my own country without being united."

"Tom!" said Edward, "I desire you not to converse with any of the people you suspect to be united, especially if they attempt to seduce you into their confederacy. It would be next thing to becoming a rebel to join them."

"And haven't you been put up, master?"

"Mullins," demanded Edward rather angrily, "has anyone had the audacity to tell you so?"

"Why, sure, sir, didn't Darragh himself, who says he knows all about these matters, tell me so not two hours ago. He said he could swear that the old gentleman you came here with had done it. Well, said I, if you can swear that, I'll be put up too. So we got a pint of whiskey, and when we had drunk a couple of rounds to old Ireland and St. Patrick, he went away to get a bible, and was bidding me stand on my feet to take the oath, when the horsemen came, and we both ran to the door to see what the crowd meant."

"So you have not yet taken the oath?" said Edward.

"No, sir; and it just came into my head when I saw you here that I would ask your honour about it, for I thought that if you were up yourself you would know whether there was any good in it."

"I am not up, as you call it," said Edward. "I am no United Irishman; and, hear me, Tom, the moment I know you to be one, I shall dismiss you from my service."

"Arrah, master, don't be angry; for if it displeases you, I won't take the oath for one of them."

After a few more cautions on the subject, and also with regard to secrecy concerning himself, Edward left Tom, and set off with O'Halloran for the castle. He was anxious to hasten his friend's departure from the town, lest his obnoxious politics, and his imprudent warmth, might betray him into some difficulties. On their way, they called at the post office, and received the newspapers, which had just arrived. They then rode on in silence, until they were nearly a mile from town, when Edward observed, that the market scenes were very amusing, but that, in this instance, any satisfaction he had experienced was more than counterbalanced by the unpleasant intelligence of the horrible murder that had been committed in Belfast.

"Sir!" said O'Halloran, "killing for self-preservation is surely no murder; and it was certainly meritorious to destroy a traitor whose longer existence would have been the destruction of hundreds."

"No man can plead self-defence," replied Edward, "unless he be personally attacked, which does not appear to have been the case with the perpetrators of this action; and deliberate assassination, in cold blood, even when the most abandoned and dangerous character is the victim, carries with it something so abhorrent to my feelings, and so contrary to all my ideas of morality, that I do not see how it can be justified, even on the supposition of it being intended to prevent occurrences by which others might eventually suffer."

"Your laws," said O'Halloran, "may acknowledge the propriety of self-defence only in repelling a personal attack, but your laws in this, as in many other cases are erroneous guides by which to estimate the morality or immorality of an action. Nature directs us better. She tells us that, by every means in our power, we should frustrate the machinations of our enemies and prevent impending evils from falling upon us by the destruction, either publicly or privately, of those who would inflict them."

"The establishment of such a doctrine," replied Edward, "as the propriety of privately destroying our enemies, would abolish all security of personal safety, which is one of the chief advantages enjoyed from governments and laws. Each individual would be constituted the sole judge of whether he is threatened with sufficient danger to warrant the destruction of his neighbour, and malice or interest would seldom fail to aggravate the slightest injury into a sanction for murder. Hence the flood-gates of all the malignant passions that generate perpetual strife and blood-shed, would be opened upon society."

At this moment the stranger who had engrossed so much of O'Halloran's company during the day, galloped down a lane from a farm-house, and joined them on the road. Edward had observed this man leaving the inn very hastily the instant the dragoons were announced. This circumstance had excited a vague suspicion that he might be one of the assassins. This suspicion almost arose to a certainty, when he read the first description, that the magistrate had attempted to apply to himself. On his approach now, Edward was more particular in observing him, and was forcibly struck with the exact correspondence of his person with the description in all its traits. He made a bow to Edward, which he returned coolly, for his soul shuddered at the idea of being in company with a murderer.

"M'Cauley," said O'Halloran, "the minions of government are now on the alert to discover those brave fellows, who have avenged their country, and saved upwards of two hundred of her patriots from the gallows, by the destruction of the perjured M'Bride. Their suspicion falls upon every stranger, and they were likely, before we left town, to give some trouble to this gentleman.

"I suppose," said M'Cauley, "your magistrate, M'Claverty, is very zealous on this occasion. But it may yet be so much the worse for him."

No reply was made, and silence continued until they were within a mile of the castle. M'Cauley then stopped suddenly. "Mr. O'Halloran," said he, looking at the same time earnestly in Edward's face, for the whole three had stopped, "if I may judge from appearance, your friend here, possesses too much honour to betray a man who reposes so much confidence in him as to entrust him with his life."

O'Halloran replied, "that he had every reliance on Edward's honour, But—"

"No buts," said the other, "if he is a man of honour, he shall know who I am, let his views of my conduct be what they may. Young man," continued he, addressing Edward, "you see before you, one whose whole heart and soul is devoted to his country; and, who to avenge her cause upon a traitor, has not scrupled to offend human laws past forgiveness; and, perhaps, in the opinion of many good men, has also violated the laws of heaven. Of this, however, he can assure you, his own conscience applauds the deed. Conviction tells him he has done his duty. He has not only prevented the lives of more than two hundred patriots from falling into the hands of tyrants who know no mercy; he has also prevented his country's enemies from becoming acquainted with the efforts her sons are making to free her from bondage. Sir, you may condemn my action. I have destroyed an enemy to my country, who had sworn to be her friend, but you must respect my motives; they were purely patriotic. I am not blood-thirsty, but in competition with my country's welfare, I value neither my own blood nor that of any other man. In short, I have destroyed M'Bride, the informer, before he got his traitorous designs accomplished, and should the gallows be my reward, I shall there glory in the deed."

The magnanimity of M'Cauley made a strong impression on Edward. He deplored his infatuation, he condemned his crime, but he admired his devoted fidelity to the cause he had espoused. He assured him, that although he would rather not have been entrusted with his secret, he should have no cause to repent the confidence he had placed in him.

O'Halloran's countenance brightened at this assurance, and with more than usual spirits he led the way to the castle. On entering, Edward was introduced to an inmate of the castle whom he had not before seen.

This was the only sister of O'Halloran, who had been some weeks absent, and had just returned a few hours before, accompanied by a Miss Agnew, at whose father's house she had been visiting. The old lady was remarkably intelligent, active and cheerful for her time of life. She was older than her brother; and might now be about her sixty-fifth year. At the early period of her life she enjoyed the sweets of matrimony for about five years, but her husband who was an extensive merchant in Belfast, was drowned in a voyage to Liverpool. His name was Brown, and, although they never had children, they were tenderly attached to each other. Indeed, so fondly did Mrs. Brown cherish the memory of her beloved husband, who had been her first and favourite lover, that she would never after his death listen to the addresses of any man.

Miss Agnew was a pretty, lively, rosy-cheeked girl of nineteen, who had lately finished a boarding school education, and possessed an easy, gay sort of familiarity in her manner, which was far from displeasing. She was, occasionally, fond of indulging in a sportive kind of wit approaching to what is vulgarly termed quizzing. This, however, if we except a little coquetry, which was natural to her, was her only foible, for she was in reality a well informed and well-bred handsome girl, with a fortune of five thousand pounds at her own disposal, bequeathed to her several years before by a deceased uncle.

This accession to the castle party was highly pleasing to Edward, as it promised not only to be the means of preventing politics from engrossing the conversation, but of affording him more of Ellen's society, who would not be so shy of her company when it would be only sought for in the presence of her female friends.

After dinner the newspapers were produced. On opening the Belfast News-Letter, O'Halloran read aloud the following paragraph:

"Barbarous Assassination. — Yesterday evening a shocking murder was committed in North Street, in this town. A respectable man named M'Bride, was shot dead at the mouth of Round Entry by some villains who had stationed themselves there for that purpose. It is supposed that the instrument used was an air-gun, as no report was heard at the time that the deed was done. Favoured by the confusion which took place the villains escaped, it is supposed, up the Entry, and have hitherto eluded pursuit. Two men, namely M'Cauley, and Kelly, were observed standing about the mouth of the Entry for some time previous to the commission of the crime; and are suspected. Descriptions of their persons are given in an advertisement in another part of our paper, where it will also be seen that a reward of five hundred pounds is offered for the apprehension of each. It is suspected that they belong to the society of United Irishmen; and that to prevent an exposure of the designs of that association, which it is thought the deceased intended to make to government, was the motive that urged these wicked and misguided wretches to the perpetration of the foulest and blackest crime of which men can be guilty."

"The editor of this paper," said O'Halloran, when he had finished reading the paragraph, "has always been a tool to the government. But let us see what the Northern Star says on the subject. The conductors of that paper are true Irishmen, men of enlightened minds and independent spirits, who cannot be bought."

"A warning to traitors. — Yesterday evening an awful but just dispensation was inflicted upon the notorious M'Bride, for an unprincipled conspiracy with some Orange magistrates to betray the cause of his country, in violation of the most solemn oaths. We are informed that this unhappy man had professed great zeal in the cause of the United Irishmen, and had consequently enjoyed a great share of their confidence. It appears, however, that this zeal was affected for the purpose of treachery. His intentions to betray the leaders of the Union into the hands of government, it is said, were only of late discovered, but discovered in such a manner as to leave no doubt on the subject. On his way to the stage office where he intended to take the coach for Dublin in order to give his information to the ministry, he was shot at the mouth of Round Entry in North-street.

"We are no friends to assassination or any other mode of destroying human life, but when the circumstances, that those who were concerned in this action, had either to do it or suffer themselves, is considered, it is hoped that the public, if they cannot altogether justify, will at least be ready to pardon them. Those at least who so loudly eulogized the destroyer of Marat, cannot with any consistency, condemn the destroyers of M'Bride. We trust that the fate of this unfortunate man will be a caution to all who would betray their country, for it demonstrates that the people have energy and promptitude sufficient to baffle the attempts of treachery, and to inflict vengeance on their enemies."

The reading of these paragraphs made an impression of deep horror on the minds of the ladies, and when O'Halloran had finished, Mrs. Brown remarked with a sigh, that the state of society must be dreadful when even its most virtuous and enlightened members, were found ready to exert their eloquence in palliating the most terrible of crimes.

"Ah! my brother!" she exclaimed, preventing him from interrupting her, "I know that you would plead necessity and self-preservation. But necessity is an old apology, and is always a dreadful one; and self-preservation, valuable as it is, is surely bought at a dear price, when assassination is paid for it."

"Sister," said O'Halloran, "we shall not at present contend this matter. The deed is done, and I hope that God will bless it, as he did the slaying of Eglon by the patriot Ehud."

He then arose, and requesting M'Cauley to accompany him, they withdrew together.

CHAP. VI.

What though no gaudy titles grace my birth, Titles the servile courtier's lean reward, Sometimes the pay of virtue, but more oft
The hire which greatness gives to sycophants, Yet Heaven has made me honest, made me more Than e'er a king did when he made a lord.
Rowe.

"Poor man!" said Mrs. Brown, when her brother had retired, "Ireland had never a warmer friend; and if his power was equal to his wishes, there would not be an unhappy individual within the limits of her four provinces. Mr. Middleton, I do not know your political sentiments, but I shall have no hesitation in telling you mine. I wish earnestly for the peace and prosperity of my country, without respect to her form of government, and have no objection to live under the protection of the British constitution, except when that protection degenerates into oppression, which, to our fatal experience, we find that it frequently does."

"Madam," replied Edward, "if you can only answer me one question in the affirmative, I shall be happy to find my opinion on these matters corroborated, and sanctioned by yours. Do you not think that conspiracy, treason, and civil war, not to speak of midnight burnings, and assassinations, are injudicious and unjustifiable methods of correcting the misgovernment, which we all acknowledge to have but too much prevailed of late years in this country?"

"I do," was the reply.

"Then we agree," said Edward.

"Since that is the case," said Miss Agnew, "we have no occasion to talk more on this horrible subject. I never hear it discussed, but it throws me into the vapours; and absolutely that dreadful story from Belfast, has depressed my spirits so terribly tonight, that I shall not be able to recover them this month. Suppose Ellen gives us a song; perhaps it may do me good. Let us have one of Mr. M'Nelvin's, and I'll try to touch the tune on the Piano."

As her aunt and Edward joined in this request, Ellen complied, remarking that, "as she was not in good enough spirits to give them an air sufficiently lively to counteract the disorder of which Miss Agnew complained, she would sing them some verses which were lately put into her hands by a friend of hers, who had once been an exile from his native country, and who to relieve the pain of absence from all he loved, had frequently recourse to the consolations of the muse."

Oft as by fair Ohio's side,
I court the solitary scene; Of hoary forests spreading wide,
Or prairies waving fresh and green; From musing on the evening ray
That gilds the glittering landscape o'er, On fancy's wings I fly away,
To Erin's sea-encircled shore.
There on the primrose covered vale,
By natal Inver's hallowed stream; Once more I breathe the scented gale,
That oft refreshed my childhood's dream: And sweet in many a tuneful lay,
I hear the warblers of the grove, Where once as blithe in song as they,
I poured the rural strains of love.
In that fair hawthorn-skirted plain,
Where youthful pleasures first I knew; I meet my long-lost friends again,
For ever loved, for ever true:

And, oh! while rapture uncontroll'd,
Bright glistens in their ardent eyes, I to my glowing breast enfold
The partners of my early joys.
Fair visions of celestial hue!
O! still possess with kindly spell, This aching heart, which but for you,
Might bid all earthly joys farewell.
From warm affection's source divine,
Your ever blissful charms arise; Oh! let that throb be ever mine,
Your rapture-giving smile supplies.

"I am still melancholy," said Miss Agnew, drawing a long sigh when Ellen had done singing, "I am still melancholy, but it is now a melancholy of a sweeter nature than I felt before. Oh! how pleasant it would have been to have wandered on the banks of the Ohio with your poet, when he produced those verses! But pray, dear, won't you tell us who is the author?"

"He is a man," replied Ellen, "whose present station in the world almost approaches that of a mendicant."

"A very poetical station, truly!" said Miss Agnew.

"But although," continued Ellen, "he has the garb, he never exhibits the meanness of a beggar."

"That is still more poetical," said Mrs. Brown.

"And although" Ellen again continued, "he has now the gravity and wisdom of sixty, he possesses all the warm-heartedness and enthusiastic benevolence of twenty."

"That is most poetical of all," said Edward.

"This person" resumed Ellen, "whom you have all pronounced to be so poetical, is no other than our Recluse, old Saunders."

"I shall visit him tomorrow," said Miss Agnew, for I won't be easy till I pay my respects to his bardship."

"But hush!" cried Mrs. Brown, "Who is you? Hah! It is Peg Dornan's coarse voice."

"Is the bonny young Dublin gentleman within?" was vociferated from the brazen lungs of Peg, to a servant in the hall.

"He is. What do you want with him?" was demanded.

"I want to see himsel. I'll tell my errand to nae body else. An'l maun see him soon, whare'er he be."

Edward went immediately to the hall. "What is the matter, Peg?" said he.

"Come awa', sir, wi' me and ye'll ken a' about it, belyve."

He followed her without hesitation till they came near to the mysterious rock, from which he first saw Ellen and her grandfather.

"They're gaen in noo," said Peg, "but when they come oot they'll, maybe, talk o't again. Ye maun wait here, gin you want to hear them; an' it concerns you nearly. I'll awa', but lie ye doon amang thir bushes, and watch them, they'll come close this way."

He had not lain long, until M'Cauley and a stranger appeared advancing from the rock. When they approached within a few yards of him, at a place where two paths crossed each other, they stopped.

"Tell me before we part," said the stranger to M'Cauley, "what is your intention with respect to this young man to whom you so foolishly entrusted your secret. If he refuses to take the oath, I advise you to despatch him, for dead men tell no tales."

"I shall be guided by O'Halloran respecting him," answered M'Cauley.

"O'Halloran is too womanish-hearted, to give good advice in this case."

"His advice I shall, nevertheless, abide by. The disclosure was voluntary on my part, and unsolicited by the young man; and I am much deceived, if I cannot confide in his honour, which is already pledged to me, almost as firmly as in his oath."

"Trust no man's honour in these times," said the other. "Happy would it be for our United confederacy, if we had trusted even fewer oaths than we have done. Government would not then have been so well prepared to give us a warm reception, whenever we shall attack it. But here comes O'Halloran himself."

The matter being referred to O'Halloran, he exclaimed with energy. "Sooner than a hair of his head shall fall, whether he join us or not, you shall pierce me to the heart. He is my guest, and my friend; and I shall protect him as such. Darragh, let us hear no more of this detestable proposal. It makes me shudder to think of it. Such atrocities only tend to weaken the best of causes. If frequently committed by our party, all virtuous and feeling men will think themselves contaminated by our connexion."

"You are right," said M'Cauley, "and the first man that raises a hand against Mr. Middleton, makes me his enemy."

"You may act as you please," said Darragh, "but I foretell that this fellow will yet make you repent your present forbearance. He must be a damned Orangeman in his heart. I could have made his servant a United Irishman today, but for his cursed interference; and now the fellow knows that I am one, and no doubt will be ready to inform on me, but, by G—d, before tomorrow night, I'll make the rascal unfit to tell stories."

"I beseech you," said O'Halloran, "not to be so rash. The poor fellow can be easily persuaded that you intended nothing but sport with him."

"Avast," said Darragh, "that won't do. If he swears to the facts as they took place, an orange jury and a pensioned judge, will never consider whether I was in sport or in earnest." He broke short the conversation by bidding them good night, in a rather surly tone, and walked off towards the town.

O'Halloran and M'Cauley moved towards the rock, and Edward, on whose mind, it will be supposed, the conversation had made a deep impression, returned to the castle. Before he reached it, however, Peg Dornan overtook him.

"Weel, sir, did you hear aucht you did na' like?"

"Too much, Peg, but how came you to know anything about it?"

"Why, sir, gin you'll no be in a hurry, I'll tell you," (for Edward's perturbation of mind made him walk very fast) "just as I was sauntering alang the shore, about an hour syne, I saw Tam Darragh, and anither doure-looking chiel they ca' M'Cauley, walking tegither — an' no' wishing to be seen by them,

I lay doon amang the bushes, an' they caM' quite close to me, an' said, the tain to the tither, that's Darragh said to M'Cauley, 'That chap at the castle maun be an Orangeman, an' will, as sure as death, tell your secret. You maun shoot him, or tak' him aff some ither way, gin you want to be safe yoursel.' What! thought I, are they gaun to kill my bonny Mr. Middleton? De'il be in my tongue, but I'll tell him every word o't. But I thoucht you would na' be likely to credit sitch an unfeasible story; so I fancied it better to gie you a chance o' hearin' about it yoursel, an' gin you should na' happen to hear it, I would then tell you. Guid nicht, an' tak' care o' yoursel, my bonny lad, for they're no' canny cheils ye heard talkin."

Edward desired her to communicate the affair to no one else; and thanking her for her timely information, he gave her half a guinea, and hastened to the castle. Just as he entered the avenue, he perceived old Saunders coming out of the gate, and not having come to any determination how to act, he thought it would be proper to consult the old man, in whose prudence he had every reason to confide. He accordingly communicated to him, the present aspect of his affairs, adding, that with respect to his own safety, he was under no concern, but how to protect his servant from the malice of Darragh, without informing upon the latter, and having him arrested, a measure to which he had the utmost aversion, gave him a great deal of perplexity.

The Recluse, after a few moments reflection, replied. "Fear nothing for your servant. I shall undertake for his safety." He then desired Edward to accompany him to William Caldwell's, where they found young Hunter, with Peggy and one of her brothers, just returned from the market. The old man requested Jemmy to go with him and Edward to the glen. On arriving there, he communicated to him the danger in which Tom Mullins then stood, and asked him if he would be willing to render Edward a service, by rescuing him from it. The generous youth, rejoiced at the office assigned him.

"That I will!" said he, seizing Edward by the hand. "I'll stand by him, and if Tam Darragh, or ony bluid-thirsty rascal like him, ventures to lay a finger's end on him, he'll find whether his bones or mine be the hardest. I ha' been made a United Irishman, but I was na' made yin to stan' by an' see my frien's murdered."

"But you must go quietly about this business," said old Saunders, "we do not wish it to be made public. You know if the kingsmen were to be informed of it, they would soon sift the matter, and bring a great many more than the guilty into trouble."

"Just tell me what I maun do, an' I'll follow your directions to a hair's breadth," said Hunter.

"You will go without delay," returned the Recluse, "with a letter from Mr. Middleton to his servant, which will contain an order for him to obey you in every particular. But first you must make haste and saddle your best riding horse, and return here with him as soon as possible. By that time we shall have written instructions prepared for you."

In about half an hour, Hunter returned gallantly mounted on a prancing steed, as boldly determined to sally forth in defence of innocence, as ever any knight of chivalry was in the days of romance. Edward gave him a letter for Tom Mullins, and the Recluse a packet of sealed instructions, which he was desired not to open until he should convey Mullins as far as Antrim, about eighteen miles from Larne. He was desired not to set out in the night, lest Darragh should suspect his designs to be discovered, and thereby be rendered more rancorous and inveterate in his resolution to destroy Mullins, but he was ordered to keep a watchful eye on the motions of the former, until the latter should be out of his reach.

Having received these instructions, he clapped spurs to his horse, and with a light heart and a determined spirit, set swiftly forward on his benevolent errand. He rode so fast that he overtook Darragh who was on foot near the entrance of the town.

"What's the matter, Hunter," said Darragh, "that you ride so fast to town at such a late hour?"

"Naething, Tam," replied the other, "but I had to tak' some lasses hame frae the market, and I thoucht I would come back an' see some mair o' the fun, an' gin you ha' naething better to do, we'll ha' a naggin together."

In pursuance of this worthy resolution, they rapped at the door of the first public house they came to, which they found locked, although there was light enough to be seen, and noise enough to be heard from within, to assure them that the inmates had still sufficient employment to keep them out of bed for some time.

"Who is there?" was demanded by the landlord.

"A friend!" replied Darragh.

"Is it you, Tam," cried the other? "It is scarcely ten minutes since the soldiers have cleared the house, though I have let in some neighbours by the back way since that. Who is with you?"

"Nobody, but young Jemmy Hunter; you know Jemmy."

"If you go round behind the house, I'll let you into a back room, and blind the shutters. You'll make as little noise as you can, and take care that nobody sees you."

They followed his directions, and were soon seated with a fuming jug of hot punch before them. "Jemmy, you have been put up lately, I'm told," said Darragh. "That was right, man. Give me your hand. I wish every stout fellow in the country was united — we would then show the tyrants that we are as good as they are, for all so much as they despise us. But I'm afraid we'll never get one half of the country united; though if I had my way, it would soon be another story, for those who would not join us from love, I would compel to join us from fear!"

"Na, Tam, that would na do either," replied Jemmy, "for it would make a great many ill-wishers to the cause join it; and they would be likely to do it mair harm than guid."

"I would prevent them from betraying us, at least," said Darragh, "by making a few examples of informers. But Jemmy, I must tell that I am myself likely to be informed on by an Up-the-country, silly fellow that I wanted to swear in this morning.

He is servant to a cursed kingsman, that I thought Mr. O'Halloran had put up, but I was damnably mistaken; for when the stupid dog of a servant went to consult him about the business, he threatened him within an inch of his life, if he would take the oath. So that after exposing myself to the rascal, I could make nothing of him; and if the blockhead should take it into his head to inform against me, you know my life would not be worth a damn. But I'll run no risks, I'll send the dog to Lucifer, before I sleep, or my name is not Tom Darragh."

"Surely, Tam," said Hunter, "you would na be sa rash; the man has done na harm yet."

"Nor, by G—d," exclaimed the other, "shall it be long in his power to do harm."

"Hoot man! dinna talk this way; it's no safe for me to hear you; you may tak' it into your head to kill me for fear I should tell that you killed him."

"I can trust you, Jemmy; you know that it is in the guid cause; and you have sworn not to betray it."

"I never swore not to discover murder if I kend o't;" replied Hunter with spirit; "I'll keep ony secret you like but that: And when the United Irishmen want my help, I'll be ready with as guid a musket as ony in the parish to tak' the field. But Tam, tak' my advice; be a little moderate. You can keep close, ye ken, if you're afeared. But let us hae na mair killing in cauld bluid — we'll hae plenty o't in warm, I'll warrant you, when the time comes."

To these remarks, Darragh made no reply, but sat for some minutes in a rather thoughtful and sulky humour. At last he took Hunter by the hand, told him he believed him to be an honest fellow, that, perhaps, he might take his advice, but that happen what would, he was sure he would not injure him.

Hunter reflecting that he himself was commissioned to prevent the threatened crime from taking place, and conceiving that it was in his power to do so, assured him that he would not inform upon him, for anything that should happen. They then drank another gill sociably together; and retiring from the house by the way they entered it, separated in the street with expressions of mutual good will and confidence.

Hunter now proceeded to the Antrim Arms, and procured admission by mentioning the letter he had to deliver to Mullins. He informed the landlord that he should lodge with him all night.

"In the meantime," said he, "let this up-the-country frien' o' mine an' me, hae a jug o' punch in a room by oursels, for I hae some cracks for his ain ear."

The landlord obeyed, and in a moment Jemmy had another fuming pitcher at his side. This important matter being adjusted, he produced Edward's letter, and desired Tom to be ready for a journey by day-break. In a short time they retired to rest without Hunter having informed him of the designs of Darragh. In the morning they both rose with the dawn, and, while Hunter went to discharge the landlord's bill, Mullins hastened to prepare the horses. He was not long in the stable until two men presented themselves before him, one holding a pistol and the other a bible to his breast.

"Swear," said Darragh, who held the pistol, "that you will never inform any one that I wanted to make you a United Irishman, or you are, this instant, a dead man!"

"I will swear anything, fairly," said Mullins, petrified with astonishment, "but, dear gentlemen, only give me time to bless myself."

"We have no time to talk with you," exclaimed Darragh, "we must be gone, swear this instant, or be shot and damned!" and he raised his arm as if to perform the deed he threatened, when that arm was seized by Hunter, who hearing the last words of the threat, sprung upon him with the force and agility of a lion upon his prey, and threw him upon his back on the ground. The pistol went off in the struggle, and grazing the arm of the man who held the bible, lodged itself in the wall of the stable. "By Jasus, he can't hurt me now," cried Mullins, "so you too shall lie down in the dirt with your comrade, my jewel." So saying, he struck the poor bible holder such a blow as almost fractured his lower jaw, and fairly prostrated him alongside his companion, while the blood gushed like a torrent from his mouth and nostrils.

The noise soon brought the landlord to the spot, who, on hearing Mullins' statement of the case, would have secured Darragh and his companion, in order to have them carried before a magistrate, but Hunter opposed this, representing it as a political quarrel of which the government might make a great handle, and that, at all events, no good could result to either party by its prosecution. On Mullins, therefore, declaring that he wished for no further revenge, it was agreed to hush the matter on condition that Darragh should swear never again to make an attempt on Mullin's life, a condition with which he, in a very surly manner, complied. When this was done he could not, however, disguise the strongly-excited malignity of his passions, and, casting a fierce look at Hunter, "I shall yet be revenged," he ejaculated.

"May God forgive you!" said the good natured youth, who had heard him. "When your anger cools, I'm sure you'll no' say so."

The victors now set off in conformity to the Recluse's instructions, but they had not gone far before Hunter reflected that an account of the morning's transactions might induce his employers to change their intentions with respect to Mullins, especially as Darragh was now under the obligation of a solemn oath not to molest him. He, therefore, thought it prudent to convey Mullins to the Recluse's cavern in order to receive further instructions.

On arriving there, Hunter hastened to the castle for Edward, who, on coming to the cavern and learning the state of affairs, declared to the Recluse his opinion that Darragh would not regard an oath into which he had been frightened; and, that while either he or his servant remained in the neighbourhood, neither of them would be safe from his malignity. He, therefore, desired Hunter to proceed immediately on his journey with Mullins, and mentioned his intention to follow them as soon as he could make a proper excuse to O'Halloran for his hasty departure.

Hunter accordingly set off with his companion, but contrived to go nearly a mile out of his proper course, to give a parting salute to Peggy Caldwell. He found her blushing like one of the daughters of the morning; and hastily seizing her by the waist, impressed a short but hearty farewell upon her lips. She burst from his arms in some trepidation, but he soon again caught her.

"Hoot, Peggy, lass," said he, in an endearing tone, "dinna be sae flirted. It's a fareweel kiss for a few days. I'm gaun on an erran' o' your frien' Mr. Middleton. But you may tell my mother an' the rest, that I expect to be back in time to help to set the potatoes in the Lime-Kiln Knowe." He then gaily mounted his steed, and Mullins and he galloped off. In a short time, however, he slackened his speed to what may be called a conversation pace, for his heart was full of Peggy, and he wished to relieve his feelings by descanting on her charms.

"Isn't she a pretty lass, that?" said he to Mullins, "hae ye ony like her up the country, amang the wild Irish?"

"In troth and we have," replied Tom, "as beautiful creatures there, as ever sat by a turf fire to sing a poor fellow's heart to rest after a hard day's digging. By the mother of me! If the sweet looks of Biddy O'Flagherty herself, my second cousin, whom the priest wouldn't let me marry, bad luck to him, wouldn't have pierced the heart of a blind man, that is, if he had eyes to see her."

Instead of attending to ToM's eulogy on the power of Biddy O'Flagherty's charms, Hunter began in the fullness of his heart, to sing from the *Gentle Shepherd.*

'My Peggy is a young thing, Just entered in her teens;
Fair as day and sweet as May, Fair as day and always gay;
My Peggy is a young thing, An' I'm no' very auld,
An' weel I like to meet her at the walking o' the fauld."

At length he stopped. "Weel, Tam," said he, "I'll no' dispute the matter o' Biddy, what do ye ca' her, being a bonny lass, but gie me my ain Peggy, an' I care na' wha gets a' the lave o' the bonny lasses in the country. I'm thinking, Tam, it's no' a bad thing to be married, when yin gets wha yin likes."

"By my shoul, and that's my own opinion to a hair, master James;" replied Tom, "and Bridget's own self, the dear creature, would have married me, but that ill-looking thief, priest O'Bletherem, said he would excommunicate us for heresy, unless we paid him twenty pounds for a pardon; and the devil a twenty pounds had poor Tom Mullins in his life. So I thought it best to go to sarvice, and left my mother, and Paddy, and Barney, and little Juddy, to work at home, until I should make twenty pounds; and my master, God bless him, for he's a gentleman every inch of him, says he'll help me to get the priest's pardon as soon as we return home."

"Damn the priest! Tam," exclaimed Hunter, "why didn't you kick the rascal oot o' the hoose, for pitting atween you an' your sweetheart. Why, man, if Peggy were yince agreed, an' wha kens hoo soon it may be sae, a' the priests on this side o' hell, wi' the wh——re o' Babylon at their back, should na prevent us fra' being married. Hoot, man, when you gang hame, marry your lassie; tak' a frien's advice. Gin your master gies you twenty pund, lay it out on plenishing, an' stock for your farm, an' ne'er fash your thumb aboot the priest and his d——d pardon."

"Master Hunter," said Tom, "I believe you are a friend to poor Mullins, after all, for my own mother never gave me such good advice. Ah! honey, why weren't you with us when we argued the case with the priest, but could make nothing of him at all, at all, but had to listen and tremble, for he swore he would never let our souls, that is after they are dead, out of purgatory, if we got married and didn't pay him."

"By Heavens! Tam," exclaimed Hunter, "had I been there, I would hae thrashed the scoundrel, as soundly as ever he'll be thrashed in purgatory, though I hae a notion that auld Satan winna spare him, yince he gets his claws on him."

We shall leave our love-sick rustics to proceed on their journey, and entertain each other in their own unadorned and homely style, and direct our attention to Edward Barrymore, who was as deeply enamoured as either of them, and at that very moment anxiously pining for an opportunity to pledge his vows to the mistress of his affections. But in order to proceed with his affairs, we must open another chapter.

CHAP. VII.

Maid of the lovely rolling eye,
Maid of each grace that kindles love, Ah! do not frown to hear me sigh,
Nor do my faithful flame reprove!
For shouldst thou unpropitious be,
My griefs in secret shall remain; Ah! never will I tell to thee,
What would the hallowed bosom pain.
Thaunus the Druid.

The reader will remember that we left Edward and the Recluse together in the cavern. The old man, reluctant as he was to part with our hero, acknowledged the necessity of his speedily withdrawing from that part of the country, since he had, however innocently and unintentionally, became an object of suspicion to some of the United Irishmen.

"The virtuous and more influential of them" said he, "I know will oppose to the utmost of their power, any attempt to injure you, and will, no doubt, succeed in frustrating any such attempt if they only obtain timely information of its being intended. But the framers of this confederacy, have not been choice in selecting its members; and the more wicked and abandoned of them pay little respect to the opinions and wishes of the wiser and more virtuous, when they do not happen to correspond with their own passions and prejudices. It is not, therefore, to be expected that the injunctions of O'Halloran, or any other of their leaders, will have much influence in restraining the violence of such men as Darragh and his companion, who would set the orders of their supreme directory itself, if they interfered with their views, at defiance."

"My friend," replied Edward, "your good sense, and the interest you have evinced in my welfare, deserve my confidence. I will, therefore, entrust the dearest wishes of my soul to your keeping. It is now become necessary that I should leave this part of the country. Not only my own safety, but, perhaps, the safety of one dearer to me than myself, demands it; for, if I should fall, who would then, with the same solicitude, watch over her and defend her from danger? Ah! sir, so strongly have my affections become riveted on that object, that I feel as if one of the strings of my heart were breaking, when I think of leaving the part of the country where she resides, and, in times too like these, when evils threaten her from every quarter. Should misfortune overtake her in my absence, my only consolation will be, a reliance on your prudence and friendship to afford her protection, until I can fly to her aid. Promise me that you will give me frequent and speedy information of whatever may befall her; and that when the storm bursts, you will, if in your power, in this sacred asylum, afford her shelter from its fury. Promise me this, and the weight of anxiety that now oppresses me, shall be greatly relieved."

"I not only promise you this," said the Recluse, "but whatever else may be in my power to do for the safety and welfare of Ellen Hamilton."

"Will you consent to be the medium of any communications I may transmit to her?" asked Edward.

"I will," replied the Recluse without hesitation, "unless she forbids it. But hasten from this dangerous neighbourhood, for here there are active and malignant spirits aroused against you, for your destruction. Farewell, and may the Almighty God of all things, protect and bless you!"

"Farewell, father," said Edward, and he hastened to apprise O'Halloran of his intended departure, and to seek a farewell interview with Ellen.

The early part of the morning had been somewhat cloudy; and one of those gentle rains, known among the Northern Irish, by the name of May showers, had fallen, and rendered the atmosphere moist but not cold. The day, however, assumed a brighter aspect, and the advancing sun had dried away all the lucid pearls that had lately bespangled the tender springing grass, the lovely richness of whose verdure has procured for Ireland the appropriate epithet of the Emerald Isle. With this refreshing verdure were intermixed innumerable multitudes of those simple flowers, so sweetly described in the beautiful pastoral song of Gramachree.

The primrose pale and violet blue, Lay scattered o'er the fields;
The daisy pied, and all the sweets The dawn of nature yields;
Such fragrance in the bosom lies, Of her whom I adore;
Ah! grá mo chrói, mo cailín óg,
Is Mailligh mo stór.

Invited by the beauty of the season, and of the weather, Mrs. Brown, after breakfast, proposed to the ladies to walk along the meadows that skirted the shore, and lay between the castle and the promontory of Ballygally.

"Miss O'Halloran," said Miss Agnew as they walked onwards, "do you think this Mr. Middleton will remain long here? If I only knew who he is, and if he were only a little merrier in his manner, he appears in other respects, such an elegant young fellow, that I could almost fall in love with him; that is, I beg pardon, if he be not already engaged."

"That begging pardon," replied Ellen, "seems to come rather awkwardly into such a fine promising speech, for I cannot see what connexion it has with any other part of it."

"Oh dear me, Ellen," cried the other, "I forgot that love is always blind, or I would have spoken more plainly. The propriety of this improperly introduced ejaculation, only consists in the desire I had to obtain the pardon of your fair self, for proposing to fall in love with a handsome young man, whom you had the advantage of first seeing, and, of course, the privilege of first loving."

"If it will be any advantage to you," retorted Ellen, "I will relinquish my privilege in your favour; and here, in the presence of my aunt, I give you full liberty to fall in love with him, as soon and as deeply as you think proper."

"Very disinterested!" exclaimed Miss Agnew; "It is not every young lady now-a-days, who will sacrifice love to friendship."

"Hush!" said Mrs. Brown, "here comes the gentleman himself, and really he is such a fine looking youth, that if I were only forty years younger, I should threaten you both with a rival. As it is, however, I have a good mind to inform him of your controversy, and let him choose between you."

"Oh! aunt," exclaimed Ellen, "do not, I beseech you, mention that we spoke of him. You know I did not — it was altogether Miss Agnew's mad talk."

"I really believe, child," said Mrs. Brown, "that you are somewhat in love. This seriousness betrays you."

"Believe what you please, dear aunt, but do not mention that we spoke of him."

"At all events," cried Miss Agnew, "don't tell him till we reach the top of the hill yonder, and then, you know, we can act the three goddesses on Mount Ida, and he shall be Paris to settle our controversy."

"I should not wish to go through such a scene," replied Mrs. Brown, "lest it should be followed by a similar result. Juno and Pallas would imbibe eternal hatred against Venus, and then, nothing but war, barbarous war, could be expected amongst us."

"O then," said Ellen, entreatingly, "let us say nothing about it. Let us meet the young man, and treat him civilly, but I would not, for the world, that he should know, he excited any particular conversation amongst us."

"We shall talk of this again," said Mrs. Brown, in a whisper to Ellen, for Edward was now so near, as to prevent her from speaking aloud, unless she chose that he should hear what she said. She then turned to him. "Mr. Middleton," said she, "if you have no better employment in view, we shall be gratified with your company during our ramble."

"You cannot be so much gratified with my company as I shall be with yours," replied Edward, "and, surely, Mrs. Brown cannot suppose me so insensible to the beauties of nature, and the charms of refined conversation, as not to prefer the enjoyment of such a scene, in such a company, to any other employment whatever."

"I expected as much from your gallantry," rejoined Mrs. Brown.

"But, aunt," said Ellen, "if Mr. Middleton has any business of importance to attend to, you know that it would be wrong that he should neglect it on our account."

He assured them that he had no business on hand of sufficient importance to induce him to forego the pleasures he felt in their company.

"How do you like the appearance of our part of the country?" asked Mrs. Brown, turning round upon an eminence to which they had arrived; and from which they had a tolerable prospect of the surrounding scenery.

"Everything in your country," replied Edward, "has had the effect of highly interesting my feelings, and exciting my admiration. The wonderful curiosities and romantic grandeur of your bold basaltic coast, could not fail to impress attention from the most unobservant spectator; while the fervid feelings which animate your people must be a subject of deep interest, not unmixed, I must confess, in these distracted times, with some concern, in the breast of every one who wishes for their happiness. In short, since I visited these scenes, I may truly say that I have lived more, that is, I have felt more of both the sweets and bitters of life, short as the period has been, than I did through the whole previous course of my existence."

"I really believe you have felt sharply of the bitters," said Miss Agnew. "Yon gulf below gave you a strong and almost a fatal sample of them."

"Had I met with nothing to make a deeper impression on my mind," replied Edward, "than the accident to which you allude, in leaving these scenes, my regret would not, perhaps, have been greater than it will be, but my recollections would have been more unmingled with sorrow. In short, ladies, I, this morning, received accounts which constrain me to an almost instantaneous departure, a circumstance which I assure you gives me a heavy heart." In saying this, he turned his eyes towards Ellen. She attempted to speak, but her voice faltered, while the blood which but the moment before had spread the bloom of roses on her cheeks, had fled and left them as pale as ivory.

"What is the matter?" exclaimed Mrs. Brown, who had observed her emotion.

"Nothing," she replied. "I felt suddenly a little dizzy. I, perhaps — I was fatigued, but I am now better."

"You are weak," said Edward, in agitation, "may I beg permission to support you?"

"It — it is not now necessary; I am quite well again."

"We had better return home," said Mrs. Brown, "Mr. Middleton you will have the goodness to support her."

Edward again offered his assistance, requesting her to lean on his arm. She reluctantly complied, but desired her aunt not to forego the pleasure of a longer excursion, as she felt perfectly able to continue it.

"Well then," said Miss Agnew, "let us proceed to the top of the hill, as we before proposed. Mrs. Brown and I shall drag each other up — and since you have become an invalid, we will permit you to engross all Mr. Middleton's assistance. Come along, Mrs. Brown, we had better take a start of them, for you see we are to have no help but our own agility in the ascent."

So saying, she dragged Mrs. Brown onwards, telling her that the two sentimental people behind would follow on the wings of imagination.

"Do not leave us," cried Ellen, "or I shall be again obliged to fatigue myself in hurrying after you."

Whether it was by accident or design, however, let love-casuists determine, instead of keeping pace with their companions, Edward and Ellen walked so slowly that in a few minutes the others were too far advanced to hear their conversation.

"Ah! Miss O'Halloran," said Edward, who gladly seized so favourable an opportunity of opening his soul to his beloved, "you cannot imagine the pangs that I feel on account of leaving this place, for you are not aware how powerful are the chains that bind me to it. I have travelled round the greater part of the kingdom, I have witnessed numerous interesting scenes, and have fallen in with company of the most worthy and attractive description, but here alone it is that my heart has been touched, here it is that my affections have become centred."

"You speak of some necessity that compels you to leave us; I hope that necessity includes no misfortune."

"I feel that the greatest misfortune attending my departure is the circumstance itself. My dear Ellen, forgive the expression, but Providence has given me this much-desired opportunity of telling you my whole heart, and I must not let it pass unimproved. You alone are the object that binds me to this spot. Ah! dare I hope that this declaration is not offensive to you? Dare I indulge the expectation that when I am afar off, you will sometimes reflect with complacency on the wanderer who, on seeing you, first saw the object to whom his soul must forever be devoted, the object that has charmed his sensations into a new feeling of existence."

"Mr. Middleton," said Ellen, extremely embarrassed, "is it proper that I should listen to this language?"

"I shall not long trouble you with it," he replied. "I know I am a stranger, in whose professions, I have no right to require that you should confide. Of my family, my prospects and my standing in society, you have no knowledge. It is, therefore, I confess, presumption in me to solicit your confidence, to request your regard, without informing you of these particulars. But ah! my beloved, say, has no youth, more fortunate than I, and known to you, and worthy of you, in all these respects, already engaged your affections? If so, my fate is decided. I shall not disturb your peace by obtruding on your notice a passion which you cannot return, nor will I endeavour to secure a place in your heart, if that heart be another's."

"Why sir," said she, "do you ask from me such a confession?"

"I have no right, I acknowledge," he replied, "to require any such disclosure from you. Forgive the freedom I have taken. All my happiness depends upon your favourable opinion of me. Oh surely it cannot be unpardonable in me to be desirous of knowing whether that heart is irrecoverably another's, which I would stop at no sacrifice, except that of virtue and honour, to make my own. Oh, Ellen! if a love as warm and sincere as ever animated a human breast, can excuse the liberty I have taken, I can plead that love, an equal to which no other woman shall ever awaken in my bosom."

"Mr. Middleton" said she, in a serious tone, "I believe you are a man of honour, and of too much generosity to sport with the feelings of an unoffending and inexperienced girl, merely for the gratification of curiosity or caprice. I feel no offence at your inquiry, although, I confess, that I am not sure whether in prudence, I ought not to be offended. Of this, however, I am certain, that under present circumstances, it would be highly imprudent to promise a return of those feelings you profess for me. I feel grateful for your preference, and as a mark of my gratitude, I may inform you that to none of your sex have I ever pledged my affections."

"Thank God!" exclaimed Edward, fervently, "then I may hope. Oh do not forget me, dearest Ellen, in my absence. I must now leave you. My soul sinks under the idea. Trouble and calamity threaten the country. They may even reach thee, pure, and lovely, and innocent as thou art, before thy lover can fly to thy aid. But I trust that God will protect thee. To his keeping I resign thee, until I again inhale love and joy from thy presence. Then, then I hope to plead my suit under circumstances more favourable for its acceptance. The Recluse will often let you hear from me."

"Hush!" said Ellen. "My aunt and Miss Agnew have turned back for us." - This either of them might have seen for several minutes before, had they not been too much engrossed with each other; in other words, had not love rendered them blind. They had made such slow progress during their conversation, that their companions, without being aware of it, had advanced nearly half a mile before them, when Mrs. Brown turning round, observed the distance, and suggested the propriety of returning to meet them. Miss Agnew and she, were in consequence within a few yards of the lovers, when Ellen suddenly observed their proximity and uttered the exclamation, "hush!" as before stated.

"You must be very weak, Ellen, otherwise you would have walked faster," said her aunt.

"Oh dear me," cried Miss Agnew, "do you not see how strong she looks? We left her as pale as sackcloth, leaning for support on the arm of that gentleman. Now she blushes like a carnation, and appears as if afraid to touch him. Come, Mr. Middleton, give me your arm. I am in more need of your assistance, after that long walk, than she is."

"And what assistance must an old frail woman like me, need, after such a walk, if a young smart chit, like you, requires any?" cried Mrs. Brown, sportively, and she also caught an arm of Edward, saying, "Ellen has monopolized you long enough; it is now our turn; Miss Agnew and I cannot bear to be longer neglected."

"Oh dear!" cried Miss Agnew. "Do not let us fight about the gentleman. I fear Ellen has not willingly resigned him, and we are intruders."

"I indeed resign him cheerfully," said Ellen, "I am now perfectly recovered, and can ascend the hill without fearing fatigue."

"So can I," cried Miss Agnew, "give me your arm, my sprightly maiden, and we shall show that gentleman and lady, that we have both life and limbs, when we choose to use them;" and she seized Ellen for the purpose of dragging her forward on a race.

"You are too wild," said Ellen, slightly restraining her, "when will you become sober?"

"Not till I fall in love," said Miss Agnew, "and then, you know, I shall be as ready to sigh and become pensive and fatigued as yourself."

They were too far removed from Edward and Mrs. Brown, for the latter to hear the last remark, which prevented Ellen from suffering all the confusion it would otherwise have occasioned.

"You insinuate then, Maria," said she, calling Miss Agnew by her Christian name, "that I am in love."

"I am sure of it," said Maria. "No female heart could withstand the partiality which that charming young man shows for you, not to mention the interesting circumstance of assisting to raise him from the dead: much as I value my own resolution, I believe, Ellen, that if I were similarly circumstanced, I should myself love him."

"Mad-cap!" said Ellen. "Quit this subject. It is all nonsense, but — but, what partiality has he shown for me? I am sure you could never have observed any."

"Rare consistence!" cried Maria. "You desire me to drop the subject; and then, you ask me a question which compels me to continue it. But this is so characteristic of a love-sick damsel, that it does not surprise me; and, dear Ellen, in pity to you, I will not drag you from the young man's company. It would be cruel as he is so soon to leave us." She then turned suddenly, and held Ellen, who blushed deeply, from advancing. "Come on," cried she, "this blushing girl and I would be at the top of the hill in a minute, did we not love our company too well to leave it."

Edward and Mrs. Brown approached. They had walked slowly, for they had conversed on the alarming nature of the times, and short as their discourse had been, Edward could easily perceive that the old lady's feelings rather than her judgment sided with the United Irishmen.

"They are my countrymen," said she, "and although their struggle may be to recover rights which you think are not lost, or to obtain objects which are but of visionary consequence — they may demand that liberty which you say they already enjoy, and may contend for an equality which instead of benefiting them, might be their greatest political misfortune; notwithstanding all this, if they be conscientious in their aims, which I believe the majority of them are,

I must regard them with complaisance. If they believe themselves oppressed, which I know they do, and ah, sir, do not some of them also feel it, resistance to oppression is natural, it is noble and manly, and must ever secure my affections to its cause."

Before Edward could reply, they were hailed by Maria, as we have already observed.

"Ah, Miss Giddyhead, I see what you wish for," cried Mrs. Brown aloud, while she advanced to Maria, "here, take Mr. Middleton to yourself. You envy everyone who has but a few minutes conversation with him, though I think you need not have become jealous of an old woman of sixty."

"A woman of Mrs. Brown's accomplishments and power of conversation, might excite my envy at any age," replied Maria; "but do you think that no other person than Maria Agnew envies you?"

"If there be anyone else, she has not, at least, betrayed it so audibly," said Mrs. Brown. "What, Mr. Middleton," she continued, "do you think of two young women in all the charms of youth and beauty, becoming jealous of old age and decayed nature enjoying a few moments of your company? You must surely have made a progress in their esteem warmer than the usual esteem of friends."

"I should be proud to excite such an esteem," said he, "but I fear I am not so happy." In saying this he cast a look at Ellen, who unconsciously returned a glance that spoke peace to his soul.

CHAP. VIII.

No titled birth had he to boast,
Son of the desert, Fortune's child.
Yet not by frowning fortune crossed,
The Muses on his cradle smiled.
He joy'd to con the fabling page,
Of prowess'd chiefs and deeds sublime; And even essay'd in infant age,
Fond task, to weave the wizzard rhyme.
Dermody.

Our party ascended to the top of the promontory, from whence they descried the gulf below.

It was the very place where Edward had first seen his beloved as if he had seen a vision of light; and where, charmed to the spot, he had lingered until he encountered death, and would have fallen in the combat, had not the same vision become his guardian angel, and sent effectual succour to his rescue.

Amidst the reflections which this scene excited, he was interrupted by Mrs. Brown, who pointed to an arbour, at some distance, made of the interwoven branches of willows, round which honeysuckles exuberantly entwined their tendrils. It was constructed in the neatest style, consistent with that rustic simplicity which seemed to have been studied by its architect. Within its sylvan walls a semi-circular range of seats were formed of earth, and covered over with a fragrant bed of chamomile and thyme. The floor was simply of nature's making, and the only furniture it appeared to contain was a small folding table placed in the centre.

"This is, indeed, a remarkable spot for a summer-house, but a very suitable one for an observatory," remarked Edward.

"It is not so much used," said Mrs. Brown, "for the study of the stars, as for the worship of the Muses. It has been erected by a young man of our neighbourhood, who, although he performs the office of a teacher to the farmers' children, contrives to find sufficient leisure to study nature, poetry and taste, in this temple of simplicity."

"I imagine," said Edward, "I have already been delighted with one of the effusions of your rural bard. Is it so, Miss O'Halloran?" he added.

"Yes, sir," she replied. "Poor M'Nelvin, as the old harper called him, the author of the verses to which you allude, is the possessor of this arbour."

"Is he unfortunate," asked Edward, "and can you tell from what cause?"

"He is unfortunate, and I can tell the cause, but, alas! it is beyond human power to relieve him. With one of the best and warmest hearts, he is a prey to a melancholy disposition, the cause of which, had he less susceptibility of feeling he would not permit to make such an impression on his mind. His body is deformed from an accidental injury he received when a child; and as the deformity cramps his personal exertions for eminence in the world, he permits his feelings of disappointment and regret, to weigh too heavily on him.

"What has lately, I believe, tended to increase his melancholy is the turn which the political prospects of the country have taken. Formerly he was affable and communicative, but, for some months past, he has become particularly reserved and averse to society."

"I should be glad of the acquaintance of this young man," said Edward, "and I am sorry that the necessity of my speedy departure will deprive me of that pleasure."

"You shall have that pleasure in five minutes," cried Miss Agnew, "for yonder he is, just appearing from the side of the hill."

They all observed him, but it was only for a moment; for he suddenly turned, and retracing his steps rather hastily, as if he wished to avoid them, disappeared.

"Shall I run after him?" said Miss Agnew. "I'll overtake him in a minute."

"I request," said Edward, "that you will not occasion him any pain on my account."

"I also request," added Mrs. Brown, "that the young man may be left to his own inclinations. He seems desirous to avoid us at present, and we have no right to force ourselves upon him."

"Well, well," returned Miss Agnew gaily, "since I am not allowed to run after young men, I shall take care to allow no young man to run after me: So, if you please, Mr. Middleton, you will either walk along side of me or before me."

They now descended the hill on their way to the castle. On coming to a smooth, gently sloping lawn of considerable extent, near the bottom, Ellen stopped suddenly.

"Here is the spot," said she, "where I felt the first thrill of patriotism that ever warmed my heart. Here it was that I first felt devoted to my country's cause; for here while only in my fourteenth year, I was present, for the first and the last time, at a review of a large party of that noble army of patriots, the Irish Volunteers. To my view, their appearance, that day, exhibited something more magnificent and impressive than anything of which my young ideas had ever formed a conception. I rejoiced to see my country's strength displayed in the unbought energies of her sons. In performing their evolutions, they appeared as if they were animated with one soul, and their dress and the brilliancy of their arms, displayed the highest polish of military splendour. I looked upon them as an irresistible band of heroes; and my heart throbbed with rapture to think that those heroes were my acquaintances, my neighbours, my friends, my protectors; and that if ever their weapons should be stained with human blood, it should be the blood of my country's enemies.

"I saw them, and became proud of my country; and frequently to this day, does my imagination present the scene before me in all its liveliness, but, alas! it is now only imagination!"

"I delight in your enthusiasm," said Edward, "and cannot but heartily condemn the ungenerous and imprudent policy which occasioned the disorganization of that gallant association of soldiers."

"I have seen," said Mrs. Brown, "various reviews of military; and I must confess that I never saw a body of men exhibit a more imposing and soldier-like appearance, than the Volunteers did on that day. I do not, indeed, wonder that they should have made Ellen proud of the country, for on that day I felt in my own breast, a warmer pulse of patriotism than I ever experienced before.

"I never again saw them embodied; for a jealous and ungrateful government, in a short time afterwards, issued its mandate for their suppression.

"Ah! little did I think when, on that day, I heard the last sound of their martial music, that it was the funeral knell of my country's liberty and peace; and little did I think, when I saw the last glimpse of their standards disappearing beyond yon hill, that I, for the last time, beheld the only soldiers whose hearts and hands were alike sincerely devoted to the salvation of their country!"

"I hope," remarked Miss Agnew, "we may yet see Irish soldiers whom no foreign authority shall have the power to disband."

"Much as I dislike the late despotic measures of the British government," replied Mrs. Brown, "I cannot yet bring my mind to consider it a foreign one. But I acknowledge that the conduct of its ministers in this country, is every day weakening that partiality I have hitherto felt for it."

"It is indeed to be lamented," said Edward, "that the interests of the government, and the wishes of the people are so opposed to each other; and, believe me, ladies, I feel as acutely as any Irishman can, for the calamities which such a state of things forebodes to the country."

"In reading history," remarked Ellen, "I have often wondered at the cruelty of all governments. They universally seem to delight more in keeping the people in subjection by terror and punishment, than in securing their affections by kindness and benefits. It is surely a strange taste in rulers, and is to me quite unaccountable, that they should take pleasure in the misery of their fellow-creatures. But rulers are generally men; methinks that our sex would both feel and act more tenderly towards those in their power."

As this opinion of the fair Ellen might lead to a controversy, which would require a more thoroughbred politician than myself to decide, and as I trust that my reader is such a one, I will leave it altogether to his disposal.

Having arrived at the castle, Edward took O'Halloran aside, and informed him of the necessity he was under of immediately leaving the country.

O'Halloran startled a little at the intelligence; and, although it was nothing but what he might have expected, he appeared very much confused.

At last recovering his self-possession, "Mr. Middleton," said he, "I did not calculate on your leaving us so soon, at least so suddenly, but if the cause of your departure be not extremely urgent, I request that you will not go until tomorrow."

Edward was himself much inclined to remain till the next day. A wish to be introduced to the poet, M'Nelvin, and a desire to spend another night, under the same roof with his beloved Ellen, predominated over his prudence; and he yielded to O'Halloran's request.

O'Halloran was not unacquainted with the danger which threatened his guest from the violence of Darragh, and some others of the conspirators; and he began to suspect that their threats had reached Edward's ears, and produced his sudden determination to leave the neighbourhood. He himself had some doubts whether the secrets of his party with which this young stranger had involuntarily become acquainted, were altogether safe in his keeping.

Although he had hitherto resisted the solicitations of his confederates to prevent his departure, by securing his person, least he should discover on them, he began now to have serious doubts as to the propriety of his so doing. In great agitation of mind he left Edward, and retired to his library to reflect on the most proper mode of proceeding. "Were I alone involved in the dangers of this young man's discovering upon us, I would then be justifiable in running the risk;" he thus reasoned with himself; "but the safety of others is also concerned; nay, perhaps, the success of all our plans to emancipate our country may be affected by either his imprudent communication, or intentional discovery of what he knows; and it is certain that he knows sufficient to ruin all. It is enough, it must be — my mind is resolved — my conscience may accuse me of perfidy to my guest, but my duty to the public cause in which I am embarked, is of infinitely more importance than any personal consideration. He must be secured, but his life must be preserved from all dangers; and he must be so treated as to have no privation of which to complain, but the loss of personal liberty."

Having brought his mind to this conclusion, he went in search of M'Cauley, and the other leading conspirators. They soon agreed on a plan for seizing Edward.

"A single hair of his head shall not fall," said M'Cauley, in the course of their deliberation, "if I can prevent it; for, I am myself to blame for too rashly communicating to him that information by which he can most seriously injure us."

Mr. Samuel Nelson, one of the proprietors of the Northern Star, a man of great intelligence, and one of the most influential leaders of the association in the North, was present at this deliberation. His opinion coincided with that of M'Cauley and O'Halloran, that Edward should be well treated, but strictly guarded. "Such a captive," he remarked, "may ultimately be of great service to us as an hostage for the safety of some of our own party; besides, as he has not yet manifested any other hostility towards us, than merely refusing to join us, it would be unjust as well as impolitic to exercise any other severity towards him, than may be absolutely necessary for our own safety."

It was then unanimously settled that Edward should be seized that evening, and confined in the Point Cave, (which was within the mysterious rock already mentioned) but that he should be there treated with every indulgence the circumstances of the case would admit.

After dinner, the unsuspecting object of these machinations, paid a visit to William Caldwell's, to make his acknowledgments for the kindness he had experienced from his family, and also with the hope that he might there meet with an opportunity of being introduced to M'Nelvin; for he understood that the poet was on a very intimate footing with this family. In the latter object of his visit, he was, however, disappointed. On his return he met with the Recluse, to whom he reported his wishes on this subject.

"You wish for a gratification," said the old man, "which it will be no easy matter to procure you. But if it be in the power of any one, I think it is in mine. You will, no doubt, be surprised when I tell you that he whose acquaintance you seek, studiously avoids yours, not from any prejudice he has imbibed against your person or principles — on the contrary, I know that he highly respects both, but he is influenced with regard to you by a delicacy, perhaps I should rather say, a weakness of feeling on a tender point. In short, he loves Ellen Hamilton with a hopeless passion, indulged in secret, and he has perceived that you are an ardent, and likely to be a favoured rival. I am the sole confidant of his sorrows. His passion is involuntarily, but it is acute; and as it is cherished altogether against hope, I pity him."

"Perhaps then," said Edward, "it is better I should not see him, for I should feel reluctant to occasion him the smallest pain."

"My friend," replied the hermit, "I should wish you and him to be acquainted with each other, as I know it would increase your mutual esteem. His personal deformity makes him shy with strangers; and the particular circumstances of which I have informed you would make him more than usually so with you. I think, however, that the first interview would be sufficient to remove this feeling. So, if you have no objection, we shall proceed to my cave, where I expect to find him very shortly. It is to him alone, besides yourself, that I have entrusted the secret of my inner dwelling; nay, it is to him alone, of all my friends in this neighbourhood, that I have as yet intrusted the story of my misfortunes, a story concerning which even to you, I must, for some time yet, take the liberty of preserving silence."

Edward acquiesced, and they soon arrived at the old man's dwelling. They were not long seated until the secret door in the bureau opened, and M'Nelvin appeared. He seemed somewhat disconcerted on seeing Edward, but at the Recluse's desire he came forward.

"Let me introduce the two most confidential friends I have in this part of the country to each other," said the old man, "and I doubt not that on further acquaintance, they will both thank me for doing so."

Edward approached, and shook the poet's hand so cordially that his reserve almost instantly vanished; and during the conversation which ensued, he became so cheerful and communicative, and displayed such an extent of information and strength of intellect, as surprised and delighted his new acquaintance. When they discoursed on politics, and M'Nelvin descanted on the natural rights of man, Edward felt within his breast a new conviction of the injustice and iniquity of arbitrary rule; and when he spoke of the benefits arising from the establishment of known laws for the regulation of society, and the maintenance of security and order among mankind, Edward could not refrain from wishing that the disorganizers of the age had only an opportunity of hearing such sentiments so enforced, but when he described and deplored the accumulating miseries of his country, it was with a fervour that almost brought tears to his own eyes, and filled, almost to bursting, the hearts of his auditors; and Edward could not avoid execrating that mismanagement, to which these measures were so clearly and so feelingly ascribed. When on the subject of poetry, he enlarged on the influence of its precepts on the conduct of men, the power which it often exerts over their dispositions, and the enjoyment it yields, by its pleasing representations of virtue and happiness, when it chooses to display them unalloyed with the sad realities of life; or, by its delightful delusions when it carries the enchanted fancy into a species of transient paradise, where the cares, and pains, and vexations of the grosser world, are, for a time, neither felt or remembered — Edward thought that he had never been before so thoroughly convinced of the benefits it confers upon mankind.

Thus the man whose poetical talents had excited his curiosity, and whose misfortunes he was prepared to pity, he found possessed of dignity which enforced his respect, and of wisdom which commanded his admiration; and he never felt so ardent a desire as on this occasion, to make amends for the injustice of fortune by some munificent testimony of his respect for merit. Accordingly, after M'Nelvin had left the cavern, which he did early in the evening, he consulted the Recluse as to the manner in which he could best serve so deserving an object.

"I know, at present, no other way," said the old man, "than by showing him your countenance, maintaining a correspondence with him, and perhaps, occasionally administering to his poetical vanity; for, like all other poets, he is vain of his profession. Pecuniary assistance must not be mentioned. In the present state of his feelings, he would look upon it as a manifestation of your superiority. His pride would be wounded, and his reserve towards you might return, never to remove. The inconveniencies of poverty, I can and shall prevent."

"I envy you," returned Edward, "the felicity of being permitted to confer favours on such a man. I trust the time will come when I shall enjoy more of both his society and yours, under happier circumstances."

He then, after requesting the Recluse to remember his wishes respecting Ellen, bade him adieu, and returned to the castle.

CHAP. IX.

Thy arm is firm, thy heart is stout,
But thou canst neither fight or flee, but beauty stands thy guard without,
Yes, beauty weeps and pleads for thee.
Hogg.

On emerging from the hermit's glen, our hero perceived four men sitting on an eminence near the path by which he was to pass. He approached, and soon knew one of them to be his new and undesired acquaintance, M'Cauley, who arose, and very respectfully saluted him.

"Mr. Middleton," said he, "I am glad to meet with you. Will you favour me with your company towards the beach?"

Edward was about excusing himself, on account of the lateness of the hour, when M'Cauley caught him familiarly by the arm, and in a half jocular and half irritating manner, swore an oath that he would not part with him for that evening at least. Edward remonstrated, and told him that he did not think it friendly, so rudely to impose on his inclinations.

"Mr. Middleton! you had as well consent," said the other, "to accompany me. I assure you no harm shall befall you; and you see," he added, looking at his companions, "that we can enforce compliance."

Edward now perceived that foul play was intended, and he demanded by what authority they attempted to detain him.

"By the authority of present strength, and a prudent regard for our own safety," replied M'Cauley.

"And where am I to go, and for what purpose?" was next demanded.

"To our head-quarters, to be both well secured and well treated," was the reply.

"Does Mr. O'Halloran know this?"

"He does; and its necessity grieves him."

"Then I submit," said Edward. "He once saved my life; he is now welcome to take it from me. Lead where you please."

The four men enclosed him round, and conducted him to the very spot where O'Halloran and his grand-daughter vanished from his sight when he first saw them on the beach.

One of them then ascended a projecting portion of the mysterious rock, and removing a loose piece of stone, which filled a narrow crevice about a foot deep, an iron ring was disclosed, on pulling which an internal bolt gave way, and permitted the upper end of a large, rugged fragment of the rock, to separate the mass with which it before seemed to have been consolidated. M'Cauley then introduced his hand and loosened the end of a rope, which, passing through a pulley fastened to the roof of the cave now visible, had its other end fixed firmly unto the moveable fragment which was thus managed as a door, its base, upon which it turned, being joined to the rock by means of strong hinges, altogether invisible on the outside. The rope being thus loosened, the fragment opened wide enough to afford space for the admission of our party in a stooping posture, but on advancing a few steps, Edward found himself in an apartment fully ten feet high, having a smooth hard-beaten artificially made earthen floor. Through this, he was conducted to another apartment, very spacious, clean-looking and lighted with several lamps. In its centre there was a large table covered with newspapers, pamphlets, letters, etc. which three genteelly dressed men seemed to have been perusing. These gentlemen accosted Edward in rather a cordial manner, and welcomed him to their habitation.

They were quite unknown to him, but one of them, he soon perceived from his accent to be a Frenchman. He now saw that he had been ushered into one of the council-chambers of the Northern conspirators, but for what purpose, he could not tell; although he was persuaded that it could not be of a friendly nature. Here the men by whom he was seized left him. By his remaining companions he was politely invited to be seated, and to accept refreshment. Conceiving that there was no use in showing ill humour on the occasion, he assented, when, to his surprise, tea was speedily produced with its usual accompaniments, and afterwards punch, of which his companions partook in a spirit of great cordiality.

During the evening politics engrossed less of the conversation than he expected. Literature, agriculture and manufactures were the prevailing topics.

On these, Edward cheerfully took a part, and almost forgot that he was a prisoner. His new acquaintances seemed highly intelligent, and perfectly conversant with every subject they discussed; they were easy and affable, and appeared to make his comfort their chief study. At length one of them requesting leave to show him where he should rest, when he wished to retire for the night, pushed a sliding door along one end of the apartment, which disclosed to view a small room resembling the state-room of the cabin of a merchant ship, and containing a bed of a comfortable appearance. On bidding good night, one of the company remarked, "I trust, Mr. Middleton, that the cause of your confinement here will soon be removed, but whether it shall be long or short, you may depend on receiving good usage."

In fact, such is the influence of civil treatment on the mind, that for some time after he was alone, Edward felt more astonishment than irritation at the occurrences of the evening. But when he reflected on the loss of his liberty, and on the share which O'Halloran had in effecting it, and which he looked upon, not only as a breach of honour and hospitality, but, from the promise he had exacted from him in the morning, as savouring of treachery itself, he became restless, agitated, irritated; and when he considered that he had done nothing to deserve being thus incarcerated in a den among traitors, his chagrin and resentment partook of a feverish violence, and sleep for that night became a stranger to his eyes.

Here for the present we shall leave him, and direct our attention to the inhabitants of the castle, some of whom, by this time, had become as much agitated on his account, as he was himself chagrined and irritated. The perturbation of O'Halloran's mind, now that a deed was done which he could not quite justify, and to which he was accessory, was such as no good man could wish even his worst enemy to experience.

"It is I," thought he, "who have in this affair committed a breach of hospitality and good faith. This young man whose disposition, I believe, to be of the most generous description, reposed implicit confidence in me; and yet I have betrayed him into captivity. He may forgive me, God may forgive me, but I cannot forgive myself. — But" — he would say, his thoughts taking another turn — "Why should I thus condemn myself! I have done no more than my duty to the great cause in which I am engaged. It is true, my private esteem for this young man would have prompted me to act otherwise, but the higher motive of duty made it imperative that I should act as I did. On escaping from us, he might league himself with our oppressors, for he is much inclined to their cause; and might think it incumbent on him to reveal those secrets which we imprudently disclosed to him. No, I will not repent it — although the deed was painful, it was necessary; it was called for by the interest of my country. Why should I grieve.

"It is weakness. Shall it be said, that O'Halloran wished to sacrifice the great interests of the great cause of Irish liberty, to private feelings or squeamish scrupulosity!"

Thus O'Halloran grieved, and reasoned, and reconciled himself to the painful duty, as he esteemed it, which he had performed. It is indeed no wonder, that he who always considered patriotism the first of human virtues, should now when that feeling was so much excited, and strengthened by resentment against national wrongs and oppressions, and by the general enthusiasm of the times, be easily prevailed on to yield the personal safety of a stranger, however well he might think of him, to his country's welfare.

But there was another inmate of the castle, whom the events of this evening agitated still more severely than they did O'Halloran. This was she, who, in the estimation of Edward, was the fairest of all Erin's daughters, and whose tears of sorrow shed for him this evening, had he known of them, would have rendered him proud and happy in his misfortunes.

Ellen was sitting alone at a window in one of the small turrets on the southern side of the castle, watching, perhaps, the declining tints of the twilight, or contemplating the dangerous aspect of the times, or, what is quite as probable, meditating on the expected return of Edward to the castle. It is certain, that from the window where she was stationed, she could survey the path by which he was to return; and if she at all took notice of the gathering shades, perhaps it was because they marked the lateness of the hour without bringing back the object of her solicitude. While she mused, the moments followed each other slowly, thought anxiously succeeded thought, but still there was no appearance of him for whom she sighed. Several people came at different times up the avenue, but Edward did not come.

"A little more patience, and he surely will appear," thought she. A well-dressed man was perceived approaching at a distance. "Ah! this is surely he?" He drew near enough to be distinguished. It was only a messenger with some news to O'Halloran.

Another came. It was only a servant who had been at town. A third, a fourth, all came who were expected, and some who were not expected, but he whom Ellen expected did not come. How provoking is suspense!

"I will go down," thought she, "to the gate: when I perceive his approach, I can easily run back and regain the castle without him seeing me."

She went to the gate. She ventured into the avenue. She saw a tall figure hastily advancing. She retreated within the gate, when looking back she perceived it to be the figure of a woman. She returned to the avenue, and met Peg Dornan. Peg was in great agitation, when she approached.

"Some yin maun help him," she abruptly exclaimed, "an' your ain bonny sel maun haste an' fin' oot that yin, or it may soon be owre wi' him; — an' he liked you weel, an' would hae run to help you in sic need, at the blackest hoor a midnicht."

"What is the matter?" anxiously demanded Ellen, "for whom do you want help?"

"For the bonniest lad that e'er caM' to thir parts — for Mr. Middleton, wham I like as weel as e'er I liked Jock Dornan, my ain sin."

"For God's sake! dear Peg, what, what has befallen Mr. Middleton?"

"He has fallen amang his enemies."

"What! have they killed him?" exclaimed Ellen, fearfully.

"No, my bonny bairn, I hope the hae na yet gane that far, but they're no to be trusted owre lang."

"For heaven's sake! tell me what you know of the matter?"

"That's what I caM' for, my bonny bairn, an' you'll hear me. I was saunterin' at my leisure aboot an hour syne, on the road to Saunders's Glen, when I saw four o' the hettist o' the warm crappies, settin' on the road side, an' thinkin' they would be talkin' politics, I did na want to disturb them; so I turned through a slap to the other side o' the hedge, an' I would na hae stapped but gane right on, but when I caM' forenent them, though they did na see me, I heard yin of them say something aboot Mr. Middleton, so I just hunkered doon to hear what it was. 'I'll warrant you he's an Orangeman,' said Sam Service. 'We must seize him, but not hurt him, let him be what he will,' said Jock M'Cauley. 'Our order is to confine him in the Point Cave, where we will soon find out whether he be friendly or not.'

"I thought it was nae time to listen langer, but to run and warn him to keep oot o' their way, as I did yince before. I e'en ran to Billy Caldwell's, whar I had seen him in the afternoon, but they said he had gane wi' auld Saunders to his glen. I let nae on, but ran there as fast as I could, for, thinks I, they'll get him in the hame comin', giff I dinna see him first. I ran like thoucht, for the deil tak' me gin I'm lazy on sic an erran'. The auld man was in the glen, I asked for Mr. Middleton. 'He left me half an hour ago,' said he. Gude preserve us! said I, then he's fa'en in wi' them Auld man, you can do nae guid. I canna wait to talk wi' you. I maun rin to the castle, for, as sure as you're auld Saunders, the crappies hae catched Mr. Middleton for nae guid. — When I said sae, he sprang — I never thoucht the auld body was sae soople. He would hae been here lang before me, had he skipt on at that gate, but he turned an' bade me haste, an' tell a' to either Mr. O'Halloran or Ellen, thinkin', doubtless, that he wad do mar harm than guid by being owre hasty."

"And are you sure they have seized on Mr. Middleton?" inquired Ellen.

"They maun ha' him," replied Peg, "for when I caM' back to whar they were sittin', they were gane. I thought he micht hae escaped them, an' won to the castle, but I met Ned Watt, the butler, just before I saw you, who says he's no come there; so I fear a's no richt."

"It is too plain!" said Ellen almost inaudibly, for speech and sense now failed her, and she sunk on the ground.

With a voice like thunder, Peg shouted for help, and in a few seconds, several of the domestics from the castle were on the spot.

Ellen soon recovered, and being conveyed to her apartment, she requested Mrs. Brown to remain with her for a short time. All others accordingly withdrew. "My dear aunt," said she, "I know your penetration has discovered my weakness. I will now therefore no longer affect to conceal it from you. My heart owns a feeling for Mr. Middleton, which is likely to be ruinous to my peace. But in loving him, I have only loved what I conceived to be excellence; and, if I have done wrong, I hope for forgiveness from my more than mother. But he is surely worthy of all the affection I can bestow on him. But, oh! I am miserable; for he is in danger.

"He has been seized by the United Irishmen, on suspicion of being an Orangeman, and heaven only knows if, at this moment, he be not breathing out his soul in agony, under the hands of a murderer. Oh! dear aunt, the idea is terrible, but I fear it is real."

She here clasped the hands of her aunt with a convulsive force, which made that affectionate relative tremble for her safety. If she considered her niece's passion to have been imprudent, and ill timed, she saw that the present was not the period to expostulate or use cool calculating arguments on the subject. She, therefore, adopted the more humane and judicious method of soothing her feelings by expressing a sincere hope, that no evil had befallen Edward; remarking that the information she had received might be partly or wholly unfounded. At all events, she encouraged her to hope for the best, at least until they should obtain more certain intelligence with regard to anything disastrous having taken place.

Ellen soon became so much quieted as to be able to relate to her all that she had heard from Peg Dornan. Her aunt then promised to communicate with her brother on the subject; and consult him as to what it should be best to do on Edward's behalf. In the meantime none of the castle servants knew of his captivity. O'Halloran himself not being present, Peg Dornan would relate her story to no one else, for she had too much regard for the United Irishmen, as a body, to propagate any report to their disadvantage.

She was also aware of the dangerous situation of an informer in those times. She, therefore, especially as she was persuaded that Ellen would lose no time in making her grandfather acquainted with Edward's situation, resolved not to mention the affair again, unless to those she could trust, and who might possess sufficient influence to serve him.

The next morning, (for O'Halloran did not appear that night) Mrs. Brown hastened to inform him of what she had heard respecting Edward's seizure by the United Irishmen. Her brother not only acknowledged that he knew of the fact, but had consented to it, and acquainted her at large with his reasons for so doing. He assured her, however, that the captive would be treated with kindness, and that his life was in no danger. Mrs. Brown, with more warmth than was usual to her, expressed her surprise and indignation of what had taken place.

"What!" said she, "has my brother; he of whose honourable and noble course of conduct, I have hitherto been so proud; whose mind, I thought superior to the narrow, selfish motives that too often influence other men, become, at last, so forgetful of his long boasted rectitude, as to betray an unsuspecting youth, who was a stranger and his guest, into the power of those who hate him, and whose hatred to those who may be in their power, is almost equivalent to destruction?"

"Mrs. Brown," said O'Halloran, rising hastily, "I have not been accustomed to hear such language from you. I have already told you my reasons for my conduct. If they are insufficient to justify me in your eyes, it is of little consequence, since they do it in my own. In the meantime my regard for a woman's weakness, must not, shall not, turn my attention from that duty, however stern it may be, which I owe to my country." He then left the apartment; and Mrs. Brown, with a heavy heart, returned to sympathise with her niece.

"Your grandfather has assured me," said she, endeavouring to comfort her, "that no attempt will be made upon his life, and that he shall experience no inconvenience in their power to prevent, except the loss of liberty."

Ellen's uncertainty respecting her lover's fate, being thus removed, the violence of her emotions gradually subsided, and was in a short time succeeded by a calm and settled melancholy. The liveliness and ingenuity of Miss Agnew, who soon discovered the cause of her friend's distress, greatly aided the unceasing tenderness and solicitude of Mrs. Brown, in assuaging the poignancy of Ellen's grief, and she was in a few weeks restored to a tolerable enjoyment of existence.

CHAP. X.

Edward sustained his misfortunes with great spirit, and however severely he felt his being thus enclosed, as it were, in a living tomb, he took care that none around him should perceive the state of his feelings.

The Rev. Mr. Porter, a Presbyterian clergyman, at this time under cover from a threatened prosecution for high treason, was his most agreeable and constant companion. Mr. Samuel Nelson, whom we mentioned before, and who at this period was a very active agent of the United Directory, was a frequent visitor at the cavern, but not being under proscription by the government, he frequented it rather for the purpose of business than concealment. His arrival always excited great interest; for he never failed to bring with him a large assortment of news, and a budget of political documents for the inspection of his coadjutors.

The Frenchman, whom we have also already mentioned, was a bustling, active sort of a character, who, on all occasions assumed an air of great importance, as being a citizen and a public, or (to speak more correctly) a secret functionary of the Great nation; for at this period, the meanest officers of the new Gallic republic exhibited a desire of being thought superior to the people of every other country; and in all companies and controversies, arrogated a distinction and authority quite inconsistent with that natural equality among mankind, which they avowed as their favourite doctrine. But the enthusiasm excited by their military successes, and the boldness of their innovations, veiled all their faults from the eyes of the United Irishmen, and among many of the zealots of the day, any indecorum might have been justified by merely asserting it to be the French custom.

From not being at first aware of this circumstance, Edward was greatly at a loss to imagine, how men of such improved minds and refined manners, as Porter, Nelson and O'Halloran, could tolerate the superciliousness and flippancy of their foreign guest; who would often, in the midst of the most serious natural discussion, interrupt the speaker by starting questions, or making observations the most frivolous and irrelevant to the subject.

For the two first days of Edward's imprisonment, O'Halloran did not visit the cave. On the evening of the third, he entered with a bundle of letters and newspapers, which he handed to Nelson. Then going forward to Edward; "Mr. Middleton," said he, "I am truly sorry that it is against your will you are here; and I hope that it will be soon otherwise. I request you will read this letter at your leisure, and seriously consider its contents."

He then seated himself at the table, and for about an hour joined his confederates in perusing the papers he had brought; after which he asked Nelson to accompany him to the castle, and they retired together.

Immediately on receiving the letter, Edward withdrew to his sleeping closet, where throwing himself on his couch, he read as follows:

My young and esteemed friend,

In consenting to your confinement, I made a greater sacrifice of feeling to duty than I had ever been before called on to make. I had a hard struggle, but my conception of what I owed to the great national cause in which I am engaged, gained the victory.

Ever since I could lay down a plan of conduct for my life, I have graduated the scale of my duties in the following manner. The first is my duty to my God, the second to my country, the third to my neighbour, and the fourth to myself. It is my pride that I have hitherto acted in conformity to this scale; and I consider no instance of my doing so, a greater triumph of my principles over my feelings, than my resigning you to a captivity, which, I trust, will not be of long continuance. This latter circumstance will, however, depend altogether on yourself. Were we certain that the secrets connected with our cause, which have come to your knowledge, would be safe in your keeping, you should not be confined a single hour. But so long as you profess a disapprobation of our designs, it is manifest that, to permit your enlargement would be unwarrantably to subject ourselves and our cause to unnecessary dangers.

I do not write to you for the purpose of apologizing for my conduct. So long as that conduct has the approbation of my own conscience, I will

*apologize to no man. But I wish to represent the affair to you in its true
light; and to assure you that you have no personal danger to apprehend,
and that you shall suffer no personal hardship nor privation, that
consistently with the precautionary views which have induced us to
confine you, we can prevent.*

*When I say that the recovery of your liberty depends on yourself, I
mean, that by evincing an attachment to our association, and by coming
under the obligations we impose on its members, you will satisfy us that
we run no risk from your disclosures, and you shall not only be
immediately set at liberty, but gladly hailed as a brother, and raised to an
honourable place in our esteem and confidence.*

*At present we make great allowances for the political principles in
which you have been educated, but we trust, that you have good sense
sufficient not to permit prejudice always to blind you to justice. For my
own part, I am persuaded that you have liberality and discernment
enough, provided you exercise them, to enable you to throw off the
trammels of early impressions, when they will not stand the test of reason.
You are an Irishman, and I believe you love your country, and wish her to
be free and happy. I will ask you can she ever be so, under a government
which derives all its authority and its impulses from a foreign country,
absolutely inimical to her prosperity; and surely a country which looks
upon ours as a conquered province, and is proud of the domination she
exercises over us, can never be likely to grant us rights and privileges, to
which, as human beings, we are entitled, and of which she herself has
despoiled us.*

*I need not enlarge upon facts to convince you that Irishmen have
nothing to expect from English generosity. You are, I doubt not, well
enough conversant in the history of our British connexion to know that it
has been pregnant with nothing but oppressions and calamities to our
ancestors and ourselves. As an Irishman, as a lover of justice and of your
country, you cannot but feel indignant at the usage she has ever received
from that nation which has so long acted, not as her sister, but as her
tyrant; and, if you feel indignant at the ages of unmerited and cruel
sufferings, that your country has sustained, we call on you, in her name,
to join with those who are resolved to deliver her from her oppressors, or
perish in the attempt.*

*It is in vain for anyone to say, that it is our own restless, discontented
and riotous dispositions, that have caused our misfortunes, and that if we*

would live peaceably, we might live happily. Ah! sir, we have tried that. We long submitted, but even then we were not spared. We were forbidden to exert our industry, but in such a manner, and in the production of such articles alone as our neighbours pleased; while our commerce was confined to such channels as suited their interest. At their caprice, we were extravagantly taxed, while we were chained into poverty — while we were forbidden to improve the natural wealth and resources with which Providence has so bountifully blessed our island, in her soil, her climate, her minerals and her situation. Three-fourths of our population, were deprived of every political privilege, and are consequently, at this day, no better than slaves, compelled to passive and degrading submission to the will of their haughty and unfeeling masters. When we patiently submitted, our submission was considered want of spirit, and we were represented as being incapable of either understanding or relishing the blessings of liberty. We then petitioned and remonstrated, and were called seditious, and troublesome, and turbulent. Our petitions were only answered by mockery, and our remonstrances with threats; and, latterly, these threats have been wantonly converted into a malignant and cruel persecution.

The state of the times, I need not describe to you. That dreadful state has been caused by the tyrannical system of vengeance, which has been adopted to counteract the natural and justifiable exertions of an enlightened people to obtain from their oppressors their legitimate and unquestionable rights. On which side is the cause of justice, your own good sense will readily perceive; and which side has the greater claim upon your good will and services, as a patriot your sense of duty to the land that gave you birth will easily decide.

As one who esteems you and feels a high interest in your welfare, I exhort you to decide in favour of an injured and oppressed nation, which claims you as her son, and to whom alone your allegiance and fidelity are due. Reflect seriously on the subject, so that if your decision be in our favour, it may be the result of deliberate reasoning and true conviction. We shall then confide in you as our friend, and I shall have the happiness of regarding you as an Irishman worthy of the name.

I am, &c.
HENRY O'HALLORAN.

To this letter, Edward wrote a very copious reply, from which the following passages are extracted.

After assuring O'Halloran that he gave full credit to the motives which influenced him in consenting to his captivity, and, on that account, let its issue be what it would, he freely forgave him, he proceeded:

But as to your attempts to bring me over to your party, it will require considerations more powerful, and arguments more conclusive, than any you have advanced, or I am persuaded have in your power to advance, to be successful. I feel as much as any man for the misfortunes of my country, and it is this very feeling that prevents me from joining in measures which, I know, will only plunge her into deeper distress.

I need not, I presume, recall to the memory of a man of your historical knowledge, the origin of those laws of which the Catholic part of our countrymen complain. Had James instead of William been the successful competitor for the crown of these kingdoms, I dare say, you will admit it to be probable, that the Catholics would have guarded their religion by statutes, at least as strong and severe as the victorious Protestants found it necessary to adopt. I need not inform you that in those countries, where the Catholics did prevail — in France, Spain, Portugal, &c. they have secured their own faith with infinitely more solicitude and zeal, than the people of Britain did theirs, for they have secured it to the total exclusion of all others. I will not speak of the use they have always made of power, whenever they happened to obtain it in these islands. You know it well, and knowing it as you do, you and the other Presbyterians who have lately espoused their cause, merit, at least, the praise of rendering good for evil, conduct which must for ever elicit respect and admiration, from every lover of generosity and magnanimity. I can, as much as anyone, appreciate the liberality of such conduct; and would be no enemy to Catholic emancipation, if brought about by legal means; for I am inclined to think that all the political privileges they desire, might now be granted to the Irish Catholics with safety, nay, with advantage to the national prosperity. They are become more tolerant than their ancestors; and, I trust, that the age is too enlightened for religious animosity and fanaticism again to produce such a degree of human misery as they did in the days of the Tudors and the Stewarts.

You must acknowledge that since the expulsion of the last mentioned family from the throne, no man is punished in these kingdoms for conscience-sake. Even with respect to the civil disabilities, which the penal laws imposed on the Catholics, they have, within the last half century, been considerably relieved from their effects; and by a proper and temperate perseverance in applying to the authority in whose hands the constitution lodges the power of redressing grievances, whatever yet remains of these laws, would undoubtedly be repealed, whenever it should appear that it could be done with safety. But I will appeal to the common sense of any man, if the present conduct of the disaffected in this island is likely to hasten that event? No; if the sword again must be used in defence of the laws and constitution of the country, I fear it will be thought necessary to make these laws stronger, perhaps severer than ever. God forbid that ever such a crisis should take place, but if it should, every unprejudiced man can perceive who are to blame for it.

With respect to the British jealousy of our prosperity, which you say has had the effect of shackling our commerce, and restraining our industry, I am of opinion, that, if fairly enquired into, it will be found to originate only in the imaginations of theorists, or the ambition of demagogues, who wish to disturb the public tranquillity. Why should Britain be averse to our prosperity? It would be directly contrary to her interests; for our prosperity is her prosperity, and our strength is her strength. As well might Middlesex oppose the prosperity of Lancashire, and the authorities of Edinburgh adopt measures to prevent the growth of Glasgow. The fact is, our trade, manufactures and capital, have more than doubled themselves within the last twenty years, and, were it not for the political broils that distract the country, it would, at the present moment, be more prosperous and happy than ever it was, during the whole course of its past history. Here, sir, you cannot deny that before the present discontents became so alarming, every peaceable industrious man had the safety of his person, property, and character well secured to him by known laws; and could sit down and call what he possessed his own, with more confidence under our government than under any other in Europe, or perhaps in the world.

You say that my country claims all my allegiance. I know it, sir, and I acknowledge it. But I cannot identify my country with that imprudent faction to which it grieves me to find you have so zealously attached yourself. I wish you to understand me clearly. I am opposed to despotism as much as I am opposed to anarchy itself. My politics are the politics of the Whigs of 1688, who expelled despotism from the throne, and by placing in its stead a limited monarch, gave the last finish to our excellent constitution.

The abuses that have crept into our government, during the lapse of more than a century, I would endeavour to reform, but I would do it by legal means; and these, if properly persisted in, could not fail to be effectual. The corruptions of the constitution, I would purify, not by violence, desolation and blood-shed, remedies infinitely more dreadful than the disease has yet become, but by the means by which Grattan obtained our free trade and independent parliament, namely, parliamentary interference, which by persevering and energetic applications from the people will always be procured. When I say that my sentiments on these subjects were the sentiments of Hampden and Russel, Addison and Steel, Chatham and Fox, Charlemont and Grattan, you will hardly think them unfriendly to rational liberty, or unworthy of an Irishman.

To obtain my enlargement, I will come under no obligations that might by any possibility be ascribed to meanness or timidity. I should scorn to act the part of an informer, against either the misguided or the unfortunate — and, with respect to you individually, to whom I am under Providence indebted for life itself, gratitude binds me too strongly to your personal welfare, to permit me either inadvertently or intentionally, to divulge any part of your conduct, or of those connected with you, that might operate to your disadvantage.

Yours, &c.
EDWARD MIDDLETON.

O'Halloran and his confederates finding that they could not shake Edward's political principles, desisted after this, from making the attempt. They also appeared more guarded when conversing in his presence, so that, during the remainder of the summer, he obtained very little information concerning the progress of their affairs.

In the meantime, the Recluse being aware of the capricious and revengeful disposition of several of those who had access to his imprisoned friend, became every day more uneasy concerning him.

With M'Nelvin, who also felt much on the subject, and who was his only confidant, he had frequent conferences on the practicability of procuring Edward's liberty, but they could devise no plan that seemed in the slightest degree to promise success. Ellen, by the assurances she received of his personal safety, and by the sympathy, and kind attentions of her aunt and Miss Agnew, became daily more resigned and cheerful, so that before the end of August, she was seen taking her usual evening walks, although it was observed that she generally walked alone, and as much as possible courted solitude. One evening, about this time, an incident took place which, as it had some connexion with those events which led to Edward's enlargement, should be related.

Monsieur Monier, the French emissary already mentioned, had fallen desperately in love with her; and having obtained her grandfather's permission to address her, had added greatly to her affliction by persecuting her with his passion for several months past. He had been lately informed of her partiality for Edward; and in consequence began to hate him as the sole obstacle to his happiness.

Edward had never esteemed this man, for independently of his criminal and disgraceful occupation, his manners were flippant, profane and arrogant, the very reverse of those he approved. In several conversations, the dissimilarity of their minds had been manifested, and on some occasions, they had taken but little pains to conceal their mutual dislike. Our Frenchman, therefore, cordially wished perdition to his rival.

On the evening alluded to, he followed Ellen into one of her favourite and lonely walks, in a small wood that skirted the Volunteer ground. She was indulging her melancholy feelings in reading Burns's beautifully tender song of *Highland Mary* when Monier approached. He had just left the company of the gentlemen at the castle, among whom the social glass had circulated freely, and was a little heated with the liquor he had drunk.

"I am right happy, right glad, maM'selle," said he, "to meet with you here. This is a fine, lovely-looking place for a lover like me to meet her he loves better than all the world."

"Sir," said Ellen, "I have often told you not to speak to me on such a subject. I now wish to be alone. You will, therefore, be pleased to walk on to wherever you were going, and leave me to myself."

"Beautiful creature, do you think I can leave you? I left my company and my wine to come after you."

"You did very wrong, sir; and I insist that you shall immediately return to your company and your wine, for whatever business you may have with them, I assure you, with me you can have none."

"Ah! my dear, with your bright eyes, with your lovely cheeks like the rose, and with your pretty bosom like the snow, I must have business. I am tired of politics, I now want to enjoy love."

"What do you mean, sir," said she, "by thus pertinaciously obtruding your-self upon me, when I tell you that your company is unwelcome?"

"Is my company unwelcome? Ah! I know somebody else, whose company you would prefer in this place."

"No matter what you know; only begone from me."

"Ah! my love, you should think how that man is in my power. He is my rival. I can be revenged. Only let me sit with you, and talk with you, and kiss your pretty hand, and he shall be used well."

"I say again, sir, begone! How dare you use such freedoms."

"It is only the way in France, maM'selle. I love you to my very soul, and I must kiss you and court you as lovers always do there."

"Your rudeness is intolerable!"

"Ah! my angel, my passion is intolerable." So saying he caught her very roughly.

"O God of mercy! Is there no one to help me?" she exclaimed.

"Villain!" cried a loud, tremendous voice, "receive that for your infamous conduct to an angel" and a tall stout man without a hat, or coat, and bald headed, struck him on the face with such force that he fell to the ground screaming, while the blood gushed freely from his mouth and nostrils.

Ellen could not recognize the stranger. "Whoever you are," said she, "may heaven bless you, for this deed!"

"Take my arm, fair innocence! I will protect you home."

She did so, and without speaking, he conducted her to the public road which led to the castle. "You are now safe," said he, "I must leave you."

"But first," she replied, "let me know to whom I am indebted for this de-liverance?"

"There are people approaching," he replied, "I must not be seen. Describe me to no one. Call with the Recluse tomorrow, at five in the afternoon. He will tell you who I am. But stop, stay — I see M'Nelvin, who knows me. He will conduct you to the castle."

The poet on seeing Ellen, was about to retire, but the stranger called him forward. "Protect this young lady to the castle," said he, "ask her no questions, but return to me in an hour. I shall explain all."

So saying he disappeared, and M'Nelvin, with considerable embarrass-ment, offered Ellen his arm.

"Oh! Mr. M'Nelvin," said she, "I shall never forget that man. I hope heaven will reward him — methinks I should know his voice."

"He is a good man, Miss O'Halloran, and you may yet know him."

"You have that pleasure it seems."

"Yes, and that pleasure is the only antidote I have against sorrows that would otherwise destroy me."

"Your unhappiness, Mr. M'Nelvin, which I have long noticed, grieves me, for I know you deserve a better fate. Can nothing be done to remove the cause of your melancholy?"

"No; nothing in this world," he replied, with a sigh, "without rendering a dearer object than myself miserable."

They had now arrived at the castle, into which the poet declined entering. But before they parted, Ellen requested him to call the next day to accompany her to the Recluse's cavern, to which he consented.

After much reflection on the Frenchman's misconduct, Ellen resolved not to reveal it to her friends. She recollected his threats against Edward, and she conceived, that by publishing his disgrace, she would only irritate his evil passions the more against his prisoner, and perhaps stimulate him to push his revenge even to assassination.

At the appointed time, she accompanied M'Nelvin to the hermit's cave, at the door of which he left her, promising to return in an hour to conduct her back. She found the old man in his usual attire in his first apartment. He informed her that he was the person who had rescued her yesterday — that seeing the Frenchman following her in a state of intoxication, and knowing how she had been lately persecuted by him, he thought it prudent to remain convenient for her protection, but not wishing to be known to him as the Recluse, he threw off part of the disguise he had usually worn since he came into this neighbourhood.

"Then you are not the decrepit, destitute old man we have hitherto taken you to be?" said she.

"No;" he replied, "but I have strong reasons for wishing to appear so for some time. This is all I must discover to you at present, but, I hope the time will come when throwing off all mystery, I shall reveal myself fully to you and to the world. In the meantime, my daughter, when you want a friend, when you need a protector, fly here, repose confidence in me, and be assured you shall receive ready and sufficient succour. I know the secret of your heart with respect to the imprisoned stranger. Be not ashamed of it. He is worthy of your preference, and in thus encouraging you to love him, you will yet find that I give a sanction to your feelings, at which your reason will rejoice. Return home now, my daughter — I may call you such, for my chief wish on earth is to see you happy; and my greatest anxiety is to guard you against misfortune. May God bless you, and be you still as innocent and virtuous as you now are, and you will deserve his blessing."

"Thank you, father," said she, "for you have spoke comfort to my soul. How shall I ever be able to repay such kindness?"

"By nursing me on my death-bed," he replied, "and shedding the tears of affection over my grave. Farewell! Visit me often."

At the door of the cave, she met the poet, who had been waiting there to conduct her home. Being thus assured of the disinterested attachment of two worthy persons, she became more cheerful in her mind, although her terror of the Frenchman was so great, that she resolved to discontinue those solitary rambles from which she had drawn so much enjoyment, least he should again find an opportunity to assault her.

CHAP. XI.

As nothing material happened to either our hero or heroine for some weeks after this period, I shall, if my reader has no objection, take advantage of this paucity of events to inform him what became of Tom Mullins and his companion.

It will be recollected that Tom Mullins, Edward's servant, set off in company with our gallant Northern peasant, Jemmy Hunter, in obedience to his master's orders, to avoid the violence of some enraged United Irishmen, who had combined against him. They rode that day, through a lovely and highly cultivated country as far as the town of Antrim, without meeting with any adventures worth relating. Here they consulted their instructions, and found that they were to remain there for two days in expectation of Edward overtaking them, at the expiration of which time, if he did not arrive they were to proceed to the seat of Sir Philip Martin in the county of Tyrone, who was a relation and a confidant of the Recluse, and whose son having been Edward's fellow-student at Trinity College, he had resolved to visit on his return homeward. They had also a letter from Edward to the Earl O'Neil, whose castle lay on the way from Antrim to Sir Philip Martin's residence.

On the evening of their second night at Antrim, as they were sitting comfortably over a mug of ale, two soldiers belonging to a regiment of fencibles that then lay in the town, and a townsman, came into the room. On hearing Mullin's brogue, and the simplicity of some of his remarks, one of the soldiers who was a Scotchman, and possessed of more mirth than good manners, thought to enjoy a little diversion at his expense. Accordingly, mimicking his tone of voice as well as he could, he approached him, saying, "Arrah, my friend Paddy, and where did yourself come from?"

Tom, however, had more mettle than he expected; and although he wished not to give offence, he replied, "I'll tell you, friend, whenever you are asked, just say I came from Kilkenny, where I don't believe in my shoul that your father was hanged, though he might have been put in the stocks for impertinence."

"What! heigh, ho!" replied the Scotchman somewhat nettled. "You maun either be a damn'd crappy, or what is worse, a damn'd papist."

"Lord! I doubt you're a warlack," said Hunter, eyeing him contemptuously, "you can guess sae weel."

"Be it sae," said the Scot, whom wrath had now reduced to his national accent, "ye'll please awa' to the guard hoose, whar weel hae you examined, an' taucht hoo to gie a ceevil answer."

"By the L—d!" said Hunter, "you maun show your warrant, ere we stir wi' you."

"The king's uniform is oor warrant," said the fencible, "didna ye confess ye war crappies."

"Confess the devil," said Hunter, "if ye don't leave the room this moment, ye'll no' leave it the next-wi' a hale skin."

"What do you mean? you rascal," cried the other fencible, "do you mean to strike one of the king's soldiers? Prepare to march!"

So saying both the soldiers drew their bayonets, and swore that they would "gut them like herrings" if they did not accompany them immediately to the guard-house. The landlord now entered, and having enquired into the cause of the disturbance, he advised our travellers to go with the soldiers, assuring them that if they could justify themselves before the officers at the guard-house, they would be instantly dismissed. Hunter swore he would not stir until absolute force should be used, or some lawful warrant for seizing him produced. An officer happening to pass at this moment, the landlord called him in. On hearing the soldiers' statement, he ordered the travellers to the guard-house without waiting for their reply. Seeing it in vain to resist longer, they complied, and in less than an hour, were both convicted by a court-martial of being United Irishmen, and attempting to abuse two privates belonging to His Majesty's regiment of Fifeshire Fencibles. They were each sentenced to receive five hundred lashes the next morning.

The townsman who had entered the room with the soldiers, and had been an observer of the whole affray, was, although a zealous kingsman, so much struck with the iniquity of these proceedings, that he resolved, if possible, to set the affair in its true light. He therefore took an opportunity of enquiring of Hunter, whether he was known to any gentleman in the neighbourhood who could have influence enough to procure a re-hearing of the case, offering to give such evidence of the affair as would entirely exculpate the prisoners. Hunter was unknown to any man of property in the vicinity, but, he said, that he had a letter from a gentleman, on whose business he and his companion, who was that gentleman's servant, were then travelling, for Lord O'Neil, who perhaps on their employer's account, might interfere in their behalf.

"He is just the man that can save you," said Thompson, which was the name of their new friend. "Give me the letter. I will carry it to his lordship, and tell him the whole truth. I know him well. He is my landlord, and a good man. He procured for me the office of gauger in this town." Without delay Thompson proceeded to Shanes Castle, long the stately and venerable seat of the O'Neil family, situated on the border of Lough Neagh, about two miles from Antrim, with the letter for its noble owner.

His lordship on hearing the circumstances, and on reading the letter, immediately ordered his horse, and set off for the town with Thompson. He called on the commanding officer, and having told him that he would pledge himself for the loyalty of the two strangers, who were then under sentence to be flogged, desired that they should have the benefit of a new trial, as he had sufficient evidence to prove their innocence.

"Whatever your lordship wishes in this affair," said the officer, "shall be done."

A new trial was accordingly ordered, at which his lordship, as colonel of the Antrim militia, was invited to preside. The soldiers testified as they did before, that the prisoners had confessed themselves to be United Irishmen, and that they had threatened violence to the deponents who in their own defence were forced to draw their side arms.

Lord O'Neil then enquired if there was no other witness, and was answered that no other had been examined on the last trial. That there had been one Thompson present during the quarrel, but, in such cases, they considered two witnesses sufficient to establish the guilt, and had not therefore examined him. His lordship desired Thompson to be called, who correctly stated to the court the facts as they happened. His lordship then mentioned that he had strong collateral evidence in favour of the prisoners, evidence indeed which went to prove that these men, so far from being conspirators against His Majesty's government, were, at the moment of their apprehension, actually flying from the threatened vengeance of a party of United Irishmen, whom they had offended by refusing to join their society.

"Here is a letter which I received," said he, "from a son of the honourable Thomas Barrymore, and a nephew to the Earl of Barrymore, one of His Majesty's privy counsellors, a young gentleman with whose principles and integrity I am well acquainted, in which letter he states that his servant, Thomas Mullins, having had a political quarrel in the town of Larne with some United Irishmen, they laid in wait for him, and would have killed him, had not his companion, James Hunter, come to his rescue, and succeeded in beating off the villains.

"He states further, that his business not permitting him immediately to leave that place, and fearing that the conspirators might renew their attempts against his servant, he has prevailed on Hunter to accompany him to the seat of his friend, Sir Philip Martin, in the county of Tyrone, and as they should pass by Shanes Castle, he took that opportunity of recommending them to my protection, in case any accident might befall them in my neighbourhood. Gentlemen," his lordship continued, "after this statement, corroborative of the positive and direct testimony of Thompson, I need not enlarge on the injustice of the proceedings that have taken place, and which, I perceive, have altogether arisen from the misconduct and malignity of two private soldiers, who to gratify their revenge on these innocent men, have not scrupled to become guilty of perjury, and upon their oaths wilfully to deceive this court.

"The testimony of Thompson, who joined neither party in the quarrel, may be safely considered impartial, and correct; and, as the matter now stands, I should suppose that no officer here will hesitate to concur in acquitting the prisoners. I also hope that the incident will impress on the minds of all present, the necessity of receiving at all times, with extreme caution, the evidence of men whose feelings are interested in procuring the conviction of prisoners, which is generally the case with informers, and of such as, in times like these, officiously display a more than ordinary zeal as partisans even in a good cause.

"I would therefore recommend it to the court both from a regard to justice, and as an example to malicious persons, to inflict a suitable punishment for perjury on the men who have been the occasion of this disgraceful business."

The court acceded to his lordship's wishes. The prisoners were dismissed; and the two soldiers ordered to receive each one hundred lashes.

Thus did our travellers escape from the unpleasant predicament, into which their evil stars had involved them. But it is impossible not to perceive that this military court was induced to do them justice, not so much from the merits of their case, as from a desire to oblige a man possessed of a title, of twenty-five thousand pounds a year, and of unlimited influence with the ministers of the day.

Under the auspices of this great man, they arrived without further accident, at the place of their destination, where Hunter left his charge, and returned home in safety, about three weeks after his departure, to the great joy of all his kindred and acquaintances, but to none more than the sweet Peggy Caldwell, whom he vowed never to leave so long again until they became 'man an' wife'.

Sir Philip Martin, to whom the Recluse had written concerning Edward's detention, being a favourer of the United Irishmen, and having by inquiries from O'Halloran, satisfied himself that his life was in no danger, refrained from acquainting his friends with the circumstance.

Lord O'Neil was ignorant of it; consequently, to Edward's relations, who had become uneasy at his long and silent absence, and had begun to make some inquiry after him, he could give no other information, than that he had received a letter from him in the month of May last, at which period he was in the vicinity of Larne. Edward had written to his friends shortly after coming to the North, that he intended, before he returned home, to visit the island of Staffa, and some other places in the Highlands. It was, therefore, concluded that he was exploring some of the remote parts of that wild, but to a mind like Edward's, attractive portion of the Empire, from whence transmitting communications by letter they knew to be rather difficult and uncertain. They, therefore, thought proper for a time to cease their inquiries after him.

CHAP. XII.

It was in the autumn of 1797, and sometime after the preceding transactions, that the melancholy event took place, which severed the last remaining link of the chain which had hitherto bound thousands of the Presbyterian community in the North, to the side of government, and gave that impulse to the wheels of the conspiracy, which no subsequent measure of either policy or force could arrest until it terminated in the fury and vengeance of a sanguinary rebellion. This event was the death, or, as the popular voice termed it, the martyrdom of William Orr.

To give a minute account of the sufferings of this greatly lamented favourite of the people, would interfere too much with the main design of this history, but his fate was too closely interwoven with, and had too important an influence on many transactions, which it will be incumbent on us to relate, to permit us to pass it over in silence.

Indeed the reader could but little appreciate those feelings, which hurried the Presbyterians of Ulster into the disastrous enterprise of 1798, unless he knew something of the story of Orr. As a body, whether we consider their numbers, or their intelligence, their wealth, their habits of industrious and active perseverance in their designs, they were by far the most efficiently powerful class of the conspirators. The majority of them, however, until the time of Orr's catastrophe, were far from being disloyal.

They were indeed greatly dissatisfied with the recent measures of the administration, but they could have been easily conciliated, for it was no trifling matter, that could totally estrange their hearts from that government, which had been the constant bulwark of the reformation. They might, and did occasionally feel some jealousy of the peculiar privileges and endowments, enjoyed by a prelatic church establishment, but they never viewed that establishment with the discontent and animosity which was felt by the Catholics; and with respect to their ideas of civil liberty they had been, generally speaking, strictly constitutional. Many of them had of late years, from a feeling of justice, warmly espoused the cause of Catholic emancipation; and when by the sagacious managers of the United confederacy, that cause became coupled with the cause of parliamentary reform, which was the great object of their political wishes, they scarcely made any difference in the zeal with which they sought the attainment of both. Still a great majority of even those among them, who had joined the United Irishmen, did not aim at a total dissolution of their connexion with Britain, notwithstanding their leaders, ever since the passing of the Insurrection law, did not hesitate to avow that such a dissolution was the great object for which they contended. Even to this period, thousands, whose political views coincided with those originally professed by the conspirators, had refused to join them, but their reluctance now vanished before the awful and exasperating spectacle of a virtuous, inoffensive, industrious and respectable man, vindictively hurried to the gallows in the face of circumstances absolutely demonstrative of his innocence; in contempt of the most earnest recommendations of a repentant jury, to mercy; and in opposition to the wishes, the expectations and the prayers of multitudes of all classes of the community.

After a year's wearisome imprisonment, this victim of executive infatuation and resentment, was brought to trial in September 1797, on a charge of administering the oath of a United Irishmen to a Scotch soldier of the name of Wheatly, an act which a clause in the Insurrection law had rendered punishable with death.

On the evidence of Wheatly, he was convicted, and sentence of death passed upon him. So notoriously bad, however, was the informer's character, that several of the jury were prevailed on to agree to the verdict, only by the cajolement and intimidation practised by others, and on the express condition that they should all join in a recommendation to mercy. This recommendation was forwarded to the Viceroy, together with the affidavits of three of the jurors, stating their solemn belief of the prisoner's innocence, and confessing

that they were under the influence of intoxication and terror when they con-
curred in the verdict.

The reader will be astonished at this confession of intoxication, it being a
direct infringement of the British law which enjoins abstinence on jurors during the solemn period of their deliberations: but it is a fact, that the jurors
alluded to, swore positively to the introduction of spirituous liquor through a
window into their chamber, and that they had used it to inebriation.

The day after the trial the informer also became conscience-struck, and
voluntarily deposed that his testimony against Orr had been malicious and
untrue. Exertions were, therefore, made by the magistrate who had originally
committed Orr upon the soldier's information, and by many other respectable
gentlemen of the county, to save him. He was, in consequence, three times
respited, and great hopes were entertained that he should finally receive mercy.
During this interval of suspense, a slanderous and unjust paragraph made its
way into a Belfast newspaper, stating that Orr had made a confession of his
guilt, and an acknowledgment of the justice of his sentence, 'which (it was
added) he had done to ease his conscience, and acquit the jury who had been
calumniated for their verdict against him.'

To repel this ungenerous fabrication, Mr. Orr despatched his brother to
Dublin with the following letter; which was delivered to the Lord Lieutenant:

May it please your Excellency,

*Having received from your Excellency's clemency, that respite from death
which affords me the opportunity of humbly and sincerely thanking you, I
avail myself of the indulgence of pen and paper, and of that goodness you
have already manifested towards me, to contradict a most cruel and
injurious publication in a late newspaper, stating that I had confessed
myself guilty of the crimes which a perjured wretch came forward to
swear against me. My lord, it is not by the confession of crimes which
would render me unfit for society, that I expect to live; it is upon the
strength of that innocence which I will boldly maintain with my last
breath, which I have already affirmed in a declaration, which I thought
was to have been my last, and which I had directed to be published as my
vindication from infamy, ten times more terrible to me than death.*

*I know my lord, that my own unhappy situation, the anguish of a
distracted wife, the mistaken tenderness of an affectionate brother, have
been resorted to, to procure that confession, and I was given to
understand that my life would have been spared on such conditions. I as
decidedly refused as I should do now, though your Excellency's pardon*

was to be the reward. Judge then, my lord, of the situation of a man to whom life was offered, upon no other condition than that of betraying himself, by a confession both false and base.

And lastly, let me make one humble observation to your Excellency, that the evidence should be strong indeed to induce conviction, that an industrious man, enjoying both comfort and competence; who had lived all his life in one neighbourhood; whose character, as well as that of all his stock, has been free from reproach of any kind; who certainly, if allowed to say so much for himself, would not shed the blood of any human creature; who is a husband and the father of a family; would engage himself with a common soldier, in any system that had for its end robbery, murder and destruction — for such was the evidence of the witness Wheatly.

If upon these grounds, and the facts already submitted to your Excellency, I am to be pardoned, I shall not fail to maintain the most dutiful sense of gratitude for that act of justice as well as mercy; and in the meantime, I beg to remain your Excellency's most obedient humble servant,

WILLIAM ORR.
October 10th, 1797.

At this period also Mrs. Orr addressed Lady Camden in the following terms:

To her Excellency the Countess of Camden,

For this freedom, grief like mine thinks not of apology. Despair and sorrow are my only companions; yet hope bids me look up to you for happiness. A miserable object, a mother and a wife, comes praying for mercy for the father of her children.

Pardon, most gracious lady, the frenzy of a distracted woman, and listen to the petition of the miserable wife of the unfortunate William Orr. I come a suppliant, a low and humble slave of misery, praying your ladyship's intercession in behalf of the life of my husband, whose existence is dearer to me than my own. O hear my complaint, and grant one beam of hope to my frantic imagination. You are the only person who has it in her power to remove never-ending misery from a wretched individual; to cheer the afflicted heart, and give comfort and consolation to her that was ready to perish. Suffer me to assure you that he is innocent

The eyes of the whole community were fixed upon these transactions, and public anxiety was strained to the uttermost respecting the fate of the prisoner. The last respite was to terminate on the 14th of October, on the evening preceding which day, a messenger arrived from government to the high sheriff of the county. It was fondly hoped and confidently expected, that he was the messenger of mercy, but no; he brought the mandate of death — a death which snapped asunder every lingering tie by which the government had yet any hold on the affections of wavering thousands. The shock which was given to the public mind is not easy to be conceived — multitudes swore that oath of vengeance, which was afterwards but too fatally performed.

On the morning of the 14th of October, he was taken from the jail. Although his long confinement had diminished the glow of health which his countenance had formerly worn, still it retained a more than ordinary degree of comeliness. His person was dignified and graceful, his stature being fully six feet, and his whole deportment such as to make a favourable and lasting impression on the spectators. As to his private character, a very candid writer of that day, who knew him well, observes that among his neighbours he was universally beloved, and in his domestic relations, as a husband, and a father, his affection and tenderness may have been equalled, but never surpassed.

At one o'clock he arrived at the place of execution, on the sea shore, about a mile to the south of Carrickfergus, in a carriage, accompanied with two clergymen, whom he had selected for the occasion. He was escorted by a strong guard of horse, foot and artillery, detached from various regiments lying at Carrickfergus and Belfast.

At the fatal spot, he sung some verses of the 23rd and 35th Psalms. On the 4th verse of the former, *Yea, though I walk in death's dark vale, Yet will I fear no ill; For thou art with me, &c.* he dwelt with particular emphasis; and also upon the following passage of the 14th chapter of Corinthians.

"So when this corruptible shall have put on incorruptible, and this mortality shall have put on immortality, then shall be brought to pass the saying, Death is swallowed up in victory. O death where is thy sting? O grave where is thy victory?"

He then addressed the by-standers, for several minutes, and boldly and earnestly declared his innocence and the falsehood of his accusers; after which he shook hands with those friends who were convenient to him, and ascended the scaffold with a firm step. When the executioner had fixed the rope about his neck, he, for the first time, exhibited some symptoms of indignation, exclaiming, "I am no traitor; I am persecuted for a persecuted country. Great Jehovah receive my soul! I die in the true faith of a Presbyterian."

He then gave the pre-concerted signal with his handkerchief, and was launched into eternity. Thus was accomplished a deed, the very mention of which, to this day, makes the blood of indignation boil in the hearts of thousands of Irishmen, even of those who are in reality friends to the constitution, and to the general conduct of the government as it has been administered since the Union. Had the administration of that day, singled out some restless, disorganizing and dangerous demagogue, some profligate disseminator of the new-fangled French doctrines of deism and equality, or the perpetrator of some act of violence or fraud, as the victim of its vengeful policy, the sensation of wrath, the passion of revenge, which seized upon, and maddened in the minds of the people, would either never have existed, or had they existed, being less defensible, would have evaporated whenever the subsiding of the first incitement of vexation and rage permitted the return of reflection.

But unfortunately Orr was not a character either dissolute or dangerous, and consequently reflection in the public mind, only gave permanence to those revengeful passions to which exasperation had given origin.

To show the impression of Orr's mind on the subject of religion, a subject on which no man who has sincere and solemn impressions, can be a bad member of society, the reader is here presented with a farewell letter, which he wrote to his wife shortly before he left the jail for the last fatal scene.

Saturday morning, Oct. 14.

My Dear Wife,

I now think it proper to mention the grounds of my present encouragement, under the apprehension of shortly appearing before my God and Redeemer.
First, my entire innocence of the crime I am charged with. Secondly, a well-grounded hope of meeting a merciful God. Thirdly, a firm confidence that that God will be a husband to you, and a father to our little children, whom I do recommend to his divine care and protection.

And my last request is, that you will bring them up in the knowledge of that religion, which is the ground of my present comfort, and the foundation of that happiness, which, I trust, I shall enjoy on that day, when we must all appear before the great Judge.

Farewell, my dear wife! farewell,
WILLIAM ORR.

It will be readily supposed that the United chiefs, who frequented the cave in which Edward Barrymore was confined, partook largely of the public excitement on this occasion. As their designs, however, were far from being ripe for execution, they had the prudence to suppress their feelings, and to act with moderation; and were, also, at considerable pains to restrain the popular fury from breaking out prematurely into acts of violence. In consequence of this solicitude to prevent atrocities that would have been detrimental to their cause, they preserved the jury that had convicted Orr, from becoming victims to the fury of some of the more daring and fanatical of their party, who had denounced vengeance against them.

One evening as Porter and Nelson were discoursing on this subject in Edward's presence, in such a manner as almost compelled him to express his opinion, he remarked that it was neither his province nor his inclination to defend the executive authority on all occasions.

"It is not necessary," said he, "that an adherent of our admirable form of government, should defend the general management of any particular administration, much less approve of any isolated act of harshness or cruelty. Still, however, before I can agree to consign the present ministers altogether to infamy, I must know the motives which induced them to permit this unhappy execution. False representations of the case, may have been made to them.

"They may have been persuaded that Orr was actually guilty of seducing the soldier from his allegiance, and therefore wished by a severe example to deter others from such practices. But, gentlemen, be my opinions on this subject what they may, I cannot help expressing my sorrow for the calamities which I perceive accumulating on the country, and which it is my sincere conviction, have had their origin in the unjustifiable and illegal attempts of secret associations to overawe the established authorities into measures, the beneficial tendency of which is, to say the least of it, controvertible."

"Sir," said Nelson, "though we dislike your sentiments, we cannot but admire the candour with which you express them; nor can we be offended at your freedom of speech, since an avowed antagonist is a much safer companion than a treacherous colleague."

The conversation was here interrupted by the entrance of O'Halloran, with a bundle of letters, one of which he handed to Nelson, saying, "Here is bad news for you. They have done what I long since predicted they would sometime do."

The transaction to which he alluded, will be related in the next chapter.

CHAP. XIII.

William Leigh Pierce.

When Nelson had finished reading the letter O'Halloran had given him, he exclaimed! "Yes, our Star is, indeed, set, but I trust that the light it has diffused through the country will not be so easily extinguished. Since the press is not now permitted to tell our injuries, we must speak them with the trumpet; and since we cannot write for the public good, nothing remains but to fight for it."

"What new atrocity has taken place? If I may be permitted to ask," said the Reverend Mr. Porter, who was at that moment preparing a communication for the Northern Star, in continuation of several ingenious letters, entitled, 'Billy Bluff and Squire Firebrand', with which he had lately amused and very much excited the minds of the people of Ulster.

"You may throw your manuscript aside," replied Nelson, "till better times. Barber's infamous dragoons have broken into my house, and destroyed our press. There is a letter from Teeling who witnessed the transaction. You may read it aloud. There will be no harm in Mr. Middleton hearing of another piece of tyranny — a ferocious outrage upon the liberty of the press, committed by a government which some men would make us believe is the grand protector of that liberty."

"Gentlemen," observed Edward, "I have said before, that an attachment to our form of government does not involve a necessity to defend every act of its administration. Some administrations may be very corrupt; nay, some acts of even a virtuous administration may be very injudicious and improper. But the constitution contains within itself a healing principle, for all mistakes or abuses, by lodging the legislative power with the representatives of the people, and giving them authority to impeach and punish a vicious ministry. The faults, therefore, of our present ministers whatever they may be, it is neither my province nor my wish to vindicate. With regard to the injury they may have done Mr. Nelson, for I perceive that they are charged with having made an attack upon his property, I do not know the merits of the case. But since you have drawn my attention to it, I shall listen to the statement you have received, provided I shall not be urged to give an opinion on it, should I wish to be silent."

He was informed that after hearing the particulars, he might remain silent or not, as he thought proper. The clergyman then read the letter aloud as follows:

October — 1797.

Dear Sir,

A dreadful scene of confusion and disaster has taken place here this morning. The vengeance of our tyrannic rulers has, at length, burst upon us, and our printing establishment is totally destroyed. I will detail to you the facts, as concisely as the nature of the affair will admit.

At about ten o'clock this morning, while I was sitting in the Star office, preparing some editorial matter for our next publication, I was alarmed by an unexpected noise of horses prancing, accompanied by a loud confusion of human voices in the yard below. Immediately one of the clerks rushed into the office, and begged me to escape as fast as possible, for the dragoons were swearing vengeance against me. I had scarcely disappeared by the back passage, before the office door was burst open, and in my retreat I could hear them exclaiming, "Damn the rascal! where is he? Ferret him out, and send him to hell!"

Every desk, draw, trunk and locker was broken open; and all our papers, books, &c. either destroyed or carried off. They beat and abused all our clerks and workmen on whom they could lay their hands. Fortunately, most of them escaped; and I am happy to understand that none of those who were seized are dangerously hurt. The windows and doors of the house were soon broken, and all our furniture, printing cases, presses, &c. hewn in pieces, and thrown into the streets. Our types are all ruined, and it is said, that several of these Vandals proposed to set fire to the premises. This was, however, opposed by some more moderate than the rest, otherwise not only we, but numbers of our neighbours, would have suffered an immense destruction of property.

It appears that the party who made the attack, had just returned from a scouring expedition round the country; and, it is said, that they made it in revenge for some observations we had published upon certain atrocities they had committed, and without authority even from their officers, much less from any civil magistrate. But the result will show whether there was any secret understanding between them and the constituted authorities. It is certain that it was nearly 12 o'clock before either the magistrates or the officers could be prevailed on to interfere, and long before that period, the destruction of our printing establishment was completed.

They then proceeded to the houses of several of our friends, and broke their doors and windows, or demolished their signboards; and, with the most infuriated madness, stimulated by drunkenness, they galloped through the principal streets, terrifying even those most devoted to the interests of government. At length the town sovereign and several other magistrates, prevailed on colonel Barber to order them into the barracks.

Thus in the most licentious and illegal manner has our establishment and property been destroyed; and it is more than probable that not one of the depredators will be called to an account for it. It is indeed strongly suspected that the rioters would not have committed such an open outrage against the common laws of the land, unless they had been previously assured that they had no punishment to dread.

I had some thoughts of lodging examinations against one or two of them whom our chief clerk can identify upon oath, but shall adopt no measure of the kind until I hear from you.

To comment to you on this worse than Gothic outrage would be unnecessary, but I may express my own feelings on the subject. They are partly those of grief and resentment; and partly of gratification. Why I should feel the former is obvious, but why I should feel the latter may require explanation. It arises from a conviction that this act of violence will do more to render our oppressors obnoxious to the intelligent part of the community than any they have yet committed. It will prove the truth of what we have often advanced, that under our present rulers the conductors of a free press cannot perform their duty to the public without danger; and that an editor who possesses sufficient integrity to despise the bribes, and sufficient intrepidity to defy the threats of the government,

*will sooner or later feel the weight of its resentment; and I rejoice, since
we have been marked out for vengeance, that it has been inflicted in this
violent and illegal manner, which will excite the public sympathy towards
us, and abhorrence towards our enemies, rather than by the more formal
mockery of a law process, the issue of which, however unjust, would not
have been so apparently flagitious to every part of the community.*

*I transmit this letter with some other documents I have just received
from Dublin, by express. Mrs. Nelson and family are well, and have
exerted more courage on this occasion than could have been expected.*

Yours, &c.
LUKE TEELING.

"Concerning this outrage," said Edward, "I will give my opinion frankly and
unsolicited. It is an instance of military violence which no rational, honest man
can justify; and which it is the duty of the government severely and promptly
to punish."

"I know the present government too well," replied Nelson, "to expect justice from it. Irishmen have been often and long the deceived satellites of
Britain, but, thank God, our eyes are now opened. Their professions can no
longer deceive us; for we know exactly the degree of credit to which they are
entitled. Now, if we want justice we must take it. Of our power to do so, our
oppressors will soon be convinced. They will, no doubt, oppose us with fire
and sword. The struggle will be dreadful, for the hatred is deadly, but the issue
will be glorious. To prepare the minds of my countrymen for the great crisis
of their national fate, I have already sacrificed my property; and my life, which
is all I can now give, is ready to be yielded, whenever my country's benefit
requires it."

"I am impatient for the day of action, that we may rid this long suffering
land of the tyrants," said O'Halloran. "Every day produces fresh atrocities,
and adds to our sufferings and their insolence. Delay may increase their
strength. It can scarcely add to ours, for we are already, in numbers, sufficiently strong. Why should we tamely continue to suffer? Why not hasten the
day of our deliverance? The people are now animated and zealous. Orr has
not died in vain!"

"Mr. O'Halloran," replied Porter, "prudence requires that we should exercise patience a few months longer. Although I acknowledge that delay by
giving the government time to prepare for the struggle, which it now evidently

expects, and, perhaps, by exposing some of our plans to discovery, may strengthen the hands of our adversaries, yet, as our adherents, however zealous and numerous, are not properly organized for insurrection, and the foreign aid we are promised, is not expected before spring, our wiser policy is to recommend our friends to a temporary submission to their misfortunes, rather than risk the ruin of their cause by a premature effort."

"Your reasoning may be correct," said O'Halloran, "but it is hard to remain inactive, and see an unoffending populace becoming every day more and more the victims of a wanton and cruel tyranny."

"We may be active," observed Nelson, "but we must be cautious. Were we, at present, to make the attempt, as we are not prepared to act in concert, the chance would be much against us. The day of retribution will come, and when we strike the blow, if it should be slow, I should like it to be sure."

"I know you are right," said O'Halloran. "My feelings, not my judgment, would hurry me into premature action. But it must not be. Necessity, hard necessity, requires that we should, for another season yet, submit to be slaves. But, I trust, that it will make our deliverance the more certain and effectual. In the meantime, Mr. Nelson, you will accompany me to the castle. Mr. Porter will examine these papers from the Directory, and tomorrow we may consult about the reply."

During the foregoing conversation, Edward's mind, as will readily be supposed, was but ill at ease. He felt no inclination to engage in it, and when O'Halloran and Nelson withdrew, he retired to his closet, there to ruminate with a heavy heart, on the rashness and misfortunes of these infatuated men, and to deplore the folly of that misgovernment which had driven them to the adoption of their desperate schemes.

CHAP. XIV.

Fair was the from that o'er him hung, And fair the form that set him free; The trembling whispers of her tongue, Sweeter than Seraph's melody.
Hogg.

The rancour and hatred which Monsieur Monier bore towards Edward, broke out in several instances of spleen and ill nature, and tended not a little, to make his imprisonment become daily more and more irksome. He publicly declared his hatred to the chiefs of the conspiracy, and insisted that such an enemy to the rights of man, and the liberties of his country, should not be permitted to live.

"If he were in France," said he, "our sans-culottes would soon have him to the guillotine; for there we know how to get rid of the enemies of the people."

O'Halloran, and the other leaders, however, resisted all his importunities, and he could procure none of the lower orders to assassinate his rival, as their chiefs were so averse to it. He, at length, fell upon another scheme of getting him out of the way. A brig freighted and cleared out of Belfast as if bound for London, but in reality intended for some French port, with dispatches from the United Irish Directory, to the Republican Government, lay in the adjoining harbour.

The insidious Frenchman meditated on having Edward carried on board of her, and despatched as a prisoner to France, where he could more easily control his fate. But even this, he could not effect without the consent of the leaders. He, therefore, applied himself to Porter, who most usually resided in the cave. This gentleman, conceiving that the principal intention of Edward's imprisonment would be answered by this means, and his life at the same time secured from any sudden impulse of resentment among his enemies, a circumstance which, while he was in their custody, could never be certain, consented, and, at last, prevailed on O'Halloran also to consent.

The Frenchman having thus far succeeded, immediately had the night fixed and the men selected for carrying him on board. It happened, however, that M'Nelvin, the poet, became accidentally acquainted with this plot. It was on an afternoon, towards the latter end of October, that he had thrown himself down amidst a thicket, a few paces from his arbour on the hill, with a small volume of Shakespeare's plays in his hand. His mind was absorbed in the romantic adventures of the *Mid-Summer's Night's Dream*, when he was startled by the sounds of voices approaching him. On looking from his thicket, he perceived the Frenchman, and Darragh, the man who had attempted Tom Mullin's life, advancing slowly. He lay quiet. When only a few yards from him, they stopped, but he was closely concealed from their view.

"They have consented at last," said the Frenchman, "to let that fair-faced Orangeman be sent to France, but I wish to Jupiter, that he could be put out of the way before he arrives there; for I understand that one cannot now get whomsoever one hates sent to the guillotine for the good of the people, as it was in the glorious days of Robespierre, when the Mountain party ruled. Our directors are now become so puny-hearted, and so full of sentiment, that they too make some fuss about a man's life, although he should be denounced in the name of the people. I am, when I think of it, somewhat afraid to trust him alive there. He might get exchanged, come home, and then disclose all. We must be more cautious than to let him off alive, say what they will about it. I have a purse of twenty guineas, and a captain's commission, to bestow on the brave man who will kill this damned heretic and lover of crowned heads."

"Jack Lafferty, and I," replied Darragh, "will do it. But not for your money. We'll do it for the good of the cause. When is he to go on board?"

"There are six men appointed to convey him on board tomorrow night," answered the Frenchman.

"Tomorrow all the country will gather to dig Robbin M'BriM's potatoes," said Darragh. "Robbin has been in jail these three months. He is a true fellow. He would not tell who put him up, all that they could do with him, although they swore they would hang him, like Orr. Long life to him! say I. We have shorn his corn already, and will dig his potatoes in rank and file tomorrow, in spite of either Orangemen or government. I'll see Lafferty at the digging, and I will take care to get the King's man snug from telling before the brig sails. Who guards the cave tomorrow?"

The Frenchman answered, that he understood that Porter intended to go in disguise with the other leaders to the potato digging; and that a man, called Anthony Allen, was selected to guard the cave during their absence.

This discovery concerned the peace of Ellen Hamilton too much to be neglected by M'Nelvin. To save Edward, therefore, from impending danger, became now the great object of his solicitude.

At first he knew not how to act, but, as he had, for several years past, been accustomed in all his perplexities to seek advice from one whose counsel had never deceived him, namely, the Recluse, he now sought him. It was soon agreed that, as this was a case which justified a disregard of the punctilios of custom, or the fastidiousness of delicacy, they should, at once, make the affair known to her whom it most nearly concerned. Accordingly M'Nelvin hastened to the castle, from whence he brought Ellen, without loss of time, to the glen.

The Recluse with as much caution and tenderness as possible, disclosed to her Edward's danger. For some minutes she remained the picture of surprise and horror, but said nothing; and so much did her emotions seem to have overcome her, that her friends began to repent having made the disclosure.

At length tears came to her relief; and she found utterance. "I feared, I feared that it would come to this at last!" she exclaimed. "Unfortunate young man! O my friends, what can be done for him? He must not, surely he must not die!"

"Can we with any prospect of success inform your grandfather of what is meditated against him?" inquired the Recluse.

"I fear not," she replied, "he is so much devoted to the will, and what he conceives to be the interest, of these conspirators, that to save his own life, he would scarcely risk a contention with them. But he must be saved. Oh! Father of mercies, assist me! I shall deliver him out of that den of tygers, or I shall perish with him. It is no time now to act the woman. Pardon me, my friends, I am resolved. I shall penetrate into their inmost recesses. I shall find him. If they have even hearts of stone, I shall melt them, or if they be too obdurate, my hands shall give him weapons; we shall clear the way, or we shall die together."

Her frenzy startled, and confounded her auditors, but it suggested an idea to M'Nelvin, which he immediately communicated; and which by infusing hope into Ellen's mind, greatly calmed her agitation.

"Tomorrow," said he, "I have learned, that the cave will be deserted by its usual inmates who are to attend the potato digging; and that Anthony Allen is appointed to remain sentinel over Mr. Middleton. He will not refuse Miss O'Halloran admittance. She may then inform the prisoner of his danger, and if we can contrive to draw Allen's attention for some time, from the door of the cave, he may escape disguised in apparel similar to hers, which she can provide for the occasion."

"I shall try it," said Ellen. "The case is desperate — I must bring my mind to make a desperate effort. Timidity, delicacy, shame, must give way to his safety."

After some deliberation, the Recluse approved of the project, as the only plausible means of rescuing his friend from the destruction that threatened him. How to manage Allen, so as to prevent him from recognising the prisoner, when he should pass from the cave, was now the difficulty. Neither the Recluse nor M'Nelvin were much trusted by the United Irishmen. They had both refused to take the oaths of fidelity to their party. But this was ascribed to a scrupulosity of conscience, with regard to swearing, and not to any disapprobation of the cause. On the contrary, they were considered well-disposed to it, but as neither of them could give much efficient aid in a military view, the one being decrepit from age, and the other from accident, they were not much pressed on the subject. Still, as they did not belong to the body, they were not trusted by it.

In this dilemma, they directed their views to Jemmy Hunter, who had served Edward so efficiently on a former occasion. Ellen now returned home to prepare the dress which was to be Edward's disguise. M'Nelvin left her at the castle gate, and went in search of Hunter. This young man, had been, for some weeks, a bridegroom, and as merry as a lark in a May morning; for his Peggy, who had long charmed him with her smiles and her blushes, had, at length, blessed him with her hand and her heart, and a happier couple could not have been found in the whole province.

M'Nelvin found the young bridegroom working in a garden adjoining his dwelling house, with a heart in a humour to be pleased with everything, and at that moment, full of the high delight he anticipated from marching with the large concourse of potato-diggers that were to assemble the next day. He was singing, "And a digging we will hie, And a digging we will hie, And we'll dig the fields of each brave man, Who in jail for truth doth lie."

M'Nelvin informed him that the Recluse had business with him, which could only be communicated in the cavern.

"Come in awee, an' tak' a dram," said Jemmy, "an' I'll gang wi' you directly. Peggy, my love, here's the poet come to see you. Gie us a drap o' the best Innishowen, for it's the native, an' pys nae taxe to support the redcoats, an' the guagers."

Peggy, with all the graceful gentility of nature, produced the cheering pitcher, but as the poet was in haste, he begged Jemmy to go with him without delay, his business being important. He promised the fair bride, however, that some evening soon he would make amends for the shortness of his present visit.

At Saunders's cave, Hunter was made acquainted with the whole affair, and was asked if he thought he could occupy Allen's attention in such a manner, that when the prisoner would pass out, he might be prevented from so closely observing him as to endanger detection.

He readily undertook to do so. "And, by heavens, if he does detect him," said he, "I'll pinion him wi' sitch a grip that he'll no' e'en stir, till Mr. Middleton be clear oot o' his reach. It will be doing mare guid, I think, to my neighbour than going to dig Rabbin M'BriM's potatoes. Damn the butchers, but we maun save the lad. He was a guid frien' to Peggy, and she aye thinks weel o' him, an' I'll no' forget him in his pinch."

The morning rose that ushered in the potato digging-day, in which numerous throngs of lads and lasses dressed in their best attire, with light and merry hearts came from all parts of the adjacent country, into the town of Larne; the lads to march to the work of charity and benevolence, the lasses to witness the procession, and reward their lovers as they passed them with their smiles. During this year, frequent assemblages of the people took place in different parts of the country to work the land, or gather in the harvest, of those who for their obnoxious politics had become inmates of the jails, or were otherwise prevented from attending to their domestic concerns. On the occasion to which we now particularly refer, upwards of five thousand men marched, in rank and file, carrying no other weapons than spades and baskets to the scene of their industry, and in the course of a few hours performed an immense quantity of labour, in raising and housing the potatoes of their proscribed confederate.

These assemblages for rural industry, were contrived by the leaders of the conspiracy, in order to display the popularity of their cause, and thereby encourage their friends to perseverance, and prevent the lukewarm and timid from defection.

Great care was taken that their proceedings should be conducted in a peaceable and orderly manner, so that no pretence should be given for magisterial interference; and, it is astonishing how well they succeeded, considering the unruly and heterogeneous multitude they had to manage. But zeal for the cause, and a general conviction that its character and success depended on the propriety with which these public bodies conducted themselves, had the effect of preventing every kind of tumult, and these assemblages generally dispersed with as much sobriety and decorum as a congregation withdraws from church.

It was in the afternoon of that day, when all the conspirators except the sentinel had left the cave, that, with an agitated and fearful heart, as if she were approaching some crisis of her fate, Ellen, in company with Hunter, hastened to the prison of her lover, with a resolution to effect his deliverance, or die with him. Often, however, the feelings of the woman would obtrude upon her, and for a moment damp the determination of the lover. But the recollection of Edward's danger still prevailed, and enabled her to persist.

Without hesitation she and her attendant were admitted by Allen. The granddaughter of O'Halloran could not be suspected, and Hunter had been long the particular friend of Allen. Besides, ever since his life had been in jeopardy at Antrim, the particulars of which story were widely circulated, he had become highly popular with his party. He remained on the outside, to converse with Allen, whilst Ellen advanced. She had now, however, to experience the greatest struggle with her delicacy that she had yet encountered, as she recollected that she was thus voluntarily seeking the presence of a young man in absolute solitude, who had professed himself her lover. Thrice after admittance, she hesitated on her step as if to argue the propriety of proceeding or returning. But her resolution carried her forward, and she appeared in Edward's presence lovely and blushing, but disconcerted and speechless with the conflict of terror, shame and solicitude which agitated her bosom. He was, at the first view, so struck with astonishment that he could scarcely believe the vision to be real.

"What happiness!" he exclaimed. "Has an angel in the dearest of all created forms, come to visit me in my prison?"

She sunk upon a chair, and almost fainted. He ran to support her, but she soon recovered her self-possession sufficiently to account for her appearance, by relating the danger she had discovered him to be in, and the means she had provided for his escape. It is needless to repeat the expressions of gratitude and rapture in which Edward now indulged. She, however, soon reminded him that there was no time for conversation, and that if he meant to escape, he must haste and depart. She now supplied him with an exact duplicate of the clothes she then wore, and in a few minutes, he was disguised.

"Let me," said he, "before I part from my guardian angel, kneel with her one precious minute before the throne of Heaven, that I may implore blessings upon her head."

They both kneeled; and he fervently caught her hand in his while he uttered the following prayer.

"Almighty Protector of innocence, and searcher of hearts, on my knees, I implore thee to be a shield to one of the fairest and purest of thy creatures.

116

Thou knowest the alarming dangers, in the midst of which I am about to leave her, but thou art sufficient to deliver her from them. Without that assurance, O God, how could I support that separation which is now become inevitable. O grant, that we may again meet under more benign circumstances, and that we may then never part until thy last summons shall call us to immortality. Preserve her for me in my absence, faithful, lovely and innocent as she now is; and hear me, while I vow eternal fidelity to her — May this heart which now beats for her alone, beat no more, ere it shall know another earthly love; and may this hand become enfeebled and withered, ere it shall grasp in the holy ordinance of wedlock, any hand but the dear one which it now holds!"

He then imprinted on her hand a fervent kiss, and bidding her adieu, rushed toward the door. Allen mistaking him for Miss O'Halloran was for running to assist him in getting out, but Hunter, who by this time had enticed him to the bottom of the rock, desired him to remain where he was, as he knew the young lady disliked to be disturbed with such attentions. He added, that though he had conveyed her here, he knew that she wished to return home by herself, and as his friend Allen was alone here today, he believed he should stay a few hours to keep him company. "Why, Allen, man," said he, "you should think o' gettin' married. I'm tauld that Jenny Davis is amaist wud aboot you; an' she's a nice lass; an' her father can gie her twa hunner pun' ony day. Lord, man, I was never sae happy, as I hae been these four weeks past, wi' Peggy. Ye ken I wad tak' naething wi' her, though her father says we'll fare naething the war o' that, or a' be owre."

Allen confessed that he had a hankering after Jenny, but feared that she liked Tam Mathewson better than him. By this time, Edward had ascended the hill that overlooked his late prison; and in a few minutes more, he found himself safe in the Recluse's habitation. His disguise was soon thrown aside.

"All has succeeded; Heaven be praised!" exclaimed the old man. "M'Nelvin waits at the top of the glen with your horse. Haste, fly, leave this distracted place, for there is no safety here; and God be with you!"

"I go, Farewell, Father! We shall yet meet again. Till then, under heaven, I charge you with the care of the angel who has delivered me."

"Adieu, my son. No earthly consideration shall prevent me from attending to that charge. Yonder is your horse."

Edward sprang forward, and seized M'Nelvin by the hand. "Farewell!" said he. "Be still Miss O'Halloran's friend; I shall ever be yours." He spurred his steed, and in three hours more found himself at the hospitable gate of Shane's Castle.

CHAP. XV.

The princely mansion of the ancient family of O'Neil, at which Edward Barrymore had now arrived, was then the pride of the surrounding country, it being the most entire and perfect specimen of the magnificence of ancient architecture to be found in Ulster. It is now no more. The fury of an accidental conflagration which took place in 1816, was sufficient, in a few hours, to convert into ashes that proud and stately structure, which had cost our ancestors the expenditure of many years of great skill, care and industry to erect. Thus adding another to those innumerable examples with which both history and experience have made us acquainted of the vanity of human calculations, and the frailty of human works.

The pleasure felt by the noble owner of this venerable edifice, as he gave the cordial welcome of a friendly Irish heart to our hero who had been so long and so mysteriously lost, is easy to be imagined.

He informed him of the anxiety of his friends respecting him, and of the unpleasant adventure that had befallen his servant. The former he had anticipated, and it had given him considerable uneasiness during his captivity. Of the latter he had never heard; for while in confinement, very little of what passed in the world, came to his ears.

After such a tedious imprisonment, he now felt how sweet it was to breathe unlimited air, how delicious to be master of his own motions. A regard for the safety of O'Halloran, prevented him from acquainting Lord O'Neil with what he had suffered, and he merely stated in general terms, that a variety of accidents had, during the whole summer, conspired to detain him on the coast.

"That part of the country abounds with the disaffected, I understand," said his lordship.

"It also abounds with steady, peaceable and loyal subjects," replied Edward. "It is a very interesting portion of the country."

"What number of the military are, at present, in Larne?" enquired the earl.

"I believe that it is thought unnecessary to keep more than a single company of Fifeshire fencibles there," said Edward.

"If that be sufficient to preserve the peace there, it is more than can be said of this neighbourhood," observed his lordship. "Here the presence of almost a whole regiment is requisite. The times are getting very awful. I begin to think that it would have been as well to have spared Orr. The people have been very much inflamed by that affair.

"But this is not the worst. French principles, I understand, have lately been everywhere disseminated with fearful success, and I am sorry to be credibly informed, that the mischievous writings of Paine are now more read by the lower orders than the Bible itself.

"I do indeed forebode very unhappy consequences to result from this state of things. It behoves all who have the preservation of social order, and rational government at heart, to be vigilant and active in restraining the excesses to which the misguided populace threaten to run."

A summons from the ladies to attend the tea-table put an end to this conversation. Edward passed a very agreeable evening in this refined society, which greatly conduced to calm the perturbation of his mind. Being in haste to return home, that he might relieve the solicitude of his friends, he, the next morning, continued his journey to the residence of Sir Philip Martin, attended by one of Lord O'Neil's servants. He arrived there on the following day, and was received with all that cordiality and friendship he expected from a worthy family, with the heir of which he had been long and intimately acquainted. Here he met with honest Tom Mullins, who was nearly broken-hearted with vexation on his master's account — for although he had no knowledge of what had really happened, he could not get rid of a vague suspicion, that the United Irishmen had done him harm. He had been detained at Sir Philip Martin's during the whole summer, at the suggestion of the Recluse, who feared that if he returned to Dublin, he might give such information to Edward's friends as would direct their attention to O'Halloran's neighbourhood, and, perhaps, bring that gentleman into trouble.

Sir Philip conversed much concerning the Recluse. He confessed that he was on the most confidential footing with him, "And you, Mr. Barrymore," said he, "have the honour to be one of his chief favourites. I have had frequent letters from him of late, in each of which you are mentioned in the most approving terms; and, let me tell you, I conceive it no slight honour to have met with such decided approbation from such a man.

"I am acquainted with every incident of importance that befell you, from your deliverance by O'Halloran, till your imprisonment for being an obstinate loyalist, a character which, I perceive, my old true-hearted friend, does not much relish. However, you and I shall not dispute on that subject.

"I shall not, as my friend did, make an attempt to convert you; although I cannot but wish that during the approaching struggle, of which I suppose you have been forewarned, the cause of the people should possess the support of more such men of talents and influence as you are, than I am sorry to find it does; and, believe me, your misunderstanding with the United Irishmen arose chiefly from their solicitude to make such an acquisition as you would be to their party.

"For this purpose they sounded you, and in so doing gave you more knowledge of their affairs than they afterwards thought it consistent with their safety you should possess. Hence they secured you. How you got out of their strong hold, unless with their permission, I cannot tell.

"I am glad, however, that you are out, for I looked upon your confinement as altogether a useless precaution against a man of your humanity and honour. You see, I know your character. Not only the Recluse, but my son has been at pains to represent it in such a favourable light, that I hesitate not to open my mind to you at once without reserve."

Edward expressed his grateful sense of the testimony his friends had given of him, and hoped that Sir Philip would never have cause to think him unworthy of it, or to repent the candour with which he had disclosed his political sentiments.

As to the mode of his escape from captivity, he did not then feel free to disclose it, but, he hoped, the time would come, when it would be his pride to relate it to his friends. Sir Philip expressed his acquiescence; and the subject of politics was dropped.

Charles Martin, Edward's fellow-student, and bosom-friend, had been absent with his sisters, two pretty and amiable girls, on a visit to a house of a neighbouring gentleman. They, however, returned early in the evening, and great was the joy of Edward and his friend on meeting. Sir Philip had not acquainted his son with Edward's imprisonment; for their political principles being somewhat different, he was unwilling to prejudice the cause of the United Irishmen, by informing him of anything that would lessen them in his esteem. Hence, when during a solitary walk, which the young friends took through Sir Philip's shrubberies, in order to relate to each other their adventures since they last parted, Charles was astonished and grieved at the extraordinary and perilous nature of those which had befallen Edward.

"I fear," said he, "that the machinations of these men against you are not over. What a pity that their connexions are so extended that we cannot bring them to justice, without involving those we love in their punishment. I agree with you, that all the circumstances considered, it is better to be silent on the subject. If you insist on immediately departing for Dublin, as your friends are so anxious concerning you, I cannot object, although I hoped to enjoy your company for several weeks here. But we shall not part so soon. I will accompany you if you will wait but a couple of days, that I may make arrangements for the journey."

This being agreed to, and Edward having one day's rest on his hands, wrote to the Recluse an account of his safety and welfare, and requesting speedy intelligence concerning Ellen and the conduct of the United Irishmen on discovering his escape.

At length, the two friends, well-armed and well-attended, set out for the capital, where they arrived on the third day without encountering any accident.

Edward was now once more amongst his relations, and the friends of his youth, an inhabitant of the metropolis of his country. But his heart and his affections were in a remote province. It was in vain that the ladies of Dublin assumed their most interesting and fascinating looks in his presence; in vain were the various pleasures of that captivating city spread before him, and offered to his acceptance. His Ellen was afar off, and, perhaps in danger, and how could he be happy? It came into his mind, that some of the most unprincipled of the conspirators might be so revengeful and unmanly, as to resent upon her, the part she had taken in his rescue. This idea rendered him miserable. He wrote a second time to the Recluse, conjuring him to lose no time in acquainting him with the treatment that Ellen had received from her grandfather and his confederates, after his departure. It was, however, only the next day after forwarding this letter that his mind was set at ease on this subject, by receiving one from the old man in reply to that which he had written at Sir Philip Martin's.

He was informed, that the United men kept the circumstance of his escape very quiet, that the whole blame was thrown on Jemmy Hunter, who was very willing to bear it.

The old man added, that he even believed that O'Halloran was secretly rejoiced at it. "He, indeed," said he, "pretty sternly and closely interrogated Ellen, as to her motives for assisting in the affair, and when she candidly told him of the plot that was laid for his destruction, he affected not to credit it. But, he said, that it was on the whole, perhaps, as well that you were out of their power, and that he had never approved of the scheme of sending you to France. He also mentioned, that if he could persuade his coadjutors that they had no reason to dread your informing on them, he should entirely approve of what she had done.

She took this opportunity to acquaint him with the whole of the Frenchman's villainy towards herself. (Here the Recluse related the incidents of Monier's attack upon her, of which Edward was ignorant, but of which the reader has been already informed.) This, at length, aroused his indignation against the foreigner; and he that evening communicated the whole to Porter, Nelson, and another of the leaders named M'Cracken. They all joined in reprobating such conduct, and agreed to induce him to leave the country, by persuading him that the government had become apprised of his residence and employment, and that his safety depended on his returning to France, in the vessel which was about to sail with their despatches for his government. And the country has, in consequence, got rid of a mischievous visitor …"

Edward resolved immediately to allay the fears of the United party, respecting the knowledge he had obtained of their measures. He, therefore, wrote a long letter to O'Halloran, in which he disclaimed any feelings of resentment on account of his confinement, which he altogether ascribed to the motives that had been assigned, the imperious nature of which on their minds he could duly appreciate.

He concluded this letter by informing O'Halloran, that as his motives for concealing his real name and character no longer existed, he would now confess that he was the apparent representative of a family, sufficiently high in office and in influence, to procure for any of his party, who wished to return to their duty, forgiveness of the past, provided they would give security for the future. He would, therefore, assume his real name, which a desire to enjoy the esteem of some who had suddenly become extremely dear to him, but whose suspicion and dislike, he believed, a knowledge of that name would have excited, had induced him for a time to conceal.

"I the more readily," said he, "give you my name on this occasion, as I flatter myself that it will confirm your reliance on my promise of secrecy respecting your affairs, by showing you that on the fulfilment of that promise, I stake the honour of a house that has never yet acted dishonourably, the house of Barrymore."

Having thus replaced Edward Barrymore, after his perilous journey to the North, in safety among his friends, we may leave him there unnoticed, for some months, as nothing remarkable happened to him during that period, and turn our attention to what, in the meantime, befell the beauteous and tender mistress of his affections.

The sentinel at the cave deceived by the disguise of Edward, and amazed by the artifices of Jemmy Hunter, did not, for several hours, discover that his prisoner had escaped. The first intimation he had of it, was by Hunter roundly saying, "I think Miss O'Halloran will noo be tired waitin'; I maun see her hame."

"Why, she's gane lang since," said the sentinel.

"Maybe sae, an' maybe no'. I'll see wha's within, however," replied Hunter.

Accordingly in he and the sentinel went; when to the astonishment and confusion of the latter, Miss O'Halloran appeared in her own identical person.

"An' wha went oot in your likeness?" inquired the wondering sentinel at the trembling girl.

She made no reply, but held down her head to conceal her shame; for she had really become innocently ashamed, while the big tears stood ready to burst from her eyes.

"Never mind," said Hunter, intercedingly, "the fault was a' mine. Ye ken, Allen, I wad na let you rin after the gentleman, when he gat oot, or ye might hae broucht him back to his prison."

"The gentleman!" exclaimed Allen. "I hope the gentleman's no' fled. Our officers will think I hae betrayed them. Some o' them may be for takin' my life. Ye ken some that wad na stap at that, if they thought I did it willingly. I should hae done my duty better."

"Fear naething," said his companion. "Jemmy Hunter will stan' by you, through thick an' thin, an' tak' a' the blame, as he deserves to do, on him. In the meantime, his honour's daughter here, ye ken, canna be in the fault. I maun just see her hame; an' I'll be back in a crack to stan' between you an' danger."

"Mr. Allen," said Ellen, who had considerably recovered from her confusion, "I shall stay here, and confess the share I have had in your prisoner's escape, rather than that you should be subjected to any trouble on its account."

"No, my lady," said the gallant Allen, "you can tell the truth as weel in the castle as here. Since he is gane, it canna be helpit noo. It's useless to fret; an' Jemmy here is willing to bear the blame o't; an' I dinna mislippen Jemmy makin' his word guid at a' risks. So, I dinna like, my lady, to see you sae vexed aboot it. When you gang hame, your aunt Brown will gie you mair comfort than I can. Jemmy, you can gae wi' her, but see that you be back in time to clear me frae the blame?"

Jemmy promised he would; and in company with his fair charge, he set off for the castle.

"Do you think he is safe?" muttered Ellen, almost unconsciously, as they went along.

"He is, I'll swear it to you," was her companion's reply.

"Thank heaven!" she ejaculated. "But alas! what have I done? What will they say of me?"

"Never mind that," replied her comforter, "you hae saved a gentleman's life, an' God will bless you for it as lang as you live; and I hope, that he winna forget me either, for helpin' in it."

"You have a good heart, James," said she, "and I trust, that you will indeed be blessed for what you have done this day."

"Thank you, thank you, lady," said he, his heart swelling within him at the praise she had so fervently bestowed upon him. "You'll mak' me prood o' this day as lang as I live."

Having conducted her to the castle, he left her, and returned with a light and satisfied heart to the cave. When O'Halloran, Porter, Nelson, M'Cracken and their confederates returned in the evening from the potato-digging, they were, at first, much surprised and chagrined at what had taken place.

"If the fellow don't inform on us," said Nelson, after his first excitement had somewhat abated, "the matter will not indeed much grieve me; for I believe we could never have prevailed on him to join us."

"Though we should, perhaps, have less cause for alarm," said O'Halloran, if he were still in our power, "yet I am almost persuaded that he has too much honour to be an informer."

"I agree with you," said Porter, "and when I reflect on the whole tenor of his conduct, while in confinement, I own that I see no great cause for apprehension."

"I am glad gentlemen," said M'Cracken, "that you console yourselves so easily; and, since the misfortune cannot now be remedied, I must acknowledge that philosophy to be the soundest, which enables us with the least difficulty to bear it."

Thus these active chiefs made a virtue of necessity; and in place of repining at any accident which would have tended to dishearten their followers, they put a good countenance upon every disaster; and, casting irremediable events as much as possible from their thoughts, proceeded to make the best of the advantages they still possessed.

CHAP. XVI.

When we think of that Island, old Nature's delight,
Where first she displayed all her charms to our sight,
Where oft we enjoyed every pleasure in store,
Of friendship and love, and whiskey galore;
Oh, sure! oh sure! that patriot glow,
Our fathers felt so long ago,
Must o'er our ardent bosoms sway,
And bid us rejoice in Patrick's Day.
Irish Soothsayer.

Although Ellen was treated with indulgence on the occasion just related, it was not long till she suffered persecution enough of another kind. A certain Sir Geoffrey Carebrow, a very formal bachelor, of great property, who had lately come, after several year's absence, to reside on an estate which he possessed in the neighbourhood, having met with her at a public ball which was given in Larne, during the Christmas holidays, became violently enamoured of her.

He was a man, who, from his youth, was noted for a union of two passions seldom found united in the same person, a love of women and a love of money. Although he possessed estates which yielded him upwards of fifteen thousand a year, with nearly a hundred and fifty thousand pounds in the national funds, he had hitherto been deterred from wedlock on account of the expense of supporting a wife and rearing a family. He fancied he could gratify his amorous propensities at a much cheaper rate by constantly keeping an obliging housekeeper, and two or three good-natured servant girls. For the offspring thus produced, he could with far less expense provide, than for legitimate children, as neither their expectations nor their claims would be so high; and, as to a wife, he sagaciously concluded, that there was no comparison between the freedoms she would naturally take with both his credit and his purse, and the trifling gratuities he might voluntarily bestow on a menial girl.

Thus he had hitherto lived in the indulgence of both lewdness and avarice, until his thousands and his bastards had become equally numerous.

At the ball we have mentioned, the exquisite beauty and bewitching sweetness of Ellen's countenance, together with the graceful symmetry of her form, and the inimitable easiness of her motions, as she threaded the mazy dance, struck on his luxurious fancy with a force altogether irresistible, and he immediately centred all his wishes and happiness in the enjoyment of such charms.

To effect this, he discovered to be no easy matter. A little reflection convinced him that illicit gratification was out of the question. Her principles were unassailable by either flattery or bribery; and as to stratagem or force, if he should by such means succeed in overcoming her virtue, the whole of that numerous party whom he knew to be devoted to her grandfather, (for he had lately become acquainted with some of the secrets of the United Irishmen) would mark him for vengeance, and his life would inevitably pay the penalty of such an offence. There remained, therefore, no other means of possessing her than by breaking through his long formed resolution against matrimony, and making her the partner of his fortune. This was a horrible alternative, but he felt that he could not be happy without her, and he resolved to adopt it. He accordingly took the earliest opportunity of making known to her his wishes.

She at once gave him an unequivocal and decided denial. In vain did he make her the most splendid offers; in vain did he enlarge on his immense wealth, and on the violence and sincerity of his passion, which he asserted would never permit him to know happiness without her. She was inexorable.

He next had recourse to her grandfather; and soon gained his favour, by suddenly becoming a warm friend to the United cause. As he had been hitherto considered, not indeed a royalist, but a very lukewarm favourer of the popular party, O'Halloran looked on his accession as a matter of great importance. At this juncture it was in reality so.

By order of the Dublin Directory, a certain quantity of arms and ammunition was to be provided by the Northern conspirators, before the middle of March ensuing. To raise money for this purpose was no easy matter. The greater number of the zealous leaders were men of broken fortunes; and the voluntary contributions of the lower orders, came in so slowly, and in such small sums, as to be of little or no service. Great was the anxiety that our Northern chiefs felt on this occasion; and frequent were the consultations they held on the subject. O'Halloran had already expended within the last fifteen months, about thirty thousand pounds on account of the confederacy; a great portion of which had gone to relieve the distresses of those whom the government had harassed on account of their obnoxious principles. Upwards of sixty thousand pounds were wanted on the present occasion. To raise this sum was beyond his power, without mortgaging his estate, and perhaps paying an exorbitant interest. This, however, he resolved to do, rather than permit the cause to suffer.

To Sir Geoffrey Carebrow, he, therefore, applied, as at this crisis he was almost the only monied man connected with the party. A mortgage for sixty thousand pounds was immediately executed, of which forty thousand were paid down, at an interest, secretly agreed upon, of ten per cent; the remaining sum being promised in six weeks. The parties to this bargain also entered into a secret stipulation that both the principal and the interest of this mortgage should be at the control of Ellen Hamilton, when she should become the wife of Sir Geoffrey Carebrow.

With the money thus procured, a vessel was despatched to Scotland, from whence she returned in a few weeks, with the requisite supply of warlike stores for the conspirators.

In the meantime, Sir Geoffrey did not fail to use the advantage which he had thus obtained over O'Halloran, in prosecuting his suit for Ellen. His vehement professions of patriotism blinded O'Halloran to his other faults; and he looked with respect upon a character whom had he known better he would have detested. But being himself the very reverse of a hypocrite, he was the less likely to suspect hypocrisy in others. Hence he firmly believed Carebrow's patriotism to be sincere. For the same reason he was convinced, that his attachment to Ellen was not only genuine, but ardent and disinterested; and being unquestionably a man of great wealth, he conceived that he consulted both her interest and happiness by ordering her to receive his addresses and to look on him as her future husband. This was a source of great affliction to this dutiful and affectionate girl.

She now felt herself for the first time obliged to disobey him who was her only parent, and whose directions she had hitherto considered as an unerring rule of conduct. Things were in this state, when that great national day which warms and elevates every Irish heart, the day consecrated to Erin's tutelary saint, arrived, and was celebrated at O'Halloran Castle by a splendid entertainment, somewhat in the character of the political dinners which the Inns and the Outs have so frequently given in the metropolis of the British empire.

On this occasion all the Northern leaders of the conspiracy who could conveniently attend were present. The room was fancifully decorated with national emblems and various transparencies, denoting but not plainly expressing the sentiments and views of the company. The figure of a harp without the crown, over which was displayed in large letters, the word Independence, and underneath, *Erin-go-bragh*, ornamented the centre of the walls, on the opposite sides of the room. On each of the two other walls was seen a figure of St. Patrick, in his ecclesiastical robes, baptizing the monarch of Ireland, who held in his hand a branch of Shamrock, over which was the inscription, "Three in One;" while over their heads were exhibited the following words, "Be free in Christ;" and at the bottom of the piece, "Love one another."

In the centre of the room, equally distant from two splendid chandeliers, which shed their brilliant illumination all around, was suspended a large transparent square, on each side of which the following distich appeared in gilt letters:

UNITE, AND THE FREEDOM OF ERIN RESTORE,

AND TYRANTS, LIKE SERPENTS, SHALL DIE ON HER SHORE.

The reader, if he has anything of a tolerable imagination, will easily conceive the nature of the toasts that were given in this assembly, but as he will readily suppose that the greater number of them were not exactly what many would consider of the most orthodox description, I beg permission to omit them here, with the exception of the first, "The memory of St. Patrick," which was legitimate enough had it not been the first, and the last, "The downfall of Tyrants," which was undoubtedly a very good toast, if the company could only have agreed with their neighbours in the application of the last word.

After supper the natural buoyancy of Irish spirits found vent in a ball, which was graced by as many beautiful female countenances as the same number of the sex ever exhibited. It was opened by the accomplished and enthusiastic Robert Emmet, then on a tour through the North, and Ellen, who decorated by her grandfather's desire, in the most tasteful manner for the occasion, tript the mazy round with a liveliness and grace which delighted everyone who beheld her.

Sir Geoffrey who was too unwieldy for dancing, had his fondness for her so excited, that he kept dangling about her and watching her motions in the most disagreeable and troublesome manner. Even the youth who was her partner, and whose heart was at that time engaged to another, could not escape his jealousy. He perceived it, and declined dancing as soon as decency permitted.

When Ellen was seated, Sir Geoffrey placed himself by her side, and exceedingly annoyed her with his importunities, but she bore them with a patience which displayed her good nature to so much advantage, that it excited almost as much admiration as her personal charms.

When the dance terminated, a new species of patriotic entertainment was exhibited. It had been invented by the Rev. Mr. Porter, expressly for the occasion, and approved of by the other leaders, as an excitement to the patriotic ingenuity of the company.

A splendid seat, approachable by steps, resembling a throne, was prepared for one of the ladies, who should be chosen to personate the genius of Ireland, in whose presence each gentleman who joined in the amusement, should stand and deliver some national sentiment. The person who, in her opinion, should deliver the most striking, tasteful and patriotic sentiment, she was to crown with a wreath of artificial Shamrock, and pronounce him the victor in this species of intellectual contest.

Ellen was unanimously chosen to represent her Country's Genius. She ascended the throne, with a wreath in one hand, and a small parchment tablet in the other. When seated, she assumed a peculiar dignity of manner, such as the imagination of Shakespeare might have conceived the genius of nature's sweetest island to possess; and addressed the company in the following words, "I invite every Irishman who hears me, to come forward, and in the presence of his country's genius express, in one sentence, the patriotic feelings of his soul; and on the brows of him who shall excel all his competitors, in the force, fervour and elegance of his sentiment, so expressed, I shall bind this wreath, the emblem of his country's faith, and the reward of his merit. But first, I require that every candidate for this reward shall inscribe his name on this tablet."

The following names were immediately inscribed; Samuel Nelson, Robert Emmet, Henry M'Cracken, Henry O'Halloran, Luke Teeling, James Porter, Geoffrey Carebrow and Thomas Russel.

After counting the names, "Eight patriots," said she, "are enrolled as candidates for this prize. If there be any other present who wishes to contend for it, let him come forward, now or never."

One of the musicians, who appeared to be unknown to the company, habited in the costume of ancient minstrelsy, with a long flowing green robe bound round his waist with a sash of the same colour, and having a hood of green velvet so constructed as to conceal his countenance from observation, now modestly advanced, and making a graceful bow to the fair genius, inscribed his name, Patrick Fitzgerald.

The Genius then called over the names, and invited Samuel Nelson, the first on the list, to deliver his sentiment.

"Fair Genius," said he, "it is my opinion that the man who will not cheerfully sacrifice both life and property, to rescue his country from a foreign yoke,
is unworthy to be called her son."

Emmet then advanced. "Genius of Erin," said he, "I consider the man
who has an opportunity, to sacrifice both life and property for the independence and freedom of his country, to be born to a happy destiny, for he is born
to immortal fame."

M'Cracken then came forward. "Genius," said he, "may the oppressors of
thy beloved Island be like the serpents they so much resemble, unable to exist
on her soil."

O'Halloran next advanced. "Genius," said he, "may the coward heart that
will not resist tyranny even unto death, never know the joys of freedom, nor
ever be found in an Irishman's bosom."

Teeling next addressed her. "Genius of this venerated country!" said he,
"in striking for her liberty, may the soul of him who dies be rewarded by the
applause of angels, and of him who survives by the long enjoyment of a nation's blessing."

Porter advanced and exclaimed, "Genius of a once blessed and sanctified,
but now unhappy and polluted country! When the crisis of her fate arrives,
may Heaven supply her sons with strength to avenge her wrongs, and restore
her ancient happiness and glory, and with wisdom to frame and adopt such
regulations as will preserve them to all posterity."

Sir Geoffrey next approached. "Charming Genius of a charming country!"
said he. "May he who will not fight in her cause, never enjoy the fruits of her
soil, nor the smiles of her daughters."

Russel now came forward and said, "Genius of my native country! May we
soon see the day when our enemies shall be compelled to confess her sons to
be invincible, her cause to be just, and their own disgrace and punishment to
be merited."

The minstrel Fitzgerald was now called. He advanced modestly, but with
dignity, and all-peculiarly as he was attired, the elegance of his figure struck
the beholders, and many of the fair ladies wished in vain for a view of that
countenance which he kept so carefully concealed. "Lovely Genius of a beloved country!" said he, "O! may that God who alone can rescue her from
misery, grant her a speedy and permanent deliverance, and render her children
happy and worthy of happiness."

"Nothing more can be wished, nor better wished, for our dear but suffering country," said the Genius. "To thee, then, pious minstrel, I award the
wreath thou hast justly won, by the noble simplicity, the affecting piety, and

the fervid patriotism of thy sentiment. Sentiments have been given tonight of high merit in these respects, but thine hath surpassed them all." She then crowned him with the wreath as he voluntarily kneeled before her.

"Genius," said he, still retaining his humble posture. "This to me is a happy night; it shall long be a proud one. I have fervently prayed to my Creator in behalf of my country, in the presence of thee, my beloved, and by thy hands is my fervency thus rewarded. This sacred prize I shall ever preserve for thy sake."

He hastily arose, leaving Ellen in extreme agitation, bowed to the wondering company, and disappeared before any of them could sufficiently recover from their astonishment, to ask him for a gratification of that curiosity concerning him which had become visible in every countenance.

"Who is he? Does anyone know him?" exclaimed several of the gentlemen.

"He is a noble, an elegant young man," thought all the ladies.

"He is an audacious intruder," cried Sir Geoffrey, "an impertinent puppy! What arrogance and impudence, to make love in this public manner to Miss O'Halloran! But I'll chastise the rascal."

With difficulty he was prevented from immediately rushing after the object of his rage in order to attempt putting his threats into execution. Although none of the gentlemen openly objected to Ellen's disposal of the wreath, several of them considered her as having displayed an erroneous judgment, in giving the preference to a sentiment, the patriotism of which was, in their opinion, at least ambiguous. Nay, some of them, among whom was O'Halloran himself, thought that they could perceive in it, an implied censure on their confederacy. It called upon heaven to deliver the country from its calamities, but it did not discriminate the party from which these calamities had sprung. Nay it even insinuated that the people were in the fault; for while it prayed for their happiness, it took care to express a wish for their amendment, that they might deserve it.

"Had it mentioned our oppressors," said O'Halloran, "and prayed either for their conversion or destruction, we should then have known the side to which this successful youth belongs. By not doing so, he has plainly declared himself, if not altogether our enemy, at least not very heartily our friend."

But no one complained in Ellen's hearing of her decision. By previous arrangement her judgment was to be absolute and final on the subject; and although among themselves, the gentlemen might animadvert on its correctness, they were aware that it would be both illiberal and unjust openly to blame her for exercising a prerogative with which they themselves had invested her, and which not one of them doubted that she had exercised conscientiously.

CHAP. XVII.

The jealousy which Sir Geoffrey had conceived against the minstrel, who had so boldly, in his hearing, and in his presence, made love, as he imagined, to his intended wife, and who had received such an unequivocal and public proof of her favour, boiled furiously within his breast, and although he had, with great effort, suppressed it, so far as not to throw the company into absolute confusion, yet he determined to spare no pains in finding the minstrel, and making him feel his vengeance.

When the company had dispersed, he demanded an interview with Ellen; for he could brook no delay in ascertaining whether she knew the youth she had so openly and so flatteringly signalized, and whether her doing so had not arisen from a softer feeling than a preference of his sentiment.

To obtain this interview for him, O'Halloran had to interfere with his authority, and she stipulated that it should be in his presence.

She positively denied any knowledge of the minstrel, or that she had been influenced in his favour by any concealed sentiment whatever.

Sir Geoffrey now urged the violence of his passion, which he confessed occasioned him to be jealous of everything she seemed to approve, while he himself was an object of her dislike.

"Lovely girl," said he, "in the presence of your grandfather, only allay my apprehension of losing you, by promising to become my wife, and I shall be happy."

She replied not.

Her grandfather urged her to speak. "My dear Ellen," said he, "consult your own welfare and mine, by accepting a man who loves you so sincerely, and who has abundantly the power of promoting your felicity. You know not how soon the arm of oppression, or the accidents of war, may deprive you of my protection; and, oh! think how it would relieve the pangs of my last hour to reflect, that you had a sure and just claim to that of a friend I so much value as Sir Geoffrey."

"Best and tenderest of parents," she replied, "since I must once more speak on this unhappy subject — O! do not attribute my refusal of a man I cannot love, to any undutiful feeling towards you. If my prayers can have any effect with Heaven, you shall long live to be my protector, but if a dispensation should take place, on which I tremble to reflect, if you should be prematurely and violently taken from me, I shall not long need a protector, for I feel, that in such a case, thy grave would soon be mine. Do not, do not, I conjure you, by the memory of the saint who gave me birth, do not compel me to do an act which would terminate all my happiness in this world."

"Ellen," said O'Halloran, "you are obstinate, but you do not know Sir Geoffrey sufficiently, or you would not scruple to become his wife. Reflect on his power, his wealth, his patriotism, his friendship for me, his love for you; and you cannot but be convinced that in accepting him for your husband, you accept a man worthy of you, and provide a permanent asylum against misfortune and sorrow. But if any absurd or romantic feeling renders you perverse on this matter, depend on it I shall consult your interest better than to indulge that feeling. It is my duty to do so. Eight days you shall have to reflect on the subject, at the end of which time, I shall expect your compliance with our wishes. If still obstinate, I shall find means to make you comply. But I trust that your own good sense will be sufficient, and render it unnecessary for me to have recourse to such means."

The harshness and cool determined tone with which this was uttered overpowered her, for she saw that her grandfather's resolution to sacrifice her to the man she detested, was unalterably fixed; and that the sacrifice must be soon made. She burst into tears, but remained silent.

"I shall urge you no more at present," said O'Halloran, rising to depart, "but remember my will, and your own interest."

"Cruel girl," said Sir Geoffrey, before he left the room, "why require such exercise of authority to compel you to be my wife, the wife of one who bears for you such unbounded love. But at the expiration of the time fixed by your grandfather, I hope your sentiments will be more favourable." He then seized her hand to kiss it on departing, which she resisted.

"Leave me, sir," said she, "nor make me more wretched, and yourself more hated."

"Then adieu, my fair one. In another week this cruelty will be useless," he replied.

When they had retired, she threw herself on her knees, and thus besought the Almighty Protector of innocence. "Father of the fatherless, I implore thee, for pity in my present distress. O! deliver me from this calamity. Open the eyes of my revered and beloved grandfather, to see the gulf of wretchedness into which his mistaken affection would plunge me.

"But if thou hast destined me to this lot, if I do wrong in opposing his desires, show me my error, and grant me fortitude and resignation to submit. In resisting the will of my earthly parent, I would not resist thine, my Heavenly father! Forgive me, therefore, if, in the weakness of my nature, I should resist. Thou hast fixed my affections on an object, whom surely it cannot be a crime to love, since it is no crime to love excellence. To him I have secretly dedicated my heart. O save me from the guilt of giving my hand to another. Alas! I am, perhaps, guilty of loving an earthly being too much, for my heart has cherished his image so fondly, that it has almost encroached on that adoration which is alone due to thee. But for mercy-sake do thou overlook my frailty, and let my Redeemer's merits plead in my behalf."

Thus did this pious young lady fly for relief in the moments of affliction to the consolations of religion, and found it. Her mind became considerably calmed, although not sufficiently so to permit her to enjoy the salutary repose, which her agitated frame much needed, of "Nature's sweet restorer, balmy sleep."

During the course of the night, the distracting idea of becoming the wife of a man whom she could not esteem, perpetually obtruded itself on her imagination, but as she could see no earthly means of avoiding it, without absolutely rebelling against the authority of her grandfather, which her habits of duty and her feelings of affection towards him, who except on this occasion, had always treated her with extreme tenderness and affection, altogether forbade, she resolved with as much fortitude as she could command, to submit to her uncontrollable destiny. The struggle, however, which took place in her mind while forming this resolution, was too great for her harassed frame, and her aunt on visiting her in the morning, found her in a high fever.

"My dear child," said that affectionate relative, "what is the matter? what has occasioned this?"

"Best of my friends," she replied, "my only mother, do not grieve for me. My grandfather has desired me in eight days to prepare my mind for becoming Sir Geoffrey's wife. I have had a hard struggle to do so. But the worst is now over. I will yield to his wishes. It is my duty, although death itself should be the consequence. I feel I shall not survive it; for O my stubborn heart has become the property of another, and I cannot, cannot help it."

"My dearest Ellen be comforted," said Mrs. Brown, "your grandfather will not, cannot persist in such harshness. I know your happiness to be dearer to him than his own. He will withdraw this cruel mandate. I will reason with him, I will remonstrate with him, I will show him the cruelty of his conduct, the absurdity of consulting your welfare by breaking your heart."

"Kindest of relatives," replied Ellen, "while thus sympathising with me, your tenderness soothes my spirits. I shall soon get better. But I do not expect you will succeed in changing my grandfather's resolution. No, I know he will persevere. He thinks it his duty, and to that he will cause every other consideration to yield."

"But dearest, patient, suffering girl," said her aunt, "it is my duty to open his eyes to your true interest. I shall this very hour let him know the worthlessness of the man's character, who has deluded him into the unfortunate opinion that he would make you a good husband. I know more of that man's demerits than even you do, and I earnestly dissuade you from consenting to become his wife."

"Only make my refusal consistent with what I owe to my grandfather," replied Ellen, "and I shall bless you, for you will save me from destruction."

Mrs. Brown went in search of O'Halloran, whom she found writing in his study. He laid down his pen when she entered.

"Sister," said he, "I want to disburden my mind to you on a subject, on which I know you will feel strongly interested. Sir Geoffrey Carebrow, who has essentially promoted the interests of our cause in this part of the country, by the pecuniary aid which he so promptly afforded us, has laid me under such obligations, that I can refuse him nothing in my power honourably to grant. You know he has long solicited the hand of my granddaughter, but owing to some unfortunate predilection which, I believe, she entertains for Mr. Barrymore, she obstinately refuses him. He has been so extremely urgent of late, that last night I was induced to lay my injunctions on her to prepare her mind in eight days to receive him.

"I know if she consents, which her sense of duty towards me, I expect will induce her to do, that she will offer some violence to her own feelings. But as this violence will only last while her prepossession in favour of Barrymore remains; and which can only be until she becomes better acquainted with Sir Geoffrey's worth, I think her permanent interests will be consulted by bringing about this union. On leaving her last night, I assure you, I felt extremely grieved at being obliged to address her in such an authoritative manner. But I perceived that nothing short of an exertion of authority would do. It was painful, but I did exert it; and must continue to do so, until this union, on which I have so fully set my heart, is accomplished."

"And why, my brother," asked Mrs. Brown, "have you so fully set your heart on this union?"

"I have strong reasons for doing so," replied her brother. "Ellen's own ultimate advantage is one, and you will readily suppose, not a slight one with me. Sir Geoffrey loves her to distraction; and will, I am persuaded, make her a good husband. I am bound to him by strong gratitude for the pecuniary assistance already mentioned; for had we not, at that time, received it, we should not have been in that state of preparation, in which we now are for taking the field, whenever the French auxiliaries arrive, who are expected in April or May next.

"He has shown his disinterestedness in this case; or rather he has shown a noble union of love and patriotism, by stipulating to place the mortgage deed, by which the money has been secured, at her disposal, as her own property, whenever she shall become his wife. This is equivalent to bestowing the money on the cause of the people; for the lands so mortgaged, I intended solely for her use at any rate. Hence on reasoning with myself, to ascertain my proper course of action, I concluded, that my duty to Sir Geoffrey, the benefactor of our country, had superior claims on my regard, than my inclination, which, I confess, would induce me to indulge my daughter's wishes, or, as I should rather say, prejudices on this subject."

"My brother," said Mrs. Brown, "I make no doubt that you have reasoned correctly enough on this subject, from what you know of this man's character; and that your decision has been conscientious, I am perfectly convinced, for your decisions have never been otherwise. But, I believe, that if you thoroughly knew this man, your determination would be very different, you would never resolve to force your dear and only child, who has ever been so obedient and affectionate to you, into the possession of a sensualist and a miser, a libertine in morals, a sceptic in religion, and of late, a hypocrite in politics; whose ruling passions are lust and avarice.

"His passion for our child has of late obtained the mastery over even his cherished avarice, and the seeming readiness with which he assisted your cause, was nothing but a bribe to secure your support to his wishes. As to the condition which he has admitted into the deeds, I can see no real generosity in it. It was, I believe, only a lure to gain, if possible, the good opinion of Ellen, and, perhaps, also to acquire a stronger hold on your esteem. He loses nothing by it; he secures your estate at all events; and he thought he might as well, at the same time, by an appearance of liberality, secure the good-will of his intended wife.

"Hence, he has merely exhibited the shadow without the least substance of generosity. Ah! Sir, I and many others know this man too well, to believe that there is the smallest particle of generosity in his disposition; and as to patriotism, he is as destitute of such a noble feeling, as I am of the power of necromancy. In lending you this money, he has taken care to have it not only well secured, but to earn by it yearly four per cent more than he could have done had he lent it anywhere else. This, one should think, savours more of avarice than of either generosity or patriotism."

"In requiring ten per cent." replied O'Halloran, warmly, "Sir Geoffrey committed no crime.

"Your rigid sticklers for the ancient and corrupt laws of Britain, may call him a usurer, but men of rational philosophical understandings, will never place a maximum on the value of money more than on other commodities. Sir Geoffrey has had the greatness of mind to act in defiance of antiquated rules and customs, but he has asked no more for the use of his money, than I think him entitled to considering the risk he runs on account of the hazardous complexion of the times, and considering also the great service his promptitude has rendered the cause of the country. I am sorry to see that more minds than Ellen's have imbibed an unwarrantable prejudice against my friend. He is called a libertine, because, until he met with a female with whom he thought he could live happy, he did not choose to marry; and no doubt evil and lying reports to the disadvantage of his chastity, may have been circulated; and because he possesses an immense fortune, and will not spend it in frivolity, or live in imitation of aristocratical splendour and extravagance, but prefers patriarchal plainness and republican simplicity, he is called a miser.

"Such may be the opinion of an unthinking and unjust world. But it is not from such a criterion that I estimate men's characters. I am in the habit, Mrs.

Brown, of examining and judging for myself; ay, and of determining for myself too, and my determination on this affair is already fixed. Ellen is my child — and me she must obey, until Sir Geoffrey Carebrow obtains a prior right to her obedience."

Here Mrs. Brown burst into tears. "I weep" said she, when she had somewhat recovered from her emotion, "for your delusion. But, ah! I weep more for the misery, which, I perceive, awaits your unfortunate child — O my brother, reflect"

"I will hear no more," said O'Halloran, "lest you stagger my resolution, which, as it is founded on reason, I am determined shall never be shaken by feeling." He then hastily left the room, evidently as much agitated as Mrs. Brown herself.

The allotted eight days elapsed, and Ellen consented to become a victim; "For," said she, "I will die before I disobey him. Oh! my grandfather, did you know what I this moment, suffer, you would have compassion on me!"

She was able to speak no more: she had fainted. In great consternation, O'Halloran and Sir Geoffrey called for assistance; for they had been both present urging her to compliance. She soon recovered, and on seeing her restored, the strength of her grandfather's determination, which her swoon had somewhat shaken, was also restored, and the day was appointed for the marriage.

The agitation of Ellen's mind now greatly subsided. She had nothing more for which to hope, and she awaited the awful hour in the calm silence of despair. Her aunt was her only comforter, but she also stood in need of comfort.

At her request, Miss Agnew was invited to the castle, to encourage and support her afflicted friend, through the horrors of the approaching ceremony.

On understanding the circumstances of the case, all the sprightliness of this lively young woman forsook her; and, although she would not desert her friend, she determined to partake of no festivity on the occasion.

"It will be a wedding" said she to O'Halloran, "that ought to be solemnized as a funeral, with the emblems of grief, for it will be death to the happiness of the loveliest maiden in the land."

"I trust not," he replied; "the consciousness of doing her duty, will of itself be a source of happiness, and her husband's worth, tenderness and affectionate assiduities, will soon obliterate this unreasonable, girlish prejudice against him, which occasions her present distress. We shall yet see her the happy, loving wife of a worthy man."

"In that case, she will not be the wife of this man," retorted Miss Agnew, with something of her usual keenness and levity, mingled with bitterness and grief.

CHAP. XVIII.

Then in that hour remorse he felt, And his heart told him he had dealt
Unkindly with his child: A father may a while refuse;
But who can for another choose.
Would'st thou, presumptuous as thou art, O'er nature play the tyrant's part,
And with the hand compel the heart! Oh! rather, rather hope to bind
The ocean wave the mountain wind; Or fix the feet upon the ground,
To stop the planet rolling round.
Rogers[1].

On the second day previous to that appointed for the marriage, the Recluse
came to the castle, and requested an interview with Ellen. He was admitted
into her chamber, for she was too unwell to leave it. She was alone. He was
shocked at the alteration which a few weeks had made in her appearance. She
who so lately was blooming in the luxuriance of health and beauty, now appeared before him the image of death, pale and emaciated, and sunk in almost
speechless sorrow.

His heart smote him. "I have neglected thee too long, suffering innocence," said he; "but if heaven permits thee to live, it is not yet too late to save
thee from misery."

"Father, what wouldst thou say?" she asked, scarcely understanding him.

"My child, if this dreaded marriage be the cause of thy affliction, I will
deliver thee from it," he replied.

"Ah! thou canst not," said she, "unless my grandfather withdraws his injunctions, for I will obey him."

"Thy grandfather will never enjoin thee to be wretched," said he.

"Alas! sir, he does enjoin it."

---

[1] In the 1824 text this was credited to Lord Byron. It is, in fact, from *Jacqueline, A
Tale* by Lord Byron's friend, Samuel Rogers.

"Then, disobey him," exclaimed the Recluse, with energy, "O thou best of daughters, and the sin be on my head!"

"What sayest thou?" cried she, starting, "Wouldst thou counsel me to disobedience?"

"I would, and will save thee from ruin," he replied. "Yea, at the foot of the altar, if I found thee there, I would snatch thee from the contaminating touch of the viper who has deluded thy grandfather, and would make thee his own to make thee wretched. No, never shall that saint who bore thee, sweet, suffering maiden, accuse thy father of standing by in heedless apathy, to see thee immolated! That father, thy own father, my child, has the first claim on thy obedience; and he forbids thee as thou wouldst value his blessing, to become the wife of Sir Geoffrey Carebrow."

"What! Oh sir," she cried, "does my father live? Does he know of my misfortunes? Am I, indeed, so happy?"

"He lives," said the Recluse. "He knows of thy sufferings; and no danger will prevent him from rescuing, and protecting thee. For what other end does he, can he live?"

"Oh! sir, where, when shall I see him? Where shall I fly to him? Only let me embrace him, and I will bless thee."

"Yes; beloved of my heart," he returned. "Daughter of my Eliza! thou shalt embrace him. The terrors of law shall no longer prevent it. Behold thy father in this disguise! I once saved thee from insult; I shall now snatch thee from wretchedness. Embrace me, my only child!"

"Oh father," cried she, straining him to her bosom; "Why did I not know thee sooner. O God! thou art merciful — my father lives! Now let me die in his arms, since I have indeed seen him. I am no longer an orphan."

Here her head sunk on his breast; for the shock of her joy was almost too powerful for her debilitated frame.

"God preserve thee, child of my love! Darling of my heart," he cried, alarmed at the changing hue of her countenance. "Am I to loose thee, in the moment thou hast found me? Art thou to be unhappy both in joy and in sorrow?"

A gush of tears from his eyes fell upon her countenance. But in the agitation of joy, although the first shock may resemble that of grief, yet the difference of its effects on the frame, is soon apparent. In place of exhausting it soon invigorates. The rays of delight soon sparkled from her dark eyes; and the flush of joy again beamed on her countenance. "It is enough," cried she. "Kind heaven! I thank thee. I cannot now be unhappy. Take me with thee, my father. Let me live alone under thy protection."

He now explained to her the necessity for his remaining concealed, on account of a sentence of outlawry under which he lay, for having killed Sir Nicholas Carebrow, the elder brother of this Sir Geoffrey, in a duel.

"He persecuted thy mother," said he, "with a disgusting and criminal passion, as his brother, almost his equal in wickedness, has persecuted thee.

"To avenge an insulted, virtuous and tenderly beloved wife, I fought him, and his death was the expiation of his offence. His friends raised a prosecution against me. I was obliged to fly. By their influence, I have been outlawed, and if this true heir to his brother's wickedness, as well as his title and estates, should discover that it was your father that thwarted his designs on you, he would prosecute me with the relentless rancour of disappointed passion. I should have either to leave the country and once more deprive you of my protection, or become the victim of his revenge."

"Oh! my father," said she, "I will save thee. I will have thee restored to me. I will deliver myself to him; I will become his — Oh! can I, can I name it? — yet it is for a father's safety — I will become his wife, on condition that he shall cancel this prosecution, and procures a reversal of the outlawry."

"No, my child! You shall not make such a sacrifice. None of my blood, I trust, shall ever be allied to such a wicked and unprincipled family. Should such a misfortune take place, all my satisfaction in this world would be at an end. Better I should die than see such a day! In my present concealment, I am safe, and in residing so near you, I am happy. I would have discovered myself to you sooner, but I found you happy in the love and under protection of your grandfather; and I did not wish to disturb your tranquillity, by apprising you of my danger in residing here."

"Father! be it as you will. Wisdom speaks from your lips. Instruct me in your wishes. It is my duty, and it shall be my study not to controvert, but to obey. Even though my venerated but mistaken grandfather should force me to the altar, I will there perish, ere the irrevocable vow which consigns me to your enemy, shall pass my lips."

"Blessed girl, image of thy sainted mother! Your grandfather will not urge you. I shall, this evening, send you a letter enclosing one to him, which by showing him that there is still in existence, one who has superior claims to your obedience, and who forbids your compliance in this affair, will make it his duty to relinquish his authority; and, you know, the moment your grandfather perceives his duty, that he will perform it. In the meantime, adieu, my daughter! Be comforted. I am safe, and thou shalt be protected. May the blessing of heaven be ever thine!" And straining her to his paternal bosom, he left her in a transport of joy and gratitude to God for her deliverance.

On her knees she addressed the Author of all good, and poured forth the fullness of her delighted and grateful heart for this signal instance of his merciful interposition in her favour. When her aunt and Miss Agnew visited her, they were surprised to find her so cheerful.

"Dear Ellen," asked her aunt "are you really become satisfied, for you appear as if you were, with this match?"

"This match shall never take place," she replied, "it is this which causes my satisfaction."

"Indeed!" said Miss Agnew, "Has your grandfather at last relented. The first time I find him dozing in his elbow chair I shall kiss him for his goodness."

"I thought" said Mrs. Brown, "that obstinate as he appeared, he could not carry his cruelty so far."

"My dear friends," said Ellen, interrupting her aunt, "you mistake. He has not yet relented, but he will relent. I dare not at present tell you more. Tomorrow, perhaps tonight, I may be free to tell you all. In the meantime, be assured that this hateful marriage will not take place, neither shall I have any occasion to infringe upon my duty to my grandfather."

"Heaven be praised for such an escape!" cried Miss Agnew. "We shall again be as merry as crickets; and laugh at the old curmudgeon of a disappointed knight. What had an old half rotten fellow of fifty, to do with a fresh blooming damsel of nineteen? It was truly abominable."

The buoyancy of this young lady's spirits now burst forth unrestrained, as if to make amends for their late depression; and she had wrought her companions into such a state of good humour, when O'Halloran entered towards the evening, that he was both surprised and delighted.

"You are, at last, reconciled, my dear Ellen?" said he "to this indispensable measure?"

"Obedience to your commands, shall always yield me pleasure," she replied.

Before he could answer, a servant entered with a letter for Ellen, which, he said, a stranger had just brought to the castle. On opening it, she found one enclosed for O'Halloran. "I expected this," said she, as she handed it to him, "only within these few hours. I believe it will reveal to you the cause of my present satisfaction. I have received intelligence that my father lives and prohibits my marriage with Sir Geoffrey Carebrow."

O'Halloran broke the seal and read as follows:

Worthy and revered father of my Eliza,

Nothing short of parental regard for my daughter's happiness, induces me to address you at present, or to interfere with an arrangement which I understand you have made, no doubt from the best of motives, for settling her in the marriage state.

It is said, that contrary to her inclinations, you have urged her, and obtained her consent, to become the wife of Sir Geoffrey Carebrow.

By the authority of a father, I have commanded her never to receive the hand of that man, whom I know to be the worthless inheritor of all his brother's baseness and wickedness. I am sorry to learn that with a view to the accomplishment of his desires with respect to my daughter, he has, by a feigned patriotism, succeeded in impressing you with a favourable opinion of his character. But on the word of whom you never knew to utter a falsehood, I assure you that his patriotism is hypocrisy, and his pecuniary accommodations to your cause, artifice.

It is not from any want of confidence in either your honour or your friendship, that I refrain from discovering to you at present my place of residence; it is from a fear that such a disclosure might involve us into a correspondence, which, by some accident, might be the means of making me known to my enemies; and after my present interference, which I do not wish concealed from Sir Geoffrey, you will perceive that there will be an increased necessity for precaution on my part; for should he now discover me, he would be goaded on by the implacable rancour of revenge for the disappointment I have occasioned him, to bring down, without mercy, that penalty which the law now holds suspended over me for his brother's death. A time may come, and I hope it is at no great distance, when I shall with safety be publicly acknowledged by my friends.

Till then, cherish my daughter as you have hitherto cherished her. But withdraw, I conjure you, as you value her, or your own peace of mind, that command, in obedience to which she has consented to marry a man she detests, and who deserves her detestation.

Should you persist in urging her to this match, which I cannot believe you will, by that prior authority which nature has given me over her, I command her to disobey you. I peremptorily enjoin her, as she values a father's love, never in wedlock to bestow herself on Sir Geoffrey Carebrow.

Receive my thanks for the tenderness with which, until this occasion, you have ever treated my child, and assure yourself that I am as heretofore, your dutiful and affectionate

FRANCIS HAMILTON.

When O'Halloran had finished reading this letter, silence for a few minutes ensued. The ladies were struck dumb with amazement. At length he approached Ellen. "My child," said he, "I rejoice that your father still lives. He was a worthy man, notwithstanding his unhappy duel. His interference on this occasion is, perhaps, fortunate. At all events it relieves me from any responsibility as to the result. I shall inform Sir Geoffrey, that I no longer possess the requisite authority to constrain your acceptance of him. I see you are all gratified. I confess that I am not much displeased myself, at the turn this affair has taken. He then withdrew.

The reader need not be detained with an account of the felicitations which Ellen received from her female confidents on this occasion. Any sensible good hearted aunt can easily imagine how Mrs. Brown expressed herself, and any lively good natured young maiden, may do the same with respect to Miss Agnew. It may be recorded, however, that this young lady observed, that she never saw O'Halloran smile so bewitchingly as when he left the room.

"Where he only thirty or forty years younger," said she, "I should certainly fall in love with him for that sweet smile. As it is, however, I shall certainly have the kiss that I threatened to steal from him, the first time I should find him asleep in his elbow chair."

Immediately on leaving the ladies, O'Halloran despatched a messenger to Sir Geoffrey, requesting his attendance at the castle as early as convenient the next morning. On his arrival he acquainted him with what had taken place.

"I thought it right," he observed, "to lose no time in giving you this information, that you might be occasioned no disappointment in your arrangement for the solemnity, that I could prevent."

With eyes flashing fire, Sir Geoffrey started to his feet. "Then you withdraw all control over your granddaughter in this case?" he demanded.

"I do, " was the laconic and firm reply.

"And Francis Hamilton, my brother's murderer, is now in the country," exclaimed the rejected knight, "and has caused this, but I shall find him, and dreadful will be my revenge."

O'Halloran was thunder-struck at such a manifestation of malignity in the man he had lately so much esteemed. He fixed his eyes steadfastly on Carebrow, and with inexpressible dignity, calmly said, "Is this the disinterested affection you professed to bear for my granddaughter? You would show your love for her by the destruction of her father?"

Sir Geoffrey resumed his seat. He remained a few moments absorbed in reflection. He saw that O'Halloran was not a man to be frightened; and concluded that he would play a surer game by pretending to submit calmly to his misfortune. "I am wrong," said he, "my friend. Excuse the impetuosity of my feelings. They are agonized by the intelligence you have given me. The warmth of my expression was occasioned by the madness of my disappointed love. But I submit. My anger was but momentary. From this instant, I shall cast the remembrance of the whole affair from my mind. But there is one piece of information," said he, somewhat sarcastically, "which, in my turn, I will lose no time in communicating, lest you, in some of your arrangements, should also be disappointed. I find it inconvenient to pay you the remaining twenty thousand pounds contracted for in the mortgage."

"That is unfortunate," replied O'Halloran, "for there is now little time to raise it elsewhere."

"The cause must then do without it," said the other.

"It will greatly cripple our exertions;" continued O'Halloran; "besides the sum being secured in the mortgage, you should in honour exert yourself to procure it, or else allow that instrument to be altered."

"As to that," said Sir Geoffrey, "the less that is either said or written on such dangerous matters, in these troublesome times, the better. The mortgage cannot be altered. But do not think that I intend to defraud you. Only, now that I think of it, our communications this evening have been mutually disagreeable. We had better, therefore, end the conference. Good night; and recollect that by withholding my bride, you have lost only twenty thousand pounds."

The man's real character now stared O'Halloran full in the face. He scorned to detain him, or reason with him. He, therefore, let him go without interruption, rejoiced that the good fortune of his beloved grandchild, had preserved her from becoming the wife of such a man.

CHAP. XIX.

When O'Halloran informed the other chiefs of the conspiracy, of Sir Geoffrey's threat, they agreed to make no noise about it, least by irritating a person so unprincipled, he might be induced to inform against them to the government.

To discover on the United Irishmen, was, indeed, the first impulse that actuated this man's mind on his rupture with O'Halloran, but he was prevented by his cowardice — the fate of M'Bride terrified him. Besides he was not sure (for he was a man of no political sagacity) which of the two parties might in the end prevail. He was, therefore, unwilling to provoke either. With respect to Ellen, his passion was not in the least diminished. He was so far from relinquishing his views upon her, that it now became his chief study, how to effect by fraud or violence, what he could not by fair and friendly means.

It was supposed, by Ellen's friends, that amusement and change of scene would contribute to remove from her mind the impression of her late sufferings, and hasten the restoration of her health and spirits. She was, therefore, prevailed on to accompany Miss Agnew on a visit to the residence of her father. It was in the afternoon of a beautiful day in April, when they set out in a one horse chair. The whispering wind waved gently over hill and valley with a balmy, genial softness, which rendered the atmosphere delightful; while the sun diffused a kindly fertilizing warmth into the bosom of the joyous earth, which produced a luxuriant, beauteous and fragrant vegetation all over its surface. The fields, the groves and the hedgerows were bursting into life; and all

nature was assuming her gay and green attire, while animation, joy and gratitude, inspired the harmonious effusions of the feathered race; and seemed to
awaken corresponding emotions in the hearts of the country people, as they
alternately whistled and sang at their rural employments.

The season and the scenery recalled to Ellen's memory, some simple verses
she had lately received of M'Nelvin's composition; and as they rode along a
fine road at an easy rate, she indulged the curiosity of her companion by repeating them to the tune of Gramachree.

A SONG FOR SPRING.

See, Mary dear, how mild the eve;
No storms molest the plain: At length stern winter calmly yields
To spring's propitious reign.
To mark the year's reviving sweets,
We'll to you upland rove; Hail Spring! fair queen of tender joys,
And meekly-smiling love. Freed from its chains, behold the brook
Winds briskly through the vale; Upon its banks, the tender grass
Yields balm to every gale: The daisy, primrose, violet, there
Are richly interwove; Hail Spring! fair queen of tender joys,
And meekly-smiling love.

The flocks and herds, that graze the mead,
And sip the falling dew: Touch'd with the vernal influence sweet,
Instinctive sports pursue: Gay chirls the plover, hoarse and loud,
And softly cooes the dove; Hail Spring! fair queen of tender joys,
And meekly-smiling love. The blackbird, thrush and linnet tribes,
In yonder grove convene, And in glad concert join their notes,
To celebrate the scene: Their little love-sick cares and joys,
Harmonious raptures move; Hail Spring! fair queen of tender joys,
And meekly-smiling love.
This morn, dear Mary, had you heard
The lark ascending sing; The distant sun-gilt hills rejoiced,
And blushed the face of spring; Your heart with mine, had softly beat,
And kind emotions strove: Hail Spring! fair queen of tender joys,
And meekly-smiling love. With careful steps, and hopeful heart,
As o'er the earth he past, The farmer blithe, his golden grain,
Into its bosom cast; While slow, before the crashing team,
The whistling plough-boy drove: Hail Spring! fair queen of tender joys,

And meekly-smiling love.
Then, as the briary bush I leaped,
A thrush out, shuddering, flew; I spied her eggs, and half-resolved
To bear the prize to you, but no; the cruel gift, I cried,
Her heart will scorn to prove: Hail Spring! fair queen of tender joys,
And meekly-smiling love.
Of youngest ivy then a wreath,
For your fair brows I twined; With loveliest flowers adorned it round,
And softest foliage lined; A purer emblem of the vows,
I made in yonder grove:

Hail Spring! fair queen of tender joys,
And meekly-smiling love. 'Tis in the woodbine thicket hid,
Where love you first confessed; 'Twas such a beauteous night as this,
In nature's gladness dressed; Come, there I'll fit it to your brows,
While passing swains approve: Hail Spring! fair queen of tender joys,
And meekly-smiling love. There oft of old, Hiberman bards
Have sat, and sweetly sung; Oft to th' inspiring charms of Spring,
Their magic harps they strung: They swept the chords with pathos strong,
Descended from above: Hail Spring! fair queen of tender joys,
And meekly-smiling love.

Ellen had scarcely finished the recital of these verses, when, in a lonely part of the road, adjoining a wood, a stranger on horseback overtook them, and addressed them in a vulgar tone, and with a face of great affrontery.

"A bonnie day, ladies! Do you gang far this way?"

"Only a few miles," was the reply of Miss Agnew; and for a short space all were again silent.

At length another unknown horseman rode forward and exclaimed, "Damn you, Jack, why don't you stop the driver? We have no time to lose."

Jack now drew a pistol from his pocket, and presenting it at the driver, ordered him to stop. He was obeyed.

"Miss O'Halloran," said the man who last came forward, "my employer desires the pleasure of your company tonight, but being afraid that you would not come willingly, he ordered us to bring you by force. You will be pleased to get behind me, and let that other lady proceed by herself. Confound your screaming! Gag them, Jack, or they'll alarm the whole country. Tear them from each other."

This was scarcely uttered when he was levelled to the ground by a tremendous blow of a large stick, which resounded from his head with a noise that startled the terrified ladies. Jack immediately discharged his pistol at the assailant, but the ball missed its object; and had he not instantly put spurs to his horse, he would have been the next moment as low as his companion.

"Let him go," cried the victor, turning to the affrighted ladies. "He will not molest you again this evening."

Ellen now recovered sufficiently from her terror to recognise the Green Minstrel in her deliverer.

"Fair lady!" said he, addressing her, and holding the shamrock wreath in his hand, "behold a man who has sworn eternal servitude to you. On the night you decorated his brow with this badge of your favour, he pledged himself to watch over and guard you, with all the zeal and assiduity of devoted knighthood; and this day has afforded him the first opportunity of proving his fidelity."

"Tell me, tell me, kind and noble youth," said she, "to whom I am so much indebted?"

"My fair mistress," replied the youth, "indulge my wish for concealment for some time. You shall know me at a more convenient season. Beware of Carebrow. 'Tis his villainy has occasioned this scene, but I shall watch him. Meantime drive on, and fear nothing. Should you again be attacked, I shall not be far off. Adieu!" and he hastily disappeared in the adjoining wood.

Having only about two miles further to ride, by a pretty smart application of his whip, which the driver now thought proper to make, they soon arrived at the residence of John Agnew, Esq. the father of Ellen's companion.

When this outrage was communicated to the united chiefs, not one of them doubted but that Sir Geoffrey was its author. They indeed soon had reason to withdraw all their confidence from him; for they received intelligence that he had made great professions of loyalty at a late public dinner given by the friends of government in Belfast; that he had, since his dispute with O'Halloran, purchased a large amount of government debentures, and was in daily expectation of being put into the commission of the peace. At the latter end of April, therefore, they held a consultation concerning him, at which it was resolved to seize his person, and confine him in their cave, before he should have time to do them mischief by the disclosures which they doubted not he would willingly make to the government.

While the chiefs were assembled at this consultation, they received despatches from Dublin, by express, containing news of a most disastrous description, which rendered it necessary for them, and for all the United Societies in the kingdom, to adopt measures of the most decisive nature. They were informed that, in consequence of one Reynolds having betrayed them, the most active members of their National Directory had been seized and imprisoned by the government; that Lord Edward Fitgerald, their leader, had been so severely wounded in the attempt to arrest him that he had since died — that Oliver Bond, Henry and John Sheares, Thomas Addis Emmet, and Dr. M'Nevin were committed to close confinement, until the formation of a special commission to try them for high treason, should be completed. They were, therefore, urged to make a grand effort either to rescue these leaders, or to seize a number of the government party as hostages for their safety. As this could not be done, however, without an absolute insurrection, they were exhorted to be ready for that measure by the beginning of June, the trial of the captured chiefs not being expected to come on before the middle of that month.

Samuel Nelson, who was now in Dublin, and at the death of Lord Fitzgerald, had been appointed to the chief management of their affairs, informed them that he should immediately despatch a messenger to France, to hasten the arrival of the promised succours; and that for the purpose of rendering the rising as simultaneous as possible in all parts of the country, he had directed it to take place everywhere on the third day after information should be received of the stoppage of the different mail coaches proceeding from the metropolis, which should be the signal of an attack having been made there.

All was now bustle and activity among the conspirators. Messengers were sent to every influential United Irishman in the country. Nightly assemblages for drilling the peasantry in the art of war, were held more extensively and frequently; and every smith who had joined the confederacy, became busily employed in the manufacture of pikes, and in the repairing of muskets and other kinds of warlike instruments. So high indeed did the excitement for insurrection become at this period, that even many of the softer sex employed themselves in casting bullets, preparing cartridges, and making cockades and insurrectionary banners.

The immediate object of O'Halloran, was to collect an additional supply of gunpowder, an article in which his district was deficient. The greater portion of what had been purchased by Sir Geoffrey's money, having been distributed throughout the adjoining counties. This distribution had been readily yielded to by O'Halloran's immediate colleagues, in reliance on being able, on account of their proximity to the sea, to procure an abundant and timely supply for themselves, with the sum which Sir Geoffrey, according to his contract, had yet to furnish them.

Sore with their disappointment, they now breathed vengeance on the defaulter; and had he fallen into the hands of M'Cauley, Kelly, Darragh, or any other of the more desperate of the party, his life would have paid the forfeit of his delinquency. He, however, having lately become a magistrate, and knowing that for that reason as well as several others of a more heinous nature, he had become obnoxious to his former friends, he confined himself as much as possible to his seat at Carebrow Hall, which he had the precaution to keep well-guarded, by supplying his domestics with arms, and ordering them every night to hold alternate watch, for fear of a surprise.

One evening he would have been destroyed by Darragh and Kelly, who were indefatigable in watching for an opportunity for that purpose, contrary to the desire of their leaders, who did not at this crisis, wish the attention of the government to be excited by any such outrage.

He was returning home from Carrickfergus, attended by two servants, (for he never at this time ventured abroad without such attendance) when coming to the border of his demesne, he ordered them to catch a favourite colt, which had broken out of an enclosure, and was playing at large on the high road. They obeyed, and he rode alone towards the house.

Darragh and Kelly were lying in wait for him in the shrubbery that skirted the public avenue, which led to the house. They were perceived by a lad about fourteen years of age, named Nelson, who knew their design, but who, on account of Carebrow having arbitrarily turned his mother, who was a widow, and her family, of which he was the eldest, out of their little holding, at the most inclement season of the preceding winter, hated him. Persuaded now that vengeance would be inflicted on the oppressor, in the excitement of the moment, he called prematurely from a tree on which he was stationed, "There, Darragh! there comes the tyrant. Now have at him."

Carebrow both heard and saw Nelson, and instantly took the alarm. He put spurs to his horse, which darting over a low clipt hedge into an open lawn, carried him at full flight towards the house. Darragh and Kelly being only armed with pistols and bayonets, conceived it imprudent to fire, as there would be little chance of hitting him, and the report would alarm his servants, and render their escape difficult. They fled immediately without making any further attempt upon him, but heartily cursing Nelson for giving him the alarm. It was, indeed, as we shall afterwards have occasion to narrate, an unfortunate incident for Nelson, resulting to him in a most melancholy catastrophe. As will be readily supposed, wrath and revenge were highly inflamed in the mind of Sir Geoffrey on this occasion, but their effects with respect to the United Irishmen were suppressed by the force of his terrors; and although he was now in the commission of the peace, and might have issued warrants for their apprehension and imprisonment, he feared their party too much to give them such provocation. He knew not but that they might in the end, overthrow their opponents, and in that case, he wished still to keep a door open for reconciliation with them. He, therefore, although he knew the Darragh whom Nelson addressed when he gave him the alarm, dared not add to the irritation of the conspirators, by having him, or any other of their associates, apprehended.

If the government should maintain its authority, this forbearance not being publicly known, would not injure him in its estimation; while, in the event of the United Irishmen being successful, it might be pleaded as a merit by which he might hope to regain their favour, at least their forgiveness.

This unsteady vacillating conduct, this endeavouring to stand well with both parties, was adopted by a numerous portion of the Irish population at this period. Some from mere timidity were entirely neutral; others from a mixture of ambition and cowardice, wished to be considered friendly by both parties, and accordingly, in a covert manner, occasionally lent assistance to both. So that, in the vulgar phrase, possessing two strings to their bow, which ever party prevailed, they were sure to be gainers. Sir Geoffrey, however, had offended the conspirators too deeply to be forgiven on account of mere forbearance towards them. But he was not altogether certain of this. He knew that they were dissatisfied and enraged at his conduct, but he did not believe that they were irreconcilably so. He, therefore, conceived it to be his interest, while he acted so as to merit the favour of the government, to give the opposite party no cause to think him their decided enemy.

His ungovernable passion for Ellen alone interfered with this wise resolution. He could not be happy without the enjoyment of those beauties, on which he had so long feasted his imagination. The cup of bliss had approached too near his lips, and had been too suddenly and unexpectedly dashed from them, to be easily forgotten and relinquished. He was resolved, therefore, to make another effort to possess it.

He knew that he was suspected for the outrage that had already been committed on her, and that consequently, the eyes of her numerous friends and connexions would be immediately directed towards him, if she were subjected to another. He felt, however, that at all hazards, he must possess her, but to succeed, and to succeed with safety, required that the attempt should be conducted, not only with great dexterity, but with great privacy. That he was foiled in his last attempt, he attributed to its having been so publicly made, in the face of day, and on the open road.

"She shall be mine," said he to himself, "if there be power in gold to hire assistants, and strength in steel to render them successful!" He had several conferences with one Philip Berwick, his game-keeper, who had often procured handsome young women for his service. It was this man and Tim Rodgers, another of his domestics, who had been his instrument in the former attempt to seize Ellen, and who for a handsome reward, notwithstanding his disaster in that affair, (for it was he who had fallen under the stroke of the Green Minstrel) was ready to renew the under-taking in whatever way he should be directed. At length their conferences resulted in the adoption of the following plan.

One of Sir Geoffrey's tenants, whose rent he attempted to raise, had a few months before, relinquished his farm, which, as nobody else thought it worth the sum he demanded for it, was now unoccupied. On this place there was a tolerably comfortable dwelling house, in a very retired situation, to which it was determined forcibly to bring Ellen, as it was believed that she could be there effectually concealed, until circumstances should permit Sir Geoffrey to carry her to an estate which he possessed in Gloucestershire, in England.

CHAP. XX.

Teeming with forms his terror grew; Heedful he watched, for well he knew That in that dark and devious dell Some ling'ring ghosts and spirits dwell, So as he trow'd, so it befel.
Hogg.

Ellen was still on her visit at Mr. Agnew's, and had recovered all her usual bloom of health and serenity of mind. She, indeed, still felt some apprehension, lest the continuance of Sir Geoffrey's passion should find out some means of disturbing her repose, but as her friends were numerous and vigilant, she confided in their zeal and ability to protect her, and did not permit this apprehension to repress the natural cheerfulness of her temper, or damp the joy she experienced from the discovery of her father, from her own deliverance from the persecutions of her tormentor, and her rescue from the violence of his menials. The brave author of this rescue, her Green Minstrel, her Shamrock Knight, was never absent from her thoughts.

"Ah!" said she to Miss Agnew, "if this young man were to reveal himself, I fear that my Edward would possess only the first share in my affections. I do not know how it is, but I almost feel as if I had two hearts, one to bestow on each of these objects, for (I am, indeed, ashamed to confess it) this noble youth intrudes himself on my mind almost as often and as intensely as he to whom my first affections have been pledged, and to whom they must be forever faithful. O! would to Heaven, that he were Edward, or Edward he!"

"You have started an odd notion into my mind," said her companion, "that they are, indeed, the same person. If they are not, they must be twins; for now when I think of them, I protest that your two stars do not more resemble each other."

This conversation took place one evening about the beginning of May, as these two young ladies walked together to visit a poor, sick man, who lived in the neighbourhood. The cause of this man's sickness being somewhat singular, and connected with the state of the times, and the popular superstitions of the country, it may be here related.

On the day previous to the visit just mentioned, Andrew Ramsey, the name of the sick man, had been on some business at a small village in the neighbourhood of Carebrow Hall. He had spent the afternoon in the enjoyment of the bottle, with some free-hearted convivial acquaintances he had met within a Shabeen house, near the village, and who being, like himself, United Irishmen, were of course, deeply versed in the politics of the times, and fond of talking on the subject.

Here it was, that Andrew was first told of the intended rising in June, and was desired to hold himself in readiness to take the field with his companions. As Andrew was not one of the most courageous of men, this news together with the accompanying requisition, struck, like a leaden bolt, upon his spirits, and it was with great difficulty that he kept them from betraying his fears, by the inspiring force of the potent liquor that he now copiously drank.

The shades of evening were fast gathering, and the time approached when Andrew must part with his cup and his company. With a doleful countenance he shook his comrades severally by the hand.

"Farewell, friends!" said he, "it's likely to be a serious time in the lan'. I wish God may preserve us through the strife. We should be a' busy praying an' preparing against the warst."

"By G——d! man, I doobt you'll greet aboot it. Fight first, an' gin you like, pray next," said an' irreverend fellow of the name of Steele, who had lately become a convert to the age of reason system, and had thrown off all the shackles of religion, as unworthy of a citizen patriot and a free born philosopher.

"Ye're prophane, man," replied Andrew, "nac guid can come o' ye, unless ye mend, but for that, I doubt Tam Paine, an' the devil, Gude forgie me for naming them, hae been owre busy wi' ye."

Several of the company laughed at Andrew's seriousness and alarm; and the more to intimidate him, as he left the house, Steele called after him, "Ye maun rin fast, Andy, when ye pass the Saut-Hole, or some ghaist will catch you there. Ye ken it's the devil's haunt."

Andrew was on foot. He blessed himself and walked onwards, endeavouring to divert his fears by occasionally whistling Patrick's Day, or humming one of the songs of Paddy's Resource. But still the terrors of the times and the awfulness of the place he was approaching, could not be driven from his recollection.

"There will be unco doings, I'll warrant," thought he. "Oh! gin yin kend wha would be slain, an' wha would be spared, in the struggle, it would be a satisfaction. Gin we had but a guid prophet noo, like Jeremiah, to tell us the warst! But Gude bless us, there's the Saut-Hole! an' the trees growin' in it, an' roon' it, whare, they say, Sir Geoffrey ravished the bonnie lass that was found dead there sax years syne. It might na' be true, for it was a lie-like story. But preserve us! What's that amang the trees! Our father! — Our father! — Ah! I canna pray. It is the White Woman hersel', that haunts here. I'm gane! I'm gane!"

He staggered some paces back, with his eyes fixed on the apparition; and then stood stock-still, unable either to speak or to move. The vision seemed to rise from the haunted hole, and advance slowly from among the trees towards him. It every now and then uttered a deep sigh, and a hollow groan. Its form was that of a handsome woman, clothed in a winding sheet of the purest white. Her jaws were tied with a fillet, and her countenance had the pale inanimate look of a corpse.

Andrew's hair now stiffened, and stood upright on his head; his teeth chattered, his knees bent under him, and his arms fell flat and useless by his sides; while his whole frame shook convulsively as the awful figure drew near and passed him.

"It will surely leave me," thought he. But it returned, and repassed him several times in the same manner. At length it stood right before him, and gave a fearful mean. "It wants me to speak," thought he. Twice he tried, but tried in vain. The third time he was more successful. "In the name of the Father, Son, and Holy Ghost, are you flesh or spirit?" said he.

"Thou hast invoked me by a name which compels me to answer," replied the vision. "I am the ghost of Elizabeth Robbins, whom the wicked master of these domains unfortunately met and forced to his loathed embraces, in yonder hollow. There was the scene of my death. I was resolved not to survive the loss of my purity, and with this knife," said she, holding up the appearance of one in her bloody hand, "as soon as the savage left me, I pierced myself to the heart. Unfit for Heaven, and yet not doomed to hell, I am permitted to wander on the earth, and am directed to show the evils that are coming on the country, to the first mortal that should invoke me by the great and mysterious name you have pronounced."

She here paused a moment, but soon resumed. "Well may the swain shudder, and the maiden mourn, for wickedness has overspread the land, and its punishment shall fall heavily on the people.

"Ah! I see the noblest in the country die on the field, and the bravest hang on the gibbet! Neighbours raise the steel of animosity and death against each other; friends are now each other's murderers — brother rushes against brother, and father and son bury the weapon of destruction in each other's bosoms!

"Mourn, ye virgins! Your fathers are captives, your brothers are slain, and your lovers are scourged, and hanged, and quartered! And ye too, ye wives, and ye widows, as well as maidens, lament; for while your purity is ravished by beastly force, the heads of those who would have defended or avenged you, are withering on high in the public places. Ah! there are now numerous and fair villages in the land, of which, yon moon, ere she twice attains her zenith of full grandeur in the heavens, shall see only the smoking ruins! She will see our hills, and our plains, and our streets, and our highways red with the blood of men! She will behold the withering features of the dead, and the writhing agonies of the dying! Hark! I hear the groans of thousands in their last struggles with the pangs of death!

"Weep ye widows, and ye orphans! Ah! Ye fill the land! Weep, for thyself, Andrew Ramsay! For thou shalt see misery: Go thy way now, and tremble, and tell the multitude to tremble also, for they would not repent!"

With an awful shriek, she flew over the tops of the trees, and disappeared like a cloud expanding along the distant verge of the horizon.

Andrew continued for some minutes, gazing, breathless and stupefied, after her. The cold sweat fell in large drops from his brows, which on the return of his faculties, he mistook for blood; and he supposed himself undone. By degrees the spasm of his muscles relaxed, and voluntary motion being thus restored, he flew on the wings of terror to the nearest habitation. The family were in bed.

"Ah! Brice Lee! Brice Lee!" cried he, "for the love of Heaven, let in a miserable frien' that is frightened to death."

The door was soon opened, but the unfortunate Andrew had fainted on the threshold. By the attention of the family, he was soon restored to sensation, and, at different intervals, gave them the foregoing account. In the morning, intelligence of his situation was sent to his friends, and he was carried home during the course of the day.

When Ellen and her friend visited him in the evening, as before stated, he was in the delirium of a high fever. They were both shocked at the recital of the story, and endeavoured to give the family what consolation they could. Ellen expressed her opinion that they had no cause to anticipate any particular calamity, on account of the prediction that had been given.

"For," she observed, "even supposing the apparition to have been supernatural, and commissioned by Heaven to reveal the secrets of futurity, it had not foretold that Andrew should feel misery; it only said that he should see it.

But even putting the worst construction on the prophecy, it might be considered as fulfilled in his present sufferings; and that whenever he should recover from the effects of his fright, all would, no doubt, be well again with the family."

Her attempts at consolation were, however, in vain; and she left the house with a sorrowful heart, at having witnessed such an example of the deplorable effects of superstition on the human mind.

"Do you not believe this story of the ghost?" asked Miss Agnew, as they walked-homeward.

"No," replied Ellen.

"And how do you account for this man's illness?" was again asked.

"Without having recourse to anything supernatural in the case," she replied, "I can account for it in two ways, either of which, to me, would be satisfactory. But, surely, Maria, you do not believe that this man really saw a spirit."

"I confess," replied Maria, "from everything I see and hear I cannot get over such a belief. I cannot, on any other supposition, account for this man's illness. But let me hear how you account for it?"

"My first method of doing so," said Ellen, "is this. I can easily conceive that the intimidated and intoxicated imagination of this poor man, after what had passed in the Shabeen house, was sufficient to conjure up at the dubious hour of darkness, all the frightful appearances which he describes as having beheld; and that such an appearance thus conjured up, might have occasioned all the disordered ideas to pass through his mind, relative to a subject which had just occupied it so intensely, that he ascribes to the revelation of the vision.

"This is my first method. My second is still an easier, more simple, and, under all the circumstances of the present case, perhaps a more satisfactory way of accounting for it. It is only by supposing it altogether a trick of Steele, or some other of his party. If you are acquainted with this person, and are really very anxious to be satisfied on the subject, I will pledge my reputation for sagacity, that by managing him properly, you will be able to obtain as satisfactory an explanation of the matter as you can desire."

CHAP. XXI.

Thaunus the Druid.

On hearing the latter mode by which Ellen accounted for the vision of Andrew Ramsay, Miss Agnew acknowledged its plausibility.

"I did not think of that," said she; "but I believe it may have been the case; for I have often heard of such tricks being practised on weak minded people, by mischievous wags. I shall make my brother question Steele on the subject."

"But, my dear Maria," observed Ellen, "there is a piece of intelligence connected with this story, which excites horrible ideas in my mind. Tell me, did you ever before hear that Sir Geoffrey was blamed with the death of that unfortunate girl?"

"I have heard it whispered," returned Maria; "but there being no proof of it, everyone was afraid, at the time of the shocking event, to mention it publicly; and I had supposed that the suspicion itself had dropped from the minds of the people."

"It is a dreadful tale, Maria. I remember the report of her death; and have often wondered that it's perpetrator has never been discovered."

"I believe," said Maria, "that there were no other grounds for suspecting Sir Geoffrey, than that he had, for some time previous, paid unusual attention to the young woman, who is said to have been remarkably handsome, and that immediately after the occurrence, he withdrew from the country, and ever since continued, until the beginning of last winter, to reside abroad. But these grounds, you know, were not sufficient to warrant magisterial interference, especially with a person of his great wealth and consequence in society."

"Thank heaven! I have escaped uniting myself to such a man," ejaculated Ellen.

At that moment, a man in a gig approached them at full gallop, followed by another on horseback. The ladies stood still to let the travellers pass, but the former stopped the gig suddenly on coming towards them.

"Fortune favours us!" cried he. "Let us seize her at once, and be off!"

So saying he sprang out; and with the assistance of the horseman, hastily secured Ellen in the gig, when gagging her with a large handkerchief, he turned his horse, and drove away at full speed.

Miss Agnew in a state of terror and distraction, fled and screamed for assistance, but before she could make herself properly understood by those who flocked to her aid, her friend was far off.

Sir Geoffrey was suspected for this outrage; and a pursuit commenced in the direction of his residence, but without success. The ruffians had taken an unfrequented road which led them directly to the untenanted house on his estate before mentioned.

The villain in the gig did not speak a word to his captive, either by way of threat or conciliation, until they arrived there. "You are safe now, madam," was his first observation; "and, thank heaven, we are safe too."

A light was soon struck, and a fire kindled, when Ellen, for the first time, recognised the two men to be the very, same that had before attempted to seize her.

"I am at length undone!" cried she, the gag being now taken out of her mouth. "For God's sake, have mercy on me! Deliver me to my grandfather, and you shall be rewarded to your utmost desire."

"We know better, ma'am," replied one of the fellows. "We shall be better rewarded by keeping you. You may as well be quiet. Here nobody can hear your noise, and come to your rescue, as that damned rascal in green did the other week. My master will use you like the apple of his eye; for he is over head and ears in love with you; and you may live like a queen, if you only take care to please him. To be sure he's a little stingy with his purse, but, I think, if you manage him well, that you may make your own of him."

To these remarks Ellen considered it useless to reply. She laid her head on a table that was near her, and relieved her bursting heart with a flood of tears, that fortunately came to her relief. On looking up after some time, she perceived that one of the men had left her, but the other sat between her and the door, and coldly remarked that, as she must be fatigued, she was perhaps disposed to go to bed.

"There is a bed in this closet," said he, as he opened a door that led into a small apartment. "It is a comfortable one, and expressly prepared in expectation of your using it."

She meditated for some time in silence. At length, under the impression that she would be freed from the observation of her jailor, she thought proper to retire.

"Won't you have a light? ma'am," asked the man.

"No," said she, and she closed the door of her apartment without waiting for more questions. She threw herself on her knees, and addressed her supplications to that God who had more than once vouchsafed her deliverance from similar distresses. "I throw myself again into thy presence," said she, "and thou art as mighty to save as ever. Add to those gracious favours thou hast already bestowed upon me, one more instance of thy goodness; save me once more from the power of this man, who has so long hunted after my ruin.

"Shouldst thou deny me the means of escape, Oh! enlighten the mind of my persecutor to see the enormity of the crime he would commit: awaken his conscience, inspire him with repentance for his past offences, and restrain him from becoming guilty of additional injury to a helpless maiden. But shouldst thou in thy providence think fit to inflict upon me still severer trials than I have yet sustained, Oh! at least, preserve me from pollution and infamy, for into thy gracious keeping I commit all my safety."

In a somewhat calmer state of mind, she threw herself on the bed, and with a trembling frame and agitated heart, passed a sleepless night. The morning only brought an increase of her sorrow, for it brought the detestable Sir Geoffrey himself.

"Sweetest of thy sex," said he, "behold in this reluctantly adopted and disagreeable measure, the violence of my passion. I cannot live without you. Be mine; make me happy as your husband; accept of me on any conditions you may prescribe. My fortune, my life — all are yours, only give me yourself in exchange."

"Son of iniquity; barbarous, wicked man, I know you now too well ever to link my fate with yours. Had I known you sooner, you should never have received even the reluctant civilities that were once extorted from me."

"My wish must be gratified!" he exclaimed. "Either voluntarily make me happy, or know, that force will compel you. I will give you till this evening to decide."

"Infamous man! Do you insult me, by calculating on my deliberate acquiescence in guilt? For guilt it would be, knowing you as I now do, to accept your proposals. I am aware that you have a villainous conscience, capable enough of perpetrating your threats, but think you that there is not a God who can blast you ere your crimes be accomplished!"

"Sorceress!" cried he, "you hate me, and defy me, but your beauty has enchanted my senses. I am mad with love! I will not postpone my bliss. The delay I proposed was unwise. Accident might once more rob me of my treasure, but now, bewitching, lovely girl, you shall bless me in spite of accident!"

So saying, he clasped her in his arms with a force and vehemence that made her tremble, and she screamed hopelessly but instinctively for help.

"It is in vain for you to resist," said he, loosening her for a moment. "My mind is too fiercely bent on you, to leave you without being satisfied. Your strength is useless, for if aid be necessary to force you, I have it at hand. As to screams, in this remote place, thank my stars, they will meet no ear but such as will listen to me alone." He again attempted to seize her, but with a desperate effort she sprang from him.

"O God," she exclaimed, "if man cannot hear me, thou canst! Save me! Save me from the murderer of Robbins."

"What meanest thou by that name?" said he, for a moment struck almost motionless by the sound.

"To awaken thy guilty conscience," she replied, "and prevent thee from being twice a murderer."

"Girl, 'tis false," he cried, in great agitation. "Thou art a fiend, but thou art a beautiful one, and thy charms shall now recompense me for this pang."

In saying this, with the fury of a tyger, he darted upon her, and threw her on the bed.

At that moment a confusion of voices were heard outside of the house, and instantaneously, the shock of a door bursting from its bolts, which was immediately followed by the discharge of a pistol in the outer room.

"Ah! villain is it you! Receive this! Where is the lady!" was exclaimed by a voice familiar to Ellen.

"She maun be in that room, gin she's on earth," was replied by a coarse female voice, and the next moment the door was laid on the floor with a dreadful crash; and the Green Minstrel appeared.

"Horrible monster!" cried he, seizing Sir Geoffrey by the throat, "have you ruined that angel?"

"Mercy! Murder! I have not injured her," stammered the terrified and half strangled knight.

"It is well for you. This hour would else have been your last," replied the Minstrel, and he dashed him to the floor with a force that made the house shake. Then turning to Ellen, "Sweet maid, are you safe?" he inquired.

"Thank Heaven, I am. My deliverer again! How providential was this?" she replied.

"Thank Heaven! indeed," said he, and he pressed her hand to his lips.

At that instant she screamed, and casting her arms about him, with a sudden effort, moved him from his position, and received the point of a dirk in her neck. It would have entered deep enough to have terminated both her sorrows and her life, had not the timely interference of Peg Dornan arrested the blow.

"The curse o' God on ye for a murderer!" exclaimed Peg, "you thoucht to kill the bonniest lad, an' ye hae killed the bonniest lass in the land."

The Minstrel turned round, and beheld the dirk in Sir Geoffrey's hand, with Peg Dornan struggling to force it from him. He also perceived it stained with the blood of his beloved. "Infernal fiend!" cried he, wresting the weapon from him; and again dashing him to the floor, he held him firmly there with his foot fixed on his neck. Jemmy Hunter at that moment entered. He had been employed in binding the legs and arms of Tim Rogers, Sir Geoffrey's servant, whom the Minstrel had knocked down in the outer chamber, on the firing of the pistol. Hunter performed the operation with great coolness and dexterity, remarking, "I wish, frien', I was tying this rape aboot your neck, to gie you the weicht o' your damned carcass at its end."

Ellen had swooned; and while Peg was running for some water to sprinkle on her face, the Minstrel who believed her to be really dead, leaned over her with tears gushing from his eyes. "Purest, loveliest of created beings," cried he, "thou art gone to a world more worthy of thee. Thou hast left thy lover. But, O! thou wert snatched from him too soon. Thou wert the delight of mine eyes, the hope, the joy of my heart — this widowed heart, that shall now never more know peace. Unmanly monster!" he exclaimed, turning towards Sir Geoffrey; "couldst thou not have aimed better, and slain me as was thy design; and not have destroyed such innocence, such virtue, such loveliness! But thy barbarous hand has left to me a living, lingering death. Ah! yet take the weapon, if thou hast any mercy in thee, and end my sorrows."

"Dinna lay in sae much to heart," said Hunter. "You should na vex yoursel' sae. It's no' reasonable to greet like a woman, (the tears at the same time swelling in his own eyes) though it's a sair an' sorrowfu' sight — for she was a weel-fared, guid young lady. But ye maunna talk o' deeing. Ye maun leeve to bring this wicked limb o' hell to the hemp rape for this wark."

Peg Dornan had now returned, and was bathing Ellen's temples and cheeks with some spirits which she had found in the outer room, when she opened her eyes and began again to respire.

The Minstrel, who had watched her with the anxiety of despair, gave a shout of joy. "My love!" said he, "speak to me. Do not you know your Edward, your Middleton, your Barrymore, your Minstrel? Live, my love, and never will I leave thy side till this execrable wretch be secured beyond the power of injuring you more."

She held out her hand to him. "I am happy," said she, "to see you living. Ah! I thought the steel had entered your body. But heaven has been more merciful. You are indeed my Edward, my Minstrel, my preserver. None else can ever be my love."

Edward kissed her hand fervently. Now indeed, he felt happiness. What a contrast! He who had the moment before been sunk into the lowest depths of misery, would not now have exchanged feelings with the proudest monarch in Christendom.

The agitation of our lovers soon began to subside.

Ellen's wound was dressed. It was found to penetrate very little deeper than the skin, for the timely interference of Peg Dornan, had given such an oblique direction to the stroke, that it had inflicted only a superficial injury, which threatened no ill consequences. Her swoon had been occasioned solely from the supposition that Edward was murdered.

Peg Dornan had by this time discovered some wine and other articles of refreshment in the house, of which Ellen partook, and in a short time her strength was sufficiently restored to admit of her being removed.

Edward had been slightly wounded in the thigh by the contents of the pistol, which Berwick had fired at him on entering the house, having grazed along the flesh, and torn part of it away. During the hurry and excitement of the preceding scene, he had paid no attention to the wound. He now, however, found it necessary to have it dressed, which was soon accomplished, and he was prepared to escort Ellen to her grandfather's, where she wished to be taken.

They were now under some embarrassment how to dispose of their prisoners. Hunter would have carried them to a magistrate for the purpose of having them committed to jail. But Sir Geoffrey threatened that if they did so, he would bring immediate destruction on O'Halloran, by disclosing his treasonable practices to the government; and Edward considering that he had not actually accomplished any crime for which he could be capitally punished, thought it better not to take this course. At the same time, he conceived it unsafe to permit him to remain at large, for then would not only O'Halloran be in danger from his disclosures, but Ellen might again suffer from his violence.

While they were in this perplexity, the Recluse and M'Nelvin arrived. They had heard of Ellen's seizure, and suspecting Sir Geoffrey to be its author, had hastened to Carebrow Hall. M'Nelvin alone entered the house, and discovered from one of the servants where Sir Geoffrey had gone that morning. "I wonder what the devil he is going to do there?" observed the servant, "for it's a waste farm."

M'Nelvin made no answer, but joining the Recluse, they hastened as fast as possible to the place, and arrived just at the point of time we have mentioned.

They were of opinion, that it would be proper to effect the removal of the captives without delay, lest some of Sir Geoffrey's domestics might arrive, and occasion them trouble, nay, perhaps, effect his rescue. It was therefore determined to deliver him, and his fellow culprit, into the hands of O'Halloran, to be dealt with as the leaders of the United Irishmen should think proper. They now proceeded by a private road to Mr. Agnew's, from whence, as soon as night came, their prisoners could be conveyed without risk or difficulty to their destination.

CHAP. XXII.

With many a vow and lock'd embrace, Our parting was fu' tender;
And pledging oft to meet again, We tore ourselves asunder.
Burns.

As the party proceeded to Mr. Agnew's, the lovers found an opportunity to ride at some distance from the rest of the company and enjoy the luxury of a private conversation. Ellen expressed some inquietude, lest Edward should, even under the disguise of a minstrel, be recognized by the United Irishmen, and involved into fresh troubles.

"I keep so close," said he, "that except when the necessity of serving you requires it, I never leave my concealment, and, on such occasions, this habit has hitherto been an effectual disguise; and you will acknowledge that my general hiding-place is well chosen, both in point of security and enjoyment, when I inform you that it is the Recluse's cavern."

"That cavern is, indeed, an endeared spot to me," said she, and she coloured as she spoke; "since it is the asylum of my two best and dearest friends."

"Ah! my heart's best treasure, sweet endearing girl!" exclaimed Edward, "how happy you make me in accounting me one of that sacred number!"

"Permit me," said she, wishing to stop his raptures, and to give a different direction to the conversation, "permit me to inquire how you discovered me this morning, in so obscure and unsuspicious a place; and also how you appeared so fortunately to rescue me on a former occasion?"

"My love," said he, "I shall explain the whole mystery. You know that after my escape from the United Irishmen, I kept up a constant correspondence with the Recluse, by whom I was informed of everything that happened to you.

"When he mentioned the persecution you suffered from the addresses of Sir Geoffrey, and that your grandfather exerted his authority over you in his favour, I anticipated some misfortune, and resolved to visit your neighbourhood, to watch over your safety, and rescue you from any calamity that might befall you. To effect this, it was necessary, for obvious reasons, to disguise myself. After my return home, I had employed one of Arthur O'Neil's pupils, to give me instructions on the harp; for I had imbibed your taste for that instrument; and having become a tolerable performer, I adopted the habit and profession of a minstrel.

"I arrived at the Recluse's cavern in the beginning of March; and by M'Nelvin's management I was admitted to perform as a harper in the castle, at the celebration of St. Patrick's Day, on which occasion you so signalized me, by bestowing on me the contested prize, as to excite the envy of my competitors.

"The jealousy of Sir Geoffrey, on that occasion, I made no doubt, was the cause of his urging you so instantaneously to accept his proposals; and I determined, at all risks, to rescue you from his power. But when I heard that you had consented to become his wife, I thought it improper to interfere, and I became almost distracted with intensity of grief; and, I assure you, that had you then married him, I should have fled my country never to see it more.

"It was then that the Recluse, in pity to my sufferings, revealed to me his relationship to you, and the other particulars of his life; and gave me assurances that, as he knew your consent had proceeded from a deference to parental authority, he would interfere with an authority of that description, which you would esteem more imperative than that of your grandfather. The happy consequence of his interference, I shall never forget. He ran some risk on the occasion, but his affection for you, and his knowledge of Sir Geoffrey's character, constrained him to overlook all hazards.

"Aware that your tormentor would adopt other methods of possessing you, I determined to keep a close watch on his motions. For this purpose, I had recourse to Peg Dornan, whose profession as a beggar would procure her constant and unsuspected admission to his house.

"Of her zeal in your cause, I was aware, and of her prudence in such matters, I had before ample demonstration. She readily undertook the office assigned her, and has discharged it with fidelity and success.

"It was she who informed me that Berwick and Rodgers, had engaged to be the instruments of Sir Geoffrey's villainy. I observed them several times suspiciously lurking in your neighbourhood, as if watching an opportunity to seize you. In all your walks and journeys, I, therefore, determined to hover near you, that in case of any attack, I might be at hand for your defence.

"Accordingly, when you set off for Mr. Agnew's, I followed you. It was fortunate I did so. But you know the result. Before Berwick recovered from the effects of the blow, you had resumed your journey, in safety from his pursuit. He did not, however, attempt to pursue; for I watched until he had remounted, and set off in a different direction.

"Since your visit to Mr. Agnew's, that I might be convenient to you, I have resided about half a mile distant, at the house of an old widow, a strenuous friend to the United Irishmen, who has carefully and kindly concealed me, under the persuasion that I am proscribed by the government, and hiding from its power.

"Conceiving, that if Sir Geoffrey renewed his attempt to seize you, he would do it in a more formidable manner than before, I thought it prudent to provide an assistant, in whose courage and fidelity I could depend. You will readily agree, that I could not have found one better qualified in these respects, than our honest farmer, James Hunter. He engaged ardently in the affair, and without hesitation took lodging beneath the same roof with me, under a similar plea. Peg Dornan, who, of course, knew where to find us, came to us this morning breathless, and in great agitation.

"Come oot," said she, "till I tell you!" I accompanied her out of doors. "They hae ta'en her, at last," she resumed, "I ca'ed at Mr. Agnew's before I caM' here, an' the servants are pursuing, yin, yin way, an' yin anither, but nane o' them the richt way; I ken that. Miss Agnew has had a'e fit o' the mither after anither, till she's amaist dead. Ye maun ken that I was sleeping in Sir Geoffrey's kitchen-neuk when Rodgers caM' hame in the night time. The master met him in the hall, for, I trow, he had no' been in bed; an' neither o' them saw me, though I was within twa yards o' them.

"Have you got her to Gorman's house?" said the master.

"We have, your honour; and a right speedy scamper we had of it," said Rodgers, "she made such a screaming, but Berwick soon gagged her. But her comrade, Agnew's daughter, ran and terrified the neighbours so much, that, late as it was, I feared we would have been catched, before we got to Gorman's. But the horses were guid, your honour; and she is now as snug for you, as if she were lodged in your own bed room."

"I immediately summoned Hunter. Our horses were soon prepared, for we kept them in an adjoining field, ready for any emergency. As Peg alone knew Gorman's place, it was necessary to take her along as a guide. She was accordingly mounted behind Hunter; and we set off at full speed. Thank Providence, our haste was not in vain. You are safe once more; and I trust your friends, in whose hands your infamous persecutor now is, will take care that he shall not again have the power to injure you."

When he had ended his recital, "Ah! generous Barrymore," she exclaimed, "what do I not owe you for so much kindness?"

"You owe me nothing," he replied. "Ah! yes;" he continued, "I do ask for

the vastness of my love, not for my services, the most valued, the most precious reward this world can afford me; I ask thyself?"

The burning blush that now glowed on the countenance of Ellen was beautiful beyond the power of genius to portray. It was like the living saffron that
irradiates the face of heaven, when the sun gilds with his golden beams, the
bosom of a snowy cloud; and the look of gladness that sparkled in her bright
rolling eyes, was like the agitated reflection of the same luminary when it glit-
ters from a liquid mirror. She replied not.

Their arrival at Mr. Agnew's prevented her, but to the penetrating eye of
Edward, her look had spoken a reply a thousand times more satisfactory than
could have been conveyed in the strongest language.

For reasons well known to his friends, Edward now disappeared. He returned to his hospitable widow, and conferring on her an unexpected reward,
told her that he must, with his companion, seek a new residence for a few
weeks. When night came he assisted his friends to convey the culprits to
O'Halloran Castle, and then retired with the Recluse to his subterraneous
dwelling.

Sir Geoffrey, and his worthy compeer, the game-keeper, were soon secured
in the conspirator's strong hold, within the Point rock, but met with very
different treatment from what Edward had received, when confined in the
same place the preceding year. The chiefs of the conspiracy, besides their
displeasure at his conduct to Ellen, detested him as an apostate, one whose
fraudulent behaviour towards them had thrown their affairs into considerable
embarrassment, and whose fears alone had prevented him from absolutely
betraying them to their enemies. They, therefore, on first receiving him,
secured him in a dark apartment, chained to the rock, where he had only straw
for a bed, and was fed on bread and water. His servant was treated more
leniently, as being only an instrument in the hands of the superior criminal. At
length Sir Geoffrey consented to purchase greater indulgence, by giving
O'Halloran an order on his Dublin banker, for the twenty thousand pounds
of which he had attempted to defraud him.

Edward having thus secured the object of his affections from the further
aggressions of her tormentor, thought of returning to Dublin. As he had lately
held no conversation with any of the conspirators on political subjects, he
neither knew, nor wished to know, the posture of their affairs.

The safety and welfare of Ellen was the great object that had occupied his
mind. He was however far from viewing the threatening aspect of the times
with indifference, but he did not conceive the stability of the constitution to

be really in danger from the present conspiracy. Had he thought so, its preservation would undoubtedly have enlisted all his energy and feelings, and been viewed as possessing a paramount claim over every other consideration, to his services. The threatened insurrection, if it did take place, as its materials were so very discordant and scattered, and the great majority of the influential men of the kingdom, its opponents, he believed, would be neither very extensive nor of long duration.

It might bring destruction on a few of its leaders and their most zealous followers, but he had no power to prevent this; he could only deplore it. In the event of an actual rebellion, the preservation of O'Halloran would be the chief object of his solicitude. He believed, however, that by ingratiating himself with the executive authorities of the day, he might acquire sufficient influence to protect this enthusiastic old man, should he fall into the hands of the government. Hence he thought it necessary to return to the capital; which he did with the less reluctance, as he knew that he left Ellen under the protection of the watchful eye of her father, the affectionate sagacity of M'Nelvin, and the energetic and faithful arm of Jemmy Hunter. Of every important occurrence, he also knew that he should receive the earliest intelligence, and could act accordingly.

During the parting interview with Ellen in her father's cave and presence, while under the influence of the warm feelings the occasion excited, he solicited strongly for an immediate marriage. "I am at my own disposal," said he, "independent as far as a competence of worldly wealth can make me so, in my own right; so that, without reference to either the pleasure or the displeasure of my father or my uncle, I think I may be justified in taking this step."

Ellen declared that in the present critical state of her grandfather's affairs, she could not consent to such a measure without his approbation, "and you are aware," said she, "that to obtain that, the obstacles are insurmountable."

Her father also declared that he would not consent to a private union, which, however, fair and valid, would carry with it something of a clandestine and improper air, and which might, from that very circumstance alone, be displeasing to Edward's relations.

"No," said he, "my young, but too ardent friend, let the crisis of the times be past, let the fate of this conspiracy be decided, and when the storm which it raises is blown over, and the affairs of our country again become calm and settled, I shall promote your views of domestic felicity; and publicly, perhaps, (for Providence may by that time restore me to society) have the pleasure, with the approbation of your friends, of bestowing my daughter on you, and giving you both, at the moment of the ceremony, a father's benediction."

Edward acquiesced, having first obtained from Ellen an assurance that she would comply with his wishes, whenever such a period as that to which her father alluded, should arrive.

"But, ah! surely," said she, "this is not a time to indulge our selfish wishes; this is no time for the mirth, or joy, or pageantry of a marriage, when our country is in sorrow, when she is about to be agonized at every pore; and, perhaps, rent in pieces by a dreadful convulsion. Ah! my Edward, I fear we have numerous scenes of sorrow to witness, perhaps to endure, before we can experience joy.

"Let us prepare our minds for the worst, but amidst our misfortunes, whatever they may be, let us be faithful to each other; for be assured, that whether in prosperity or adversity, I shall be faithful to you."

"My only love!" replied Edward, touched to the heart by her fervency, "that God who loves purity, will avert from thee the calamities thy toe timid mind forebodes; and as to the fidelity of my heart's affections, the moment of its first wandering from thee, shall be that of its last pulsation. No; Ellen, I have rivetted thy image, I have rivetted thy virtues and thy loveliness, too strongly here, in my heart, ever to displace them, and they never shall be displaced." He warmly caught her hand, and kissed it. "God preserve thee, my espoused," he exclaimed, "for whatever man may say or do, thou art mine in the ordination of Heaven. God preserve thee, until I see thee again!" and he rushed from her in violent agitation, and departed.

Volume II

CHAP. I.

The moment came, the hour when Otho thought, Secure at last the vengeance which he sought. That morning he had freed the soil bound slaves, Who dig no lands for tyrants but their graves. Such is their cry; some watch-word for the fight, Must vindicate the wrong, and warp the right. Religion — freedom — vengeance — what you will — A word's enough to raise mankind to kill.
Byron.

It was on the evening of the fourth of June, that a messenger arrived from Belfast, at O'Halloran Castle. He delivered to its owner the following note, and passed on to circulate others of a similar import throughout the country.

June 4th, 1798.

The signal is given. The mail coach has not arrived. Our informant says it was stopped yesterday at Swords. The south is in arms — Wexford is taken. Let the rising be on the 7th inst.

The general rendezvous for this county is Donegore Hill. The small parties of the military quartered in the country towns must be captured, if possible, by surprise. The bearer will proceed with intelligence along the coast.

You will despatch messengers through the interior, by Ballynure, Ballyclare, Ballyeaston, Ballymena, &c.

Expedition is requisite.
HENRY M'CRACKEN.

O'Halloran immediately assembled his coadjutors, and couriers were soon despatched agreeably to the foregoing instructions.

All was now preparation, bustle, and eagerness, among the populace of Larne, but everyone was unusually sober, and good humoured. Not a drunken man was to be seen, nor even a woman heard to scold, during this awful period of secrecy, suspense, and anxious activity. Even the military were treated with more than usual complaisance, and all men were not only quiet, but apparently contented and happy. Thus in a profound calm were the populace of this district employed in collecting all the elements of irritation, hatred, and ferocity, which were soon to burst into the most dreadful storm of destruction that ever swept that unhappy country.

The sixth of June, the eve of the insurrection, came. Mirth seemed to engage the young; friendship, good humour, and hilarity, the middle aged; while the old looked on in portentous silence and meditation. All business, every species of labour, spontaneously ceased after mid-day. The merchant, indeed, still kept his shop open, but it was only to lean over his counter; for he neither desired, nor obtained customers. The mechanic also kept his work-shop open, but in it there was no sound of hammer, nor saw, nor axe, nor shuttle to be heard. Spades, mattocks, and hoes were thrown aside, or disappeared as if they had in reality been converted into swords and spears. Towards the evening, an increased degree of mirth and jollity pervaded the younger part of the community; while even the more sedate and advanced in life, relaxed, or, growing weary of their thoughtfulness or their idleness, joined in athletic sports, such as wrestling, running, leaping, hurling, and various other kinds of rural pastimes. Such an unusual degree of mirth and idleness among the people, excited the attention of the friends of government, and a vague whisper of some disturbance being intended during the night, reached the ears of the commander of the small party of military then quartered in Larne.

This party consisted of about fifty of the Tay fencibles. Their captain's name was Small. In consequence of the rumour which had reached him, he thought proper strictly to enforce the general orders which had been several months before issued to the military dispersed over the country, to cause all persons in the disaffected towns and villages to keep within doors after nine o'clock at night, but the execution of which, from the continued appearance of tranquillity in his neighbourhood, had been lately induced to relax.

He therefore as soon as tattoo was beat, which for many months had been regularly done at nine o'clock at night, paraded the streets with a patrol of twenty men, and compelled the people to relinquish their sports, and retire to their respective homes, under pain of being taken to the guard house. Men, women and children, all complied, and the streets, which a few minutes before displayed such a full scene of life, resounding with all the noise of rural mirth and manners, were now totally deserted, and as silent as the habitations of the dead. The soldiers had retired to their barrack, and a deep portentous calm

continued for several hours. During this interval, a number of the most in-
trepid and zealous of the United Irishmen, stole cautiously to their appointed
rendezvous, at a place called the Green Holme, about a half a mile from the
town. It was a solitary spot, at the foot of a high hill, a short distance from the
public road, from which it was screened by two intervening thick hedges, and
was selected for their meeting, not more on account of its privacy and conti-
guity to the town, than on account of a cold, clear and beautiful spring of
water it contained. Here O'Halloran and M'Cauley arranged the plan of an
attack upon the barrack, the other leaders having gone off to head the insurrection in different parts of the country.

It was about one o'clock in the morning, and everything was quiet in the
town, when O'Halloran, after having distributed among his little band, whiskey, and other refreshments, gave orders for proceeding to the attack. They
were about eighty in number; about thirty of whom were armed with muskets,
and the remainder with pikes. Their plan was two-fold:

If the soldiers were retired to sleep, which they presumed would be the
case, but which they could easily ascertain by the show of resistance that would
be made on their first appearance in the street that contained the barrack, they
should proceed at once to the assault. But if their adversaries should be on the
alert, they were to retreat so as to attract them in pursuit, while M'Cauley
should hasten with a body of twenty men, twelve of whom had muskets, to
form an ambuscade behind the wall of a rope factory, which joined one of the
streets, and to which O'Halloran at the head of the main body, should direct
his retreat, in order to bring his pursuers between two fires.

The barrack was situated near the centre of a long street, on arriving at the
upper end of which, the insurgents perceived that they must relinquish their
first plan, as the garrison were evidently on the watch.

Captain Small, who was a vigilant and active officer, had kept above a third
of his troops under arms, for fear of a surprise, and had ordered the rest to
sleep in their clothes, that they might be ready for action at a moment's warning.

M'Cauley was now despatched to lay his ambush, and Darragh was ordered
to pass through a by street, at the head of twenty men, to possess himself of
the barrack, in case Small should leave it with his whole force in pursuit of
O'Halloran.

Having made these arrangements, and given the detachments time to exe-
cute them, which as it was considerably dark, and as they kept very silent, they
accomplished without alarming their enemies, O'Halloran ordered his men to

advance a few paces into the street containing the barrack, and, after discharging several muskets at the garrison, to retire immediately to the shelter of that adjoining.

They fired.

In a moment the royal drums beat "to arms," and the troops to the number of forty — the remainder, in conjunction with some loyalists who had joined them on the preceding evening, being left to guard the barrack — formed in two lines, and, each taking one side of the street, marched at a quick pace towards the insurgents. But before their approach, O'Halloran had eluded their attack by removing to another street, at the end of which he stopped for a moment, to fire on the advancing troops, by which several of them were wounded. He then continued his retreat into the Rope-walk street, where M'Cauley lay concealed, and halting at the upper end of it, awaited the approach of his pursuers, who steadily advanced until they were within three hundred yards of him.

Not a shot having been as yet fired in this street by either party, Small stopped, and exclaimed, "Front division, ready! Now my lads, fire sure, and cut down the rebels!" Immediately a volley of musketry from behind, brought six of his own men to the ground. He turned round, but no enemy was visible. His van had fired at O'Halloran's party, two of whom were killed and several wounded. They immediately returned the fire, and two more of the soldiers pressed the ground. Small now gave orders for a retreat, when O'Halloran's pikemen rushed down upon him. But he checked them by his front presenting bayonets, and his rear division advancing and firing amongst them, and they were obliged, in their turn, to withdraw and seek shelter at their former stand. He had just ordered his opponents to be pursued, when another volley from his invisible assailants, brought down four more of his men.

A retreat, at all hazards, was now necessary to save the remainder of his troops. It was, therefore, again attempted, but on coming opposite the rope-walk gate, M'Cauley, with the view of capturing Small, rushed with his little band of pikemen upon him, but they were too weak to make any impression, and a front of bayonets being instantly presented to them, they were compelled again to seek refuge behind their wall, though not until M'Cauley, with his own hands, had given Small a dreadful wound in the groin with a pike.

As O'Halloran's men appeared coming to the aid of their companions, the troops did not think proper to pursue M'Cauley, but hastily passed on in their retreat to the end of the street, where they only halted to reload. They then continued their retreat, practising for their safety the same expedient that the insurgents had practised in drawing them into the ambush.

On coming opposite a lane through which Darragh's small party were retiring, after having made an unsuccessful attempt on the barrack, they were
fired on by this party, and two of their number killed. They returned the fire,
but it did no execution; for Darragh's men, immediately on discharging their
pieces, had taken refuge behind a low garden wall which formed one side of
the lane. After this their progress to the barrack was unmolested.

On arriving there, Captain Small found that he had left seventeen of his
men in the hands of the Insurgents, and of those he had brought back, five,
besides himself, were severely, and four slightly, wounded.

Thus one half of the soldiers who had gone out on this skirmish, were now
unfit for duty. During the affair, only two of the insurgents were killed, and
about seven or eight wounded. So that, although they had failed in their object
of reducing the barrack, they had obtained a considerable advantage; they had
weakened and disheartened their enemies.

Darragh's attempt on the barrack, had failed from the weakness of his
party. He had, indeed, been directed to make no attempt, unless the whole
strength of the troops should be drawn out in pursuit of O'Halloran. But, as
from the number which appeared to be drawn out, he concluded that very
few, indeed, could be left, he was induced to hazard an effort. Accordingly, he
advanced boldly with his followers into the middle of the street, when he was
assailed with such a firing as, although his men escaped uninjured, convinced
him of his inability to succeed. He, therefore, withdrew, and was on his way
by a circuitous route to join O'Halloran, when he encountered the retreating
troops as before-mentioned, and added to their misfortunes.

The inhabitants of the town, by this time, were flying in every direction, as
their wishes or their fears prompted them, either to join that party to which
they adhered, or to seek refuge in the country from that fate, to which many
of them believed, that all who remained in the town would be doomed. During
the skirmish they had, in terrible suspense, awaited the issue; those, especially
of the popular party, who had relatives engaged in the affair, endured a dreadful agony of mind, not knowing but that every shot they heard was the death
knell of a husband, a brother, a son, or some other dear relative or friend. The
shouts of the combatants, as either side gained the advantage — the groans of
the wounded and the dying — the shrieks of the alarmed women and children,
who, even from within their houses, loudly proclaimed their fears, formed a
scene terribly painful to the imaginations of all, but such, if there be such
monsters, as delight in human misery.

Notwithstanding his success, O'Halloran did not think it prudent, immediately, to renew the attack on the garrison. His strength was every minute

increasing, and he expected in a few hours, to be able to overwhelm all opposition. The distance to Donegore Hill, the appointed rendezvous for the county, where the great stand was to be made, and where it was his duty to be with his followers, at four o'clock that afternoon, was only about fourteen miles. He had, consequently, sufficient time to wait for such an accession of strength, before he renewed his attack on the troops, as would render resistance hopeless, and, perhaps, lead to a surrender of the place without bloodshed.

To these suggestions he yielded as much from humanity as policy. In the meantime, he was not inactive. Small parties were despatched in every direction to arouse their friends, and intimidate even their enemies, to come to their assistance.

Multitudes came voluntarily, but it must be confessed, that numbers whose fears or principles rendered them reluctant, were compelled to take the field with the pike at their breasts. These recruiting and impressing parties, were ordered to be again on the ground by eight o'clock in the morning, at which time it was intended to make a grand assault on the barrack.

In the meantime, every avenue to and from the place was strictly guarded, so that none of the loyalists in the country could join the garrison, nor any of those in the town carry intelligence from it. The garrison, however, notwithstanding their disaster, had been joined by nearly a hundred of the town's people who were attached to the government, and many more would have flocked to their aid, had they not been forced either to conceal themselves, or to fall into the ranks of the Insurgents.

CHAP. II.

Sir, you may counsel though you are our foe,
Because you are an honourable man;
We'll hearken to you, and those friends of yours,
Whom we have vanquished, may have terms of truce,
If they will take them of our framing, for
'Tis not our wish that human blood should flow
For useless purpose. So haste on the treaty.
The Irish Soothsayer.

O'Halloran was afraid that before he should have numbers sufficient to over-come the garrison, after it became strengthened by the loyalists of the town, as has been just mentioned, a detachment of the army which lay in considerable force at Carrickfergus, only nine miles distant, might come to its relief. He, therefore, took the precaution to station scouts on horseback on the roads leading to and from that place, so that he might have the speediest intelligence of any such detachment, and be enabled to meet it on suitable ground.

When the time fixed for assaulting the garrison arrived, he found his party about twelve hundred strong. Not more than three hundred of them, however, had firearms, the rest being armed in the most miscellaneous, and some of them in the most unserviceable, manner. About four hundred had tolerably good pikes, the handles of which varied from ten to fifteen feet long, and consequently in close combat, possessed a great advantage over the guns and bayonets of the king's troops; and were expected by the projectors of the insurrection, to be capable of doing so much execution, as almost to atone for their deficiency in firearms and ammunition. The remainder were armed, some with common hay forks, some with scythes fixed on the ends of poles, and many with dung-forks, spades, or other implements of rural industry.

O'Halloran having made the necessary dispositions for the attack, in order to animate the courage of his men, addressed them in the following words, "Irishmen! you have this day, with a glorious effort, thrown off a yoke which for centuries bound your ancestors to the feet of tyrants. A great task is yet to be performed, a mighty struggle is yet to be maintained, before you can convince your oppressors that they cannot replace you in your former degradation. You are now freemen. I congratulate you! But remember that it is only while you have arms in your hands, and your enemies are unable to wrest them from you, that you are so.

"Be united in sentiment, and firm in combat, and the latter will never be the case. Oppression will be driven out of the country, and your freedom will be established forever. You will then have your prosperity as a nation in your own hands. No foreign power, actuated by jealousy or fear of your growing greatness, will presume to set bounds to your external commerce, or to lay restrictions on your internal industry.

"But why need I allude to the attempts of your late masters to keep you in poverty. Had they done you no other injury, you might have forgiven them. But have they not shackled the consciences of two-thirds of your countrymen and do they not compel them, together with nine-tenths of the other third, to support an expensive and extravagant prelatic church establishment, which their consciences disapprove, and their feelings detest? Have they not driven thousands of your ancestors into exile; and have they not plundered and disinherited thousands more?

"As to yourselves, have they not of late years, heaped on you insult upon insult, injury upon injury, until your hearts have bled with agony? Have not your unoffending neighbours been dragged in hundreds from their firesides, and treated as malefactors? They have been lodged in loathsome cells and dungeons; they have been scourged, and hanged, and shot, and gibbetted, without the common formality of law; without even the appearance of justice. But this was, perhaps, a more merciful mode of destruction; at least it was a more honest and courageous species of tyranny, than indictments before pensioned judges, and bribed and drunken juries.

"But I need not recount your wrongs. Your hearts feel them, and rankle with them, and burn this day for vengeance. Ah! I see rage against your oppressors sparkle in your eyes, and fury is now the expression of your countenances. But let justice rather than rage direct your conduct; and be brave for freedom rather than vengeance. In aid of the multitudes of your compatriots, who are this day in arms for the same holy purpose, you will be strong, not so much, I trust, with a view to revenge, as to terminate your sufferings. Like men, we shall conquer our enemies; and, like Christians, we shall forgive them: for it will be glorious to show them, that we can feel and practice towards them a virtue which they never felt, which they never practised towards us — the virtue of mercy.

"This evening we must join our countrymen at the county encampment on Donegore, there to assist them in the glorious struggle. But we cannot leave our homes at the mercy of our enemies. We must capture those troops we have already defeated, if, in our absence, we wish our wives, our children, and our properties to be safe. Should we depart without taking this garrison with us, the look that we should give our habitations from yonder hill would be the last. We might return victors over our oppressors, but we should return to desolated streets and ruined walls. Be strong, my countrymen; consider the object for which you are to fight, your families and your homes. Remember the cause in which you are engaged is the sacred cause of your country. Fear nothing. Your quarrel is righteous; and God is on your side. Resolve, each man who hears me, resolve now to conquer or die. Let our war word be, Erin and Freedom!"

He was answered by loud acclamations, and the sounds of 'Erin and Freedom', for several minutes continued to reverberate through the air.

By dividing his men into two parties, one of which he entrusted to the command of M'Cauley, he made dispositions to attack the barracks in both front and rear at the same time.

The standard of the United Irishmen was now hoisted. It displayed a gilded harp formed on a banner of green silk, surrounded with the mottoes of, '*Erin-go-bragh*' and 'Liberty and Equality'.

In martial music the insurgents at Larne were deficient; for they had only one drum and one fife, but these animated their spirits with the sounds of national airs, and they had just begun their march to the tune of, 'The Volunteer's Quick Step', when an accession to their strength of nearly two hundred men arrived from one of the adjoining parishes, bringing with them as a prisoner, George M'Claverty, Esq. the magistrate, who, as the reader will recollect, examined Edward Barrymore so closely at the Antrim arms, when in pursuit of the murderers of M'Bride.

O'Halloran halted his men, and they hailed the arrival of their confederates and their prisoner, with loud huzzas. On being informed of their design to attack the garrison, M'Claverty, who, although disliked among them on account of his political principles, was much respected for his other amiable qualities, attempted to dissuade them from it.

"The capture of such a handful of men," said he, "will tend nothing to the ultimate success of your cause, and forbearance may induce the government to forbearance with you on some similar occasion."

"Sir," replied O'Halloran, "you are now our prisoner; as such we shall treat you as well as circumstances will permit, but we do not wish you to be our counsellor. We know your feelings towards us too well for that. In the meantime, I may inform you that we do not attack this garrison from any thirst of revenge or fondness for blood-shed, but, as we cannot remain here to protect our families and properties from their violence, we are resolved that where we go, they shall go also."

He then gave his men orders to proceed. But an incident at that moment occurred, which, by delaying their march for a space, gave M'Claverty another opportunity to interfere. A man of the name of Shaw, an inhabitant of the town, who had borne a captain's commission under George II in his German wars, and had fought at the battle of Dettingen, and was an enthusiastic loyalist, excited to a temporary madness by the scenes he beheld, rushed out of his house, armed with a drawn sword, in spite of the entreaties and tears of his three daughters, into the midst of the insurgents; and with the most terrible imprecations on them as rebels, called on them to lay down their arms and disperse. A man whom he attacked was about thrusting a pike into his body, when M'Cauley rushed forward, and saved him. He was instantly disarmed, and delivered to his daughters, with strict injunctions to confine him, under a threat, that if he again molested them, his life should be taken.

Struck with the humanity and magnanimity of this action, M'Claverty determined to make another effort to prevent the effusion of blood.

"Summon the garrison," cried he, "before you attack it. You are all my neighbours and friends, and this action makes me proud that you are so. I, therefore, earnestly entreat you to consult your own safety and welfare on this occasion, and avoid the useless destruction of human lives, even if they should be those of your enemies. Send a flag of truce to the garrison. Its commander will, perhaps, treat for its surrender, and human lives will be spared, while your interests will not be injured."

O'Halloran now consulted with the other officers of his small army, and gave it as his opinion, that M'Claverty's advice pointed out nothing more than their duty; and that policy as well as humanity required them to adopt it. They were all of the same opinion, except Darragh, who observed that, if they should now fight, they would be certain of victory, but if they negotiated, they might be out-witted, and lose, by the deceit and cunning of their enemies, all the advantages they had gained by their own valour.

"However," said he, "if you are all agreed to this measure, I won't resist it: but in managing it, I beg you to keep your wits about you."

O'Halloran approached M'Claverty. "Sir," said he, "we esteem you for the sentiments you have expressed; and shall take your advice. But first it is necessary, that we should apprize our enemies of our strength, in order to convince them that resistance is useless. They will believe your statement. Write to them an account of our number, our unanimity, and our enthusiasm; and exhort them to deliver themselves, and those loyalists who have taken refuge with them, together with all their warlike stores, into our hands; and we promise them, that not only the troops, but the refugees, shall be well treated, and their families and properties protected from injury."

"I shall make this statement," said M'Claverty, "but I would not encourage you to expect that they will agree to such an unconditional surrender. However, I shall open the negotiation, and ulterior arrangements may be afterwards discussed."

He accordingly wrote as follows:

I am now a prisoner in the hands of the insurgents; and you may be sure I am well treated, when I inform you that I have had influence enough to persuade them to postpone an attack, which, just as I was brought here, they were on the point of making upon you.

I know your gallantry would induce you to make a brave and persevering resistance, but their numbers, (they are now about sixteen hundred strong) and their enthusiasm, make them formidable, and would ensure them ultimate success, although, doubtless, at the expense of many lives.

However, I will not assume the responsibility of advising you to an absolute surrender. Your duty forbids such an alternative, until resistance is proved beyond doubt, to be useless. But I entreat you to open a door for negotiation.

Something short of unconditional submission may probably be obtained. The cause of humanity will be consulted, and, perhaps, His Majesty's interests also, by means of a treaty the terms of which it may be in your power honourably to accept.

I have just witnessed an instance of magnanimity which speaks much for the humane dispositions of those people; and renders them entitled to more indulgence, than, as rebels, they would otherwise deserve.

I have the honour to be, &c.
GEORGE M'CLAVERTY.

This letter was accompanied by the following from the insurgent leaders:

Sir, we are to the number of sixteen hundred men in arms, prepared to attack the garrison under your command. But to give you an opportunity of saving your soldiers from destruction, we have thought proper, first, to apprize you of our intention, and to summon you in the name of our country, to surrender your party, both military and others, with all your warlike stores, into our hands.

As our prisoners your lives will be safe, and as much attention as possible paid to your comforts. The lives, families and properties of such of our town's-men as have joined you, shall also remain unmolested. Our attack shall be suspended, in expectation of your compliance, for three quarters of an hour, but no longer.

We have the honour to be, Your obedient humble servants,
HENRY O'HALLORAN,
JOHN M'CAULEY,
WILLIAM JOHNSTON,
Commanding the army of the United Irishmen in Larne.

In less than twenty minutes the following answer was received:

Sir, enclosed is my reply to the rebel chieftains. By it you will see that you anticipated truly, when you supposed that I would not agree to an unconditional surrender. I am sorry that you are in their power, but it is pleasing to find that they are not disposed to abuse their good fortune, by acts of wantonness or cruelty. It may yet be in my power to show that I can esteem humanity, even in such an enemy.

I have the honour to be, &c.
JAMES SMALL, Capt. &c.

The following was the reply received by the insurgents:

Gentlemen,

In answer to your message, I have to inform you that rather than comply with your demands, my party and myself are resolved to meet destruction amidst the ruins of the place, which it is our duty to defend. Do not, however, suppose that we shall fall an easy prey. It is true, your

186

*number exceed ours by ten to one, but were they a hundred to one, as we
are fully supplied with the means of defence, we know too well how to use
them, not to make our enemies deplore the dearness of any victory they
may gain over us.*

*In your case, it is apparent that victory is at least doubtful. Some traits
of humanity displayed by you have been communicated to me, in
consideration of which I give you my promise, and all the gentlemen of
the town, who have so gallantly come to my assistance, will guarantee its
performance, that if you lay down your arms, and return peaceably to
your allegiance, all that you have yet done shall be overlooked, and
pardoned, and the full and free protection of the laws of your country
shall once more be extended towards you. Should you reject this offer, I
can only deplore your infatuation; I must resist you unto destruction, and
the blood of those who may fall on both sides, be upon your heads.*

JAMES SMALL, Capt. &c.

The insurgent officers now held another consultation, in which it was agreed
to send a second message to the garrison, proposing to withdraw peaceably
from the town, if Captain Small, and the loyalist gentlemen who were with
him, would guarantee the safety of their families and properties after their departure.

To these proposals Small replied that he would agree, provided, the insurgents would liberate George M'Claverty, Esq. Sir Geoffrey Carebrow, and a
Mr. John Hill, together with the wounded soldiers they had captured.

O'Halloran replied that he would, without reluctance, deliver up the
wounded soldiers, but on no account would he part with the three gentlemen,
except in exchange for an equal number of the United Irishmen then imprisoned in Carrickfergus, and for whose safety he would keep these prisoners as
hostages.

"Tell Captain Small," said he to the messenger, "that this is our last proposal. If it is not acceded to in twenty minutes, the barrack shall be attacked
in front and rear; and for whatever blood shall be shed, let him be accounta-
ble."

Small held a short consultation with the gentlemen of the town who had
joined him, who, willing to prevent matters from coming to an extremity, advised the acceptance of these terms. Within the prescribed time, he therefore,

returned an answer to that effect. The articles of the treaty were soon exchanged in proper form, and the wounded soldiers given into the hands of Dr. Ferral, who had them safely conveyed to the barrack.

As nothing now remained to prevent the insurgents from proceeding to the Donegore encampment, O'Halloran ordered them to take some refreshment, and prepare for the march. But being anxious to know what success his coadjutors had met with in raising the people in other parts of the country, he committed the command of the party to M'Cauley, and accompanied with ten men, well mounted and armed, departed without delay to Donegore. Before setting off, however, he gave M'Cauley directions to bury the soldiers who had been slain in the skirmish, with due respect, in the adjoining church-yard; and to follow immediately after, at a steady pace, so as to arrive at the encampment about four o'clock in the afternoon.

M'Cauley obeyed in every particular. The bodies of the soldiers were interred with military honours. Funeral music accompanied the procession to the burial ground; and when the grave closed on the dead, three rounds of musketry were fired over them, by twelve men selected for the purpose. It is said that M'Claverty was so much affected on seeing this generous proceeding, on the part of an enemy from whom he had expected nothing but outrage and ferocity, that he shed tears; and turning to his fellow prisoner, Sir Geoffrey Carebrow, he exclaimed, "What a pity it is, that men of such generous hearts should possess such erring judgments!"

Sir Geoffrey made no reply. He and Berwick had been brought from their confinement in the Point cave, in order to be conveyed to Donegore with the other prisoners. Those who conducted him from the cave, had diverted themselves with his fears, by informing him that he was going to be tried for his crimes by the victorious United Irishmen; and that he should undoubtedly be hanged before the evening. He was in consequence much depressed in spirits, and in no humour to interchange ideas of a pleasant nature with the more courageous and liberal minded M'Claverty.

CHAP. III.

Gray.

M'Cauley now assembled his men on a height to the north-west of the town, where he occupied about the space of an hour in arranging them into companies, and putting them through different military evolutions, after which they proceeded to Donegore Hill.

They had scarcely departed, when a detachment of cavalry, about eighty in number, who had been for some time concealed behind the heights to the southward of the valley in which Larne is situated, now entered the town, in great fury, under the command of a Captain Claverill, and was preparing, in the wantonness of revenge, to set fire to the houses, when Small informed them of his treaty with the insurgents, and declared that he would, with all the force under his command, cause it to be respected. The loyalists of the town joined him in the declaration, protesting that they would oppose with their whole power any infringement of the treaty.

"If you violate this contract," said they, "the first news you may expect to hear from the rebel camp, will be that M'Claverty and his fellow prisoners have fallen victims to your perfidy."

By this firmness the town was saved from the destroying hands of barbarians, who had not the courage to show themselves while it was occupied by that enemy, whom they now affected to despise and detest.

When the first intelligence of the insurrection at Larne reached Carrickfergus, this troop of cavalry had been detached there to assist the garrison in suppressing it. On arriving at the vicinity of Larne, they were informed that the soldiers had been defeated, and nearly all slain; and that the survivors, who with their wounded captain had taken refuge in the barrack, were expected soon to surrender to the insurgents, whose numbers, courage and warlike equipment were described in the most exaggerated terms. Intimidated by this account, they did not venture to enter the town, until the enemy had departed.

At about eleven o'clock, O'Halloran arrived at the place of encampment. He had expected to find thousands assembled, but he only found about a hundred and fifty men busily employed entrenching the ground. These, however, soon satisfied him that there was no want of zeal in the country.

They informed him that, less than half an hour before, upwards of five thousand men had marched thence, under the command of Porter and M'Cracken for Antrim, in order to dislodge the military stationed in that town, and to capture a number of magistrates, who, they were informed, had appointed to meet there that day on some county business.

At this intelligence, O'Halloran's heart leapt light within him. He put spurs to his horse, and followed by those who had attended him from Larne, in less than forty minutes overtook the insurgent army.

It had just halted at the entrance of the town to form its plan of attack. His arrival was hailed by loud cheers from the assembled multitude; and on relating the occurrences that had taken place in Larne, the air again rang with acclamations; and Porter, M'Cracken, and all the other chiefs, as well as the whole body of the insurgents, with one voice, requested him to assume the command. He consented, on condition that Porter and M'Cracken, should be considered as having equal authority, as well as equal responsibility, in all the measures that should be adopted. "For," said he, "I am determined to adopt none of which they shall disapprove."

He then inquired into the strength of the opposition they were to encounter, and was informed that there were two hundred and fifty infantry, and one hundred and fifty cavalry, stationed in the town, under the command of a Major Siddons, which force would perhaps be augmented by the junction of from fifty to a hundred loyalists. It was stated, also, that they had three or four pieces of cannon, but it was supposed that their ammunition was not abundant.

O'Halloran now reviewed the strength and appointments of his own party, and found that it consisted of between seven and eight thousand men, who were promiscuously armed with pikes, muskets, swords, hayforks, &c. They had also two small pieces of cannon, with some experienced cannoniers, who had formerly been in the royal service, to manage them.

By people from the town, he was informed that Major Siddons, apprised of the intended attack, had drawn up his men in the main street, in the open area, between the market-house and the entrance of the street, his cavalry forming a compact body in front of the market-house, and his infantry lining the sides of the street.

On hearing this, O'Halloran made a short encouraging address to his men, which he concluded by observing that they were to fight this battle almost in view of the residence of William Orr, the most lamented martyr in these latter times, for the cause of Irish liberty, that glorious, animating cause for which they had now taken up arms. He exhorted them to fight valiantly in order to avenge his death. "Reflect," said he, "that his disconsolate widow, and bereaved children, will, this day, hear the dying, repentant cries of his destroyers, and that your shouts of victory will be to them the intelligence, that a portion at least, of their proud and relentless oppressors are humbled to the dust. Let, therefore, our word of battle be 'Remember Orr!'"

He now selected five hundred men whom he put under the direction of Samuel Orr, the brother of their favourite martyr, with injunctions to take a circuitous route towards the Shane's-castle road, and enter the town from the south-west, while the main body should, as soon as they ascertained the proximity of Orr's approach to the enemy, enter from the eastward by the road on which they were already stationed, by which means the enemy would be attacked on both sides.

As O'Halloran expected that Major Siddons would endeavour to disperse his men, as soon as they should enter the town, by a charge of cavalry; he placed in his van a phalanx, consisting of four hundred pikemen, forming a compact square of twenty men on each side. This phalanx was divided into five files, each containing four men in front, and the whole range of the twenty men in depth. The second and fourth of these files, were ordered, as soon as the expected charge should be made, to give way and permit the horsemen to follow into the spaces they should thus leave vacant, while the first, third and fifth files remaining firm, should fall upon them on all sides with their pikes.

A considerable number of musketeers were ordered to station themselves in the houses of such of the inhabitants as were friendly to their cause, and, from thence, to direct their fire upon their troops.

The four hundred pikemen, composing the phalanx, were selected both on account of their enthusiasm and their personal activity. They were supplied with the best manufactured pikes in their whole army, and each division or file was under the conduct of an officer who perfectly comprehended his duty.

A promiscuous multitude of thousands on whom no regularity could be imposed, and over whom it was impossible to exert any control, followed close to the phalanx, which insured its steadiness, while their officers took care to prevent the pressure from being so great as to derange its operations.

In front of the whole, their two pieces of cannon were placed, but it was not intended that they should take them farther than the bend of the street, which opened on the military. At this place O'Halloran wished to await the attack of the cavalry, whom he hoped his cannon would throw into some confusion, as they advanced. For this purpose, he also placed a number of men with muskets on the sides, and somewhat in advance of his phalanx, who were directed to keep their station, and not fire on the enemy until the latter should approach to the charge. They were then to retreat by the sides of the streets, and leave the phalanx to its operations.

Having made all his dispositions, and having no time to lose, as he understood the loyalists were in momentary expectation of a reinforcement from Belfast, O'Halloran on ascertaining that Samuel Orr's detachment had nearly reached its destination, rode up to the van exclaiming, "Lead on, my boys! Remember Orr!"

"Remember Orr!" was reiterated by the whole multitude, and they immediately moved forward.

On arriving at the end of the street, whence they had a full view of the enemy, they fired both their cannon and their muskets with such effect that about twenty of the dragoons, ten or twelve of the infantry, and all the men who were stationed at one of the enemy's cannon, were killed. The fire of the troops did comparatively little execution, the insurgents having chiefly withdrawn themselves behind the corner of the street. Five or six, however, were killed, and one of their cannon was dismounted!

As O'Halloran had expected, Siddons supposing their disappearance, at that moment, a mark of their intimidation, thought to decide the affair at once by a charge of his cavalry. He accordingly gave orders to that effect; on perceiving which, the insurgent musketeers speedily retreated, as they had been directed, which encouraged Siddons hastily to advance at full-gallop, calling on them as rebels to lay down their arms and disperse.

On the approach of the cavalry, the front men of the three divisions of the phalanx that were to remain firm, presented their pikes, and prevented their progress, but the other two divisions retiring as they were directed, the cavalry followed into the vacancies; and, in a few minutes, every man and horse was prostrated to the earth. A torrent of pikes which they could neither escape nor resist, rushed upon them from every direction. It was in vain that they called for quarter. Their cries were either unheard or disregarded, in the terrible tumult. The fatal war-word 'Remember Orr' alone resounded from every quarter, and deafened the voice of mercy.

Siddons, on seeing this disaster, rode back to call his infantry into action, but they were panic struck, and on the appearance of Samuel Orr's party had fled behind the wall that surrounded Lord Massareene's castle, which fronted the end of the street; and even of this refuge they would have been deprived, had it not been for the cowardice of Orr. On perceiving them flying towards the castle, past the one side of which he was entering the town with his men, he supposed that they were advancing to attack him. He, therefore, took the alarm, and putting spurs to his horse, set off on an absolute flight. His men seeing their leader fly, without staying to inquire the cause, followed his example, and dispersed in all directions, in consequence of which Siddons's infantry were enabled to effect their escape into the castle yard. Siddons seeing it vain to attempt to rally cowards, and in despair for the fate of his cavalry, galloped back to the scene of slaughter, to beg quarter for such as survived, or to die along with them.

O'Halloran, who had been unable to restrain the fury of the insurgents, or to save a single horseman, perceiving his approach, and aware of his danger, burst furiously through the crowd, calling after some men who were rushing towards Siddons, to halt and not slay him; and he reached them just in time to arrest the arm of one man who had aimed at him a deadly blow. Although broken in its force, the weapon still descended and knocked off Siddons's hat, without, however, inflicting any wound. O'Halloran ordered the man to lift the hat, and present it to Siddons, and was obeyed.

"I am your prisoner," said Siddons, and he held out the handle of his sword to O'Halloran, which was accepted. O'Halloran hastily gave him in charge to three men, who stood convenient, and returned to where the work of destruction was still going on upon the cavalry. He had scarcely done so, when some of the troops firing from behind the wall where they had taken shelter, upon Siddons's guard, brought the whole three to the ground. Siddons immediately turned his horse, and in another moment was also in shelter of the castle wall.

The carnage of the cavalry was now nearly over, and O'Halloran had succeeded in saving only five from destruction. He found afterwards, however, that Porter and M'Cracken had saved seven others, but four of them were supposed to be too severely wounded to survive.

In a few minutes his attention was drawn to another fatal incident, which was taking place near the Court-house, which stood between Lord Massareene's castle, where the infantry had taken refuge, and the scene of battle. He perceived a gentleman on horseback hastily advancing, and four men rushing to attack him with pikes. He clapped spurs to his horse to save him, but he was too far distant, and before he could reach the scene, not only was the stranger wounded in several places, but three of his assailants were shot dead, by a volley fired from the troops from behind the castle wall. O'Halloran, however, approached, screened from the fire of the troops, by the Court-house; and ascertaining that the stranger was the Earl O'Neil, whose private character he much respected, he caused him to be carried into a house, and ordered him to be well treated; and immediately despatching a messenger for surgical assistance, again joined his companions.

CHAP. IV.

But that vain victory has ruined all,
They form no longer to their leader's call;
In vain he doth whate'er a chief may do,
To check the headlong fury of that crew;
In vain their stubborn ardour he would tame,
The hand that kindles cannot quench the flame;
The weary foe alone hath turned their mood,
And shown their rashness to that erring brood.

Byron.

Although the insurgents had gained a complete victory and were in absolute possession of the town, Massareene Castle excepted, their exultation was but short lived. Indeed they had scarcely time to be sensible of its existence before they were thrown into great perplexity by the hasty arrival of some of their friends, with very discouraging intelligence. They informed them that General Nugent was rapidly advancing, and was now only a few miles distant at the head of two thousand men, and a heavy train of artillery, in order to attack them.

Various were the opinions now given concerning what measures should be adopted. Some were immediately for storming the walls behind which Siddons's infantry had taken shelter; others were for marching to meet Nugent, and attack him in the open country; while some, more timid or less zealous than the rest, hinted at the propriety of taking advantage of their recent success, by opening a negotiation with the approaching army.

Great clamour and confusion took place in expressing these different opinions. Scarcely anyone was silent; and so many spoke at once that scarcely anyone understood what another proposed. O'Halloran at length obtained a hearing among the principal officers, who, after several unavailing attempts to procure silence and attention amidst the irrepressible confusion of the multitude, separated themselves from it.

After deploring the unmanageable dispositions of their followers, "My friends," said he, "we must even with such materials, attempt by some means to stem the tide of misfortune, before we give up all for lost. We must not despair — brave men never despair in a good cause. The irregularities of these people may grieve you; the timidity of some, the fanaticism of others, and the ungovernable temper of all, may excite anxiety in your minds concerning our approaching enemy. But in the midst of anxiety, duty must be performed; by what method, reason must be consulted. The unthinking and giddy crowd, will not, cannot reason. You must, therefore, both reason and decide for them, otherwise they will become a feeble, and almost resistless prey, to their enemies. I shall give you my opinion.

"It has been proposed to negotiate, but unless you intend absolutely to abandon the cause, to assert which, by force of arms, we have been so many years preparing, and for which you have this day so gallantly fought, and obtained, by the blessing of Providence, so signal a victory, you will not listen to this proposal. By our enemies nothing under present circumstances will be expected but unconditional surrender, which would be followed by unmerciful slaughter. We have commenced, we must go on with the work — it would be ruin to go back.

"As to the proposal of attacking Massareene castle, the advancing enemy is too near, according to our information, to permit that. It is evident that their coming on us while engaged in such an attack would be attended with the most disastrous consequences.

"No rational counsel, in my opinion, has yet been offered for your consideration. The most salutary that has been offered seems to be that which advises you to march out and oppose Nugent on the field; as in so doing you might have a chance, though I think it would be but a very slight one, of overcoming so numerous and well-appointed an army as his.

"My opinion, taking all circumstances into view, is that we should immediately withdraw from the town, and return to the encampment at Donegore, where, during the evening, we may expect to be joined by large reinforcements from all parts of the country, and where from the entrenchments already thrown up, and the nature of the ground, no army can attack us but at a great disadvantage. There we may await the occurrences of favourable opportunities to harass our enemies, or if they shall have the hardihood to attack us, the chance of victory will be much on our side."

The officers agreed to the wisdom of this opinion, and having by great exertions, at length procured an audience from the multitude, earnestly pressed its adoption. But that multitude was now greatly diminished — more than one-half of its number had disappeared. Some were panic-struck at the approach of so formidable an army; some were horror-struck at the scene of carnage they had just witnessed, and could not bear the idea of seeing it repeated; while others were disgusted at the dissonance of opinion, clamour and confusion which had taken place, and anticipating that numbers would imitate the treachery of Orr's party, and desert the cause, since there was no authority or regulation by which defection could be prevented, resolved not to be the last to get rid of so troublesome and perilous an enterprise.

From these various motives, while the leaders were deliberating on what measure to adopt, several thousand had withdrawn from the insurrection standard; so that when they came to make known their decision, as before stated, they found that nearly one-half of their number had left them.

The brave phalanx, however, to whose intrepidity the victory they had gained was altogether owing, still remained. It had lost about a third of its original number. But the gallant spirits who composed it, were elevated by the excitement of their successful fighting, and by the plaudits of their companions. They now received the thanks of O'Halloran, delivered publicly in the name of the other officers, and of their country, for their good conduct, and the services they had performed.

"Had Orr's party only acted with half your heroism," said he, in concluding his address of thanks, "we should now have been in possession of Massareene castle; and, protected by its walls, we might have bade defiance to the coming enemy. As it is, we must now withdraw to Donegore, and, fortified in that position, where we shall receive large reinforcements, we can await with advantage the assault of our opponents."

A headstrong enthusiast of the name of Campbell, who had during the battle performed prodigies of valour, now stepped from the ranks, all covered as he was with blood and dust, and addressed O'Halloran.

"Why should we retreat?" he exclaimed. "We have gained a great victory. Let us wait for the enemy here. I'll warrant we shall give a good account of him. It is time enough to fly when we are beaten. Surely, Mr. O'Halloran won't turn coward, like Orr."

"Bravo! bravo!" shouted numbers of the most violent and determined. "Campbell is right! We shall fight them here!"

It was in vain that O'Halloran expostulated with them, and represented the imprudence and even madness of their determination. They could not understand his reasoning. The majority had indeed, by this time, become too intoxicated to understand it, for they had plundered the ardent spirits contained in the houses of the royalists. O'Halloran deplored their infatuation and misconduct, but he determined not to desert them.

"Perhaps," said he to Porter, "some means may yet be found to save these people. It is our duty to stand by them, and to do our best to avert their ruin."

He then told them that although he disapproved of their wishes, he would comply with them; and make an immediate stand against the enemy. "But we must choose better ground," said he. "Will you submit to my directions? Heaven may yet grant us success."

He was answered by loud cheers of approbation, and he immediately commenced making his arrangements for receiving the enemy.

At the eastern entrance of the town there was a large meadow, surrounded by a thick hedge, at one corner of which two roads met. Along one of these roads it was known that the enemy was advancing, and here O'Halloran was determined to make his stand, with the view of having the other road, which led to Donegore, open and convenient for his men, in case they should be worsted, to retreat to that rendezvous, without being scattered in a confused flight, which he knew would be the case if they should be defeated in the streets. He lined the whole range of the hedge, along the road on which he expected the attack, with musketeers, directing them to remain in shelter of the ditch, to be steady and not to expend their fire until they were sure of their object. His phalanx was not of much service, in its embodied form, in repelling an attack to be made, as he expected, with firearms; nay, that very compactness which, together with the nature of its weapons, rendered it so formidable to a charge of cavalry, or of the bayonet, would here have been a disadvantage. Instead, therefore, of arranging it as formerly, into the form of a solid square, he drew up the men who composed it, into that of a semi-circle, and stationed them a few paces behind the musketeers, with instructions, in the event of being attacked with artillery or musketry, to throw themselves flat on the grass, but, to fall immediately into their former compact square form, in case they should be attacked with the cavalry or charged with the bayonet. His few pieces of artillery, he planted at the eastern end of the field, on the left of his phalanx, and in such a situation as would permit them to be the most efficiently employed against the enemy.

The rest of his followers not being under much discipline, nor, indeed, as he plainly perceived, likely to be of much service during the conflict, he placed in various groups about the field, desiring them, while the fire of their adversaries continued, to shelter themselves as much as possible among the long meadow grass, or in the ditch that surrounded the field, but if a close charge should be made, to be prompt in assisting the phalanx to repel it.

He now, after exhorting them to firmness and bravery, reminded them that Donegore Hill was the place of rendezvous, to which, in case of a defeat, every man should be careful to direct his course. He had scarcely finished this exhortation when the eastern hill, at the distance of about a mile, began to glitter in the sun, and a forest of bayonets appeared gradually approaching. The whole hill became covered with the scarlet uniforms of the royal troops, who kept steadily advancing to the military music of 'Croppies lie down'. They halted when within a quarter of a mile from the field occupied by the insurgents. Immediately nine pieces of cannon were wheeled round, and drawn at full gallop somewhat nearer, to the top of a rising ground, and their muzzles turned to the field. Four companies of infantry were at the same time marched into an adjoining pasture field.

As yet not a shot was fired, and every voice was silent for a few minutes; even all motion seemed suspended, while the insurgents gazed, during this dreadful pause, on the terrible army that was thus brought against them, with the most intense anxiety and awe. But this pause was indeed short; for on the other road, on which no enemy was expected, a large body of both horse and foot made their appearance.

Nugent, who had reconnoitred the position of the insurgents before he appeared in view, had detached this body by a circuitous route, under the command of Colonel Lumly, to attack them on that side, by which means they would be nearly surrounded.

In a moment the cannons opened their mouths, and a destructive fire was at the same instant poured both by Lumly's troops and those which occupied the pasture field, on the unfortunate insurgents. The cannon of the latter, was also fired, but it was only once, for their cannoniers either fled or fell, while the terrified musketeers, who were concealed behind the hedge, discharged their pieces at random and fled also. The pikemen also started up to fly; for a fiery death was around them, and fast enclosing them on all sides.

As Lumly's party occupied the road by which they endeavoured to escape, O'Halloran at the head of a considerable number of pikemen, the majority of whom belonged to his heroic phalanx, made on it a rapid and resolute charge, which succeeded in throwing it into confusion, and opened the way for escape. Immediately the whole insurgent force rushed in desperation to that quarter, for unabated destruction continued to assail them from every other; and by the weight and fierceness of their attack, and the length of their pikes, overthrew all opposition.

O'Halloran individually fought with wonderful energy and success. Twice when Lumly had rallied a portion of his troops to arrest his progress, at the head of his chosen body did he break his way through. A third time Lumly attempted it, and it proved fatal to him.

"That officer must be slain or we shall not escape," exclaimed O'Halloran, who perceived the whole of Nugent's force fast approaching from behind; and as he made the exclamation, he dashed his horse forwards, and Lumly and he instantly met. Their swords were in a moment shivered to pieces, but a stump of O'Halloran's still remained, with which, at one blow, he brought his antagonist to the ground.

"To Donegore, my men!" said he. "Stop for nothing." And without minding the fallen Lumly, they rushed over him with the speed and ferocity of wild animals, presenting a terrible front of pikes, which cleared the way as they flew along. Lumly's party seeing their commander fall, did not, however, offer much more opposition, so that the way was easily kept open for their flight. Nugent now despatched his cavalry in pursuit of the fugitives, who soon scattering, fled in all directions; not, however, until numbers of them had fallen victims to the firing of the carbines of their pursuers.

As they took into the fields or into the by-roads and private avenues, the cavalry separated into small parties, in order to follow them. One party pursued some of them as far as Templepatrick, to which town, after pillaging it, they set fire, and consumed upwards of a hundred dwelling houses, besides committing many acts of violence and cruelty on the inhabitants. Night alone put an end to the havoc, destruction and horror of this disastrous day; and, at a late hour, the pursuing cavalry rejoined their companions in Antrim.

Such of the wounded of the insurgents as had fallen into the hands of the victors, were carried to the court-house, and in a summary manner tried by martial law, and sentenced to die the next morning. Between seven and eight hundred of them had been killed during the day, and between eighty and ninety were now under sentence of death.

Of the military, about one hundred and seventy had fallen in both actions. But the deaths which the royalists most lamented were those of Lord O'Neil and Colonel Lumly. The latter, on being unhorsed by O'Halloran, had received a mortal stroke with a pike from one of the insurgents, another of whom had rolled him into the ditch, by the road side, where, after the conflict was over, he was found by some of the soldiers just expiring.

Lord O'Neil suffered extremely from his wounds until the next morning, when he also expired. He had begged Nugent, almost with his last breath, to spare the lives of the deluded people, and not to permit any feelings of revenge to excite him to unnecessary severity in the execution of his duty. For the prisoners now under the sentence of death he particularly pleaded, and had their lives granted to his intercession.

CHAP. V.

Lo! comes a flag to summon their surrender. To fight or yield is now the question with them: To fight for what? — a cause they scarce approve of, And which, even if they did, they see is hopeless.
To yield unbargained, would betray too much Of cowardice, as if they feared a battle.
It would be madness too without conditions, To throw themselves into the power of those Whose power they have insulted. But negotiate! Negotiate! is the cry — get terms or fight.
Irish Soothsayer.

O'Halloran, after the discomfiture of his forces, rode in company with M'Cracken, Porter, and a few others, at full speed to Donegore, on reaching which he found that his old associates from Larne, had just arrived. A vast concourse from other parts of the country had flocked to this rendezvous; and the number was every moment increasing; so that before night came, it was supposed that the encampment contained no fewer than ten thousand men. They were not all, however, equally zealous.

The news of the defeat at Antrim, filled some of them with considerable dismay; and a great many took advantage of the night to withdraw from such a dangerous enterprise. When the morning came, the diminution of their numbers, from these desertions, was very perceptible; and seemed very generally to shake that mutual confidence in each other, which is so necessary to the success of warlike operations. Hence doubt and perplexity began to reign over the whole camp, a circumstance which did not escape the penetration of M'Claverty.

He conceived it to afford a favourable opportunity of once more attempting to dissuade them from persevering in their designs. He accordingly addressed them, promising to negotiate for them, an absolute pardon for all they had done, if they would quietly lay down their arms and disperse.

He was listened to with the more attention, even by those who were not intimidated by the preceding day's misfortunes, (and who still formed a sufficiently numerous body to enforce the adherence of the rest, if they should think proper to do so) by intelligence which had been just received of the massacre of the Protestants at Wexford, and the other atrocities committed by the insurgents of the Catholic persuasion in the South.

The nine-tenths of their number being Presbyterians, were easily excited on this subject, and without much difficulty made to believe that they had entered into a rebellion which was likely to be converted into a war of religious vengeance, like the former Irish rebellions, against the atrocities of which they had, from their infancy, been taught to feel the most inveterate abhorrence.

M'Claverty was well aware of this circumstance, and did not neglect to avail himself of it. After enlarging on the extreme improbability of final success attending their exertions — "And for what is it, my friends," said he, "that you are making these exertions, at the awful risk of your lives and of everything else dear to you? Your views, no doubt, are confined to the acquirement of some civil or political right, of which you suppose yourselves deprived, whereas, you may rely on it, that by far the greater portion of your confederacy, at present in arms throughout the kingdom, have very different views. Theirs is a religious warfare.

"They regard civil grievances as of comparatively little importance, to those religious restrictions which they conceive an heretical government has imposed upon them. Wishing for your aid, they have, until they got you, as they supposed, too far involved to retreat with safety, kept the real object of their sedition out of view. But they have now thrown off the cloak. They have put themselves under the absolute direction of their priests, who alone govern in their counsels, and command in their battles; and whose chief desire is the extirpation of that religion you profess, and the infliction of a malignant, but as they teach their fanatical followers, a holy revenge on its professors.

"In selecting their victims, you perceive that already they do not inquire, are they royalists, but are they Protestants? Lay your hands upon your hearts, and ask if your conscience will justify you in fighting with such confederates, in such a cause? Pause, I beseech you, and reflect that the moment the power and influence of Britain is expelled this country, Protestantism is also expelled. You would have neither equal numbers, nor equal ferocity with your Catholic confederates; you would, consequently, be utterly unable to prevent the establishment of Catholic supremacy and intolerance in the Island.

"Oh! my friends, withdraw from this unnatural confederacy ere it be too late. Perhaps there are some among you who think that it is already too late; who will tell you that you have even now gone too far to retrace your steps; that you have offended the constituted authorities past forgiveness; and that you have no alternative but to persevere. Do not listen to such deceitful language. You have not yet done anything, as a body, but what I am persuaded, the government will freely pardon, on condition of your returning peaceably to your allegiance. Now is your time successfully to negotiate for pardon. You are still in force, with arms in your hands, but after your defeat, and that defeat is easily foreseen, from the force which is now coming against you, you may in vain implore from the clemency, what you can now in some measure demand from the policy of the government.

"General Nugent whose victorious army will be here in a few hours, is my friend. With him, if you permit me, I will negotiate for you, and I pledge my honour, that in doing so I shall consult your interests as faithfully as if I were of your party."

The majority of the insurgents listened to this reasoning with seeming approbation, but there were a few who acted very differently. They were either Catholics, or Protestants who had already so openly signalized themselves in the rebellion that they were hopeless of pardon. These began to raise the cry of cowardice and treachery, against all who appeared wavering, which soon produced much dissention throughout the camp; and the approaching army was considerably advanced, without any resolution being formed either for battle or negotiation.

At length the royal standard was seen floating in the air, and all the glittering pomp of war perceived, at the distance of a few miles, to be approaching the hill. Contention ceased for some minutes, while every eye contemplated this imposing spectacle in profound and awe-struck silence.

M'Claverty sprung again to his feet. All eyes were directed to him. "O, my neighbours, my friends!" he exclaimed, "Negotiate now or perish! Another hour may place pardon beyond your reach."

"We will, we will negotiate," was the spontaneous cry which now burst from almost every mouth.

O'Halloran, M'Cracken, Porter, M'Cauley and Darragh, (the two latter of whom were Catholics, and the whole five either already proscribed or without expectation of pardon) at first endeavoured to check the expression of this resolution, and to inspire the multitude with more firm and courageous sentiments. But they soon found themselves obliged to yield to the torrent.

O'Halloran, indeed, now began to perceive that the cause had become desperate. No French aid had arrived to afford its adherents a rallying point, while the bigotry and cruelty of its friends in the South, cooled and disgusted those in the North, and tended more to its abandonment and ruin than the whole power of the government. He, therefore, who was still recognized as their commander, made but a faint opposition to the cry for negotiation.

M'Cracken and Porter soon also withdrew their opposition; perhaps as much from having fallen into a similar train of reflection, as from the apparent impossibility of resisting the general decision.

They were employed in drawing up proposals to be presented to General Nugent as the conditions of their surrender, when an officer from the royal army appeared advancing on horseback towards the hill, bearing a white flag. O'Halloran, M'Claverty, and one Watt, an influential man among them, who had been very strenuous in recommending negotiation, were appointed a committee to receive the messenger, and report his business to the people. They advanced some distance down the hill to meet him, carrying with them the propositions they had prepared.

M'Claverty soon recognised the flag-bearer to be an intimate friend, a Captain Hutton, whom he knew to be a man of honour and humanity.

"What!" said Hutton, as he approached M'Claverty. "I understood you were the prisoner of these people. I now perceive you to be one of their confidential agents."

"Fate has, indeed, made me their prisoner," said M'Claverty. "But humanity has at present induced me to become their agent, and they have had sufficient confidence in my honour to entrust me with the office."

"I am glad of it," returned the other, "for it augurs favourably for the termination of the business with which I am entrusted. I have been sent to summon these people to deliver up their arms, and throw themselves on His Majesty's mercy."

"Surely," said O'Halloran, "your commander does not expect an unconditional surrender from men with arms in their hands, strong in numbers, strong in position, and if urged to extremity, strong also in courage and determination. To prevent the effusion of human blood, we will disperse if the requisite terms are granted us. If they are refused, however, we can fight, and a few hours may give us the power of dictating instead of begging terms."

"I look on myself," said M'Claverty, "as a mediator in this case. To the government I am attached from principle, and to those whose prisoner I am, and who, confiding in my pledged word, have deputed me to assist in the management of this affair, I am bound by honour. To them I am also bound by gratitude for the respectful treatment I have received since I fell into their hands.

"In giving my advice, therefore, both parties may be assured that I do it with a view to their mutual advantage. I can conceive of no detriment that the government would sustain by granting an absolute pardon to these people for the delusions and errors into which they have fallen, on condition of their returning quietly to their duty; and to accept of such a pardon, I believe, they are already convinced is to consult their true interest."

"Gentlemen," said Hutton, "my powers do not extend to the granting of a pardon. I have been merely sent to demand an unconditional surrender, but whatever proposals you may please to make, I shall convey them to our commander, and return in one hour with his answer."

"Here are our proposals," replied O'Halloran, producing the written documents to the messenger. "Submit them to your general and tell him, that rather than submit to terms less favourable than these, we are resolved, in God's name, to try the issue of a battle."

The officer received the papers, and was about departing, when M'Claverty called on him to stay a moment. "Convey my earnest request to General Nugent," said he, "that he will sooth the feelings of the people as much as possible. They now see their delusion, and are desirous of reconciliation with the established authorities, not so much from fear, as from conviction of their error. The accounts from Wexford have made great impressions on them and, I believe, that they sincerely repent having joined such a confederacy. Tell him also, that I, and their other prisoners, have been treated well and that, notwithstanding their irregularity and total want of discipline, they have hitherto committed no excess repugnant to humanity."

"I shall with pleasure deliver your message," replied Hutton. "Good morning, gentlemen. I sincerely hope this affair will terminate without more bloodshed." He then spurred his horse, and hastened towards the royal army.

Nugent having perused the proposals, called his officers together to deliberate concerning them. They were to the following effect:

"That General Nugent and the principal officers under his command, shall guarantee to the army of the United Irishmen, now encamped on Donegore Hill, a full and free indemnity for all past transactions, in which indemnity, all the United officers as well as private men, and all the prisoners for matters of state, now in the jails of Carrickfergus and Downpatrick, or at the camp of Blarrismoor, or in the towns of Belfast, Lisburn, Antrim and Ballymena, shall be included; on which conditions the said army of the United Irishmen, shall immediately, without committing any further act of hostility, disband, and the individuals composing it, return to their respective homes."

"Gentlemen," said Nugent, "you will perceive that some of these demands are absolutely beyond our power to grant. We have no control over any prisoners but those we have ourselves taken and have now in custody; neither can we fly in the face of the civil authority, by guaranteeing a pardon to several individuals now known to be in the rebel camp, who are already in a state of proscription for their crimes and treasons. It is my opinion, therefore, that we cannot, in duty, listen to these terms, but on account of the favourable report given by Mr. M'Claverty, of the present dispositions of these blind-led people, as well as from humane considerations, I will, should it meet with your approbation, make another effort to induce a submission without blood-shed."

It was then agreed that Hutton should return to the insurgent camp with the following note:

"General Nugent, and the officers under his command, find some of the terms required by the insurgents on Donegore Hill, beyond their power to grant. They cannot interfere with the intentions of government respecting any prisoners, but such as they have themselves taken, and have in their immediate custody. These they are willing to discharge. There are several individuals in the insurgent army, already pointed out by the government as persons whose offences render them unworthy of pardon. Over the fate of these persons they have no control; neither do they think it their duty to include, in any promise of pardon, those mischievous men, whose delusive doctrines have seduced their fellow-subjects into the criminal and unfortunate measures they have adopted.

"From the general pardon, therefore, which they agree to guarantee to all others now assembled on Donegore Hill, who shall, within one hour after they receive this notification, deliver up their arms and return peaceably to their homes and employments, they exclude the following persons, and description of persons, viz. Henry O'Halloran, the Rev. James Porter, Henry M'Cracken, Thomas Story, Thomas Archer, and all who may have been guilty of assassination, or of wantonly burning the houses, or otherwise destroying the properties of the loyal inhabitants of the country."

CHAP. VI.

Alas, poor country!
Almost afraid to know itself! it cannot
Be called our mother, but our grave; where nothing, But who knows nothing, is seen to smile;
Where sighs, and groans, and shrieks, that rend the air, Are made, not marked; where
violent sorrow seems A modern ecstacy; the dead man's knell
Is there scarce asked for whom, and good men's lives Expire before the flowers in their caps,
Dying or e'er they sicken.
Shakespeare.

Previous to the return of Hutton with the foregoing note, containing Nugent's ultimate offer, a man on horseback, who said he had travelled all night, arrived at the insurgent camp, with the following letter for O'Halloran: Letter

June 7th, 1798.

Dear Sir,

It has fallen to my lot to communicate to you the unfortunate news of the forces we assembled this morning, being completely defeated and dispersed, after a severe conflict with a large body of the King's troops, near Ballynahinch, in which it is supposed, that we lost upwards of one thousand men.

According to previous arrangement we began about midnight to assemble in the neighbourhood of Saintfield, where we had a slight skirmish with a small body of militia stationed there, over whom we obtained the advantage, having, with only the loss of one man, killed six of theirs, and compelled the rest to retreat.

We then proceeded to Ballynahinch, and encamped on Lord Moira's demesne adjoining the town. Here our numbers increased so rapidly, that before noon, we were nearly twelve thousand strong. Colonel Munroe joined us about ten o'clock with a large body from the neighbourhood of

Lisburn and Hilsborough. About one o'clock the King's troops arrived from the camp at Blarrismoor, and halted on a hill opposite, part of the town being between us.

They soon commenced a cannonade, which we attempted to return, having three small field-pieces, but we could not manage them to much advantage, whereas their fire annoyed us extremely. Being conscious of our superiority in point of numbers, it was, therefore, agreed that we should rush over the intermediate ground, and charge them with pikes. For this purpose, we had completed the necessary arrangements, and were proceeding forward, when we were attacked with a volley of musketry from behind, by a party, which, unnoticed by us, they had detached round the hill, and which thus took us in the rear by surprise. Many of our men immediately fled, but the greater number rushed on to the intended attack.

When within thirty yards of our opponents, we received a dreadful discharge of musketry, which checked us for an instant by levelling hundreds of us to the ground. My left arm was broken on this occasion, but I was impelled along by the press of the multitude, which had resumed its motion forwards.

We soon reached our adversaries, and made on them a very effective charge, for in a few minutes they were compelled to retreat some distance from the hill, but there, facing about, they poured upon us another fire so destructive that hundreds fell to the ground, while hundreds more threw down their arms and fled.

At this important crisis, the troops behind us also repeated their fire and increased our confusion. To prevent our rallying, for though much broken, some of us would still have made a stand, their cavalry now galloped furiously amongst us and completed our defeat.

The cavalry in continuing the pursuit, committed dreadful havoc throughout the country. The greater part of Ballynahinch, the whole of Saintfield, and country houses without number, have been consigned to flames, and are now only smoking ruins.

The destruction is not yet over. From the hill on which I am concealed, we can see every moment new volumes of conflagration arising. My heart sickens at the disasters of the day. I trust in God, you have been more fortunate in your county. If not, I much fear that the cause for which we have been so long and so anxiously preparing to make this struggle, is indeed lost, and that we shall now have, each of us to await with what fortitude we can, the fate which an oppressive, cruel and highly incensed government, may think fit to award us.

The unfortunate religious jealousy that exists among the people has been one great cause of our failure. Some accounts of the misconduct of the Catholics in the South arrived here the day before yesterday, which cooled the ardour of the Presbyterians, in whom consisted our main strength. Not one in ten of that persuasion, in whom we confided, have joined us; and although, as you well know, the Catholic population of the county is not one to twenty, yet more than the half of those who took arms were of that body.

If you be yet in force, endeavour all you can, I beseech you, to prevent the poison of the Wexford news from infecting the minds of your men, otherwise all hopes of liberty for poor Ireland will indeed soon be over.

It is to put you on your guard in this matter, that I make such haste to dispatch this courier, who, as he is acquainted with the country, and has the advantage of the night to travel in, will, I hope, reach you in safety.

Munroe and several of our leaders have been captured. Death, no doubt, will be their portion. Their doom is perhaps already awarded, for our merciless pursuers will lose no time, when they seize any of us, in glutting their vengeance.

May heaven preserve you from such misfortunes as we have experienced! I am, with an aching heart,

Your friend,
M. R—Y.

When O'Halloran had communicated the contents of this letter to his fellow chiefs, "It is in vain," said he, "to contend longer. A battle here, even if we could persuade our men to risk one, would only be additional slaughter. A victory itself could scarcely retrieve the prospects with which we set out. It is our duty, therefore, for the sake of these people, to accept whatever conditions may be offered. For myself, should I be demanded as a sacrifice, I am resigned to my fate, and shall submit, I hope, without murmuring. I did not engage in this enterprise without calculating on the chance and consequences of failure, and preparing my mind, if it should be necessary, to endure the severest forms of death."

Porter and M'Cracken deliberated a few moments. They then exclaimed, "It must be so; we must yield to fate! Since we can do no more for our country, we care little for ourselves; and to whatever lot Providence has ordered for us, we shall, as becomes us, submit. But Nugent's messenger returns; let us hear the terms, and then, all resistance out of view, we can decide as to the steps we must take."

The reply of Nugent to their proposals was given to O'Halloran. He read it aloud to the people. When he had done, all remained silent in expectation of receiving his opinion; he perceived it; and spoke as follows:

"My friends, you have sufficiently proved your attachment for the cause of liberty and your country. Fate forbids that cause to prevail; and it is now become necessary for you to relinquish the pleasing hope, and yield once more to that government you have attempted to resist. These are the terms offered for your submission. You will obtain no better. From their benefits, I and some of my dearest friends are excluded. But we must give way to our destiny. I should abhor myself, if from any personal consideration, I could be withheld from giving you what I conceive to be the most salutary counsel, in your present situation.

"You ought to accept of these conditions, and surrender. I have just become acquainted with circumstances which leave you no other alternative. Our friends in the county of Down have met with a total and irretrievable overthrow. Farewell! I and my proscribed friends, will provide for our own safety, as prudence may dictate."

He immediately mounted his horse, and accompanied by Porter, M'Cracken, and the other exempted persons, galloped from the hill. The multitude, struck with admiration, for several minutes gazed after them in profound silence. M'Claverty then addressed the people. "My friends and fellow subjects," said he, "I admire the magnanimity of your late leader, and sincerely hope that he may ultimately escape the dangers that surround him. A free pardon is offered to you, will you accept it? The messenger awaits your reply."

"We will — we will accept it," was answered by a thousand voices. A man of the name of Quin now stepped forward, and said aloud to M'Claverty, "Sir, be our representative in this affair. Be it your care to prevent any infringement of these conditions."

"It shall be my care," replied M'Claverty.

The people then threw their arms on the ground, and returned every man to his own home.

Thus terminated this insurrection in the North, the only part of the kingdom, of which, from the intelligent and persevering character of the people, the government was seriously apprehensive; and thus, in a few days, was blown into air, those magnificent but impracticable schemes of social equality, and national independence, over which the fond imaginations of thousands of Irishmen had for years been brooding.

The impolicy of the Southern insurgents in betraying so early a zeal for the destruction of that religion which was by far the most prevalent among their Northern coadjutors, unquestionably contributed more to the speedy over-throw of this ill concerted conspiracy, than either the vigilance or force of the government. Indeed so much were the Northerns disgusted and alarmed at the conduct of their Southern confederates, that out of the nine counties of Ulster, which contained upwards of two hundred thousand United Irishmen, in only two had the insurrection been of any consequence; and in these two, a coolness in the cause was immediately manifested by the populace when intelligence was received of the Southern atrocities.

CHAP. VII.

Still as I haste the Tartan shouts behind,
And shrieks and sorrows load the saddening wind; In rage of heart, with ruin in his hand,
He blasts our harvests, and deforms our land; Yon citron grove, where first in fear we came,
Droops its fair honours to the conquering flame: Far fly the swains, like us, in deep despair,
And leave to ruffian hands their fleecy care.
Collins.

After leaving Donegore Hill, O'Halloran and his companions did not relax their speed until they reached Ballyclare, a town about five miles distant. Here they stopped for some refreshment, and with a view to consult on what measures they should adopt for their safety. But here they had not been many minutes, until the town was beset by a troop of horse, that had just arrived from Larne, on their way to join Nugent in his attack upon the insurgents at Donegore.

These were the men who, as the reader will remember, entered Larne the preceding day under the command of Captain Claverill, and would have set fire to the town after the insurgents left it, had they not been prevented by Small and his party. They were now informed of the encampment at Donegore being broken up, for which the valiant Captain Caverill swore he was damned sorry, as he had expected to have some good fighting with the rebel rascals that evening. "But come, my lads," said he to his dragoons, "this cursed town has been a nest for rebels. Apply your matches and burn the damned hole."

The dragoons obeyed him after having for some time galloped through the streets, uttering the most horrid imprecations against the inhabitants, who were mostly women and children, for the majority of the men had been at Donegore, and were not yet returned. In a few minutes the town was emptied of these miserable inhabitants, terror driving them in all directions, over the surrounding country.

O'Halloran and his companions had also started off. But the troopers having received some intimation concerning them, they were pursued. The fleetness of their horses, however, saved them all, except Porter, whose horse stumbled and threw him, in consequence of which he was taken.

When O'Halloran and M'Cracken had reached Ballybolly Hill, about two miles distant, perceiving that the pursuit had ceased, they slackened their pace, and turning round, perceived the town in flames.

"Ah!" said M'Cracken, "what have not these villains to answer for?"

"Regret is now useless," replied O'Halloran, "but I am afraid that we also have some of this to answer for. But our motives were good; our judgments only were in error."

"Surely," said M'Cracken "you do not repent your efforts in the cause of your country's freedom."

"I meant well for my country," replied O'Halloran, "but my efforts have only increased her chains. I wished to make her happy, and more prosperous, and I have contributed to make her more miserable and degraded!"

M'Cracken only replied with a sigh; and in this tone of mind, each absorbed in his own reflections, they rode slowly and silently until they came to a small cottage on the verge of Agnew's Hill. They stopped at the door, and a neat, cleanly looking, middle aged woman, with a child in her arms, opened it. She appeared to have been weeping, for the tears still shone in her eyes. On first seeing the gentlemen, she startled as if she apprehended some danger, but soon recognising O'Halloran, her fears vanished, and being asked if they could obtain some refreshment, she replied, "Yes, and welcome; such as I have."

They now alighted and entered. Upon a small table, near a blazing turf fire, over which a teakettle was suspended, they found a large bible, lying open, on looking into which, O'Halloran's attention was arrested by the following con-solatory passage, at the beginning of the 46th Psalm.

God is our refuge and strength, a very present help in trouble. Therefore will we not fear, though the earth be removed, and though the mountains be carried into the midst of the sea; though the waters thereof roar and be troubled; though the mountains shake with the swellings thereof.

He read the passage aloud; and turning to M'Cracken, "I am not supersti-tious," said he, "but really there is consolation here. Dependence on God is, indeed, the firmest rock on which to build hope, and the unlooked-for occur-rence of this passage, appears to me something like an assurance that heavenly power will protect us from our enemies."

"Mr. O'Halloran," replied the other, "you are surely not serious in laying such emphasis on any accidental incident? We must expect no miracles now-a-days; and I believe that the best way to preserve ourselves from our enemies is to keep out of their reach."

"I believe, however," observed O'Halloran, "that whether out of their reach or in it, we require the protecting arm of Providence to accomplish our safety. I confess that from the time that we left the camp, until this moment, I felt much dispirited. I felt as if I had no support in my distress, no refuge to fly to from the vengeance of our pursuers, but this passage has, in an instant, dispelled my fears, or rather it has restored my courage, for it has reminded me that, come what will, I have an unchangeable friend, who will not desert me in my need."

M'Cracken, astonished at the seriousness of his companion, replied, "I hope, however, that, in relying on preternatural protection, you will not neglect the usual earthly means of safety, a proper concealment from your enemies."

"I will not neglect earthly means," said O'Halloran, "for it is my duty not to neglect them, but I shall not, henceforth, be so solicitous about the result; for should my enemies find me, here," said he, placing his finger on the passage, "here is my support."

The woman now modestly observed to O'Halloran, "Ah! sir, that is, indeed, a comfortable passage. I also, just before you came, derived great consolation from it; for I have been, both yesterday and today, in great trouble, but this precious book has enabled me to support it. I have passed the time in reading the various promises which God makes to his children in affliction, and I have had my sorrows sweetened. But, gentlemen, as I find you have been at Donegore, may I ask you if there has been any blood shed? My husband left me yesterday to join the United Irishmen there?"

"At what time of the day did your husband go," inquired O'Halloran.

"In the afternoon, Sir."

"Then" said he," be comforted, for he is safe. There was blood shed at Antrim, but none at Donegore; and your husband did not depart in time to have reached Antrim before all was over. You may expect him home this very evening, for the people assembled at Donegore, have voluntarily dispersed, after having stipulated with the government for a pardon.

"O God! I thank thee, that my children are not yet fatherless!" she cried, falling on her knees. "Thou hast heard my prayer, and hast protected him. Make me thankful all the days of my life, for thou hast delivered me out of this great calamity."

She then rose with a countenance brightened with joy, but still serious. "Gentlemen," said she, "you must excuse me; for really I could not refrain for returning instant thanks to the Author of all good, for this unlooked for mercy to me and mine. But you must want refreshments. Shall I prepare you any?"

They assented.

She called aloud, "Paddy!" and a little boy of about ten years old appeared, whom she directed to lead the gentlemen's horses into the stable, and give them oats.

The gentlemen seeing the boy so small, went to assist him. When they returned they found a comfortable meal prepared for them. During the repast, Mrs. M'Kinley, with a countenance expressive of some anxiety, requested to know if the pardon they had mentioned, extended to all who had been in arms on Donegore Hill, for, said she, "You were there and yet you speak of being in danger."

"The pardon was not granted to all," replied O'Halloran, "but very few were excepted, and it was our fate to be among the unfortunate number. You may be assured, however, that your husband is included in it."

"Gentlemen," said she, "I am sorry for your situation. In this remote place, however, you are in the meantime safe; and my husband will gladly contribute all in his power to your concealment. Poor man! He left me yesterday with a sore heart, but, he said, he must go, as his oath compelled him."

Shortly after tea was finished, little Paddy came running into the house, with intelligence that he saw his father coming, and then ran off with the fleetness of an arrow to meet him. Mrs. M'Kinley hastily got up, and was speedily in her husband's arms. "Thank God! thank God!" was all she could utter for some minutes, while her husband kissed off the tears of joy that trickled down her cheeks. He now perceived O'Halloran and his companion and advancing respectfully towards them, welcomed them to his house.

"Gentlemen," said he, "you must be carefully concealed, for Claverill's dragoons are scouring the whole country. They have caught Porter; and had it not been for M'Claverty, they would have put him to death in Ballyclare, but he prevailed on them to send him to General Nugent, to be disposed of as the government may order. It was well for us all that M'Claverty came with us to Ballyclare, as they would otherwise have discredited, or at least disregarded, our having obtained pardon and many would have fallen victims to their ferocity. They had more than three-fourths of the town in flames, when he arrived, but by his exertions the remainder has been saved."

O'Halloran signified his intention, if M'Cracken would accompany him, to proceed, as soon as it should be dark, by unfrequented roads, to his own castle, in the neighbourhood of which, they might find means of concealment till an opportunity should offer of escaping to Scotland, whence they would easily obtain a conveyance to America. M'Cracken at first preferred taking the road to Slimiss mountain, where M'Cauley, Archer, and the other unpardoned insurgents had proposed to take refuge, as they believed that they might there, for a long time, elude the pursuit of the government, but the advantage of being near a sea-port, from which means might be found to escape to another country, appeared so inviting that he yielded to his friend's proposal. They accordingly set off as soon as it became dark, expecting to arrive at O'Halloran castle long before day break.

When within two miles of the castle they were surprised to find the road, at the house of a man named Howley, guarded by armed persons in military uniform, on whom they had advanced before they were aware. They turned suddenly back and endeavoured to escape at full flight, which they would both have done, had not a shot, fired at them by one of the military, wounded M'Cracken's horse. The animal immediately fell with his rider under him, who was instantly seized by three men who had followed in pursuit of them.

"Who is your companion?" demanded they.

"A gentleman," he replied, "whom I pray heaven you may never discover."

"Where were you journeying to at this unseasonable hour?" was the next question.

"To Larne," was the reply.

"We'll send you there tomorrow," said one of them; "but tonight, you must be so good as to lodge with us. Culbert and Craig," continued he, addressing two of his party who had come forward on horseback, "pursue the other runaway! They must be a couple of the damned rebels who are now flying from justice."

They obeyed him with all their speed, but O'Halloran was considerably in advance of them, and knew the country so well, that although their horses were fresh and swift, he finally escaped. However, as he was now obliged, if he continued on horseback, to keep the main road to Larne, which he wished to avoid, judging rightly that it would be the whole of the ensuing day beset with parties of military and royalists, in pursuit of their prey, he thought it best to abandon his horse, and seek safety on foot. He, therefore, turned into an avenue leading to a farm house, with the principles of whose owner he was acquainted, but not wishing to disturb the family, for fear of attracting his pursuers, he threw his saddle and bridle into a ditch and turning his horse loose betook himself for shelter to one of the out houses.

He had scarcely secreted himself when he heard the sound of his pursuers galloping rapidly past the avenue to the house. He, therefore, conceived that he was for the present safe; and endeavoured to compose himself to rest on some straw that he found on the floor. For a considerable time, the agitation of his mind, on account of M'Cracken, kept him awake, but the fatigue of his body, together with his having slept none for the two preceding nights, at length overcame him, and he fell into a slumber, from which he did not awake until he was startled by the entrance of a man in the morning.

He arose, and found that the threshing floor of a barn had been his couch. He also found that the man whose entrance had aroused him, was the owner of the place. His name was Blair; and although he had not been active among the conspirators, his sentiments and feelings were known to be on their side. He conducted O'Halloran to the dwelling house, and ordered breakfast to be prepared for him in a private room. O'Halloran recounted to him the incidents which had brought him there, and requested to know by what accident the military were stationed on the road at Howley's house.

"They are a party of the Glenarm yeomanry," said Blair; "and, I believe, it is for the purpose of making a parade of his loyalty that Howley has brought them to his house. The United Irishmen had taken him prisoner, in Glenarm, on the morning of the rising, and carried him to their camp on Belair Hill, adjoining that town. The Catholics from the northern part of the county, who disliked him on account of the officious discoveries he had made of their smuggling, by which he impoverished many of them, would have put him to death but for the opposition of their leaders.

"The yeomen of the place and a few Scotch fencibles, forming the whole military force stationed there, took refuge from the people, in Lord Antrim's Castle. No bloodshed, as far as I can learn, took place, and on hearing this morning of the defeat at Antrim, the United men thought proper, spontaneously to disperse. Howley pretending great fear of assassination, obtained from the commander of the yeomanry a guard of twelve men, who escorted him home; and these men, whom from either excess or affectation of fear, he has kept as sentinels about his house, are those you encountered."

"Then M'Cracken is, indeed, among his enemies!" said O'Halloran, with a sigh.

Towards the evening he was informed that M'Cracken had been sent forward to Carrickfergus, to be imprisoned in the county jail. Blair had gone himself to O'Halloran Castle to inform Mrs. Brown and Ellen of the place of his concealment.

In the evening, therefore, his sister visited him, the distance being little more than two miles. She told him that Ellen was in a state of dreadful anxiety for his safety; and that it was with great persuasion she was prevented from accompanying her to see him, being prevailed on to stay behind only from the consideration that her visit might excite suspicion, and lead to a discovery of his retreat.

"The Recluse has been our only comforter," continued Mrs. Brown. "He is a worthy, and a wise man and has visited us frequently since you left us. When we proposed the Point Rock as the place of your concealment, 'No,' said he, 'Sir Geoffrey is acquainted with it, and it will unquestionably be searched before many days.' He then mentioned that he had an apartment in his subterraneous dwelling, in which he thinks you might be comfortably and safely concealed until a vessel can be provided to convey you to Scotland."

"That meets my own views exactly," said O'Halloran. "In this country I never can be safe and breathe the air in freedom. To Scotland I shall go, and thence, if the government still pursues me, I can find a ready passage to America."

As the vicinity of Howley, who with his twelve yeomen had become very active in hunting after the proscribed rebels, was considered peculiarly dangerous, with Blair's assistance, O'Halloran was that very night conveyed in safety to the Recluse's dwelling. His astonishment at the accommodations it afforded and the furniture it contained, were strongly expressed, but the Recluse soon explained the matter.

"It is now no time," said he, "to be mysterious or reserved with you. I am not the poor destitute Sanders you have hitherto supposed me to be. I am your son-in-law, Francis Hamilton. I make the explanation now that you may know how much I am interested in your safety, and to satisfy you that, should your affairs take the worst possible turn, she, for whom you have hitherto displayed the tenderness and solicitude of a father, will not want a protector. It is true, I cannot as yet publicly acknowledge her as my daughter. The vengeance of the disappointed Sir Geoffrey, armed with the power of those laws I was so unfortunate as to offend, would be let loose without mercy upon me. But I can reside near her. I can watch over her, and render her all the effectual advice and assistance, that I could, if I enjoyed the privileges of an unoffending subject."

At this moment Ellen entered. "Oh! my grandfather!" she exclaimed, as she rushed into his arms. "God be praised, you are safe!"

"Yes, my child, I am yet safe," he replied, "but how long I shall be so, God only knows. I have no doubt that I have much persecution to suffer; for my enemies are inveterate and will not be at rest until they effect my destruction. But, my daughter, whatever may now be my lot, I can bear it with resignation, since I shall not leave you destitute of parental protection. Your father has revealed himself to me; and I feel now that death has lost its sharpest sting.

The hand of fate cannot now be so grievous, fall upon me in what manner it may. Very different are now my feelings and views respecting death from what they were when I left Donegore Hill. Then, I could have braved that king of terrors as a soldier; now I can submit to his summons as a Christian, who considers it as an invitation to a better country." He then strained her to his bosom, and kissing her with parental affection, "May the God of Heaven bless thee," he added, "and never leave thee destitute of a friend as sincerely solicitous for thy welfare as thy grandfather!"

CHAP. VIII.

With speed the furious troopers come, In hopes to catch our chief at home, but his more kindly stars prevail; — Hence they in dreadful wrath assail;
Doors, windows, closets, ceilings, walls; And many a stately chimney falls.
But as for plunder there is not An article that's worth a groat: —
For which their raging leader frets, And wreaks his vengeance on the cats.
Major Trip.

Ellen left her grandfather with her mind much relieved of its anxiety, but still labouring under the oppression of foreboding fears. The Recluse accompanied her to the castle. As it was a fine moonlight night, and as O'Halloran had retired to rest, he indulged himself, on his return to the glen, in a walk along the beach, to contemplate the great scenery of nature, and lose in the sublime feeling of its immensity and magnificence, the sense of all his earthly cares and sorrows.

There was a perfect stillness in the air; not a leaf moved in the groves, nor a wave swelled on the sleeping waters. He looked to heaven, and beheld the vast extent of that space through which the moon seemed scarcely to move; he looked on that boundless expanse of ocean which commenced at his feet, and the greatness of Creation's Architect rushed forcibly upon his mind; and he could not help exclaiming in the words of inspiration, "Ah! what is man, that thou shouldst think of him? Or the son of man, that thou shouldst regard him?" and applying the thought to his own situation and feelings, he continued:

"What am I, or my friends? what are their sufferings or mine, that we should repine at them?

An insect is trodden to death; it is of no consequence. Man also dies; of what importance is it?

Short, indeed, are the insect's joys and sorrows; and of what duration are those of men, in the eyes of immortal beings to whom a thousand years are but a day? But man is also immortal; and the time will come when he shall wonder that he considered the pains or pleasures of this transitory existence worth a sigh of sorrow or a throb of exultation."

He was here interrupted by the appearance of a tall figure, coming along the beach, towards him. He looked at it for a moment with some surprise; and then proceeded to meet it, although, with all his philosophy, he was somewhat disconcerted; for it was a late hour, and he could not conceive why any single human being should be traversing there, at such a time. He stopped, but the figure continued to approach, although slowly. He now placed his back against a rock, the better to defend himself against the attack of some nocturnal marauder, or, if the object were really preternatural, to support himself during the interview which it evidently sought with him. At last it approached near enough to speak; and he at once recognised the voice and person of Peg Dornan.

"I hae been watching for you" said she, "in the glen for mair than half an hoor. I'm just come wi' a' the speed my legs could carry me frae Larne to tell you, gin you ken if Mr. O'Halloran be here, or near han' this place, ye maun gar him get aff before the mornin', for Claverill's dragoons, wi' Sir Geoffrey at their head, will be here, an' they will herry up every pit and cave, an' hole an' neuk, to come at him; an' mair than that, Ellen maun also be ta'en oot o' the way, for Sir Geoffrey swears that he'll hae her noo, in spite o' a' the crappies in the country."

"How did you obtain this intelligence?" inquired the Recluse.

"Why, sir, I went yesterday to the toon for news o' the folk that had come hame frae Donegore. Ye ken my sin Jock was there.

"I was smoking a blast, an' talking wi' him, quite blithe to see him, an' a' the lave hame again safe an' pardoned. Weel, thinks I, they're no' sic ill bodies, thae government folk, after a', gin yin tak's the richt way o' them. When, 'what's that? mither,' quoth Jock; an' we baith ran to the door, an' saw the dragoons galloping doon the street wi' their drawn swords in their hands, till the very fire flew oot o' the pavement. They went to the schoolmaster's hoose, but he had cannily gi'en then the slip. Howsomever they set to wark, hacking an' hewin', an in a crack wrecked his hoose, an' ruined a' his guid plenishin', an' books, an' 'mathical instruments.

"Then, in less time than you could say Jack Robinson, they galloped to baith the ministers, an' took them an' thirteen or fourteen ithers prisoners. They had na' gane to the hill; so you see the hill folk, wha had the maist spirit, hae come the best aff. Nae doobt the prisoners will be a' hanged, or shot, whilk is amaist as bad."

"But tell me, Peg," said the Recluse, "what you heard concerning O'Halloran?"

"Why, that's what I'm comin' to," she replied. "The dragoons cam' to the barracks wi' their prisoners; an' I followed doon to see them, an' I sune observed Claverill, an' Howley, an' Sir Geoffrey, talking together in a corner o' the yard. Thinks I, they're hatching some mischief, but deel be in my lugs, gin a dinna find it oot, an' gie warnin' o't.

"I cannily slipt ahint a door near whare they were standin', an' heard every word they said, for I was na' three feet frae them. They were plotting to catch Mr. O'Halloran in his castle the morn; or gin he should na be found there, to rummage the hale neighbourhood till they gat him.

"Sir Geoffrey tauld them that gin he were within five miles of the place he could ferret him oot, for there's no' a creek or cranny about the castle, where a cat could hide, but he said he was acquainted wi' — nor is there a den or cave in the neighbourhood but either Berwick or he could lead to it. 'There's yin,' said he, 'where the scoundrel kept me a prisoner twa or three weeks, which we maun search thoroughly; and if he is no' found there, we maun ransack, to its foundation, the cell o' an auld hypocritical beggar, wha lives like a hermit. But the girl, captain, we maun hae her secured; and you know whenever you want a magistrate to help you oot o' a scrape, I am at your command.'"

"May Heaven disappoint their wickedness," said the Recluse. "But, Peg, we have no time to lose. I must go immediately to acquaint O'Halloran with his danger. In the meantime, tell Jemmy Hunter to be at my cell in half an hour, but you need not mention for what purpose, for there are more ears in the world than we think of when we are telling secrets."

Peg proceeded to obey his directions, which she did very discreetly.

"What want you? Peg," demanded Jemmy, after she had bawled several times through the window to him to arise. "Auld Sanders wants you fast," she replied; "he's in a pinch, an' ye maun help him."

Jemmy required no more solicitation, and in a short time, he was at the cavern. The Recluse soon informed him of O'Halloran's danger, and required that he should assist in getting him off without delay.

With his usual alacrity, Jemmy consented; observing, "You maunna tak' him farther frae the coast, for there are parties o' yeomen parading aboot and searching the hale country."

"Hasten then to the gully," said the Recluse, "where the pleasure boat lies, and have it ready. O'Halloran and I shall follow you in a few minutes."

While Peg had been gone for Hunter, O'Halloran and the Recluse aware of the danger of removing farther into the interior, on account of the numerous scouting parties of military with which it was overrun, concerted the plan of retiring to Island Magee, the inhabitants of which were well disposed to the insurgent cause. To reach this island, or more properly, peninsula, they had only about three miles to sail across the bay which forms the entrance of Larne harbour, a task which would require them no long time to accomplish. O'Halloran was landed without accident at Brown's Bay on the peninsula, and was kindly received by a warm friend of the name of Barry, who immediately assigned a private apartment for his use. In less than two hours from their setting out, the Recluse and Hunter returned, and having, with Peg's assistance, removed out of the cavern whatever could excite suspicion of its inhabitant being anything else than he seemed, to the beach, the whole was there safely buried in the sand.

How to dispose of Ellen was the next consideration.

As the leader of the dragoons could have no legal, or in any respect, justifiable plea for seizing her, all that was thought necessary for her protection, was to convey her and her aunt to the house of a Mr. Wilson, a neighbouring gentleman of an honourable and humane character, attached to the government, but who had not interfered with the political transactions of the times. This gentleman received them with great kindness, and when informed of the threatened depredation on the castle, he was shocked at its wantonness and barbarity, and ordered his servants to assist those of O'Halloran in removing to his house all the furniture and other articles of value they should have time to bring away.

"De'il a hait they'll get noo," said Jemmy Hunter, who, in company with a number of his neighbours, had also assisted in the transportation of O'Halloran's goods to a place of safety, as he finished loading the last cart. "De'il a hait they'll get noo, but the stane wa's, gin they should rage their sauls oot; an' they may owreset them if they please, though it would be a pity too to see the douce auld biggin battered to the yearth."

The Recluse had also taken care to have the horses, cattle, and almost every valuable kind of stock removed from the demesne, rightly judging that between the affected zeal of Howley, the inveterate revenge of Sir Geoffrey, and the wanton brutality of Claverill, nothing belonging to O'Halloran, on which it would be worthwhile to exhibit resentment, would escape destruction or pillage.

At length, about nine o'clock in the morning, the glittering armour of the cavalry was seen by many an anxious spectator, glancing in the sun, as the troops gained the summit of a rising ground about a mile and a half distant. The cavalry then with a quickened pace rode down the descending road, until they again disappeared. In a few minutes they ascended the last hill which obstructed their view of the castle; then continuing on at full speed, they halted not until they arrived at its gate.

"Let two men guard every out-let," said Claverill.

This being done, the whole troop, to the number of forty, occupied the yard. Not a sound but such as was made by themselves had they yet heard.

"Why, all is as quiet here as in a desert," said Claverill. "I believe, in my soul, that the people within, care no more about our visit, than if we were a drove of sheep. Sergeant Duff! Advance with twelve men, force your entrance, and seize the rebel if he is to be found in the inside of these walls."

A thick massive door was thrown open by Duff's men without resistance; and they proceeded with drawn sabres through a large square hall, from whence they ascended a long flight of stone stairs, which winded to the top of the castle, interrupted only by a landing place at each floor. At the first landing place, they divided, part entering a long passage communicating on each side with a range of apartments, while the remainder continued their ascent. But everywhere all was silence, emptiness, and desolation. At the suggestion of Sir Geoffrey, another party of six men was sent beneath to explore the cellars, while, with Berwick, and several others of his own servants, the knight followed the ascending party for the purpose of seizing and carrying off Ellen.

In vain did he penetrate into every chamber and closet. No animated thing belonging to the castle was perceived by any of them, until the first ascending party had reached the garret, when two cats leaped from under an old bench, that had not been thought worth removing. One of them running across the steps of a dragoon, he stumbled, and fell with a great shock, and a greater oath; while the cat whose leg he had broken, gave at the same time a tremendous squall, which alarmed Howley, who was advancing behind, and who conceiving the noise to be occasioned by some persons making resistance, shouted, "Damn the rebels! Kill every soul of them!"

Immediately a dragoon with one stroke cut off the cat's head, roaring out at the same time: "By G—d! sir, the other has escaped!"

Claverill at this moment coming to the top of the stairs, and labouring under the same mistake as Howley, who had kept back from fear, cried out, "You damn'd villain, you must find him then."

"By the Lord," exclaimed one of the dragoons, "he has jumped out of the window, and is now, I suppose, fast sticking on the top of the roof."

"Run down, Andrews," cried the Captain, who was convinced that none but O'Halloran himself could have taken such a desperate step, "run to the outside, and order him down, or blow his brains out. I'll give a guinea for his head."

"Yes, your honour," said Andrews, "I'll fix him."

Down he ran, and seeing the poor cat perched on one corner of the roof, took so good an aim that he sent a bullet through its body. It instantly rolled down to the no small diversion of his barbarous companions.

"That shot is worth a guinea," said Andrews, and with his sabre severing the head from the body, he hastened in to claim his reward.

By this time Claverill was apprised of his mistake; and he felt horribly chagrined, when, as the cat's head was presented to him, and the promised guinea demanded, the whole party burst into an incontrollable fit of laughter.

"Damned villains!" cried he, "Whom do you laugh at? But it was your confounded stupidity, Howley, in mistaking cats for rebels."

"My guinea, your honour!" said Andrews, putting his hand to his cap.

"Begone, scoundrel!" cried Claverill, "No more impertinence here with your damned cats."

The story may be here interrupted for a moment, to state that while Claverill remained in that part of the country, he was known by no other name than that of the 'Cat's Head' and to this day, it continues proverbial in the neighbourhood, to say of a man who makes a ridiculous mistake, or a blundering bargain, that, 'He has given a guinea for a cat's head.'

Irritated by this incident, and full of impatience at not having met with his prey, Claverill ordered the floors to be torn up, and the ceilings, petitions and wainscottings to be demolished, lest peradventure they might conceal a rebel. This work of destruction was vigorously commenced, and forty men boiling with resentment, because they were disappointed in their high flown expectations of rich plunder, soon completed it. Having satisfied themselves that there was no human being secreted in the castle, they proceeded to the out houses.

"If there be any persons in these," said Claverill, "we shall make speedy work of them; the flames shall drive them out."

In a few minutes the whole range of the stables, cow-houses, barns, coach-houses, &c. were in one broad sheet of conflagration, to the great horror and consternation of hundreds of spectators, who from a distance beheld the scene.

"Not a man, woman, or child," said Howley, to Sergeant Duff, "is to be found on these premises."

"No, by Heavens!" replied Duff, "And what is worse, there is not so much as an old trencher to be plundered."

Having left this stately building, and all its offices, a complete wreck, the magnanimous party proceeded, under the guidance of Sir Geoffrey, to the Point cave, the scene of his late imprisonment. As, however, he was not acquainted with the secret of its entrance, a circumstance to which he had not before adverted, he went repeatedly round and over the rock, examining it in all directions, but to no purpose.

"What," exclaimed Claverill, losing all patience, "am I to be fooled here also? What a wise set of companions I have got? One mistakes cats for rebels; and another solid rocks for prisons. Damn such stupidity!"

Sir Geoffrey insisted that the rock before them was hollow, and contained two or three apartments, appealing to Berwick as corroborative testimony.

"Confound his testimony," cried Claverill. "Have you not told me already that he will swear whatever you bid him."

Berwick, whose confinement in the rock had not been so rigid as his master's, had, once or twice, during its continuance, been permitted to walk, for exercise, along the beach, in company with a sentinel, and therefore had some faint knowledge of the machinery by which the entrance was opened and shut. He knew that the end of some rope or chain must be pulled on the outside, but where to find it he could not at once discover. At last he recollected that the sentinel always ascended to a particular prominence in the rock, previous to opening it, when they were to enter. He accordingly soon discovered the ring, and the party obtained admittance.

Here they found some books, a large file of newspapers, and a great many of the official papers of the United Irishmen, which they eagerly seized as a prize to be forwarded to the government.

"We have at last discovered the rebels' den," said Claverill, "but the beasts are flown."

"We may yet find some of them, not far distant," replied Sir Geoffrey. "They were afraid, I suppose, that as I knew of this place, I should lead you to it, and have therefore avoided it. But Berwick is acquainted with another cavity in the neighbourhood, which they may imagine to be a less suspicious refuge."

"Lead on then," said Claverill, "for there is nothing more to be got here."

The squadron now proceeded to the Recluse's cell, a knowledge of which Berwick had acquired, when skulking in the neighbourhood, for an opportunity to carry off Ellen. There was no obstruction to their entrance, for the Recluse himself conducted them in, in order, that whatever suspicion they might have of his being accessary to the concealment of O'Halloran, might be removed.

"My old buck!" said Claverill, "have you any rebels within?"

"No, Sir; I never approved of rebellion."

"So far you were right, old hypocrite! But we cannot take your word."

"Enter then, and be satisfied, although, I believe, that to utter a falsehood would be as grievous to me in these rags as if I wore epaulets."

"You are a saucy dog," said the captain; "but lead us in, and be thankful that we do not blanket your old bones."

The old man led them through his cell, and without reserve showed them everything it contained. "All these are but little worth," said he, "but an old man like me requires little."

"None of your preaching!" cried Claverill, "we shall search and begone."

They then raised the flooring, and drove their sabres into the roof and sides of the cave to ascertain whether there was a vacuity in which any person might be secreted. At length, finding that it was all vain labour, they withdrew; Claverill exclaiming, "Come along, boys, out of this damned hole. The five hundred pounds set on the old rebel's head will not, I perceive, be found here."

The party started away at full speed, their commander grumbling that he was both hungry and thirsty, not having obtained so much as a glass of whiskey on this unprofitable expedition.

CHAP. IX.

But while these riotous troops were cursing their ill luck, in not meeting with the proscribed chief, that unfortunate man was already in the hands of his enemies.

We have mentioned his removal to the house of one Barry, in Island Magee, where his friends supposed that he was perfectly secure. But fate had ordered it otherwise, although neither the instrumentality nor the wishes of his entertainer, were to blame in the affair.

As the inhabitants of the Island Magee had been deeply implicated in the rebellion, and as it was expected that many of the proscribed insurgents would seek concealment among them, for the convenience of getting off to another country, the commander of the garrison at Carrickfergus had sent a company of infantry to be quartered on them, for the purpose of detecting any such fugitives. As this company had only arrived the day previous to O'Halloran's taking refuge on the Island, its presence there was unknown both to him and his friends.

From an expression of Claverill on leaving the Recluse's cell, the reader will have gathered, that government had offered a reward of five hundred pounds for his apprehension. This sum was to be paid to his captors; and to the person who should give such information as would lead to his capture, whether dead or alive, an equal reward was promised. This was enough to excite the cupidity of a certain tide-waiter, named Conly, a young fellow, who was on a nocturnal visit of courtship to one of Barry's maid servants, and was concealed in her chamber, at the very time O'Halloran arrived. The apartment allotted to him adjoined this chamber.

Through a chink in the partition the gallant discovered who this unseasonable visitor was. From that moment avarice predominated over love in his bosom, and he resolved to lose no time in earning the five hundred pounds. He accordingly the next morning, gave his information to the commander of the troops on the Island, in consequence of which Barry's house was soon surrounded by about fifty soldiers.

O'Halloran was demanded. He was denied to be present. But the doors were soon burst open, and the soldiers, conducted by the informer, entered, without stopping, the very room in which the object of their search was secreted. With great delicacy Captain Dougal, their officer, exonerated Barry from the infamy of having betrayed him; and declared explicitly from whom he had received the information. O'Halloran was conveyed on horseback to the county jail, in company with the informer, for that wretch knew that unless he were so protected, his life would be sacrificed to the vengeance of the defeated party.

When intelligence of O'Halloran's capture reached Larne, the disappointed Claverill was about setting off with the prisoners he had there seized, being seventeen in number, for Carrickfergus. On reaching the village of Ballycarry, Sir Geoffrey, who accompanied him, perceiving a lad of fourteen years of age, named Nelson, who has already been introduced into this work, and immediately remembering the injury he had done the lad's family, and their consequent antipathy to him, and also recalling to mind the attempt to assassinate him, in which he considered Nelson to have been concerned, although it was the lad's premature exclamation which gave him the alarm by which he avoided his fate, he determined on revenge.

"Seize you young fellow," said he to Claverill, "he lately attempted to murder me, and I have besides sufficient proof against him for being an active promoter of the rebellion."

Orders were accordingly given, and Nelson was seized and bound, and conveyed with the other captives to prison.

It was towards the evening, when the Recluse heard of O'Halloran's misfortune. He felt the stroke severely, but he was not one of those whom grief deprives of energy. Now was the time for serviceable action; and he would not waste it in useless lamentation. He immediately sat down and wrote as follows to Edward Barrymore:

The crisis is at last arrived. The long anticipated calamity, to secure your co-operation in preventing which, from falling too heavily on us, I was first induced to solicit your confidence and friendship.

230

*O'Halloran has this day been imprisoned for treasonable offences,
alas! Too notorious to be difficult of proof. His sentence is already
certain. A court martial at Carrickfergus will, perhaps, in a few days,
pronounce it. No time is to be lost in exerting your influence to save him,
and should you be successful in your application for mercy, equal
expedition is requisite in making the result known, for much time, we may
be assured, will not intervene between the pronouncing of the sentence
and its execution.*

*I send this, both for the sake of speed and certainty, with an
extraordinary but faithful courier, whose zeal will outrun the post, and
whose profession will obviate the interference of suspicion to occasion
obstruction or delay.*

*I am too much agitated to give you particulars, or to make comments,
even if time permitted. I know not whether Ellen has yet received
information of the disaster. I dread the effect it will have on her, and must
hasten to her support.*

The courier being despatched with the necessary instructions, the Recluse hastened to Mr. Wilson's. The family had heard a report of O'Halloran's capture,
but not being certain of its truth, they had not communicated it to Ellen or
Mrs. Brown.

The Recluse, whose real character was unknown to Mr. Wilson, entered in
his hermit's habit. Ellen had seen him coming round the house, and ran to
meet him. She led him into a chamber.

"Have you yet heard from my grandfather?" she inquired, at the same time
ejaculating, "What a providential escape he has had!"

"My child," he replied, "I have heard from him, and I fear he is not yet
secure from his enemies, but I have hopes that even if he were in their power
he might be saved. He has many influential friends."

"If he were in their power" said she, "I should have no hope. He has been
too conspicuously active against them. They thirst for his blood, and will not
be satisfied without it."

"Child," he returned, "it is your duty not to distrust Providence. Even if
the worst should take place, it is the will of him who disposes of all events,
and we should submit without complaining."

"I trust I should submit even to his death without complaining," she replied, "but I should not do it without feeling."

"Well then," my child, "be resolute and resigned, for I fear that he is in danger. The place of his concealment has been discovered."

"Tell me, tell me all," she exclaimed, the truth flashing on her mind, more from his manner than his words. "Is he in their hands?"

"Not in the hands of his worst enemies, thank God. No, Sir Geoffrey nor Claverill has captured him. Their malignant rancour and cruelty might have made short work of it."

"But he is taken, tell me plainly — he is taken?" cried Ellen, interrupting her father and catching him by the hand.

He paused to make a reply.

"Ah! It is over, then," she exclaimed; and bursting into tears, she gave vent to the fullness of her grief without uttering a word for some minutes. She then lifted her swimming eyes towards Heaven, and spoke, "Alas! They will drag him to a violent death! Oh! God! support him in that last trial!"

"Compose yourself my child," said her father, "if you would not inflict infinitely more agony on my heart, than it at present bears!"

"I will try to be composed," she answered. "It is God's will, and I must submit. But where have they taken him? I shall go to him; I will soothe, I will comfort him. Ah! greatly now will he need a comforter; nor will I leave him, when doomed to die, until his soul be no longer an inhabitant of earth. Ah! His poor sister! What will become of her? He was her stay, and her pride. I will now see her and let her know her misfortune."

"It is right," said the Recluse, "that she should know it. But remain here; I will bring her to you. You will support each other."

It now occurred to the Recluse that Mrs. Brown was as yet ignorant of his relationship to Ellen, and that she would now require a friend to look up to for support in her affliction, over whom there should be no mystery, and in whom she could without reserve repose confidence. He therefore authorized his daughter to embrace the first opportunity that should offer of revealing his secret to her aunt, well knowing that it would be safe in her keeping. He then communicated to the old lady her niece's wish to see her. She followed him into her presence.

On seeing Ellen in tears, "Alas! I perceive there is bad news," said she.

"Your resolution, my dear aunt!" replied Ellen, "is stronger than mine; and I hope you will bear with more Christian calmness, the misfortunes of a brother, than I can of such a parent."

"What then, is my brother no more?" she exclaimed.

"He is still alive," said Ellen, "and, perhaps, his cause may not be so hopeless as we imagine. But he is a prisoner in the power of his enemies; and, alas! There is much to dread."

"This is, indeed, a heavy stroke," said Mrs. Brown, bursting into tears, "but I have been long preparing for it; and am not taken by surprise. Oh, my child!" Here she clasped Ellen round the neck. "This indeed requires fortitude to bear. But dry up your tears. God will not desert us under this stroke. He will not leave us destitute! Oh my brother! He was indeed a kind brother, but I knew we must separate sometime. The Almighty alone regulates the time, and the manner of separation. It is our part to submit; we may grieve, but we must not repine."

Mrs. Wilson, who had received a confirmation of the report, now came to condole with her guests, and the Recluse took his leave. During the evening, Ellen had an opportunity of communicating his secret to her aunt.

"I rejoice," said the latter, "that your father lives, but it adds to my anxiety to know that he lives in a land of danger."

"But," returned Ellen, startled at the idea, "he is safe, I hope, in his concealment."

"I hope so, child," said her aunt, "but we must speak on this subject with caution, as there are too many who would be tempted by the reward offered for his apprehension, to betray him."

Ellen's fears now took the alarm. She put her finger to her lips in token of silence; and felt as if she feared that her very thoughts would expose her father to danger.

CHAP. X.

Accompanied by Mr. Wilson, Jemmy Hunter and two servants, Ellen and her aunt proceeded the next morning to visit O'Halloran.

When they reached Carrickfergus, they were shocked at the multitude of prisoners with which it was crowded, the number of whom was every hour augmenting. The county jail was filled almost to suffocation, and it had become necessary for the military commanders, whose will now superseded all law, to appropriate not only the jail belonging to the town of Carrickfergus, which is a county in itself, but also to convert the fortress into a prison.

O'Halloran was confined in the county of Antrim jail, in an apartment about twelve feet square, in which he had for companions in captivity, five of the prisoners from Larne, two of whom were Presbyterian clergymen, and young Nelson.

On the application of Mr. Wilson to the commander of the garrison, O'Halloran's friends procured an order for admission into his apartment during certain hours in the day, although such an indulgence was generally denied to the friends of the prisoners, on account of their being so very numerous.

Ellen, who had never before been within the walls of a jail, was much shocked at the mixture of corruption, wretchedness, and wickedness which she now witnessed. She was accompanied only by her aunt and Mr. Wilson, Hunter and the servant not being included in their order for admission.

On passing the outer gate, they found the yard into which it led, filled with soldiers, whose profane oaths and coarse jests, uttered with indelicate broadness, together with their familiar and impertinent looks, so intimidated Ellen, that had she not been supported by Mr. Wilson, she would have sunk under the impression, before she could have reached the flight of stone stairs which led to the principal door of the prison. Here they were shown into a long narrow gallery, at the further end of which, on the left side, was the room which contained O'Halloran and his fellow prisoners.

The room contained no other furniture than one bed, one small table, and a few chairs, all of the most indifferent quality. O'Halloran and the two clergymen sat on the bed, and the other prisoners on chairs. They were all pinioned.

As soon as Ellen perceived her grandfather, she rushed forward, and falling on his neck, without speaking a word, burst into tears. His sister at the same time caught one of his hands, and ejaculating, "Oh my brother!" wept also.

He entreated them to be resigned, as he assured them he was, to whatever fate was in reserve for him. "For my sake," said he, "endeavour to be courageous on this occasion; for I know of nothing that will tend so much to shake my fortitude as witnessing your distress."

"With the help of God," replied his sister, "we will be resigned. But, oh, Henry! this a terrible blow — too terrible for the infirmity of our nature to bear, without grief, heart-rending grief."

At this moment, Claverill and Sir Geoffrey entered the room. When Ellen and her friends crossed the jail yard, Sir Geoffrey, who was conversing with Claverill and some other officers at a small distance from the gate, had observed them, and although he knew that the publicity of the place and the company that attended her, rendered it impossible for him to attempt any outrage on her person, he could not resist the desire he felt to follow her. An opportunity to be again in her presence, although it should be as an avowed enemy, was to him too great a luxury to be neglected.

He, therefore, took Claverill aside; and desired him to accompany him into jail, and he would there shew him the only woman he ever considered a perfect beauty. "And you know," said he, "that I ought to be a judge of this matter, for I have been a pretty general admirer of the sex."

"This is the lady, I suppose," replied Claverill, "whom you expected to capture at the old castle yesterday, but, by Jupiter, she had better fortune; and I am glad of it, although her granddad is a rebel. But come along; I must see this beauty of the North. Yet, hark ye! You may blackguard and threaten the other sex as you please, but to ladies, especially handsome ones, he is unworthy of wearing breeches, who would give an insult, and of wearing a sword, damn me! Who would tamely see one given." Here he strutted big, and attempted to look very fierce.

It must not be supposed, that this ruffian officer spoke these sentiments from any generous feeling towards the sex, or that he felt the least spark of that manly courage, the appearance of which he assumed; for in real danger, his conduct disgraced the King's livery; he was a mere poltroon. But like most other cowards, he was a perpetual and arrogant boaster wherever he had nothing to fear. He had, besides, more penetration than Sir Geoffrey; and knew that the surest mode of preserving that ascendancy which he had acquired over the redoubted knight, was to keep him in awe, by making him believe that he had to deal with a man of a very irritable and daring temper. He, therefore, frequently affected to be in a violent passion with his companion, when he only wished to terrify him into his purposes, or to perplex him for his diversion. He knew that Sir Geoffrey would not dare to resent this conduct; for, besides his effeminacy and natural cowardice, he held him in complete check by being the confident of many of his villanies, and by threatening, if ever he offended him, to expose them to the world.

Sir Geoffrey was particularly afraid that in some angry humour, he would disclose the offer he had made him, when soliciting his assistance to seize Ellen, to prostitute his authority as a magistrate to his views, and to procure the testimony of Berwick and Rogers in support of any charge he might wish to substantiate against any of his enemies.

On the other hand, Sir Geoffrey felt great mortification, and sometimes even displayed considerable impatience, under the domineering control of his military confederate, but he was destitute of sufficient energy to break the shackles which bound him to submission. He, therefore, viewed Claverill as a hateful tormentor, with whose caprices and humours necessity at present obliged him to comply. Thus, as is uniformly the case with vicious friends, Claverill utterly despised his friend Sir Geoffrey, while Sir Geoffrey was in perpetual terror of his friend Claverill.

On entering the room in which O'Halloran was confined, they found Ellen still weeping on his shoulder; and Mrs. Brown holding his right hand, in all the agony of affectionate distress.

"'Fore Gad, Sir," cried Claverill, addressing the prisoner, "I see you have got an addition to your company, and a damned agreeable one too. But I think, my old Donegore general, you would be better employed in psalm-singing, or in prayer-making, than in fondling this pretty girl, now when you are on the brink of hell; for you have a damnable account of rebellious sins to answer for when you get there."

"I am bound," said O'Halloran, looking contemptuously on him, "otherwise, captive as I am, you dared not insult me or my grandchild, in so wanton a manner."

"Hey day! You would still be a hero, I perceive," returned Claverill. "I like to see so much metal in your gizzard, although, my old cock, we'll try to get it out of you in a few days by breaking your neck. Nugent, after he has hanged your cropped-eared comrades in Belfast, will be here, the day after tomorrow, and then we'll make short work of you. As to you," turning to the Clergymen, "my pious parsons, you should exhort this old rebel to restrain his temper, for his soul's sake."

One of the clergymen, who was a man of spirit, replied, "Sir, over misfortune you may play the coward's part of triumphing, when you can do it with impunity. But do you suppose your general, of whom you have just spoken so insolently, will tolerate your unmanly conduct? Will he not, when we inform him of it, make you repent your having—"

"By Heavens!" exclaimed Claverill, interrupting him. "I'd have you repent this audacity among your other crimes, as soon as possible. So to your psalm-singing, while you have breath, or the halter will soon choke your music. Come, Sir Geoffrey, let us leave the rascals. But first let us salute the ladies, by way of amends for the lectures we have received. Kiss you the old dame, and I'll kiss the young one. By Heaven!" said he, gazing licentiously at Ellen, "I must taste those rosy lips. It will be so sweet after such unpalatable lectures!"

So saying he seized her round the waist, when O'Halloran, by a violent effort, broke the cord which tied his arms, and unexpectedly struck him a blow which laid him senseless on the floor.

"By Jove! it was well done," said M'Claverty, who had just entered the moment before, and unseen by Claverill, had witnessed the rudeness he had offered to Ellen. Had you not been beforehand with me, Mr. O'Halloran, I should myself have knocked down the scoundrel."

Sir Geoffrey without waiting to ascertain which side M'Claverty took, had hastened to alarm the guard. M'Claverty suspecting his intention, after assisting Mr. Wilson to disarm Claverill, and to drag him out of the apartment, followed the knight, and perceiving him leading a file of soldiers across the yard, he desired the jailor to refuse them admittance. He then returned to the apartment, and receiving an accurate statement of the whole transaction from Wilson, he hastened to communicate it to the commander of the garrison.

That officer said he was aware of the outrageous disposition of Claverill, and would prevent him from visiting the jail until these prisoners should be disposed of.

"But he may repeat his outrages on the ladies in other places besides the jail," observed M'Claverty.

"I shall let him know" said the officer, "that they are under my protection, while they remain in Carrickfergus; and that if he insults them, it shall be at his peril."

M'Claverty having obtained an order for the guard not to interfere with what had taken place, returned to the prison with intelligence of what he had done. He then offered to accompany the ladies to the inn, in order to show the military that he would defend them from any unwarrantable liberties. At the inn, he candidly told them that he had little expectation of any favour being extended to the prisoners, none of them being entitled to the conditions of the surrender at Donegore. He added that the system of intimidation was still persisted in by the Irish Cabinet; and that it was now more strictly enforced in consequence of the excesses committed by the rebels in the South.

"Letters were received yesterday," said he, "from the Secretary's office, ordering speedy examples to be made of the rebel leaders. In consequence of which, M'Cracken, Porter, and one Story were to be executed in Belfast. The court martial for the trial of the prisoners here will commence its sittings the day after tomorrow. Who will be the first to suffer, I cannot tell, but, ladies," he continued, "I trust you will keep up your spirits, and not dishearten your unfortunate friends on this trying occasion. Perhaps it would be better for them and you both that you should be absent from a scene, the solemnity and horror of which, you may not be able to support."

"I wish indeed that Ellen would return home," said Mrs. Brown. "She is here exposed to dangers from which I am exempted. Besides her inexperience of affliction, will render her less capable of bearing its presence. For me, I must stay to support and comfort my brother; and, I trust, God will give me strength to do so until the last scene shall be closed."

"Ah! my aunt," replied Ellen, "do you think I have no experience in affliction? Did I not lose my mother just when I began to know her value. Did I suffer nothing from a man whose violence and hatred we now all experience. And have I not for a long time past been preparing my mind for the approaching catastrophe? No; I cannot leave you in this hour of tribulation. Desire me not to go; and whatever I may feel, I shall endeavour to confine to my own breast. As to personal danger, the friendship of these gentlemen, and the order of the Governor will, I should think, be ample protection from any."

"Well," said M'Claverty, "if you will stay, I shall take care, as much as lies in my power, to provide for your safety. Mr. Wilson, I suppose, will remain with you."

"No consideration," replied Mr. Wilson, "will induce me to part with them, while they desire to remain; neither will I, in a matter which so nearly concerns them, urge them to relinquish that desire."

"You are perhaps right," said M'Claverty. "In the meantime, my friends, I must take my leave, and may heaven support you through your misfortunes, and grant us soon to see better times."

CHAP. XI.

The Court Martial.

The day for proceeding with the trials now arrived.

The martial tribunal was organized, and assumed its functions, in the county court-house. O'Halloran, and the prisoners who occupied the same apartment with him, were the first ordered to the bar, and the trial of young Nelson was the first proceeded on, not so much to gratify his accuser, Sir Geoffrey, as to prove to the other prisoners, that, if one of his tender age could not be spared, they had no room to expect mercy.

He was charged with, "joining others in an attempt to assassinate Sir Geoffrey Carebrow some weeks previous to the insurrection; and also with having, in the morning of the insurrection, in company with some other rebels, forced into the dwelling house of the said Sir Geoffrey, and seizing certain of his male servants, compelled them, under peril of their lives, to proceed in the rebel ranks, to the encampment at Donegore."

The first charge was positively sworn to by Sir Geoffrey himself, and the second by Tim Rogers, his bailiff. No defence being made, he was pronounced guilty.

The president then addressed him, descanting on the enormous character of his crimes. "Wickedness," said he, "unfortunate boy, must be engrained in your very nature; since at such an early age, it has broken out with so much ferocity. In mercy to your country, you should be cut off; for if your evil disposition were to increase with your years, horrible indeed would be their effects on society. Still we shall spare your life, on condition of your entering the army, where you will be taught to behave better, if you inform us who were your accomplices in the attempt to murder Sir Geoffrey Carebrow, and who instigated you to threaten and force his servants into the rebellion."

"I never attempted to murder Sir Geoffrey," said the boy, "though I know who did. But I will not tell you, for you would then take two lives instead of one; for there were two of them; and I should then be guilty of murder to save myself. But I will not talk to you more, only to say that if you should cut me to inches, I will not inform against any one."

Every one present was struck with astonishment; and not a few with admiration, at this resolute answer from one so young; and when the sentence that he should the next day be taken to the house of his mother, and should be hanged by the neck until dead, in front thereof, was pronounced, a half stifled murmur of indignation burst from the spectators, and was perfectly audible over the whole court.

He was then remanded to prison, and O'Halloran was put on his trial. His indictment contained a variety of charges, the principal of which were, 'That in conjunction with a number of other traitors, he had negotiated with the enemies of the country for the purpose of procuring their assistance in overthrowing the established government, and substituting another in its stead; and that he had not only been active in seducing numbers of the people from their allegiance, and in administering to them treasonable oaths, but had actually at the head of a numerous party of his deluded followers, levied war against the King, whereby the peace and tranquillity of the country was, and still is, very much disturbed, to the great destruction not only of the properties, but of the lives of His Majesty's loyal subjects, &c. &c.

'Further, that he had in an illegal and felonious manner, by the aid of his fellow conspirators, seized and imprisoned certain of the peaceable and unoffending inhabitants of the country, for no other cause than their having resisted his attempts to seduce them into his traitorous association. And, that he had, with his own hand, cruelly murdered one of the officers of His Majesty's army, for attempting, in the discharge of his duty, to suppress that rebellion which his wicked machinations had so effectually contributed to excite in the country.'

To prove these charges, Sir Geoffrey Carebrow, Philip Berwick, and Anthony Burdolph, a private soldier belonging to the regiment lately commanded by the deceased Colonel Lumly, were brought forward.

The first deposed, "That he and the prisoner were at one time on an intimate footing, during which period the prisoner had made frequent attempts to prevail on him to join the society of the United Irishmen; that in consequence of his constant refusal to do so, he had caused him, and one of his servants, to be seized by some of that society, and imprisoned in a cave near his (the prisoner's) habitation, where they were confined until the breaking out of the rebellion; when they were carried to the rebel camp at Donegore, and regained their liberty only in consequence of the submission of the rebels assembled there. That while in their custody, he knew of various meetings between the prisoner and some French emissaries taking place in the cave in which he was confined, when they freely conversed on the aid the conspirators were to receive from France. That while he and the prisoner were on a friendly footing, he had lent the latter a large sum of money, without knowing to what use it was intended to be applied; that, while imprisoned in the cave, he discovered that it had gone to purchase arms and ammunition for the conspirators; and was informed that since he had shown himself an enemy to the conspirators, he should not receive payment. It was even told him, that he might think himself fortunate, if he did not lose his life as well as his money, for his enmity to their cause."

Berwick's testimony was merely corroborative of his master's — that of Burdolph, the soldier, went to prove that, "On the seventh instant, near Antrim, the prisoner, with a large broad-sword, struck the deponent's commander, Colonel Lumly, a blow which knocked him off his horse; and in consequence of which he was found dead that same evening, near the spot where he fell, with a terrible fracture in his skull. This witness also swore that he saw the prisoner very active that day, leading on and encouraging the rebels to attack and destroy the King's troops, and that he fought more with the fury of a lion than the consideration of a man."

The evidence being closed, O'Halloran was called on for his defence.

"Gentlemen," said he, "as I know that my death is already determined on, to address you for the purpose of defending my life would be a mere waste of words, but part of the testimony you have heard, has gone further than merely to affect my life, it has gone to affect my character as an honest man. On this account, I should think it wrong to let it pass without animadversion. I am also anxious that my country should be acquainted with my real motives for taking so active and conspicuous a part in behalf of that cause for which I am to suffer; for erroneous impressions on this subject, impressions injurious to my reputation, may go abroad, which I now conceive it my duty to make some effort to prevent.

"Indeed, I acknowledge, that at this moment, however little I may be shaken by the terrors of death, I feel sensible on the point of character; for, if in the full enjoyment of health, competence, and security, I have often felt the

pride of an unstained reputation; if I then congratulated myself on the possession of a character unslandered either in honour or morals, and until this hour,
I believe, that I have been in this respect as fortunate as the majority of men,
now, when I am on the verge of eternity, I must, and do feel that pride of
character more intensely than ever, and am really anxious to leave behind me
the good name that I have hitherto enjoyed. I must, and shall, therefore, endeavour to rescue it from the malicious misrepresentations of a false witness.

"I may here remark that I bear that witness no ill-will for coming here
today, to testify against my political conduct, for, I am aware that had he not
done so, there are many others who could, and no doubt would, have furnished you with enough of information to justify you, according to your ideas
on the subject, in dooming me to destruction. But it would, I believe, have
been difficult to find any other who would have voluntarily and unnecessarily
impeached the integrity of my private character.

"When that witness first succeeded in gaining my confidence, I was a zealous United Irishmen. I was so, because I considered it my duty to my country,
to join that portion of her people who had resolved to vindicate her rights and
break those shackles of oppression with which strangers had long kept her in
bondage. It is unnecessary to enter into a long detail of those grievances for
the redress of which, after we had in vain repeatedly petitioned an unjust and
unfeeling government, we resolved to take arms. It is sufficient to say that we
felt them severely, and the circumstance of our risking so much for their removal is ample proof that we did so.

"To induce others to engage in a cause, in which I had thought it my own
duty to embark. I could not conceive to be a crime; nay, I considered that the
same obligation which bound me to to enter into the union of my countrymen,
bound me to make all the exertions I could, to strengthen that union by increasing its adherents. Among others, I prevailed on Sir Geoffrey Carebrow
to join us. But, as under our circumstances, there was no good in having numbers, without having them armed, and as Sir Geoffrey, who then professed
great zeal for our cause, was known to be a money lender, I hesitated not to
borrow a large sum from him on the security of my estate, for the purpose,
then explicitly avowed to him, of purchasing arms and ammunition, a purpose
which he seemed very zealous to promote. It is not true, therefore, that he was
deceived concerning the intended appropriation of his money.

"His assertion that I attempted to make his desertion of our cause, a plea
for refusing him payment, is also unfounded. He must have uttered it here
today, only with the base and malicious intention of wounding me in a point,
on which, he knows me to be sensible, that of my character for honour and

personal integrity. I here, in the presence of this court, and on the word of a man who is shortly to meet his God, deny that I ever intended, much less expressed an intention, on any plea, whatever, to refuse refunding his money; and having made this solemn denial, I shall dismiss this part of his evidence, by leaving to his conscience the task of reconciling it to truth.

"The deposition that I caused his imprisonment, is equally untrue. I knew nothing of it until he was brought to the place of his confinement. He himself knows too well the cause of it. It had no connexion with politics, nor were they United Irishmen who did it. Let him put his hand to his heart, and say if it was not done to prevent female innocence from being exposed to his villainy? But it is a subject I shall leave unexplained, on account of her whom he would have destroyed.

"With respect to the testimony of his servant, he has only repeated that given by the master. I strongly suspect he has obeyed his instructions in so doing, and the same remarks will apply to both. I shall only make this additional one, that as the servant was the accomplice of his master in the frustrated outrage against innocence to which I have alluded, it is not surprising that he should be capable of assisting him in the perjury of this day.

"Against the evidence of the soldier I have nothing to say, but of the charge in the indictment, founded on a part of this evidence, I must complain. I was at the battle of Antrim; I did meet Colonel Lumly arm to arm, and I met a brave man. We fought, for we were arrayed on different sides; and I was victorious. My success may have been his death, as his success might have been mine, but this is the first time, I ever heard the destruction of an enemy, in the heat of an open battle, in which thousands are engaged on both sides, stigmatized by the harsh epithet of murder. What! Is there a gentleman in that box, who after he had fought zealously, and contributed by the work of his own hands to the discomfiture of his enemy, would tamely assent to the propriety of being called a murderer! Surely to soldiers, it is unnecessary to enlarge on the wide distinction between a murderer and a victor. The common sense of mankind has long decided on the subject; and the cruel application of the former epithet to me, must only have proceeded from a disingenuous and overstrained affectation of zeal against the cause for which I fought.

"The merits of that cause have long, and will long be a disputed subject. I shall not, therefore, enter on it. It is sufficient justification of my conduct, to my own conscience, that I believe the cause to be righteous; and that it was my duty to lend it my support. With respect to the views of such of my unfortunate coadjutors, as were active in this disastrous attempt to emancipate our country, so far as I am acquainted with them, they were directed only to her benefit. If they had any sinister views of ambition or personal aggrandizement, or the introduction of any favourite national establishment, whether civil or religious, inimical to true liberty, I know nothing of them. What would have been their conduct had we been successful, I cannot say, but I can state what I believe would have been my own. I never should have consented to the establishment of a French influence in the government of this country. We solicited the aid of France in the struggle for our independence, but not at the price of permitting her government to infringe that independence. I believe that my colleagues were of the same mind with myself on this subject. In our conversations, we have often agreed in the sentiment, that if we must yield to a foreign connexion in matters of state, it should be a connexion with Britain, in preference to any other country.

"The form of government I should have preferred, would have been a republic of the democratical kind, but so constituted, as while it allowed the people their just ascendancy in the national affairs, it would have afforded strength and energy sufficient to the executive for every useful purpose, whether external or internal. Should the attainment of this desirable species of government have been impracticable, the state of things that I would have next preferred, would have been British connexion without British authority. I should have no objection for the King of Great Britain to be our king, constitutionally limited, and without the power of appointing any foreigner our viceroy, if it were found that such a state of things would be necessary to the preservation of peace between the two countries.

"The United Irishmen have been charged with the intention of establishing the Catholic as the national religion. Whatever dispositions of the kind they may have lately evinced in the South, it is absurd to suppose that in the North, where nine-tenths of their number were Presbyterians, they should have ever meditated such a design. We never talked of a national religious establishment. The general understanding was, that on this subject, all men should be as free as the Creator made them. Should uncontrollable events, however, have occasioned the reverse to take place; should the absurd and inhuman doctrine of extirpating heresy, have again became the fashion of the day, I would have withdrawn from my ill-fated country, and lamented her delusion, conscious, at the same time, that I had done my duty towards her, in assisting her to throw off that yoke of foreign oppression, whose weight had bowed her to the dust.

"But it is now over. She is destined longer to wear the chains; and I fear that they will be more firmly than ever rivetted around her. Every prospect of deliverance from her evil destiny, is now far distant. Long, long will it be ere she shall lift her head among the nations, proud and independent as she ought to be. But although I expect not her independence, yet, if I could hope that her stronger and victorious neighbour would treat her with that kindness and justice which true policy would dictate, I should die satisfied, for she might then be prosperous and happy as a British island, although she should never be great and glorious as an Irish nation.

"Now, gentlemen! you have heard my sentiments, and know the motives that actuated me during the late unfortunate transactions. It only remains for you to do your duty according as your consciences may prescribe. I shall submit to your decision without murmuring; and, I hope, without weakness. About nine months ago, the illustrious Orr stood to receive his doom on the very spot on which I now stand to receive mine. Here he displayed a firmness which I shall try to imitate; and at this moment his beatified spirit is not unobservant of the scene that passes here. Glorious martyr of oppression! When thou sawest thy country enslaved, thou couldst not look on and be idle; and for thy love to her, to this place thou wert dragged, and doomed to that fate, which I am now, like thee, ready to receive. Oh! That he whose mighty aid sustained thee in the day of thy suffering, may also sustain me!"

After a short address from the president, the court in a few minutes, produced its verdict of, "Guilty of all the charges except that of murder."

The president now rose to pronounce the sentence of death. "Mistaken, and ill-fated man," said he to the prisoner, "it is now my fate to deliver the opinion of this court, and pronounce according to its award, the awful words that shall cut short your earthly existence.

"Before performing this duty, it may not be improper to say a few words on the fallacy of those doctrines which hurried you into the commission of the treasons for which you are to suffer.

"Your infatuated imagination has been carried away by the theories of a new race of visionary philosophers, whose notions of government are as inapplicable to the proper regulation of a human community, as the means they have resorted to in making the experiment, have been destructive of human happiness. Men who know less of human nature than you, men less capable of reasoning on the nature of their passions and interests, and less aware of the necessity of governing and restraining them, for the safety and benefit of society, might have been excusable in becoming deluded by the fascinating, but absurd doctrine, of absolute liberty and equality. But you, from your education and opportunities of knowing, can have no apology.

"What subordination to the laws of a country can be expected from the uninformed minds, and ill-regulated passions of the peasantry, when such men

246

as you, to whom they naturally look for an example, teach them that there is virtue in resisting, even unto blood, every regulation of which they do not happen to approve. Such men as you cannot but perceive, that in a great community, consisting of many millions of individuals, and containing many different interests in direct opposition to each other, difference of sentiments on even the most evidently useful measures of government will often arise, for every mind as well as every interest, has its own mode of viewing such things. Would not then the establishment of your disorganizing doctrines be a source of endless calamity to our age; would it not make the state of civilization, laws, and government, a more wretched state than that of savage life itself. The best institutions that human wisdom ever framed, or ever will frame, for human happiness, will have opponents. Is it, therefore, proper that, whenever a portion of the community chooses to be dissatisfied with the existing state of things, they should take up arms and wade through bloodshed and destruction to enforce a change? Should not those who not only entertain, but propagate and act on such dangerous principles be punished as enemies to social happiness. The peace and welfare of their fellowmen demand it.

"That you, Henry O'Halloran, to the great detriment of your country, have been guilty of such offences, has been amply proved against you. This court has, therefore, awarded you a punishment, by which you are to atone for this guilt; and which it is my duty now to pronounce. You are to be taken tomorrow, to the place of your late residence, in sight of which you are to be hanged by the neck until you are dead, and the Lord have mercy upon your soul!"

O'Halloran was then conveyed back to the prison, and the court adjourned.

CHAP. XII.

When Ellen and her aunt visited their unfortunate relative after his condemnation, they found him in an apartment separate from the other prisoners.

He had requested that they would not be present at his trial, lest the horror with which they should hear his doom pronounced, should overpower them, and their distress tend to weaken his own fortitude. As they expected the result, they were not surprised, when informed of it. But when they visited him, the sad reality being now before them, they gave way to all the softness and affection of the female nature, and long and loudly wept beside him.

While they were thus venting their grief, the Recluse, and the poet, M'Nelvin, entered the prison. They obtained this permission, by means of M'Claverty, who, on this occasion, exerted himself to procure for O'Halloran and his friends, every possible indulgence, and it was by his management that they now enjoyed the convenience of a separate apartment.

After the first salutation, M'Nelvin became downcast and silent. The Recluse spoke some words of consolation, but his own agitation made him a bad comforter, and he soon also became silent. For some time the same gloom and silence pervaded the apartment, as if O'Halloran's soul had already taken its flight. He was himself by far the least agitated; and perceiving the faculties of his visitors to be absorbed in sorrow, "My friends," said he, looking round with a cheerful countenance, "the muteness of your grief shows its intensity. But for my sake, I beg you will not give way to such weakness, otherwise I may not be able to support my own strength of mind. Indeed I cannot bear to see my friends in such affliction. But for what are you afflicted? Because one of your friends, who has been upwards of half a century in this world, is about to leave it for a better! Rather rejoice with me, that I shall so soon be released from all my sorrows and vexations. Is it the manner of this release that effects you? God has willed that it should take place in this manner; and will you offend him by repining? And what, after all, is there peculiarly distressing in this mode of changing existence? As to its suddenness, an apoplexy would be more so. As to the pain it inflicts no man should regard that. It is soon over; the torments of many diseases are far more excruciating, and infinitely more tedious. As to ignominy, there is none attending it, for this path to eternity, has been trodden by many virtuous and great men, whose memories are hallowed in the affections of all the wise and good of their species.

"It can be no disgrace for me, to tread the path that was formerly trod by Sidney and Russell, and latterly by Orr, and only yesterday by Porter and M'Cracken. Our enemies may indeed cut short the thread of our existence here, but they cannot deprive us of the esteem of our friends and countrymen when we are gone. These are comfortable considerations. But they are not the only considerations that support me under this dispensation. Here is my grand support," said he, lifting a small bible which lay on a table near him, and opening it. "Here is the support with which God himself graciously furnished me, when a wanderer from Donegore, and driven to the very verge of despair. In the midst of my anguish, this consolatory passage was opened to me, in an hospitable cottage, and from that moment, my soul has never known despondency, or distrusted its Creator."

The Recluse now drew near him. "Forgive my weakness," said he; "my mind is agitated from more causes than grief. Suspense tears it to pieces, but I must not disturb your serenity by communicating the cause of my anxiety."

"What!" said O'Halloran, with some alarm; "I trust you forebode no more misfortune to my grandchild! Oh! Ellen, my child, your exposed state alone causes me to feel uneasy. But to the care of that God, in whom I trust, I commend you; and you have near, dear, and vigilant friends, even in this world. But oh! Never forget to repose your chief confidence in the protector you have in heaven."

The Recluse assured him that he knew of no evil threatening Ellen; that his suspense was occasioned by his entertaining hopes for him which he feared were likely to be disappointed.

"If that be all," replied O'Halloran, "you may cast aside your suspense. My hopes are sure, and will not deceive me, for they are fixed on Heaven."

A messenger now entered from the commander of the garrison, requesting to know if O'Halloran desired the society of a clergyman; and if so, to signify his commands on the subject, and they should be attended to. The attendance of one of his clerical fellow prisoners was requested, and obtained; the other being appointed to attend young Nelson. The ladies, and O'Halloran's other friends, now left him to the conversation of the clergyman, and withdrew to the inn. The next morning, they again visited him.

He had enjoyed a good night's sleep; was very much refreshed, and somewhat more cheerful than on the preceding evening. "Now my sister," said he to Mrs. Brown, "I do not wish you to accompany me today. Let me bid you and Ellen a last adieu. After the pang of this separation, for I feel indeed a pang," and the tears started into his eyes, "all my earthly cares will be over, and I shall have nothing to do but to die."

"We will accompany you part of the way," said they.

"I would rather not," he replied, "your presence would remind me of earthly enjoyments; and I wish nothing at that period to attract my thoughts from Heaven."

"Well, then, Henry!" said Mrs. Brown, "farewell! In Heaven I hope, soon to meet you."

"Farewell! my sister. We shall meet there;" and he embraced her.

"Now, thou daughter of my only child!" continued he, turning to Ellen, "the only offspring I leave in this world; thou hast long been the darling of my heart and the object of my care, farewell! I resign thee to the care of the Almighty. May his blessing forever rest on thee!" He then gave her a parting embrace, and her aunt and she, were led out of the room by Mr. Wilson and the Recluse.

It was about eight o'clock; and they had scarcely reached the inn, when the sound of military music drew their attention. They looked from the windows and beheld a regiment of infantry marching from the castle towards the jail. Their hearts sank within them; for this was the commencement of the procession to the fatal spot.

The regiment halted; and was drawn up before the jail. In a few minutes, they saw Nelson brought out, on a common farming car, surrounded by soldiers. His coffin was behind him, and a man who, as they were informed, was the executioner, sat on the other side of the vehicle. It stopped a few minutes in the middle of the street; when one of the clergymen before mentioned, placed himself alongside of Nelson, with a bible in his hand.

In a short time, another vehicle of the same sort, appeared. It contained O'Halloran, his coffin, and his clerical attendant. The ladies saw but one glimpse of it; for they could look no more. Their hearts became faint, their vision indistinct, and their heads swam dizzily, as they were removed from the appalling view.

The heavy monotonous sound of the muffled drums, now beating time to the music of a dead march, informed them that the procession was departing on its fatal errand; and when the ladies had recovered sufficiently to look into the street, all was there as still and quiet as if nothing of importance had taken place.

The procession having taken the road to Ballycarry, Mr. Wilson, and the ladies, attended by their servants and Jemmy Hunter, set off on another road, to avoid passing it, towards Larne.

The military with their prisoners, halted about half a mile to the south of Ballycarry, (at the northern end of which village, stood the cabin in which Nelson's mother resided) to give the soldiers time to form their ranks for marching through the village. The slow pace, the dead music, and the solemn beat, was again heard, and continued until the car on which Nelson was seated, came opposite his mother's door. The whole then stopped, and Nelson's mother suddenly fainted in the arms of her son.

The executioner selected an ash tree, which grew near the end of the house, for the gallows. The car was soon drawn forward under the spreading branches of that tree on which Nelson had often ascended in pastime with all the sprightly playfulness and innocence of childhood. After the affecting ceremony of bidding farewell to several of his friends and playmates, who were permitted to approach him, the clergyman commenced divine worship by singing the forty-third psalm, in which Nelson and several of the by-standers joined. The clergyman then addressed the throne of heaven in a style so fervent and pathetic as to draw tears from the eyes of all present, not excepting the rough soldiers themselves. When he had finished, he asked the youthful victim, if he had anything to communicate to the people, concerning his death.

He replied that he had nothing more to say, than that he died innocent; for he had never murdered, nor intended to murder anyone — that on the day of the rising, he had gone with a message to some of Sir Geoffrey's men, who were United Irishmen, to call them out, but that he had no arms with him, nor had he threatened any of them. That he was willing and ready to die; since he was sure that as he died innocent, he would go to heaven. The executioner now adjusted the rope, and asked him if he was ready. He replied that he only wished to see his mother once more, and then he would be ready.

His mother was supported forward to him, for her distress rendered her unable to support herself. "Oh! my William! My lovely child!" exclaimed she. "They murder thee—" She would have continued, but grief choked her further utterance.

"Mother!" said he, stooping to catch her in his arms, "won't you kiss me, and bless me before I die?"

She raised her eyes, swimming in tears, and with an almost convulsive effort, clasped him to her bosom. "May the God of heaven bless thee, my dear son!" she cried. "Thou wilt soon be with thy father, and I will soon follow thee."

"Amen," replied the victim, and giving a sign to the executioner, his mother was removed, and the work of death proceeded on. It was soon finished amidst the agonizing horror, but profound silence of the assembled multitude. His body was then cut down, deposited in the coffin, and delivered, a melancholy, heart-rending present, to his disconsolate mother.

Long, long will the maidens of the surrounding country, pause to drop a tear, as they pass the spot where the remains of this youthful martyr are deposited; and with swelling bosoms, adopt the language of Ireland's sweetest melodist, when they pathetically express their sorrows for his cruel fate.

"Oh! breathe not his name, let it sleep in the shade,
Where cold and unhonoured, his relics are laid;
Sad, silent, and dark, be the tears that we shed,
As the night dew that falls on the grass o'er his head:
But the night dew that falls, though in silence it weeps,
Shall brighten with verdure, the grave where he sleeps,
And the tear that we shed, though in secret it rolls,
Shall long keep his memory green in our souls."

CHAP. XIII.

Down yonder hill with headlong flight, Swift as a swallow to the sight,
With rapid course, he cuts the wind; Trees, fields, and hedges, roll behind;
The thickening clouds of dust that rise, He leaves afar to seek the skies;
For love, and friendship, urge his speed, A friend in need 's a friend indeed.
Irish Soothsayer.

After completing the foregoing tragedy, the military procession resumed its march toward the place appointed for accomplishing another. We have already mentioned, that Mr. Wilson and the ladies, for the purpose of avoiding this procession, had taken another road on their return homewards. It so happened, however, that they overtook it at the entrance of Larne where the two roads joined.

"Oh! I shall see him again," cried Ellen, "before he dies."

Mr. Wilson wished his party to avoid an interview, which, he said, would only cause additional distress to both parties.

But Mrs. Brown cried out, "Since Providence has once more brought me so near my brother while he lives, I must see and speak with him."

The procession had stopped to form into ranks for marching through the town. During this interval, Mr. Wilson's carriage, containing himself and the ladies, drew forward to the car on which O'Halloran sat. Ellen, and her aunt, were soon in his arms, and the commanding officer had the politeness to postpone the march, until the first burst of their feelings subsiding, should allow them to separate.

"My dear sister! My beloved daughter! Do not go with us further." O'Halloran was thus replying to their earnest entreaty to be permitted to remain with him to the last, when their attention was drawn to a man on horseback, who was galloping down the hill, behind them, at the most furious rate, with the dust all rising in clouds around him as he flew along.

The commander was about to desire the ladies to resume their seats in the carriage, and to order the procession to proceed, when he perceived the advancing horseman. "It is, perhaps, some express," said he to Mr. Wilson, with whom he had been conversing, "I shall delay a few minutes."

As soon as the horseman approached, "Oh! Father, it is Edward Barrymore," exclaimed Ellen. "He is come to see you die."

"Are you the commander of this party?" inquired the rider, who was indeed Edward, as he advanced hastily to Colonel Parker.

"I am," was the reply.

"Then, your duty is over on this occasion," said Edward, at the same time handing the colonel a letter signed by the Lord Lieutenant, accompanied with one from the governor of the fortress of Carrickfergus.

"This, I am glad to see, is a conditional pardon for our prisoner," said Colonel Parker.

"You will also observe that I am to be his jailer, until the condition is complied with," replied Edward.

"What, sir, are you the Mr. Barrymore here mentioned?"

"That is my name, sir."

"Why, you were zealous, indeed, to be the courier in this case."

"It was a desperate case; I could entrust no one else," said Edward.

"You were right," returned Parker. "I respect your feelings, and shall for ever thank you for taking this disagreeable business off my hands. Guards, untie the prisoner! He is pardoned."

Shouts of joy arose, and continued to rend the air for many minutes, from an innumerable multitude of people of all descriptions. Edward, in the meantime, flew to his beloved, who on the first mention of pardon, almost fainted with excess of joy. He caught her gently by the arm. "Miss O'Halloran, I hope you know me?" said he.

She turned round at the sound of the well-known voice. "Yes, O yes! It is you who have saved my grandfather's life. Oh let me thus return you thanks," and without considering what she was about to do, she attempted to throw herself on her knees before him.

But he caught her in his arms. "No, my love!" he whispered, "God alone must be thanked in that posture."

"Oh! yes," cried she, recovering her recollection, "I knew not what I was doing. But I shall thank God all the days of my life, for this kind providence."

Mrs. Brown now approached Edward. "Ah! Mr. Barrymore! what do we not owe you?"

"I am already full repaid," replied the youth, as he gently pressed Ellen's hand. Immediately a burning blush tinged her countenance; and sweet confusion sparkled in her eyes. Edward now handed the ladies into the carriage; and

254

at Mr. Wilson's request took his seat along with them, that gentleman intending to go on foot with O'Halloran to the inn.

The press of people, however, became so great round O'Halloran, every one anxious to congratulate him, that he was obliged to accept of Jemmy Hunter's kindness, who rode in among them, and offered him his horse. The crowd soon spontaneously formed into two parties; one of which followed O'Halloran with loud acclamations to the inn, while the other assembled round his deliverer. A vague and exaggerated story had got among them, that in his haste to bring the pardon from Dublin, he had killed four horses, and by means of such velocity alone had he been able to arrive in time to save O'Halloran.

An immense concourse gathered around the carriage, in which he and the ladies were seated, and unharnessing the horses, drew them in triumph to the inn, while the women from the doors and windows of the houses, showered blessings on his head.

The party remained at the inn only until another carriage was prepared, in which O'Halloran and Mr. Wilson proceeded to the residence of the latter, followed by Edward and the ladies, amidst the blessings and acclamations of thousands of joyful spectators.

When the party, after arriving at Mr. Wilson's, had partaken of some refreshments, and their minds were somewhat composed after the high excitement of the day, O'Halloran requested a private interview with Edward.

"It is a beautiful evening," said he, "suppose we walk out to the shrubbery. Methinks the free enjoyment of woodland air, after my late confinement, will be refreshing and tranquillizing to my spirits."

The shrubbery led to a small cascade or linn, as it is called in that part of the country, to which an imperceptible continuation of their walk soon led them. This cascade, although small, was romantic. It was formed by a rivulet which ran through the shrubbery, and emitting itself at this place, rushed over the edge of a rocky precipice, about thirty feet high, into a wide dell, or low level lawn which spread towards the east, being bounded by the sea shore. This lawn was clothed with the deepest verdure, intermingled with myriads of wild flowers, with the stream formed by the waters of the cascade, rolling placidly through the midst of them. To the westward, the side by which our gentlemen approached this dell, it was bounded by a semi-circular extension of a grass-covered bank, varying from twenty to thirty feet high, continued from each side of the cascade about half way round the small valley. On the brow of this bank, at a place where it declined with a gentle slope into the valley, the gentlemen sat down to contemplate the scene.

The saffron hue of the sky indicated the setting sun behind them. Before them were to be dimly seen, the blue hills of Scotland rising like mist from the ocean at the extremity of the horizon. Beneath them a flock of sheep, and several cows, were enjoying the luxuriant herbage; while a thrush seemingly delighted with the tranquillity and beauty of the scene, expressed her joy in the full swelling rapturous melody, peculiar to that charming bird.

"What a contrast" said O'Halloran, "is this holy scene, to that which I have so lately left! This pure wholesome air to the suffocating loathsome vapour inhaled by the unfortunate inmates of the prison from which I have just come! How different are my feelings now, from what they were at this time yesterday evening! From the windows of my prison, I then beheld the reflecting rays of the setting sun, as I supposed for the last time. I can now turn to that glorious luminary, and behold him setting once more, with the pleasurable sensation of hope, that I may yet many times view the same scene. It is only a few hours since I thought I should never again see the most splendid of all created objects, taking his diurnal farewell of my native hills. Oh! What do I not owe to your active friendship, to which, under Divine Providence, I must ascribe this unexpected happiness?"

"In serving you," replied Edward, "on this occasion, I have only discharged a debt which I owed you for my life; and we have now, to speak in mercantile language, only balanced accounts."

"Ah! sir," exclaimed O'Halloran, "my subsequent harsh conduct, did more than cancel any claim I may have had on your gratitude for that service. You were my guest; I broke the laws of hospitality, and treacherously made you my prisoner.

"Yes, hurried away from the dictates of my better feelings, by an over anxious solicitude for the success of an unfortunate enterprise, I forgot the duty I owed to the sacred claim of a stranger under the protection of my roof. It was a crime, it was a foul crime, which, even in my then perverted state of mind, I could not altogether justify to my conscience, and which has since given me more uneasy feelings than any other event of my life. Your magnanimity now in preserving your persecutor, demands all the atonement in my power to make.

"To give this explanation of the state of my feelings towards you, I have asked your privacy. I need not entreat your forgiveness, for you have proven already that you have forgiven me; but I wish to convince you of my compunction for the injuries I have done you."

"I beg," said Edward, "that you will not think of that affair. Even when it took place, I was conscious of your motives, and felt more for the pain which

256

the struggle between your inclinations and your sense of duty occasioned you, than for the temporary confinement to which I was subjected.

"And, O! Sir, let me disclose my whole mind to you. I do not regret that captivity, for it resulted in one of the most pleasing events of my life. It brought an angel to unbar my prison doors; and proved to me that I was not indifferent to the loveliest of all created beings. I have said that you owe me nothing. But if I have nothing to demand from obligation, I have a precious gift to ask from kindness. I love Miss O'Halloran; the hopes of my life depend on her; consent that she shall be mine, and you will make me happy; refuse me, and you will render me indeed miserable."

"Refuse you!" cried O'Halloran; "No! Not if I had an empire to give you with her;" and seizing Edward by both his hands, he continued, "O God, under whose canopy I now live, and breathe, make me grateful for thy goodness, in thus providing for the child of my heart a protector, and a lover so worthy of her. Young man, I shed tears, but they are tears of joy. I have shed none such, since the day that the wife of my affection, presented me with my only infant, and said 'Behold our child!'

"I felt I was then a father, I blest the babe, and wept. I am still a father; that infant's child is still left to me; and can I but weep at this prospect of her happiness? But," said he, suddenly changing his tone, as if some new suggestion had occurred to him, "Mr. Barrymore, are you not too precipitate in this matter? In the first impulse of delight at your proposal, I did not recollect that you have relations rich and powerful. Have they been consulted on the subject?"

"I confess," replied Edward, somewhat embarrassed with the question, "that I have not as yet spoken to them concerning it. Having no hopes of obtaining your consent, to the accomplishment of my wishes, since I had incurred your displeasure, and knowing that without yours, hers could not be obtained, I did not wish to acquaint my friends that I cherished views of happiness which had so little prospect of being realized."

"Then," said O'Halloran, "there are obstacles I did not before perceive; and for the sake of my child's peace, I request that this affair shall not, for the present, be pushed farther."

"What obstacles!" cried Edward. "I cannot think that my father will oppose me in a point which so nearly concerns my welfare. He has no son but me. He is an affectionate father, and will not command me to be wretched. Besides, what objections can he have? Her beauty, her sweetness of disposition, her virtue, her connexions—"

"Ah! Stop," cried O'Halloran, "there lies the obstacle. Her connexions. Will the powerful, the rich, the constitutional, the loyal family of the Barrymores degrade itself by an alliance with a traitor, a rebel, a ringleader of rebels, a man scarcely escaped from the gallows! No, sir; by strongly wishing for it, you may force yourself to expect it, but cool reason tells me that it cannot be."

"If I have any knowledge of my father's character," replied Edward, "he has too liberal a mind to permit the errors of one individual to influence his estimation of another, however nearly they may be connected. Your being concerned in the late conspiracy, will not, in his eyes, diminish the worth of your granddaughter; nor, since you have done nothing unworthy of a man of honour and a gentleman, can any errors of a mere political nature, communicate anything degrading to one, who is in herself all purity and excellence, and worthy of the best and noblest in the empire."

"You may think so, my young friend," said O'Halloran; "but your relations will not look on her with your eyes. In the meantime, much as I should rejoice at your union with her, you must permit me to retract my assent, until it receives your father's; for unfortunate, poor and persecuted as I am, I am too proud to permit my child to be taken into a family, the head of which may look on her as unworthy of such a situation."

"Wherever Ellen is known," said Edward, "she cannot be thought unworthy of any situation."

"But," returned O'Halloran, "her grandfather's unworthiness may be reflected on her."

"Oh, sir," said Edward, in a tone of entreaty, "I shall procure the approbation of my family. You will surely then be satisfied."

"Not only satisfied but rejoiced," replied O'Halloran. "That they will yield to your wishes is my earnest prayer, but whether they yield or not, I shall ever be equally solicitous for your happiness as for hers to whom I should wish you united. For the present, however, we must drop the subject."

They arose; and ascending a small eminence on their way to the house, they perceived the country for several miles round, studded with bonfires; while the frequent shouts of mirth, that broke upon the air, proclaimed the joy of the people for O'Halloran's safety.

"This is a brilliant and romantic, and must be to you, a very gratifying scene," observed Edward, "for it proves how much you are esteemed by these people."

"They are a kind people," replied O'Halloran. "I only wish they were happier." He heaved a sigh, and silence ensued, until they arrived at the house.

CHAP. XIV.

Major Trip.

Edward anxious for an interview with the Recluse, that very evening, after parting with O'Halloran, visited the cell before M'Nelvin had left it.

"Ah! Sir," cried the Recluse, as soon as he perceived him, "never did the arrival of a mortal messenger yield more heartfelt delight than yours did to-day."

"My friends," said Edward, addressing them both, "you have had sad times here since I left you. The storm is now, however, abated, and I trust in God that our country will never witness such another. Perhaps some lives may yet fall; but I have reason to think that the councils of the nation will soon be regulated on wiser and milder principles, for Lord Camden is recalled, and the benign Cornwallis has by this time assumed the reins of government."

"Cornwallis! did you say?" exclaimed the Recluse, hastily.

"Yes, father, Lord Cornwallis is now Lord Lieutenant."

"Thank heaven!" ejaculated the Recluse, "both for my country and for myself. The benevolent Cornwallis will restore my country to peace; and I shall be restored to my country. In a short time I shall no more tread my native soil as a disguised outlaw."

"You are then acquainted with Lord Cornwallis," asked Edward.

"Yes," said the Recluse. "I was his bosom friend, during his campaigns in America; and, on a certain occasion, had the felicity to save his life, for which he has never since ceased to remember me with gratitude."

"Through his means might you not long since have procured a reversal of your sentence?" asked Edward.

"No, sir. On my return from America, he did apply for my pardon, but the influence of Sir Geoffrey Carebrow and others of his connexions, counteracted his exertions. I have never since permitted any application to be made. For some years I travelled on the continent; and having, at length, settled here and adopted this disguise, I became satisfied with my lot. As, however, late events have induced me to discover myself to a few friends, whose society I should be glad to enjoy without restraint, and one of my best friends has it now in his own power to remove the legal terrors that hang over me, I shall avail myself of the opportunity which is thus providentially afforded me, to become again an acknowledged member of society."

He then inquired of Edward at what time the courier he had despatched with the account of O'Halloran's capture arrived in Dublin.

"On Wednesday evening," replied Edward. "She was diligent and expeditious, but how did you think of such an extraordinary messenger?"

"I could not, with safety," said the Recluse, "have waited till the succeeding mail left Larne. Besides, I understand that the transportation of letters by mail has, since the troubles commenced, been very irregular, and I was well aware that a single day's delay might be fatal. I had some thoughts of sending James Hunter, but his unlucky adventure at Antrim, taught me that he was not one of the fittest people in the world for such an errand in such times. Peg Dornan appeared a much more suitable messenger. Her strength was equal to the task of travelling night and day for that distance; her zeal and perseverance I knew would be indefatigable; and her sex, manners, and attire, were the best passports she could carry to secure her an unsuspected and uninterrupted journey."

"The perseverance and zeal of Peg have fully equalled your expectations," remarked Edward, "but I believe that her strength has not held out so well. I left her absolutely crippled with fatigue."

"Poor creature!" ejaculated M'Nelvin.

"But she will be well attended to," continued Edward; "and I make no doubt that such a constitution as hers will soon repair the damage it has sustained. It was about four o'clock in the afternoon when she arrived. I was sitting with my friend, Charles Martin, in the drawing-room, when we heard a loud rapping at the street door. The butler happening to be in the hall, and thinking, perhaps, from the nature of the noise, that some distinguished personage wanted admittance, flew to open the door, but was so disappointed at seeing the uncouth figure which presented itself, that he would have instantly closed it again, had not Peg by main strength, half thrust herself into the hall.

'I want to see Mr. Barrymore. I'm tauld he bides here,' cried she.

'You're tall enough, and impudent enough too; you hussey!' exclaimed the butler.

'I maun see him, she resumed; for the life o'a man, an' a guid man, depends on it; ye unceevil, ill-mannered tyke.'

"The altercation now induced me to look from the window, when I immediately recognised Peg. She was holding fast by the door frame, from which the man was endeavouring all in his power to disengage her, and thrust her into the street. I ordered him to desist, and ran down stairs to secure Peg a welcome reception. She gave me no time to speak, but taking your letter from her bosom, the moment she saw me.

'Read that, sir, quoth she, and ride to Carrick, as fast as the best horse in this muckle toon can carry you, gin you wad save him. Heigh, sirs; but I'm tired! — but dinna wait, dinna wait — I have been owre lang a coming.'

"I was not too much absorbed in the contents of the letter to hear more. Having read it, I ran upstairs. Martin! Said I, see that woman below taken care of. These are horrible times! I must be off immediately to the Castle, and thence to the North. A friend's life is in danger. I have no time for explanation.

"I then ordered Tom Mullins to follow me hastily with two horses to the Castle. I knew every minute was precious, and hastened onward at a pace which made the people stare as I passed them. When I reached the Castle, I found that his Excellency had just set off for the Phoenix Park. I rushed out to follow him on foot, when I fortunately perceived Mullins advancing with the horses.

"I mounted one, and ordered him to wait for me, with the others, at the commencement of the northern road. Lord Camden had just reached the Phoenix Lodge when I overtook him. Surprised to see me riding with such speed, he stopped till I approached.

'What is the matter, Barrymore,' said he; I hope no fresh insurrection has broken out?'

"No, my lord, I replied, as I dismounted, I came to solicit your Excellency in favour of a very dear friend, who is confined for treason, and even while we are speaking, may have sentence of death pronounced and executed on him, by the military in the north.

'Is that all!' said he, 'then let us walk in. I have of late received so many expresses about insurrections, and battles, and massacres, that I imagine every person who approaches me, to be the bearer of some such intelligence. But let us have a glass of wine, and then you can explain your wishes.'

"This comported little with my impatience, but I was obliged to submit. After we were seated; 'Who is this friend of yours,' he asked, 'that has got himself into captivity?'

"O'Halloran is his name, my lord.

'What! The chief instrument of the rebellion in Ulster? I am glad of it. I expect that now we shall soon be able to reduce that province to order.'

"I came said I, to crave your Excellency's pardon for this unfortunate man, whose excellent private character, would, if your Excellency were acquainted with it, be sufficient to procure your forgiveness for his public errors.

'How! Edward Barrymore', said he, are you become an advocate for a man who has been so fatally active in stirring up this horrible rebellion? A man whose destruction will be of more advantage to the country than that of any thousand rebels in it.'

"My lord! Said I, this man once saved my life; and oh! If ever my friends or my family, have rendered your, or His Majesty's government, any service, gratify me with an opportunity of repaying him the debt. The destruction of one individual, even of the most important description, will not add much to the success of the royal cause. Your leniency will attach him and all his friends to the existing authorities; and I, for my part, shall be bound to you by ever-lasting gratitude.

'It cannot be, Edward,' he replied. 'To extend absolute pardon to such an offender would afford an injudicious example of leniency, now when energy and wholesome severity are so much required.'

"Anything, my lord," I replied, "anything short of death will be acceptable — but if he be permitted to remain in the country, I shall be security for his good behaviour in any amount you choose to name.

'You are very pressing, Edward,' said he. 'Stay for dinner. I shall reflect on what is best to be done. You cannot, at any rate, despatch an express before the morning.'

"I shall be the express myself, my lord, I replied. The moment I obtain your Excellency's order in his favour, I shall set off. In such emergency I cannot trust another.

'You are indeed very zealous in this matter,' said he. 'But I must reflect a little. I wish to oblige you; yet I must do my duty to the state. Dine with me, and if during the evening, I receive no more news of bloodshed, burnings, and murders, committed by those wretches, I may be in a better humour to spare one of their ringleaders.'

"I was obliged to comply. At about eight o'clock, an express arrived from the castle with a letter to his lordship. I trembled lest it might contain intelligence of a nature to irritate him against the insurgents, and frustrate my application. In a few minutes he laid the letter on the table.

'So you are to have a new viceroy,' said he. 'Mr. Pitt don't think me enough of a soldier for these hot times. Cornwallis will arrive tomorrow to assume the government. He is a brave man, but too tender-hearted, I believe, when severity is requisite. I am glad, however, that he comes. The responsibility of conducting the country through these perplexing times, shall be taken off my hands. But, as to your affair, I must oblige you while I have the power; and in despite of all that has been said of the cruelty and harshness of my administration, I shall end it with an act of clemency.'

"He then retired to an adjoining chamber, and wrote the following letter, which he presented to me, saying, 'Read that, sir; I expect it will answer your purpose.' "

June 14, 1798.

Sir, being informed that you have the rebel chief, O'Halloran, in custody, I am induced, in consequence of some representations made to me in his favour, by a person well acquainted with him, to pardon his offence, on condition that he shall pay a fine to be assessed by you to any amount, not exceeding ten thousand pounds, which sum shall be appropriated to the relief of those royalists who have suffered from the rebellion in the county of Antrim.

The prisoner may be given over to the custody of the Hon. Edward Barrymore, who is chargeable with his safety until the fine be paid, and who will with any other person you may approve, enter into recognisance for his subsequent good behaviour.

CAMDEN.

"Having received this anxiously-desired document, I hastily expressed my acknowledgments, and withdrew.

"I found Mullins waiting at the place appointed, and we proceeded onwards at a very rapid pace. At the instance, or rather the remonstrance of Mullins, we stopped at Swords to refresh the horses; during which interval, I endeavoured to relieve my impatience by writing to Charles Martin. I informed him of the cause of my hasty departure; and requested him to recommend Peg

Dornan to the care of my friends, under the assurance that she had rendered me an important piece of service, while I was in the North last summer.

"Martin had proposed to accompany me to my favourite shore as soon as the troubles should be over. I now requested him to follow me whenever circumstances would permit. I informed him that I should be found either at the Antrim Arms in Larne, or at O'Halloran castle, the residence of the Northern beauty I had so often described to him. Alas! Said I, in concluding my letter, she is at this moment in great affliction. I figure to myself her luxuriant black hair all dishevelled, and flowing round her, as she buries her lovely face in the bosom of her unfortunate grandfather, who is the cause of her sorrows, in order to conceal the crystal tears that shine with heart-piercing lustre through her dark eye-lashes. The rosy hue of her cheeks, and the coral of her lips, are, perhaps, now pale. I cannot bear to dwell on the image that her distress at this moment presents to my mind. Loveliness in distress — and such loveliness as hers! Oh, Charles, I must quicken my pace, that I may have the supreme luxury of drying those tears, of removing those sorrows. I can write no more, my heart is too full.

"We soon again proceeded on our journey, and reached Newry the following night. The horses being unable to go further at such a rapid rate, I, the next morning very early, procured a fresh one, and desiring Mullins to follow more leisurely with the others, set off alone, and reached Carrickfergus about eleven o'clock. You may imagine my consternation, when I was informed that O'Halloran had been taken away some hours before, to be executed at his own castle. The governor of the place, however, on reading the Lord Lieutenant's letter, observed that as the party would be detained sometime at Ballycarry, in putting Nelson to death, by taking the shorter road over the mountain, I might, by swift travelling, overtake it in time to prevent the catastrophe. Observing my horse to be greatly fatigued, he ordered out his own, and giving me a note to the commander of the party I was to pursue, 'Don't spare the horse,' said he; 'and may heaven prosper your journey!'

"The horse seconded my impatience with great spirit, and you know the fortunate result."

"The hand of Providence has been remarkably manifest on this occasion," said the Recluse. "How much reason have we to be thankful to the Great Ruler of the universe, for this signal deliverance! Two hours more would have rendered this pardon useless."

Edward now took leave of his friends, and returned to Mr. Wilson's.

CHAP. XV.

Thompson.

The next day, while O'Halloran was employed in attending to congratulatory messages and visits from his friends, his servants assisted by a number of mechanics, commenced repairing the castle, that he might with as little delay as possible, return to his ancient residence.

The Governor of Carrickfergus, having the discretionary power over the fine to be inflicted on him, fixed it at three thousand pounds, for which Edward, who transacted this business unknown to O'Halloran, immediately gave a draught on his Dublin banker. He then, with Mr. Wilson, became security to the amount of ten thousand pounds for their friend's future submission to the established government.

When these two gentlemen went to Carrickfergus for the purpose of transacting these matters, which they did the day but one succeeding that on which Edward arrived with the pardon, they found the courts-martial still busied with the state trials. But these terminated before they left the place, by the arrival of a proclamation of a general amnesty issued by Lord Cornwallis in favour of all, except a few individuals therein named, who should within the term of six weeks from the date thereof, make their submission to the government. Of this merciful measure all the prisoners in Carrickfergus instantly availed themselves, and were set at liberty.

Edward and Mr. Wilson returned in company with a number of the prisoners, who had been taken from the neighbourhood of Larne. On hearing their expressions of sorrow of the rash step they had taken, and their protestations of gratitude to the new viceroy for his clemency, he was forcibly struck with this proof of the advantage of conciliation over coercion in securing the tranquillity of a country. Here he saw men whom Camden's oppressive policy had rendered bitter enemies to the government, now, in consequence of Cornwallis's clemency, manifesting by every expression of sincerity, their resolution to live and die its friends and supporters.

"Ah!" thought he, "how happy it would be for society, if governments would hearken to the lesson taught by such an example! But pride and passion too often blind them to their own and their people's interests. All history proves the falsity of the barbarous doctrines of making public examples. The tyranny of the duke of Alva caused Spain to lose the Netherlands; the cruelty of the Catholic Mary strengthened the protestant cause, and powerfully contributed to its permanent establishment in these countries; while the inhumanity of Jefferies, of Dalzel, and of Claverhouse, hurled from the throne, the family they attempted to support!"

Full of these reflections, and cheered with prospects of peace and prosperity which, under the auspices of the new viceroy, he perceived again to be dawning on his afflicted country, he approached the house of his companion, as yet the temporary residence of his Ellen, with light and joyous spirits. Here he had the pleasure to find the agreeable Miss Agnew, for whom he had contracted a sincere friendship.

This young lady ran forward to him with an air of great liveliness; exclaiming, "Welcome, Mr. Middleton! Oh! I forgot, Mr. Barrymore. But, indeed, I am so glad to see you that I cannot help blundering."

"My fair friend!" replied Edward, unthinkingly, "either of the names will be agreeable to me that shall be most acceptable to you."

"Upon my word," she cried, "very gallant; a fair proposal, all at once, before one has time to bless one's self. But what, my tender Damon, if I accept neither of these names?"

"I must then bear the misfortune, with as much fortitude as I may," returned Edward, perceiving the turn she had gaily given to his expression.

"Well! then, prepare to exert it," said she, "for the old Scotch name of Agnew sounds so well to my ears, that I am determined to change it for no other, but if I had to bear the awkward Granuwale one of Halloran, I would soon adopt one of yours in its stead."

"I love my own country too well," observed Ellen, to whom the last remark had been slyly directed, "to prefer either a Scotch or an English name to one of true Irish growth; and while my native appellation distinguishes me as an Irishwoman, I shall neither envy you your Scotch title, nor the gentleman both his English ones. But, Mr. Barrymore," she continued, turning to Edward, "what news have you brought from Carrickfergus?"

"I have brought good news," he replied. "The state prisoners are all discharged in consequence of a general amnesty proclaimed by the new Lord Lieutenant. Mr. Wilson and I returned in company with some of those belonging to this neighbourhood."

"Heaven be praised! we shall yet see happy times," exclaimed Ellen.

"This is indeed pleasing intelligence," said Mrs. Brown, who had entered the room, as Edward was relating it. Mr. Barrymore, you are always the bearer of good news.

"Are you a mere man, or a magician?" asked Miss Agnew, looking him archly in the face.

"Why, mad-cap! such an absurd question?" demanded Mrs. Brown.

"Let the gentleman answer first," said Miss Agnew.

"I can scarcely tell," he answered, "but I believe, I am enchanted here."

"That is but just," cried the arch lady, "for I am sure you carry enchantment to every place else you visit. You must certainly have some power of necromancy about you. The sea cannot drown you; the strength of rocks cannot confine you; at the power of your words the chaplet prize goes over the heads of all your competitors, and alights on yours. When your friends are assaulted, you drop as if from the clouds, to their assistance; the shades of night, or the intervention of hills, cannot conceal your enemies from your penetrating eye; nor protect them, though assisted by doors, and bolts, and guards, and pistols, from your vengeance. Neither is it in the power of steel to pierce you; for when the assassin lifts his arm, either an angel, or, what answers the same purpose, a saint, protects you from the blow. If your friend is in danger, from the distance of a hundred miles, you wing your flight, and in a few hours armies are dispersed before you, and your friend is rescued; or if you only visit the prisons where hundreds of captives are confined, whom you compassionate, the prison doors fly open, the prisoners' chains fall off, and they are set at liberty. O! Sir, the African's ring had not more power over time and space, nor was his wonderful lamp more capable of surmounting all the obstacles of nature, and overcoming all the opposition of men, than your talismanic influence."

"What, a lecture on necromancy, I protest," cried Mrs. Wilson, who had just entered. "Why, I believe, girl, you are really mad."

"She is only labouring under the delirium of a joyous fever!" said Ellen.

"I am indeed in a delirium of joy" returned Miss Agnew, "to see all my friends so happy. But I have also spoken truth in my delirium. No one can deny that many miracles have been wrought in our favour by that conjuror from the South."

"If our fair enigmatical lecturer," observed Edward, "labours under any malady, it is that of a warm heart, accompanied with a lively imagination, and an irresistible command over metaphorical ideas and expressions."

They were now summoned to dinner. Several gentlemen of the neighbourhood were of the party, and among others, their friend, M'Claverty. As soon as this gentleman perceived Edward, he appeared somewhat startled.

"Sir," said he, approaching him, "I think I have seen you before."

"Yes," replied Edward, "You were then on an important duty."

"I remember having examined you rather roughly," returned M'Claverty.

"That is nothing," said Edward. "Your duty required you to examine me. I was a stranger; and you were in pursuit of the perpetrators of a crime, of which, for aught you knew, I might have been guilty. I was a little peevish under your interrogatories at the time, but I afterwards blamed myself for being so foolish. I have since that time, heard enough of your character, to convince me, that your conduct did not proceed from either the pride or petulance of authority."

"Well I hope," returned the magistrate, "that we shall be good friends on further acquaintance."

After an hospitable dinner, which, like every other dinner given by people of fortune, displayed all the luxuries of the season, the cloth was withdrawn; and the ladies soon following it, the gentlemen addressed themselves, like true Irishmen, to the conviviality of the social cup; and the time passed away in the enjoyment of much good humour and hilarity.

CHAP. XVI.

We may roam through this world like a child at a feast, Who but sips of a sweet, and then
flies to the rest;
And when pleasure begins to grow dull in the east, We may order our wings and be off to
the west:
But if hearts that feel, and eyes that smile, Are the dearest gifts that heaven supplies,
We never need leave our own green isle, For sensitive hearts and sun-bright eyes.
Moore.

The principal gentlemen in the neighbourhood, now gave a routine of dinners and balls in testimony of their satisfaction at O'Halloran's escape from the dangers into which he had been involved, and of their respect for the high character he had supported through the trying scene.

Edward and Ellen were, of course, always invited to these parties, and the easy urbanity, the respectful kindness, and cheerful politeness of the Northern Irish, made an indelible impression on Edward's mind in their favour. He the more zealously cherished this impression, because he had been taught to believe, that they were a race of stiff, plodding, narrow-minded, avaricious people, the descendants of Scotch adventurers, so dry, so inhospitable, and so selfish in their manners, that they scarcely deserved to be considered Irish.

"How much have I been deceived," said he, in a letter, written about this period, to a friend in Dublin, "in the character of these people?

"Are these the cunning Scotchmen, the bigoted, ignorant Presbyterians, whose study is to cheat, and whose business is to grow rich, that have been said to inhabit Ulster. They deserve a character the very reverse. Their peasantry have all the good nature, simplicity and kindness of Arcadians; their merchants and manufacturers possess all the honour and punctuality once said to be naturalized on the Exchange of London; and their nobility and gentry, all the high-spiritedness, gallantry, and generosity of the days of romance. These people are indeed Scottish in their industry and intelligence, but they are altogether Irish in their manners and feelings. I am in reality proud to call them my countrymen."

The industry and zeal of the workmen employed at O'Halloran castle, soon repaired the damages it had sustained; and, in a few weeks, the family were reinstated in the Hall of their ancestors. It is the custom in that part of the country, when a family removes from one dwelling to another, to assemble a large party of its friends and neighbours to an entertainment, called 'heating the house.' By a man of O'Halloran's disposition, a custom of this kind could not be neglected; and as so many respectable people had of late shown him so much kindness, the party he invited was more than ordinarily numerous.

After the usual entertainments of dinner, desert, tea, &c. the party in the height of glee, mirth, and enjoyment, resorted to a large room, where flaming chandeliers gave an artificial day, and harps, violins, and flutes, poured an animating stream of lively sounds, to give motion to their flowing spirits in the buoyancy of the bounding dance. It was about an hour before this sprightly and exhilarating amusement commenced, that a messenger arrived with the following note to Edward:

Dear Barrymore,

I have at length followed you. Excited by my ardent desire to see the peerless beauty, who could so completely subdue a heart which was impregnable to all the attacks of the Dublin fair, I eagerly embraced the first moment, in which I could, with propriety, undertake the journey. The day before I left the city, I waited on the Lord Lieutenant, with the letter you enclosed from the Recluse, who, I understand, is to be no longer a mendicant, but is to appear in society in his own proper character of Francis Hamilton, Esq. of Hamilton-hall, in the county of Tyrone.

His Excellency was much pleased to hear from him; and, without delay, not only granted to him his request, but wrote to him a long letter, which on finding I was about to take a Northern trip, he entrusted to my care.

Your favourite, Peg Dornan, had a pretty smart fever, and was unable to walk for nearly a couple of weeks: but she was in a convalescent state when I left Dublin, and as she was getting very home-sick, I suppose she will, in imitation of your humble servant, speedily honour the Northern folks with her presence. Your father informed me that he would send her in the stage. Both he and your mother have been as attentive to her as you could desire.

By means of Lord Camden, your father has become acquainted with your intercession for the Insurgent Chief. He is pleased enough with your conduct in that affair, only he thought you might have made him your confidant. But I told him you had not time; which settled the point. I will give you no more city news till I see you. Indeed I should not have given you so much in this way, but having to send you a letter, I could not properly do so without putting something in it, and news answered the purpose as well as anything else. I shall only add that I am impatient to see the old chief, with the fame of whose exploits, the whole city rang for some days before I left it.

Yours, &c.
CHARLES MARTIN.

Edward instantly acquainted O'Halloran with his friend's arrival. A messenger with an invitation to the Castle, was despatched for him; and he arrived just as the party had finished the first set of country dances.

Charles Martin was a lively young man of the middle height, rather slender, with dark hair, and a glowing complexion. Though inferior to Edward in manly proportions, he was, on the whole, an interesting youth, gifted with the easy, affable, and polished manners of a gentleman.

Edward was conversing with a group of ladies, consisting of Ellen, Miss Agnew, two Misses Simpsons, and a Miss Moore, who had just sat down from the dance, when Charles was announced.

Edward hastened to meet him; and taking him to his own chamber, Charles was speedily transformed, from a hardy traveller, into a "gallant gay," ready to wait on the fair, and join in the mirthful revelry of the evening. Before they entered the brilliant scene of hilarity, joy, and beauty, he stopped Edward near the door, where unseen they had a full view of the whole party.

"Stay, Edward," said he, "I, for a moment, wish to view at a distance, a constellation of charms, the splendour of whose beams, if too suddenly approached, might dazzle and confound me."

"Right," said Edward. "Let me see if, among all the fair, you can single out she whom I hold fairest?"

The young man's glance speedily traversed the whole room. At last, resting upon a group of ladies to the right, who were sitting in a kind of semicircle,

"If your goddess be within those walls," said he, "yonder she is, surrounded by her attendant nymphs; the lady with the damask rose on her breast. I know her by the glowing descriptions you have so often given me. The sparkling brilliancy of her black eyes; her high and circular forehead, as smooth as ivory; her well-formed Grecian nose; her rosy cheeks; and coral lips. Ah! She smiles! No wonder you were enchanted. What an expression of heavenly things is there in that smile! See! Her gauze handkerchief moves to one side. Oh! What a sight is revealed! What snowy whiteness of skin — what delicate fullness — what gentle swellings mark that half concealed seat of tenderness and love's emotion!"

"Hush!" cried Edward. "Profane not — you will turn me distracted!"

"I knew it," replied the other, "and do not wonder that you have been overcome. Indeed, did I not know how that lovely object has already disposed of her heart, I could not answer for the safety of my own. But mark! who is the lady to the right of this high beauty? She who has just turned her face towards us? The lady with the green sash round her waist? Let me see; I can hardly describe her. She is a brunette — my favourite colour; and the most becoming one, I protest, I ever saw. What simplicity and archness in the expression of her oval countenance! What ease and liveliness in her looks! What a well formed neck; What a well formed waist! In the name of all the Graces, Edward, who is she?"

"She is the Miss Agnew I have so often mentioned," replied Edward. "She is the greatest coquette in the company; and when she is in the humour, a considerable quiz, but one always overflowing with kindness and good nature."

"By Heaven! Edward," exclaimed Charles, "you charm me. She is just such a one as I have vowed to love, if I could ever find. Serious beauty is too sublime for me. Give me life in my lady; a sprinkling of Attic salt to season her charms. No offence, Edward; I acknowledge your enchantress to be the more perfect beauty, according to the usual notions of such matters. But she is, perhaps, too exquisite for me. You are more highly gifted than you friend; and the eagle alone you know can look at the sun without injury. Methinks I could feel more at home basking in the less resplendent beams of that little luminary whose countenance seems to say, 'Here wit, and love's bewitching wiles, Unite with gay good humour's smiles.' You see she makes me poetical. Hasten forward, and introduce me to the Circean group. I long for a nearer view."

"Check your rapture first," said Edward; "and do not play the fool when we approach. Why, I believe your heart is already lost; your making poetry is an infallible symptom of such a misfortune."

"It is lost" replied Martin, "past redemption, unless you show me some fault in that lady; for I confess that I shall never see any myself. But, lead on. Give me the pleasure of an introduction. I hope to conduct myself so as not altogether to forfeit my claim to the possession of common sense."

They now advanced directly to the ladies.

"Miss O'Halloran! this is my friend, Mr. Martin," said Edward.

Ellen rose, and with a smile extended her hand to him, saying, "You are welcome, sir, to this part of the country. I hope so long as you remain here you will find it agreeable to your taste."

She resumed her seat; and Edward introduced him to Miss Agnew, who, without rising, made an assenting motion with her head, and said in a somewhat fluttered voice, that she joined in the welcome her friend had given him.

A nod from each of the other ladies, as they were severally named, returned by a bow from Martin, concluded the ceremony of the introduction.

Martin was next made acquainted with the gentlemen, who, each of them, gave him a hearty Irishman's shake of the hand, in token of a cordial welcome to their society.

A second country dance was now proposed. It was led off by M'Claverty and Ellen; while Edward followed with Miss Agnew for his partner, and Martin succeeded with the elder Miss Simpson. The whole set consisted of eighteen couples, who threaded the mazy rounds on the light fantastic toe, to the animating music of various instruments, with as much enjoyment as ever the inhabitants of this world experienced on such an occasion.

"Why you have completely done me out," said M'Claverty, wiping the perspiration from his brows with a handkerchief, after the set had broken up, to his fair partner, who appeared as free from fatigue as at the commencement. "An old half worn-out fellow like me, should never engage with so youthful and vigorous a partner."

"Why you have done better than I expected," replied Ellen; for she did not indeed expect much agility from her partner, who was now nearly fifty years of age, and had not latterly been much accustomed to mingle in such active pastime.

"I suppose so," said he; "but twenty years ago, had you seen me, you would have both expected and found that I could have tired out the best of our youngsters here. But there is a time for all things; and I am now hanging between the sober methodical feelings of your grandfather, and the warm impassioned throb of the young Barrymore, who, I think is the best winded youth in the company. And now, my dear madam, since I have acted my part with the juniors, I must go and recover a calmer and graver mood, in more venerable, but certainly not more delightful society."

So saying, he joined a party of the elder gentlemen, who, in a recess at one end of the room, were enjoying themselves in the less fatiguing, less animating, but, to them, not less interesting amusement of the 'Spoiled Fifteen'.

The company (to employ a usual phrase) enjoyed themselves to a late hour, and separated highly pleased with their entertainment, and congratulating themselves on having added one more happy evening to their lives.

CHAP. XVII.

What mighty power adheres to certain names! — When written on a little slip of paper;
They can convert it to a talisman. There is a magic in the very letters,
To raise the humble, to debase the proud,
To shield the weak, to overwhelm the mighty, To chain the conqueror to a desert rock,
And from a hermit to produce a courtier. —
Oh that such names were still the friends of virtue!
M'Carrocher.

The next morning Edward and Charles Martin called on the Recluse, with the Lord Lieutenant's letter. They found M'Nelvin with him; and both, especially the Recluse, seemed to be much dejected.

"My friend," said Edward, as he approached the latter, "I have taken the liberty of introducing into your habitation, a friend whom I believe you have never seen, but of whom you have often heard. This is the only son of your correspondent Sir Philip Martin."

"I am happy to see your father's son," said the Recluse to Charles. "You bear a near resemblance to what he was before my misfortunes began. Ah! you recall those days to my recollection, when your father and I were college classmates. The same was our age, the same were our studies, the same were our pursuits, and nearly the same were our opinions and principles. But different, far different has been the tenor of our lives. His has been smooth, calm and unruffled; for he was never the victim of those fierce passions which have brought on my head the storms of misfortune."

"Your misfortunes, sir," replied Martin, "are I believe now at an end; and, I hope, that my father and you, have, in the evening of your lives, a long period of tranquillity and happiness before you."

"My friends," observed the Recluse, "I will never distrust the kindness of Providence. But you will pardon my present seriousness, when I inform you that I have received news of a melancholy nature. You know, Mr. Martin, that I never had a sister, and but only one brother; now I have neither."

"What!" interrupted Martin, "is Sir John Hamilton dead?"

"Yes; and the manner of his death, is what, at present, so much afflicts me," answered the Recluse. "M'Nelvin has just brought me a letter, which he received last night from the post office, written by your father, in which he mentions that my brother who had, as you know, never been married, and had for a number of years past become a perfect sot, and associated with none but jockeys, huntsmen and profligates of every description, was found dead a few mornings since in a ditch at the road side, about two miles from his own house. There were no marks of violence on his person. His watch, his money, and every other article about him, remained undisturbed. But it was known that he left a neighbouring public house at a late hour the preceding night, in a high state of intoxication.

"These, and some other circumstances, induced the coroner's jury to return a verdict on the case, of 'Death by drunkenness', a death which I consider to be in no respect less horrible than suicide.

"Oh! I feel it awful to reflect that my only brother, who, however exceptionable his character might be in other respects, was always kind to me, should come to the termination of his existence in such a manner."

"Sir Francis Hamilton!" cried Martin, extending his hand to the Recluse, "permit me to address you by your proper title. You are now a free man. I hold the document in my hand which absolves you from the effects of your unfortunate duel, and restores you to society. May you long enjoy your freedom, friends and property!"

M'Nelvin's eyes sparkled at this intelligence. "God Almighty be praised for this addition to his other signal mercies!" he ejaculated, while Sir Francis hastily glanced at the signature of the letter.

"I expected this," said he, "from his Excellency's friendship. I see that it is his own hand writing."

"I sincerely congratulate you," said Edward. "This is a turn of Providence from which, I trust, will proceed many years of happiness to us all."

"But my poor brother!" said Sir Francis, his mind still full of his catastrophe. "O! That he had died a less sudden death!"

"Sir," said M'Nelvin, "in the midst of so many blessings, we ought not to repine, if the great Ruler of all, does not send them unmixed. His ways are inscrutable; his dispensations are frequently mysterious, but they never fail, in some shape, to redound to the advantage of his creatures. That your brother's death has answered some kind purpose of Providence both to himself and to others, it would be impious to doubt."

"My friend," cried Sir Francis, catching M'Nelvin's hand, "your words to me have ever been wisdom. I shall endeavour to grieve no more. God has removed him in the way he thought best. His will be done."

It was proposed that Sir Francis should without delay, relinquish his disguise and resume his proper appearance and station in society. To this he agreed, adding that he had the means at hand, and should, in a few hours, meet them at the Castle, free, fearless and undisguised.

Edward and Charles now left the cell, and with joyous hearts turned down the glen towards the shore; while M'Nelvin set off for Jemmy Hunter, in order to send him express to the sheriff of the county with information of the pardon his friend had received. Jemmy was soon on his journey; and that very evening returned with the following note from the sheriff, addressed to Sir Francis Hamilton:

Dear Sir

It is with great satisfaction that I acknowledge the receipt of yours of this morning, covering the commands of his Excellency, the Lord Lieutenant, respecting you, which, of course, it is my duty, as well as my pleasure, to obey. I shall make the agreeable communication known without delay to all the justices of the peace, jailers, and other officers, whom it concerns, so that you will be in no danger of personal molestation; and may appear in public whenever you think proper.

I have the honour to be, &c.

Edward and his friend having reached the beach, "Do you behold yon rock" said the former, "at the foot of the precipice to the right hand. It was from its summit, I first beheld the mistress of my heart."

"And it was there too," observed Martin, "I understand, that you were kept in durance for about four months, without once seeing the light of the sun."

"But," returned Edward, "it was there, I was more than compensated for that privation, by the light of her lovely countenance visiting me, and showing me the way to liberty."

"You are a happy man, I acknowledge," said Martin. "O! That my sweet brunette were to render me such a service."

"It is remarkable," observed Edward, "that we have been both doomed to lose our hearts in this bewitching country. After the warning I gave you of its

Circean influence, I think you displayed but little prudence in venturing to visit it."

"Ah! my friend," replied Martin, "I confess I am indeed caught. But I rejoice at it. If I am a captive, I have, at least, the grace to be content with my chains. Methinks I would not fly from my charmer, even if my flight were to deliver me from a rocky prison."

"Yours is the superlative of love, I admit," said Edward. "I could wish we had the proof of its sincerity. But shall we explore the interior of the rock?"

"Yes," replied his friend; "I am full of curiosity to view that nest, in which so many ill-formed projects of rebellion have been hatched."

"But, not so fast," interrupted Edward. "I see our two enchantresses yonder. It will, methinks, be pleasanter to join them. On some other occasion, we may visit the curiosities of this rock." As they walked towards the ladies, Martin observed, "Since you have the key to my feelings, Edward, you cannot but know that I am unhappy; for, I perceived that my little sly tempter looked rather askance on me last night. Whenever my eye caught hers she suddenly looked in another direction, and, as I imagined, attempted to appear sulky; and if her countenance was not too pretty to be ill-natured, I fear it would wear a perpetual gloom in my presence."

"Have courage," said Edward; "you must have your day of trial as well as others. I underwent a long heart-burning season of suspense. I endured insults, threats, ran the risk of assassination, and suffered under a long deprivation of the light of day, before I became certain that my fair one loved me. My sufferings at length softened her, and she confessed."

They had now advanced within hearing of the ladies. After the first salutation, "If it will not be intrusion" said Edward, "we should wish to share the pleasure of your ramble."

"We do not intend going far," replied Ellen. "We were just about returning when we saw you approaching."

"Could we prevail on you to extend your walk," said Martin, looking timidly at Miss Agnew, "we should be much gratified."

A pause ensued, each lady expecting the other to reply. At length, Ellen said, "If our company could indeed be of any service to you, gentlemen, we should cheerfully afford it."

"I assure you, ladies!" replied Edward, "there can be no species of recreation which we would prefer to your company."

"Nor," added Martin, fervently, "would we exchange that company for any other under the sun."

"You, Dublin gentlemen," said Miss Agnew, "have a bold knack at complimenting. Is such language frequent in your city?"

"I protest, Miss Agnew," said Martin, with simplicity, "I only speak what I feel to be true."

"Ah! young man," she returned, "you are now fallen from the sublime. I should like you to take another flight towards the sun — but no, the clouds will be high enough; for I should not wish you to be overcome with fatigue, if you are to be our companion when you descend."

"I am, indeed, too much overpowered by my present feelings to venture on any flight," replied Martin.

"Our presence is, perhaps, oppressive to you," said she. "We had better, therefore, separate."

So saying, she affected to turn away from him, but with a smile of such sweet good nature as threw him totally off his guard.

"Oh! no, Miss Agnew," he exclaimed, "do not leave me until I lay my heart open before you."

"Lay your heart open before me! What a sight it would be!" she exclaimed. "Why this must be another of your Dublin customs."

During this conversation, Edward and Ellen had proceeded some distance in advance of their friends, so that Martin perceived that he had an opportunity of expressing himself more freely and explicitly on the subject of his new born love.

"I shall now speak plainly to you, my lovely banterer," said he. "The language of feeling and of love is everywhere the same. It does not consist so much in the words, as in the manner and looks of the speaker. Ah! Have you not perceived, from the confusion of my eyes, the agitation of my manner, that you have become too interesting to me, too essential to my happiness."

"Sir," said she, interrupting him, "this is strange discourse; but we must follow our companions."

"Ah! let us imitate them too?" said he, "by loving each other."

"They know each other better than we do," she replied, "and are consequently more excusable in yielding to the impulse of mutual affection with which their virtues have inspired them."

While speaking this, she hastened so rapidly forward, that they had nearly overtaken their companions, before he had time to ask, "When I am better known, may I hope?"

"Perhaps so," was the only reply he received; but it was accompanied with a look that gave pleasure to his heart.

Ellen, conscious that the state of her feelings were too well known to permit an over-strained reserve to appear natural, had without hesitation accepted her lover's arm as they walked forward.

Her gentle pressure communicated a thrill of delight to his whole frame, and he could not help exclaiming, "Ah! Life of my heart! When shall I have a legal and exclusive claim to call thee my own, and to support thee thus in our walks, careless of observation, in the face of the world?"

"In that respect, I am not at my own disposal," she replied. "My father must act for me, or rather his wisdom must show me how to act, but my father dares not now act openly; and I should very much question the propriety of giving away my hand, while he lives, unless he appeared publicly on the occasion, to sanction the deed."

"And publicly he will appear," replied her lover. "His danger is over, and his disguise will be thrown off this very day. The new viceroy is his friend; and has reversed his outlawry."

"Oh, Edward, do you indeed speak the truth?" she exclaimed. "But why do I doubt? This consummates the blessings which Heaven has so graciously, so abundantly showered on us of late. Lead me to my father, that, in his presence, I may thank my God."

Miss Agnew, who had heard her last expression, was astonished at her fervency, but on learning the cause, she partook warmly of her joy, and earnestly joined in her thanksgiving.

Edward now informed Ellen, that he expected her father had, by this time, thrown aside forever, his disguise; and that in his own proper person, he would very soon appear at the Castle to confirm the intelligence with his own lips. "Even at this moment, he may be there," said he, "anxiously waiting to gladden the heart of his daughter with the certainty of his safety."

As the party approached the Castle, they were overtaken by M'Nelvin, in company with a stranger of a genteel appearance, who seemed somewhat beyond the middle age of life. He advanced towards them with a firm step and an air of courtesy, with a smile playing on his countenance, while M'Nelvin introduced him to them by the name of Sir Francis Hamilton.

Ellen startled, supposing that it might be her uncle, of whose death she had not been informed. "Sir John Hamilton, I rather suppose," said she.

"No; I have made no mistake. Sir Francis is his name," returned the poet.

"Yes, my daughter," exclaimed Sir Francis, "and I am thy father, the old Recluse, who have for six years been content to live as a hermit, because you were near him. He saw you all he wished you to be, and he was happy, although covered with the garb of poverty."

"You are indeed my father!" cried she. "That you are now safe, thank Heaven; but how have you become Sir Francis Hamilton. Has the Lord Lieutenant also given you a title?"

"No, my daughter. I have my title by inheritance. My brother, your uncle, is dead."

"Dead!" she exclaimed.

"Yes," replied her father. "He was a kind relative; and I cannot but feel much for his fate, it was so unexpected."

"But, I trust, he has gone to a better world," said Ellen, heaving a sigh; "the same journey is destined for us all."

They soon arrived at the Castle, where O'Halloran and his sister being informed of the revolution in the affairs of the Recluse, partook of the general thankfulness; and the whole party enjoyed several days of more felicity than usually falls to the lot of mortals.

CHAP. XVIII.

A FEW evenings after the foregoing incidents, Edward expressed a desire to view the celebrated cliffs called the 'Gabbon Heughs', being the only part of the Antrim coast which he had not formerly visited. The young ladies, Martin and O'Halloran, agreed to accompany him; and it was settled that they should set out after breakfast the next morning.

An invitation in the meantime was sent to the eldest son of Mr. Wilson, a youth who was well accustomed to navigate the coast, to attend with his sister, a young girl scarcely fourteen, which was accepted. Two of O'Halloran's servants were also taken along for the purpose of managing the oars in case of a calm.

The weather was as favourable as they could wish and at the time they left the shore the sun had dispelled every cloud, and was ascending towards his meridian altitude in unveiled majesty. The water was smooth and glossy; for there had been no high winds for several days. A moderate and favourable breeze sprung up from the north-west, and filling their sails, soon blew them from the land.

In about twenty minutes, they were opposite the mouth of Larne harbour, and perceived the ruins of Old Fleet Castle, at about two miles distant, standing on the narrow stripe of land called the Curran, which projects from the bottom of the valley in which Larne is situated, into the harbour, which expands southward into a large lake, extending upwards of five miles, between the main land and the peninsula of Magee. Our party perceived the bosom of this lake to be studded with merchant vessels of various sizes, while numerous yachts, barges and fishing boats, plied in the strait between the Curran and the peninsula. They soon, however, doubled one of the points of the latter, and lost sight of this animating scene. They now passed rapidly along Brown's Bay, at the eastern extremity of which O'Halloran informed them that there was to be seen one of those ancient monuments of superstition, called Rocking Stones, by the instrumentality of which, the druidical priests are said to have imposed on their followers, the belief that they possessed preternatural powers. The party stopped to examine this curiosity, and found it to consist of a prodigious rock, upwards of fifty tons weight, seated on two points so firmly as not to be displaced by the united strength of twenty horses, but so delicately poised as to be easily moved by the little finger of the gentlest lady of the party.

"What think you of this?" said Edward to Sir Francis. "Do you suppose that this rock was placed here by human means?"

"Tradition says so," replied Sir Francis, "but tradition ever loves to ascribe wonders to our ancestors. It particularly delights to magnify their personal prowess; and, indeed, if we could believe that the raising and fixing of this extraordinary balance was the work of our forefathers, we must acknowledge that they were a wonderful race, every way equal to those giants in strength and stature, to whom popular opinion has ascribed the construction of the celebrated Causeway at the lower end of this county. But I have formed a theory concerning these moving rocks, which, indeed, ascribes their construction to human hands, but does not require that they should be larger or more powerful than our own.

"Respecting this one in particular, I can see nothing absurd or improbable in the supposition that some dexterous mechanical genius finding it favourably situated for his purpose, attempted, and succeeded in the attempt, to afford it the small capacity for motion, which it possesses, by removing obstructions in some places, and placing impediments in others.

"But that it was raised and fixed in its present situation by human means, is not to be credited, for even if our remote progenitors had possessed machinery sufficient to lift and adjust such an enormous weight, it would have been nearly impossible to have hit upon the proper adaptation of its axles and their corresponding grooves, at the first trial, and they must have had to lift and re-lift it an innumerable variety of times, before they could get it to fit."

"What learned disquisition is this?" said Miss Agnew, coming round to the side of the rock where Edward and Sir Francis stood.

"It is concerning the creation of this moveable rock," replied Edward. "Sir Francis thinks that nature, in one of her wanton freaks, left it here by chance, either just as we see it, or more than half prepared to be made what we see it, by the chisel and mallet of some ingenious mechanic."

"So he thinks that giants had no hand in the affair," said Martin, who had followed Miss Agnew's footsteps.

"None in the least," replied Edward. "Nay, he scarcely believes that in the days of the Druids, our fathers were much larger or stronger than ourselves."

"That is consolatory to our modern dignity," observed Martin; "for what a degenerate race we must be, if our fathers could have set a rock of fifty tons weight, on a place, and in a position, where we could scarcely fix one of five hundred pounds!"

"It is time," said Sir Francis, "that we should prosecute our voyage, if we mean to visit the Gabbons, and return home by day light."

The party accordingly once more betook themselves to their bark, and scudded gently forward, before a pleasant breeze. They withdrew some distance from the land, in order to double a small island called 'Muck', the strait between which and the peninsula being too narrow to admit of an easy passage. When they had cleared this islet, the whole party being in high spirits, felt disposed to enjoy the luxury of music on the water. Edward and Martin had provided for such an enjoyment, by bringing flutes with them. After playing a few tunes in concert, they requested of the ladies a song.

Ellen, after stipulating that Miss Agnew should yield them a similar gratification on their return homewards, complied, and sang the following verses, the production of M'Nelvin, to the tune of Coolin, her favourite air, which the gentlemen had been just playing.

Oh the best spot on earth for delight to be found,
Is at home, where with joy our affection is crowned;
Where the wife of our bosom still meets us with smiles,
And the mirth of our children each sorrow beguiles.
In the walks of ambition, with power and with fame,
We may shine in full pomp, and establish a name,
but the flower of content, in the soul will not bloom,
Unless it first springs from our comforts at home.

When disease overtakes us, and wealth flies away,
When foes triumph o'er us, and flatterers betray;
Ah! where shall we find the true cordial of life,
But at home, in th' endearments of children and wife!
Whenever my sum of contentment is low,

When a bankrupt in bliss, and embarrassed with woe,
At home I still find, in the charms that are there,
A fund that o'erpays, and discharges my care.

The domestic contentment and tranquillity expressed in verses so finely sung, contrasted with the political exasperation and disasters of the times, made a deep impression on all present, which had not altogether subsided when they approached the tremendous Gabbons, the very name of which, to this day, makes the Roman Catholics of the North of Ireland shudder. O'Halloran related the story of the dreadful retaliation which, during the rebellion of 1641, the Presbyterians of the neighbourhood inflicted on the Catholics for a barbarous massacre which the latter had committed on the Protestants inhabiting the borders of the Blackwater, in the county of Armagh.

"The English garrisons had been drawn from that quarter," said he, "to assist the parliamentary army in making head against the famous Roger Moore, who had raised the standard of rebellion in aid of Tyrconnel, and a great many of the zealous Protestant inhabitants accompanied the troops as volunteers. This afforded an opportunity to the discontented Catholics, of avenging what they considered the cause of their country and their religion, on a proud progeny of foreigners and heretics.

"On an appointed night, they accordingly arose in arms, and seizing the Protestants of all sexes, ages, and ranks, murdered them, and threw their corpses into the Blackwater. Intelligence of this transaction soon reached the garrisons of Belfast and Carrickfergus, among whom were many of the Blackwater volunteers, whose families had suffered. Inflamed with grief and rage, and giving way to feelings of barbarity unworthy of the milder spirit and more philosophical doctrines of their religion, they resolved to inflict a terrible example of retribution on their enemies. Assisted by a large party of the Protestant inhabitants, the garrisons sallied out, and seizing about fifteen hundred Catholics of both sexes, bound them together in pairs, and drove them to the edge of that very precipice," said he, pointing to a long continued perpendicular range of limestone cliffs soaring upwards of two thousand feet above the surface of the sea, and sinking beneath it perhaps as many, "and from the top of that awful cliff, the very sight of which turns one dizzy, those unfortunate beings were whirled into the air, whence they plunged into the watery gulf below, for there is here no beach, where they sunk to eternity.

"The place is called, to this day, the 'Catholic Leap' and it is currently believed by thousands of that persuasion, that the blood of those who were

bayoneted previous to their being thrown over, which streamed down the
white front of the precipice, still does, and shall to the end of the world, remain
there as a testimony against the heretics. In this last part of their statement,
however," he continued, "they are mistaken, for no traces of blood are to be
seen along the whole course of this tremendous coast. "There are, indeed, at
the top of the cliffs some veins of a reddish ochry substance, which, in wet
weather, is apt to be washed down the precipice, and, at a distance, may be
mistaken for blood, and has, no doubt, given origin to this absurd story.

"The Catholics, indeed, seldom give themselves an opportunity of being
undeceived on this subject, for they abhor the place too much to visit it; and,
it is said, that none of their body have ever ventured since the occurrence of
this unjustifiable transaction, to reside on the peninsula, for, although it is really very fertile, and its present inhabitants prosperous and wealthy, they look
on it as an accursed place."

Having contemplated this sublime shore, with an intensity of interest, and
solemnity of feeling, which at length became painful, at the request of the
ladies, they turned their prow homewards.

Everyone was so much absorbed in the reflections naturally produced by
the foregoing recital, and the awfulness of the scene before them, that, for
some time, they all kept silent. No sounds, but those occasioned by the flap-
ping of the sails, or the rushing of the boat through the water, were heard to
interrupt the perpetual clamour of the multitude of gulls, curlews, herons, and
innumerable other species of sea fowl, that flew to and from the cliffs where
they had erected their airy nests, until the party had cleared the Gabbons, and
came opposite to the place where the green land shelves towards the shore.

Miss Agnew was then the first to break silence. Addressing Ellen softly,
she said, "Ah! there is the green earth again! I begin to breathe easier."

"Oh! how pleasant," returned Ellen "are the haunts of man, full of care,
and sorrow, and pain, and strife, as they generally are, to those who have just
emerged from such a scene of wildness, terror and awful sublimity, as that we
have just left behind!"

CHAP. XIX.

He prospered in his crimes — but what of that —
Twas but awhile — for soon a dreadful end
Arrived, and conscience — scorpion conscience,
stung Him to the very marrow, and the frown
Of overwhelming and eternal justice, Darkened his dying moments with despair.
Irish Soothsayer.

On reaching Isle Muck, it was determined to land there, to take some refreshment, and give the ladies an opportunity of recovering their spirits.

The surface of this islet consists of a green sward of about three acres in extent. It is uninhabited by man, but commonly contains a flock of sheep, and constantly a multitude of rabbits. It has a fine spring of fresh water near its centre, in consequence of which it is a favourite place of resort for boating parties of pleasure, from the neighbouring country. Our party, after partaking of a cold dinner, materials for which they had taken care to bring with them, spent some time in rambling over the islet, and viewing from different points, the magnificent and picturesque scenery of land, and water, and rocks, and ships, and castles, and cottages, that at various distances surrounded them. They at length seated themselves on a hillock, to enjoy the sweets of song and music before they departed. Miss Agnew was now called on for the performance of her stipulation with Ellen. She complied, and Edward accompanied her voice with the melody of his flute, while she sung, with much sweetness, the following words, to the tune of Burns's, *Bonnie Doon.*

Ye natal hills! that softly throw
Around my soul, a mystic charm,
Oft have ye seen the former joys,
That did my youthful bosom warm;
When blest with Ellen's lovely smiles,
I stray'd your verdant scenes among,

The singing was finished, and the company preparing to depart, when two men on horseback were perceived galloping with great speed along the beach of the peninsula, opposite the islet. In a few seconds, a body of ten or twelve countrymen, in pursuit of them, also appeared, who on seeing our party drew back, but not until they had fired some shots at the fugitives, one of which brought the foremost horseman to the ground. Our party had brought some fowling pieces with them. O'Halloran, Sir Francis, Edward and Martin, each seized one, and ran immediately to the boat. In a few minutes they were on the opposite shore, and had rescued the wounded man and his companion from their assailants. But what was their astonishment to find the fallen fugitive, no other than the notorious Sir Geoffrey Carebrow?

Compassion predominated over resentment in their bosoms; and without hesitation, they resolved to yield all the relief in their power to the man they had so much reason to detest. They instantly placed him in their boat, and, at the earnest entreaty of his attendant, the infamous Berwick, who represented that he had no other mode of escaping from his pursuers, they received him also on board.

They had scarcely regained the Isle Muck shore, when they perceived a man, waving a white handkerchief, running down the declivity which led to the beach, towards them. He soon reached the bottom, from whence he suddenly ascended a high rock connected with a headland which overlooked the islet, from which it jutted, forming a kind of terrace, hanging over the narrow strait that separated the two shores. Approaching the edge of this, he stood still and beckoned to our party, who advanced towards him. He appeared to be a very large active man.

His head was wrapped in a red handkerchief, wound round the forehead, extending down the cheeks, and covering the chin, so as effectually to conceal his features. He wore a short roundabout of brown cloth, with buckskin breeches, and had a leathern belt round his waist, from which was suspended something like a sword or huge dagger.

When near enough to be distinctly heard, he called out, with a loud voice, "Be joyous! Be joyous! Do not interrupt your pleasure. The blood, the tortures, the groans of your countrymen pass for nothing. Be joyous. Follow your revels. Let the pleasant melody of your flutes delight you; and let your pretty ladies sing to you to wantonness. Why should you be sad! The desolation, the ravaging, the destructions, the burnings, the bayonetings, the shootings, the hangings, the gibbetings, cannot reach you. They are destined for us, an unpitied, execrated, persecuted, proclaimed, outlawed, miserable race; whose homes are ruined, whose families are scattered, and whose heads are sold for a price.

"But I am not come to reproach you. Among you, we have friends, in whose safety we rejoice. But why prevent us from taking a sweet revenge on our enemies? They are also your enemies, and have sworn lies to bring some of you to destruction; and even now, when you return them good for evil, gall is boiling in their hearts against you, and they would rejoice if that isle would turn a volcano, and swallow you in its flames, if they themselves could escape. They have hunted us here in our hiding places, from hatred and from avarice; for they would earn the price set upon us, while their hearts would riot as in luxury, at the spectacle of our destruction.

"But although they were strong, and we were weak; although they had a band of soldiers in their train, we had prevailed over them, and had you not interfered, their carcases would have soon bleached on the cliffs of the Gabbons, a feast for the eagle and the seafowl. When we first saw you there today, we took you for enemies looking for our concealments, and were about sinking you, by sending a volley of balls through your boat. But God prevented a deed for which we would have sorely lamented. We described your ladies, and concluded that your errand was pleasure, and not treachery. We now know you, and ask you to give up our enemies and yours. If you will not, however, be joyous, we will not molest you. But how can you feel joy in shielding the murderer of Nelson from justice?" He paused as if he had asked a triumphant question, and waited for an answer.

O'Halloran waved his hand, and endeavoured to address him in his own wild style. "Hear me," cried he, "and hear the voice of a friend. Our enemy is now helpless, and in our hands. We know his wickedness; we have felt his villainy, but his punishment does not belong to us. We form no tribunal in the country. We cannot, therefore, chastise the guilty. This man is wounded; I fear, for your sakes I fear, mortally wounded. We will try to save him that we may do the duty which man owes to man; and also that you may be free from his blood. If he dies, I trust God will forgive you. To God alone, vengeance for such crimes as his, belongs."

"Depart then," cried the man on the rock. "Since you will have it so. This dagger, which I hoped to have plunged into the heart of the destroyer of Nelson, since it cannot perform that office, shall never perform another; and I shall never have peace on earth, since I cannot have vengeance."

So saying, he ran to an angle of the rock, which overhung the sea, and with a mighty force cast the dagger from him. With the rapidity of a thunderbolt, it whizzed through the air, and sunk to the bottom.

"So sink to fathomless perdition the betrayers of their country!" exclaimed the man, and he darted from his airy stand with the headlong speed of a falcon, towards his companions.

On his disappearance, O'Halloran informed the astonished party, that he believed him to be M'Cauley, one of M'Bride's assassins, and one of the proclaimed rebels, who had no mercy to expect. "Poor fellow," said he, with a sigh. "His whole soul is devoted to an unfortunate cause, but a cause which he conscientiously believes to be just. But how did he allure Sir Geoffrey into this ambuscade?" said he, turning to Berwick, for Sir Geoffrey himself was unfit for conversation.

"Here is a letter," replied Berwick, "which will explain that matter."

O'Halloran at once declared the hand writing to be M'Cauley's. He read it aloud as follows: "Sir Geoffrey Carebrow is informed by the writer of this, who wishes to share with him the reward offered for the heads of M'Cauley, Darragh, Archer, Kelly, and some others of the proscribed rebels, that if he will meet him at the uninhabited house near Isle Muck, tomorrow afternoon, the writer will go with him, and point out a cave amidst the cliffs of the Gabbons, where they are secreted. This cave is accessible only by a very intricate path, which will be discovered to Sir Geoffrey. He may bring his servant Berwick with him, but must bring no military, lest alarm should be excited. The writer not wishing to be known, if military be brought, or any other servant than Berwick, whom he thinks trustworthy, he will not appear."

"Notwithstanding this caution," said Berwick, "my master brought fifty soldiers with him, but left them about half a mile from the place of meeting, and ordered me to accompany him there. The place is just behind that hill. On our way, after leaving the soldiers, I hinted to my master, that there might be treachery in the affair. This seemed to alarm him, but he persisted in going forward, saying that the rebels were now too much frightened to do any more mischief. Being well mounted, we soon arrived in sight of the 'Old Ruins', where we were to meet our unknown confederate, when perceiving the muzzles of two guns projecting out of one of the broken windows, my master's fear overcame his resolution, and we turned round to fly, but our flight towards the military was intercepted by a number of armed men, who were advancing on us. We had, therefore, nothing for it, but to take the road to the beach, which we did in such terror, that we scarcely knew whither we fled, and should undoubtedly have fallen into their hands had not your appearance checked their approach."

As Sir Geoffrey seemed to be in great torture, our party hastened homeward with all the sail their boat could carry, in order as soon as possible to procure for him more comfortable accommodations and surgical assistance; for they did not conceive it safe or humane to re-land him on the peninsula, now the resort of his infuriated and determined enemies. It soon became so calm that their sails were not of much service. They were therefore, furled; and the servants set to the oars. Sir Geoffrey becoming very faint, they gave him some wine, and laid him on the bottom of the boat, in as comfortable a position as their circumstances would permit.

His groans and ejaculations, indicating great torment of both mind and body, made a strong and melancholy impression on all present, especially the ladies. Cheerfulness, joy and mirth, vanished, and anxiety, gloom, and compassion occupied their places. In the mind of Ellen, as she saw her dreaded persecutor, the arch enemy of her peace, and the perjured betrayer of her grandfather's life, lying before her in all the agonies of mental despair and bodily pain, a suppliant for the compassion of those who had suffered so much from his wickedness, a mingled sensation of horror and pity arose, accompanied with an awful impression of the power of Providence, in frustrating the machinations of the wicked, and inflicting a just retribution for their crimes. Her feelings on this subject, became so intense, that she almost fainted, as she leaned on the breast of her father, but tears, the holy tears of heart-felt compassion, came to her relief.

"Why do you weep, my child?" asked her father.

"Ah! father," she replied, in a low tone, "I have been overcome by reflecting on that signal example now before us, of the certainty of vice meeting with punishment. That man's great wealth and influence seemed to place his crimes beyond the reach of human power to punish, but a mightier power, one that can be neither eluded nor withstood, has taken up the sword of justice. Oh! That it may be exercised in mercy, and not in proportion to his guilt! I cannot but feel for his severe anguish. He is one of God's creatures; and if his crimes have been great, his sufferings also are great."

"Be comforted, my daughter," said Sir Francis, in a soothing manner. "This sight must indeed be appalling to you. But remember that if God punishes severely here, it is for gracious purposes hereafter."

Edward who during this conversation, sat beside her, did not utter a word. He was alarmed for the effect of such a spectacle on her mind, and became quite impatient for their reaching home. He threw off his coat, and flew to one of the oars, which was wrought by a man who seemed rather fatigued; and putting to it his whole strength, gave such an increased impulse to the boat's motion on his side, that two men had to work the corresponding oar on the other, and the boat moved through the water with almost double velocity. The promontory of Ballygally soon drew near, and the bay in which O'Halloran Castle is situated, opened before them, and, in a short time the boat rested alongside of a small pier, where she was usually kept.

Sir Geoffrey was immediately conveyed to that Castle, which he had been so lately active in damaging, and the generous hospitality of which, he was now thankful to accept. Messages, at the same time, were despatched to request the attendance of Doctor Ferral, and Mr. M'Claverty. It was thought desirable that the latter should be made acquainted with the circumstances of the case, lest the government, or Sir Geoffrey's friends, might imbibe any misapprehension on the subject. The doctor attended immediately; and on examining the wound, unequivocally declared that it would be mortal.

When informed of his situation, he became greatly dismayed, and overcome with the dread of death. When the first shock of his terror somewhat subsided, the propriety of sending for a notary and a clergyman was suggested to him. He at first opposed this, but musing for a few minutes, during an interval of ease which medicine now procured for him, he ejaculated, "Yes, it must be so! My days are finished. Send for the Rev. Mr. Nichols, and for any notary you think proper, but let them come soon. In the meantime, request Miss O'Halloran to speak with me. A dying man cannot harm her; I wish her grandfather also to be present."

With trembling steps, Ellen approached his bedside, supported by O'Halloran.

"This is kind in you," said Sir Geoffrey. "I have asked you here to request forgiveness from you both, for the injuries I intended you. After which I shall, with an easier mind, solicit the forgiveness of Heaven."

They both assured him, that they forgave him with all their hearts.

"Dost thou, fair lady," said he; "thou whom I loved more intensely than ever I did any of thy sex; thou whom I so severely, so cruelly treated; dost thou really say so? Or is it only a fond illusion of my mind?"

"I do really say so," replied Ellen. "I do indeed sincerely forgive you, and may Heaven forgive you also!"

"And you pray for me too," said he. "Oh! Then, I may indeed hope; for Heaven will surely hear the petition of innocence and virtue like thine."

Then turning to O'Halloran, he said, "Much injured man, dare I hope that you also will pray for your enemy?"

"Yes," replied O'Halloran. "Unfortunate man, fervently do I pray, that the Almighty will grant you repentance, and pardon for all your crimes and he is able to pardon them, be they ever so aggravated and numerous."

"And art thou he," exclaimed the conscience-struck criminal, "to effect whose destruction, I did not, in the height of my vengeful feelings, scruple to sin against my soul? Ah! that lies heavy on me!"

"For that too," said O'Halloran, "I hope you will be forgiven."

"God bless you," cried the penitent, "and hear your prayers on my behalf. And oh! May you never feel the pangs of conscience, which I now feel. Oh! The sting — the fiery sting of conscience, that burns within me. Oh! Pity me — pray for me! But you have promised it, and you are not liars; you are not perjured criminals like me! O! My vile passions, revenge! — lust! — avarice! To what have you brought me? You have brought on me — wretched me — a load of guilt, greater than I can bear. Oh! That murdered innocence! That too was passion. Ellen, thou knowest of it. Didst thou not once speak of it? But hush — no — thou needst not hush; for God knows of it. Ah! I could not hide it from him; and he is now my judge! Oh! Pray for me, pray for me, that he will have mercy! But I had not mercy. She pleaded on her knees for mercy, but I would not hear her. Oh! There can be no mercy for me! O God of justice thou art terrible!"

He here convulsively covered his head, as if to conceal from his view something too dreadful to behold. Ellen could endure the scene no longer; for she had never conceived of anything so appalling as the horrible contortions of despair that disfigured Sir Geoffrey's countenance, and the wild flashing terror that gleamed from his eyes. She was therefore, obliged to withdraw from such a distressing spectacle of human misery.

CHAP. XX.

Beside the bed where parting life is laid;
And sorrow, guilt and pain by turns dismayed;
The reverend champion stood.
At his control Despair and anguish fled the struggling soul.
Comfort came down the trembling wretch to raise,
And his last faltering accents whispered praise.
Goldsmith.

Prompt to the calls of duty, the Rev. Mr. Nichols soon arrived; and never had a sinner more need of the consolations of the most merciful of all religions, than the despairing object to whom they now administered.

"No matter how great your crimes may be," said the holy man, when he found Sir Geoffrey had become sufficiently calm to listen to him, "an infinite propitiation — an omnipotent atonement has been made for human guilt. Put your trust in the great Redeemer, who died to ransom such as you, from the effects of their transgressions, when they feel a genuine contrition; and, acknowledging their offences, throw themselves on his mercy for pardon. Your penitence may be late; yet, it will be accepted, if it be sincere. He who could pardon the malefactor on the cross, is the same today, in power and in purpose, that he was then.

"Do not think that he died and suffered in vain, or that there can be any crime too great to be propitiated by such a sacrifice. No, the sufferings and death of the Son of God were a sufficient ransom for all the crimes committed by ten thousand worlds, although each of them were ten thousand times more heinous than the most heinous of yours. He who pardoned the guilt of the royal adulterer and murderer, he who cleansed away the abominations of Menasseh, and forgave the cruelty of the persecuting Saul, can blot out your iniquities; and no one who sincerely sought for his redemption ever sought in vain: for he is long-suffering, and full of kindness towards his creatures, and he has expressly said that, in the event of their repentance, although their sins be as scarlet, he will make them white as wool."

After this encouraging exhortation, followed by a fervent and animated address to the throne of Divine Mercy, the patient's mind became considerably composed, and, on the arrival of the notary, he was in a capacity to go through the task of arranging his temporal affairs. This being accomplished, he desired to see O'Halloran; and taking from his pocket a key, he presented it to him, together with a newly written paper.

"This key," said he, "opens a small set of ebony drawers, which you will find seated on a shelf in the south-eastern angle of my library, and this paper is a deed of gift of these drawers, and all that they contain, with the exceptions I shall immediately mention. This deed I now make over to you in the presence of this notary. In the drawers, there are testimonies of crimes I have committed, of which, I hope, through the merits and sufferings of my Redeemer, to obtain eternal forgiveness, but the promulgation of which, while it would do the world no good, would uselessly bring ruin on the reputation, and embitter the lives of several individuals, who may have yet long to live. The exceptions to which I have alluded, are three certificates of money I possess in the national funds, which are to be disposed of as mentioned in my will. Everything else contained in these drawers of value, or not of value, is bequeathed to you."

O'Halloran assured him that he would cheerfully take charge of these things; and endeavour to fulfil his intentions, as far as lay in his power, concerning them, and concerning all other matters that might be entrusted to his care. The patient was then left quiet, and the anguish of both his mind and body being greatly relieved, he fell into a slumber, which, although an uneasy one, continued till near the morning. When M'Claverty arrived, he was awake and considerably distressed from a recurrence of his bodily pain.

"In the name of heaven?" exclaimed M'Claverty, on entering and seeing the ghastly countenance of Sir Geoffrey, "how has this happened?"

"My evil career has been cut short," replied Sir Geoffrey. "I was shot at yesterday by a parcel of men, I believe some of the outlawed rebels, whose place of concealment I was endeavouring to discover. A ball has entered beneath my ribs, and I feel that my existence here will soon terminate."

"Shall I write this down?" asked the magistrate, "as your declaration of the means by which you came by the accident."

"You may, and I will sign it," was the reply.

This being done, he again fell into a slumber, which his pain did not permit to continue long; and he awoke with the hand of death upon him. He requested to see Ellen. When she entered his bedchamber, "Bless me, fair saint," said he, "and I shall die contented."

"May the God of Heaven bless you," she replied, while the tears filled her eyes, "and take you to himself."

"Amen!" he tried to utter, but the word died on his lips; and he sank back on the pillow, in the agony of death. Ellen gave a scream of terror, and was led from the appalling sight, almost senseless with horror. In a few minutes Sir Geoffrey was no more.

On investigating the circumstances of the case, the coroner's inquest gave a verdict of, 'killed by a gunshot wound, received from some person unknown, but supposed to be one of the rebels now in a state of proscription'.

After the funeral, the notary signified to Messrs. O'Halloran, M'Claverty, and Wilson, that they were appointed by the deceased, executors of his last testament, and requested their attendance the next day, at Carebrow Hall, in order that the manner in which he had disposed of his property might be made known to all whom it concerned. They accordingly met, and the will was read in the presence of all the testators and relatives who could conveniently attend, of whom a married sister, and two female cousins, both married, were the nearest of kin.

His whole property, both real and personal, was bequeathed to his sister, with the exceptions mentioned in the will, of which the principal was his government stock, amounting to £150,000, for which he held three different debentures. The first marked No. 1, for seventy thousand pounds, he bequeathed to Ellen, as an atonement for the persecutions his uncontrollable passion had obliged her to sustain. The others were to be equally divided between his two cousins.

The ebony drawers with all they contained, excepting these debentures, being bequeathed to O'Halloran, he proceeded according to the express direction of the will to examine them in private. In the first drawer, he opened, he found the debentures. In the second, he found the mortgage which he had given for sixty thousand pounds on his own estate. He immediately relocked the drawers, and returning to the company, desired so much of the will to be a second time read, as would enable him clearly to understand the testator's meaning, in bequeathing to him the ebony drawers, and their contents.

This being done, "Gentlemen," said he to the other executors, "I am so delicately situated, with respect to this legacy that my judgment cannot, at once, decide how to act. I shall, however, be governed by your opinions. I borrowed, as is now publicly known, a large sum from the deceased, and gave him, for security, a mortgage on my landed property, which mortgage, to my astonishment, I find in one of these drawers."

"Then it is undoubtedly yours," observed M'Claverty. "This explains the mystery of his anxiety to give you the key of these drawers, before he died, and, perhaps too, of his requisition that you should examine them privately, lest some interested person might displace that important paper."

"I am not clear on that point," returned O'Halloran. "This instrument might have been there without it recurring to his memory, when he dictated the will. For you are aware of the dreadful state of mind he was in at that time."

"But," replied M'Claverty, "if he could recollect where he kept the government securities, he might, it is to be presumed, easily recollect where he kept your mortgage."

"Gentlemen," interrupted the notary, "with your permission, I can, at once, decide this controversy. When writing that part of the will, the deceased declared to me that his intention was to give up to Mr. O'Halloran the incumbrance that he held on his property. He added, that he took this method of doing so, as he felt a repugnance to mention this mortgage in a will which might become public, and, at all events, would go down to the posterity of his relatives; for in several transactions connected with it, he had not acted in a manner satisfactory to his conscience."

"Since that is the case," said O'Halloran, "I believe I need not scruple to avail myself of this unexpected kindness of the deceased, who had an undoubted right to dispose of this part of his property as he pleased."

"Upon my soul," exclaimed M'Claverty, "you seem as much afraid of touching what is decidedly your own, as if you were committing theft. But I wish you joy of your good fortune, and on account of this business, I shall, notwithstanding all his faults, respect the testator's memory as long as I live."

The government debentures being now produced, each of the female cousins received that appropriated to her; and at the desire of his co-executors, O'Halloran placed that bequeathed to Ellen in his pocket-book, and in company with Mr. Wilson, returned home on horseback, ordering his servants to follow with the ebony bureau in the carriage.

That evening after tea, Mrs. Brown had left the room on some domestic business, and Martin had accompanied Miss Agnew on a ramble into the fields. Edward and Ellen, were therefore left to the unobserved and delicious enjoyment of their own society. They had been for some time conversing on late events, and were now indulging their imagination, in sketching scenes of future felicity, of which they were to be long in the enjoyment; or, in other words, they were building delightful 'Castles in the air', when O'Halloran entered. The 'baseless fabrics' immediately 'dissolved' and the lovers on again descending to the earth, found themselves in the midst of a castle of more durable materials; one whose rocky foundations and strongly cemented massive walls of stone and lime, had already withstood the pressure of several centuries, and were likely to withstand that of several more.

When O'Halloran approached, "My love!" said he to Ellen, "since God has, I hope, removed to himself, the man who lately so much disturbed your peace, I trust that any resentment you may ever have felt against him, is buried in his grave; and that you harbour no wish injurious to his memory."

She looked steadfastly in his face, and repeated, "Harbour, a wish injurious to his memory? No, my grandfather, my worst wish concerning him is that his soul may now be in Paradise."

"For that sentiment, dear, forgiving girl, then," said he, "receive this;" and he handed her the paper by which she became a government creditor, to the amount of seventy thousand pounds. "This shows, at least, that he wished to make some atonement for what he caused you to suffer. He has bequeathed you this."

She looked at the paper for several seconds, as if involved in some doubt concerning it. "And am I free to receive this legacy?" she asked. "As perfectly free," he replied, "as if I had myself willed it to you, on my death-bed."

Edward here started as if from a reverie. "Miss Hamilton," said he, "if your grandfather has no objection, I wish just now to speak with you a moment on this subject by ourselves."

"With all my heart," said O'Halloran; "but remember that it is not in the power of Sir Geoffrey's executors to make any other disposal of this property. So fastidiousness may only occasion unnecessary perplexity."

"I shall counsel her to accept it," replied Edward and O'Halloran immediately withdrew.

"As I trust," said the young lover, to the mistress of his heart, when they were alone. "As I trust that your fortune and mine, will soon be the same, for a letter containing my father's consent to my happiness, I expect daily, I hope that it will not be considered officiousness in me to suggest my wishes respecting your disposal of this legacy; for I perceive that you must receive it, although you are not obliged to keep it.

"My fortune does not require any addition. My present income, independent of my friends, is ample, even for the support of splendour; and the entailed estates of my father and my uncle, for the latter it is not likely will ever marry, will, in the course of time, descend to us or ours. But your grandfather is involved in a large debt to the estate of this very Sir Geoffrey, who has made you so considerable a legatee, and it would almost appear that he had done so to enable you to relieve from this incumbrance, a man whom he had so seriously injured."

"It is right! Edward," she replied. "How kind you are to advise me thus. My grandfather's debts shall be discharged immediately out of this sum. Let us hasten to him, for I shall not be easy until it be done."

O'Halloran had gone to his library. They followed him, Ellen still holding the paper in her hand.

"What," said he, as he saw them approaching, "have you decided already? I see you are a persuasive adviser, Mr. Barrymore."

"Grandfather!" said Ellen, running to him, and catching him by the hand, "you must grant me one request."

"Be assured, my dear," he returned, "that I shall grant you anything in reason."

"In reason, or out of reason," she observed, "you must grant me this one."

"That is very provoking, Ellen, you did not use to be so unconscionable. But what would you have? my child."

"I would have you to receive this," said she, presenting him the government note.

"If it be to manage it for you, I shall receive it with pleasure," he replied.

"No," said she, "manage it for yourself, my grandfather. I do not wish Sir Geoffrey's successors to have any claim upon you."

"They have no claim upon me," he replied. "But, if they had, do you think I would rob you to satisfy them? No, I would rather sell my last acre."

"Are you not largely indebted to Sir Geoffrey's heirs?" she asked.

"I do not owe them a fraction, my child," he answered. "But I cannot, indeed, I cannot bear this!" Here tears of fondness and joy swelled in his eyes. "Your affection makes your old grandfather weep like a babe. Come to my arms, and let me embrace the daughter, the delight of my old age." So saying he impressed a parental kiss on her glowing cheek, and sat down for a few seconds, to recover from his agitation. Then again rising, "Edward! Ellen!" said he, catching a hand of each, and joining them, "May your children, and your children's children, love you with a love like this, and make your hoary age as happy as you now make mine!"

"Thank you, father, for this inestimable gift," cried Edward; and forgetting himself in the delirium of the moment, "Permit me too to embrace such excellence," said he to Ellen, and he also impressed a burning kiss on her cheek ere she was aware. In an instant, she burst from his embrace, and ran to conceal her confusion in an anti-chamber.

Edward immediately perceived that he had acted rudely, and had given offence, and heartily condemning himself, he begged O'Halloran to intercede for his pardon. "I am mad!" cried he; I have insulted an angel. I know not what I am doing."

"Young man!" said O'Halloran. "I confess you are rather vehement. But, be at ease, I shall try to procure your forgiveness."

He then sought Ellen, and leading her back into Edward's presence, "You must forgive this rash youth," said he, "for I set him the example; and he only forgot that he had not the weight of nearly threescore years on his head, to entitle him to such privileges."

"Pardon me, Miss Hamilton!" said Edward, imploringly. "By Heavens! you know I would rather cut off my right hand than offer you an intentional insult."

"Well, sir," said she, "to please my grandfather, I will overlook this piece of folly. But you must remember never to treat me again with such disrespect!"

"Never, never, my beloved!" he exclaimed, as he fervently kissed the hand she held out to him in token of reconciliation.

"Well!" said O'Halloran, seating himself on a chair, and laughing heartily at them. "What fools you are! What a love-scene you have acted in the presence of an old man! It will be well for you if I do not discover the whole to Miss Agnew. She would, undoubtedly, divert young Martin with it for a month to come."

They both begged that he would not mention the incident, it was so ridiculous, and was now no more to be thought of by themselves. He cautioned them to keep their own secret, and he should certainly not betray them.

"But!" said Ellen, wishing to turn the conversation into another channel, "You refuse my offer; may I ask the reason?"

"Because, my child," said O'Halloran, "I do not need it." I have a clear income of five thousand a year, which is more than enough for an old widower of fifty-nine, who has no longer any ambition to become conspicuous in the world."

"How is this! grandfather," said she, "pardon my enquiry, for you know your welfare is necessary to mine."

"I know it, my daughter, and shall satisfy you."

He then produced the mortgage, and informed them that he also was a legatee of Sir Geoffrey, at least to the amount mentioned in that instrument, but to how much more he did not himself know, as he had not yet examined all the ebony drawers.

"Then, sir," said she, "I suppose I must keep my legacy."

"I suppose so," he replied; "and I shall just mention one thing to you, my daughter, not for the purpose of stifling the feelings of generosity in your bosom, which I hope will ever remain active there, but to remind you that property honestly obtained, should not be thrown away. You may have children, and grandchildren."

Edward and she instinctively exchanged looks full of meaning and emotion, and in much confusion she hastily left their presence.

CHAP. XXI.

My safety thy fair truth shall be,
As sword and buckler serving; My life shall be more dear to me,
Because of thy preserving; Let peril come, let horror threat,
Let thundering cannons rattle; I fearless seek the conflict's heat,
Assured when on the wings of love, To Heaven above,
Thy fervent orisons are flown,
The tender prayer Thou putt'st up there,
Shall call a guardian angel down, To watch me in the battle.
Popular Song.

That very evening one of O'Halloran's servants brought from the post office, a letter to Edward from his father, and one to Sir Francis Hamilton from the Lord Lieutenant. Edward's was as follows:

My Son,

A few days ago, I received from you a very foolish letter, requesting me to consent to your marriage with a woman I never saw, nor, until that very moment, ever heard of. I took, of course, some pains to inquire concerning her, and her connexions. The only person from whom I could obtain much information, is your old mendicant protégé, who praises her in a style that I cannot well understand, but from which I can gather that she is a great beauty. I presume, therefore, that in the ardour of your admiration, you have endowed her with angelic qualities, for in the eyes of every love-sick young man who has a handsome mistress, she cannot be aught else than an angel.

But, sir, how does it happen that you could suppose your father as easily blinded as yourself on such a subject? Or how could you imagine that bright eyes and a fine complexion, could make up in my estimation for obscurity of birth, and rebellious connexions; — for I understand that the lady in question, is daughter to an outlaw, and granddaughter to a rebel; and a rebel too of the very worst stamp; one whose influence in the country has been wilfully perverted from preserving its tranquillity to promoting its destruction. How could the loyal, the virtuous, the patriotic Edward Barrymore, he of whose promising talents and acquirements, his friends have been hitherto so proud, degrade himself, and the family whose representative he is, by such a connexion?

I speak nothing of the lady's want of fortune, although I am informed that her grandfather, on whom she totally depends, has mortgaged his property for more than it is worth, for the wicked purpose too of procuring supplies for the rebel armies.

If ever the fomenter of a country's ruin deserved death, this jacobinical old man, according to all accounts, did so. But your boyish and imprudent attachment for a handsome face, interfered and snatched him from justice. When I first heard of that affair, I was silly enough to approve of your conduct, as I ascribed it to a generous impulse of humanity and gratitude for one who had, as it is reported, saved your life. But I now see that a foolish passion for a pretty girl, was at the bottom of your apparent benevolence. What your uncle will say on this subject, I cannot tell, for I have not yet communicated it to him. But as he scarcely approved of your interference in behalf of the old rebel, I presume he will utterly disapprove of your intention to contaminate the purity of your family blood, by marrying the granddaughter. — But enough on this subject.

Ah! Sir, is it a time for any of the house of Barrymore to bask indolently in the rays of beauty, or in the enjoyment of female blandishments, when the fabric of society is tottering to its very foundations? When your country is assailed at once by domestic traitors and foreign invaders, ought you, in the vigour of youth and activity, to desert her cause, and lie supinely sunk under the fascinations of love and luxury?

I call on you, I order you, to throw off your disgraceful chains and fly to the standard of your King and country. The French have landed, in what force it is not exactly known, on the Connaught coast. But it is certain that they will form a rallying point for insurrection. It is said that the peasantry have already swelled their ranks to a countless multitude. I take the field tomorrow, as commander of a regiment of cavalry, in which I have preserved for you the rank of a captain.

*Cornwallis has placed himself at the head of the troops; and I trust
that we shall all exhibit a zeal and soldier-like conduct, worthy of our
cause, and of such a renowned commander.*

*I shall expect you to join us, wherever we may be encamped, in a week
at farthest from this date; and, if you do your duty on this occasion, as
becomes you, your late errors will be forgiven, by your indulgent father,*

THOMAS BARRYMORE.

The Lord Lieutenant's letter required Sir Francis Hamilton's immediate attendance on the army.

** * * * * * * * At what an awful crisis have I been entrusted with the
government of this unfortunate country? Treason, rebellion, massacre,
and invasion, have shaken her to pieces, and have prostrated her into the
depth of misery.*

*I remember you were ever proud of being an Irishman. Show yourself
now worthy of the name, and fly to the standard which is raised for the
preservation of whatever your country yet possesses of law, order,
civilization, and rational freedom.*

*I want such men as you about me. Your counsels whether as a
statesman or a soldier, to me will be valuable; and they will be the more
acceptable, as I know that they will be given with uprightness, and with
the feelings not only of a wise man, but of an Irishman, anxious for the
safety and welfare of his country.*

*I hope you have, before this time, availed yourself of the exertion of the
executive prerogative which I made in your favour. I need not say how
happy I felt at being thus able to pay the debt of gratitude under which
you laid me on that terrible night at Yorktown, when the furious
American, Colonel, Scammel, made his desperate attack on our defences.
On that dreadful night, his brandished weapon hovered over my head,
and would have cut short my existence, had you not heroically interposed
and clove him to the earth.*

*I could, with much gratification, dwell longer on those trans-Atlantic
subjects, but with me time is now precious; and I hasten to request you to
lose none in coming to resume your former station in my military
household, as my confidential aide-de-camp.*

I have with true and undiminished esteem, the honour to be, &c.

CORNWALLIS.

Edward and Sir Francis made hasty preparations to set off, in obedience to these requisitions, the next morning.

Edward saw that, with respect to Ellen, his father had received some gross misrepresentations, which caused him, in the meantime, to labour under several grievously mistaken impressions, but which he knew that, at their first interview, he could, by a simple statement of the truth, easily remove. He did not, therefore, think proper to disclose to either her or her friends, this part of the intelligence he had received; for, besides his reluctance to wound their feelings, he did not wish to occasion a renewal of O'Halloran's interdiction, to address her on the subject of love, which interdiction he had just withdrawn, under the conviction that, from the nature of her present circumstances, her future prospects, and recently discovered parentage, there was but little danger of the Barrymore's offering much opposition to the intended union.

Ellen was much agitated on parting with her lover. "You are going," said she, "into danger. I may never see you again. Oh! I thought — I presumptuously thought, that all my misfortunes were at an end — but I may yet have the greatest that could befall me, to endure. And my father too — to be torn from me. Oh! Heaven grant that I may not have just found him only to lose him forever!"

"Dearest Ellen," replied her lover, "be comforted. This new disturbance, this daring invasion will not be long able to withstand the power that shall be led to its suppression under the direction of such an able commander. When we shall have driven our enemies from the country, no impediment, my love, will then exist to the completion of our happiness. I must now assist my country to the best of my abilities, but fear not but that I shall soon return safe and victorious, and shall then claim her fairest daughter as the dear reward of my services."

"Go, then, my Edward; and, if my unceasing prayers can prevail on Heaven to protect thee, thou shalt indeed return safe and uninjured."

"Then, my love," said he, "heaven, I am assured, will hear thy prayers; and I shall have nothing to fear."

They now exchanged vows of lasting fidelity; and Ellen retired to seek sympathy from the friendship of Miss Agnew. But Miss Agnew was in almost as much need of a comforter as herself. She had just taken a tender farewell of Martin, who had resolved, in this alarming juncture, to volunteer his services to the government.

Sir Francis requested Jemmy Hunter to accompany him, as his attendant, to which he readily agreed after a reluctant and weeping consent was obtained from his Peggy, to whom he gave a tender embrace at parting; and with a full and manly heart said, "May God keep you and the wean, frae a' ill till I see you again!"

With her child, (which was now about six weeks old) in her arms, she followed him to the door. "You were aye kind to me, Jemmy," said she, half choked with grief, "but you are noo gaun in a lawfu' cause, and in guid company. May Grace gae wi' ye! — an' may He keep you that can keep you, an' bring you safe back to your wife an' wean!" She then retired to offer up to heaven, in simple but fervent language, the artless wishes of her soul for the husband of her affections, the father of her child.

As Jemmy rode to the castle to join the gentlemen, previous to their departure, he thought intensely of his Peggy. "Gude keep her for a guid creature, and the wee helpless wean — how it looked at me!" Here a few tears swelled in his eyes.

"But I maunna be such a chicken as this," thought he, and he wiped them off with a courageous resolution, that they should have no successors.

CHAP. XXII.

Popular Song.

The French under the command of General Humbert, an experienced and active officer of revolutionary origin, landed about the middle of August, to the number of between eleven and twelve hundred men, at Killala, in the west of the island. They brought with them a large quantity of arms and warlike stores of every description, for the supply of the multitude of insurgents, whom they expected immediately to join their standard; and, in some degree, they were not disappointed; although the conciliatory measures so prudently adopted by the new administration, prevented their hopes from being altogether realized.

Landing in a Catholic district, they were indeed joined by a considerable number of the more zealous of the lower orders of that persuasion, but they were denied the more efficient aid of the influential and wealthy portion of the community, who had universally embraced the terms of the late proclamation of indemnity, and remained at peace.

The French, with their Irish auxiliaries, soon advanced upon Castlebar, the capital of Mayo, the county in which they landed, and there briskly attacked and defeated General Lake, who commanded a small division of the royal troops. This success opened their way into the interior of the country, and, besides increasing the number of their insurgent allies, spread consternation among all ranks of the royalists throughout the kingdom. Cornwallis, however, was soon on his march at the head of ten thousand men, in order to wrest its short lived triumph from the invading standard.

He was about three day's march from the metropolis, when Edward Barrymore and his friends joined him. Sir Francis Hamilton received from the Lord Lieutenant all that cordial and friendly welcome, which, from his knowledge of that nobleman's warmth of heart, he expected; and was immediately appointed to the office which he had been solicited to accept. Edward's father was so well pleased with his orders having been so promptly obeyed, that he received his son with much kindness.

"This is right, Edward," said he, taking him aside, "you will now have a more honourable employment than sighing at the feet of a woman."

"Ah! sir," replied Edward, "you do not know that woman, otherwise you would not speak so lightly of her."

"So you think, foolish boy. I see she has you still in her chains. But I shall not at present reproach you. I indeed admire your obedience and zeal on this occasion the more, that I perceive what they have cost you. But when you choose a wife, if you would please me, you must choose one well connected."

"Oh father, this lady's connexions are not properly known to you."

"I have heard of them."

"But permit me to say that you have heard misrepresentations."

"Was not her grandfather a rebel chief, condemned to the gallows?"

"Yes, sir, but deservedly pardoned. He was always virtuous, humane, and honourable."

"Is her father not an outlaw for murder?"

"No, sir!"

"And what is he?"

"His name is Sir Francis Hamilton."

"What! he who came here today with you, and whom his Excellency esteems so much?"

"The same is Ellen Hamilton's father."

"Why, I was told that O'Halloran is her name, and that her grandfather to save her from the disgrace of bearing that of a murderer, gave her his own."

"He gave it to her from affection, as he brought her up from her infancy, her father having had to fly the country."

"It is true then, he was an outlaw?"

"Yes, but not for murder. His wife's honour was assailed by a villain. For her he fought, as, in similar circumstances, you would have done, and conquered."

"Well, my son, we shall speak more of this hereafter," he said, perceiving the Lord Lieutenant and Sir Francis Hamilton advancing towards them.

"Mr. Barrymore," said his Excellency, "permit me to become acquainted with your son, of whom my friend, Sir Francis Hamilton, whom I beg leave to introduce to you, speaks so highly." The introduction having taken place, the party accompanied Lord Cornwallis to his quarters.

They had scarcely sat down, when an express arrived with intelligence that the enemy had penetrated as far as Tuam, in the county of Gallway, little more than a day's march distant, where they had chosen ground for an encampment, which they had commenced entrenching, as if they intended there to await an attack. Their number was not ascertained, but, including the French, it was supposed to be nearly twenty thousand.

Orders to move forward were immediately issued. The trumpets sounded, the drums beat to arms, and in a few minutes the army resumed its march.

The honourable Thomas Barrymore at the head of a squadron of horse, led the van. His son had a station assigned to him in the same corps, in order that he might be near his father.

That night brought them within ten miles of the enemy; and, at about nine o'clock the next morning, they perceived the insurrectionary banners in the vicinity of the tri-coloured flag, floating in the air on the opposite hill, about a mile distant, which was covered with a countless multitude, but who were evidently, with the exception of the French, quite destitute of everything like military discipline.

Humbert had indeed made every arrangement in his power, to repel the formidable attack which he knew he was about to sustain; and something like a regular division of his forces into four bodies appeared to have taken place. His own men were in the centre, where the ground was most accessible. Behind them, and on each side, large bodies of the Irish, covering almost the whole rising ground, were placed. The French artillery was stationed at intervals along the front of their line.

Between the two armies there was a low broken hedge, along which, on the side next the royal army, ran a small stream, but which, at this time, owing to a long series of dry weather, contained very little water. However much assured of victory, the military caution of Cornwallis, would not permit him to make the attack until he had ascertained the most practicable spot for passing the obstruction with his cavalry.

For this purpose he despatched Colonel Barrymore, with a party of about fifty horsemen, up the streamlet, while another trusty officer, with a similar party, went on the same errand in the opposite direction. Edward attended his father on this duty, and Jemmy Hunter who had, on his arrival at the camp, obtained permission to join the cavalry, was also of the party. The detachment which went down the stream soon found such a passage as their general wanted and immediately returned. As the Barrymore detachment, therefore, gained the brow of a small hill, about half a mile distant from where they had set out, they heard the royal trumpets sounding; and immediately a heavy cannonade was commenced by the King's troops, reciprocated almost instantly by their opponents. Knowing by this, that the object of their search was elsewhere discovered, they were about returning to their former station, when they observed a body of about a hundred and fifty insurgent horsemen descending the hill, leading from the extremity of the enemy's right, and approaching towards them at full speed. They immediately formed into a compact body, and riding briskly among the insurgents, whose very speed had deranged their order, if they had ever possessed any, in a few minutes put them to flight with considerable loss. They had scarcely pursued the fugitives to the bottom of the hill, when two men on horseback were perceived rushing furiously down in order to rally them.

One of these men in particular displayed great energy. With a drawn sabre he endeavoured to arrest the progress of those who seemed resolved to fly past him, exclaiming, "Cowards! see what a handful of men you fly from! Turn, for heaven's sake, and fight. This day decides the fate of your country. Follow me; if ye are men, follow me!"

Only about thirty of the most resolute reined their horses and followed him, as foremost and almost alone, he rushed on his opponents. The first and second of Barrymore's horsemen he met scarcely obstructed his flying speed. He gave each only a passing blow with his sabre, by which he clove them from their horses, as if he had struck twigs from their stems. Opposition seemed to give way before him; and, almost unobstructed, he directed his fearful course towards Colonel Barrymore.

Edward, alarmed for his father's safety, galloped forward to arrest the death-blow, which he saw aimed against him, but ere he could prevent it, that blow was given, and his father had fallen. With uncontrollable fury, he rushed to meet his terrible antagonist, who perceived him, while he was yet some paces distant; and re-dashing his spurs into his horse, darted towards him.

The horses met with a dreadful momentum, and were both overthrown. But in an instant, their riders had gained their feet. The same instant they recognised each other, and paused, as if surprise had for a moment paralyzed their strength.

Edward first exclaimed, "M'Cauley!"

"Barrymore!" was the immediate reply.

That moment Edward heard a groan from his father as some person raised him from the ground. "Villain! die! you have killed my father," he shouted, flying with the force and agility of a lion on his antagonist, who, however, coolly parried the attack without returning it, crying out, at the same time,

"By the life of him you saved from the gallows! Barrymore, I will not hurt you, if you should slay me on the spot."

An instinctive feeling of reluctance to destroy a man thus voluntarily throwing himself in his power, occasioned Edward to desist from the attack.

Another of the insurgents now rode forward, crying out, "Slay him, M'Cauley! Down with the young traitor. Had you slain him when I advised you, at the Point Rock, you would not now have to fight him. But, by God! There's another traitor that I'll smite to the earth."

He had that moment seen Jemmy Hunter, who was advancing to Edward's assistance. He hastened towards him, exclaiming, "Accursed villain! I owe you a deadly debt. Receive this!" But before he could wield his weapon, Jemmy's sabre had fallen with well-aimed and resistless force, on his neck; and his head hung half severed from his body, as if a schoolboy's wand had broken down the head of a thistle, and he immediately reeled from his horse.

"Darragh! you were owre lang a gettin' this," cried Jemmy. "Had I gein ye't a twal month ago in M'Gorley's stable in Larne, ye would hae gane to your lang hame wi' fewer sins on your head."

"Is it you, traitor!" cried M'Cauley; "but you shall pay for it;" and he aimed a fierce and sudden blow at Hunter. But the stroke was dexterously avoided, although it did not fall without mischief, for Hunter's horse received it in his neck, and tumbled to the ground. M'Cauley would have repeated the blow with fatal effect, had not Edward sprung forward, and struck the falling blade with such force that it almost forsook its owner's grasp.

"Desperate wretch!" cried he, "will you commit another murder in my sight, and expect I will look tamely on it? Ah! Hear you my father's groans? O Heaven! He has been slain by an assassin — a monster!"

"Assassin!" reiterated M'Cauley, assuming the countenance of a fiend. "By Heaven! that word has sealed thy doom. Away with it!" cried he, as if he was discharging some troublesome feeling that seemed tenaciously to harbour in his breast. "Away! All regard for the preserver of O'Halloran is now fled."

So saying, he withdrew a step backwards, as if to come forward with a surer aim, and redoubled force. Edward met him with equal force; and his father's groans still ringing in his ears, with a higher degree of rage than he had ever before felt.

Fury flashed from the eyes of both, and when their weapons met the clash shook the air, the fiery sparks fell around them, and they both reeled with the concussion.

Edward was an expert and educated swordsman; and he now applied his science for his safety.

A forward thrust by M'Cauley, who conceived that he had a fair opportunity for such a manoeuvre, was so well observed and so dexterously turned aside, that the weapon passed without doing injury, while Edward's was instantly buried in his antagonist's body, who fell, but uttered not a groan.

Edward immediately ran to his father, whom he found almost speechless. But on hearing his son's voice he faintly uttered, "Pursue the enemy!"

A sense of public duty rushed on Edward's mind, and mounting the horse of a man whom he ordered to remain with his father to support him and keep his wound staunched, he galloped after his men, who had again discomfited the insurgent party, and were just commencing a new pursuit. Having followed them to the very verge of their camp, which was now getting fast into confusion, he withdrew them back to the scene of his late action, in good order, no attempt being made by the enemy to follow them.

Indeed by this time the attention of the insurgents all over the hill was principally engaged in providing for their own safety. Cornwallis had ordered a large party of both horse and foot to march by the passage over the stream, that had been discovered as before mentioned, for the purpose of out flanking the enemy's left, while his powerful artillery continued to commit great havoc among them in front. As soon as this detachment reached its destination, and opened its fire, the insurgents on the whole of the left and rear of the French, fled in all directions, and were pursued with a too terrible slaughter by the cavalry.

General Humbert seeing that it was in vain to resist longer, hoisted the white flag. The firing immediately ceased on both sides, and after a short negotiation, the French having lost about one third of their number, surrendered themselves prisoners of war. The insurgents to the right of the French, now followed the example of those who had occupied the left; and in a short time, there was no enemy to be seen on the field.

Being persuaded that the rebels were thoroughly dispersed, and that there was no danger of them rallying again to give any more disturbance, from motives of humanity, the viceroy soon ordered the pursuit to cease, so that this complete and decisive victory, which terminated the disastrous insurrection of 1798, was achieved with far less bloodshed than from the numbers arrayed on both sides, previous to the engagement, could have been expected.

This was undoubtedly owing to the judicious and humane plan which the viceroy took to disperse the insurgents, rather by intimidation than actual slaughter, in which he completely succeeded, as well as to his ordering the pursuit to be so soon relinquished. It was fortunate also, that there were few such resolute and daring men among the Southern conspirators as M'Cauley, otherwise the resistance, and consequently the slaughter, would have been infinitely greater.

That unfortunate man, on hearing of the landing of the French, had left his concealment at the Gabbons, and, in company with Darragh, and eight or nine more of the proscribed Northerns, joined the invaders on their march from Castlebar to Tuam. These men all met with their death in this engagement.

When Edward had obtained accommodations for his father in the house of a gentleman in the neighbourhood, and had left him under surgical care, he returned with Jemmy Hunter to where M'Cauley and Darragh lay, in order to ascertain their fate. The latter was dead. He had died almost instantly, his head, as has been already observed, having been nearly separated from his body. The former was still alive, but very much exhausted.

Edward proposed that he should be carried to a house, and receive the care of a surgeon, but to this he would not consent.

"Here," said he, "is the most honourable place for me to die, and I rejoice that my death has been occasioned by honourable hands. My life was rendered miserable, but my spirits were never depressed; nor was I ever so irresolute as to abandon my purpose, for fear of dying an ignominious death and Providence has been kinder to me than I perhaps deserved.

"I have not always squared my actions by the rules of conduct, or the notions of morality generally adopted by men. An instinctive perception — some might call it the impulse of feeling, but I have flattered myself that it was the dictate of conscience that generally directed me in my path, and pointed out what I should do. To neglect the inspirations of this instinct, which I had made my guide, I considered as great a crime as to infringe the prohibitions of a divine law; and the most questionable action of my life, the destruction of M'Bride, I considered a positive duty, because it was suggested by this regulator of my conduct.

"Mr. Barrymore, I die because I was an assassin, as you please to term it; for had you not enraged me by pronouncing a word which I considered an insult, I should not have fought you; and you would not have slain me; neither could you have done so today, had I been naturally of a more blood-thirsty disposition, for then, fifteen months ago, I should have taken the advice of the wretched man who lies there, and sent you unseen, or unheard of, to the grave. But my inward monitor forbade me, and I dared not do it. And now, if I have really been such a pest to the world, such a monster of mischief to society, as my enemies have called me, by my own forbearance you have lived to avenge the world, and rid society of me.

"Hear now my last words; for I feel that I shall not be able to speak much longer. Let not my death misgive you anything; for to you it was no crime. Vexation for the fall of a beloved father, prompted you to utter harsh expressions; these expressions occasioned my death, by causing me to draw upon you. But it is a death I rejoice in; the death of a Hampden, on the field of glory, in my country's cause, and by the hand of an honourable man. What can be a happier consummation!

"But, oh! Farewell. Tell O'Halloran that I died blessing my country."

The last words were almost inaudible, and he expired in a few minutes after uttering them.

When Edward beheld him dead, his heart smote him. "It is the first death that has ever been occasioned by my hand," he exclaimed. "And, oh! May heaven grant that neither duty nor accident may prevent it from being the last!"

CHAP. XXIII.

What is the worst of woes that wait on age? What stamps the wrinkle deeper on the brow
To view each loved one blotted from life's page, And be alone on earth as I am now.
Before the chast'ner humbly let me bow,
O'er hearts divided, and o'er hopes destroyed; Roll on vain days, full reckless may ye flow,
Since time has 'reft what'er my soul enjoyed!
Byron.

When Edward returned to his father, he was given to understand that the latter had not many hours to live.

"Oh father!" cried he, catching his hand and bathing it in tears; "how soon has it pleased God to take you from me! You have been to me a good father. You have ever been to me an example, a director and a friend. Ah! Who can to me supply your place?"

"Edward," said his father, "grieve not thus. I must now repeat what I have often inculcated on you. Bear misfortunes with the spirit of a man, and the resignation of a Christian. Show yourself, whether in prosperity or in adversity, worthy of the house of Barrymore. It is useless, it is unbecoming, to lament in this manner. And why should we lament for the result of this day? It ought to be esteemed a day of rejoicing, and not of grief. We have crushed a mighty rebellion; and ere I die, I have the satisfaction to know that the decisiveness of this day's victory, has secured to my country, and my children, the blessings of just laws, and a well-regulated government. A government equally removed from despotism and anarchy.

"These, my son, are blessings worth fighting for, worth dying for. Edward if you inherit any of your father's principles and feelings, you will not, if fate requires it, regret to die for them. When you have children I know you will not, for the power of transmitting such a legacy as our incomparably happy form of government, cannot be purchased too dear. Ah! What would be my pangs on this death-bed, if I perceived the enemies of that truly free and rational government, triumphant, and all its wise and venerable institutions in

"

danger of being subverted by the demons of anarchy, bigotry and massacre. But thank God! In the midst of my country's madness, in the midst of her delirious attempts at self-destruction, the weapon has been wrested from her hand; and although, in the blind fury of her paroxysm, she has inflicted dreadful wounds on her welfare and prosperity, yet, I trust, that the regenerating soundness of her constitution will soon repair her injuries, and restore her once more to vigour and happiness.

"Your mother, and your sister, will now look to you as their protector. I know that you will treat them with all the care and tenderness, with which I have treated them. Be to them in my stead — be to your country in my stead."

"My father," cried Edward, "I shall, with all my soul, endeavour to be so. But who shall be to me in your stead?"

His father paused a few moments, and then replied, "My son, you have a heavenly father; never, never forget that. But there is also one man on earth to whom, if he will accept them, I will resign my rights over you. I hope he will be to you a parent, such as I have been. I wish to see Sir Francis Hamilton."

That gentleman in company with the Lord Lieutenant, was just approaching to enquire after his situation. When they entered his apartment, "My lord," said he, "I congratulate you and the country, on this day's victory. I hope it will terminate this unnatural rebellion."

"I hope so," replied the viceroy; "but we have purchased it dearly, with your loss."

"My lord, I am happy to die in such a manner, and in such a cause. My country will experience but little injury, for I shall leave her this young man, my only son, to fill my place; and to him, Sir Francis Hamilton," said he, looking at that gentleman, "I wish you to fill mine. I am no stranger to his ardent attachment to your daughter; and although I have never seen her, the circumstances of her being your child, and his choice, are to me sufficient for wishing her to become his wife; and if you have no objection to receive him as your son-in-law, when I am no more, the reflection that he has such a prospect of happiness before him, will contribute much to sooth my dying moments."

Sir Francis grasping the hand of the patient, which was extended to him, replied, "I am sorry that my Edward, for I will now call him mine, so soon, so suddenly loses such a father. With all my heart and soul, I shall endeavour, however imperfectly, to supply the loss; for if I were to search the whole civilized world, I should not find a man, whom my heart would prefer to him, as a husband for my daughter."

"Then, Edward," said the Colonel, "give me your hand. May you soon be happy with the woman of your choice; and may Heaven bless you and her with every virtue that may entitle you to happiness!"

Not many hours after this, Colonel Barrymore closed his eyes upon all earthly scenes. His body was carried to Dublin, and thence to Barrymount, the family seat, and there buried with his fathers, in the presence of a large concourse of real mourners. His brother the Earl, being now much advanced in life, for he was upwards of fifteen years older than the Colonel, laid his death so much to heart, they having ever lived on the most affectionate footing, that from being only infirm, he became diseased, and soon felt such a change for the worse in his constitution, that he prognosticated that he was speedily approaching to his last illness.

"And I am content that it should be so," said he to Edward's mother and sister, (who now resided at Barrymount for the purpose of giving him their society) for since my beloved brother has left this world, it is become to me a world of desolation.

"O! I wish, fervently wish, to follow him to that world of happiness, which he now inhabits, and where when we once meet, we shall never part."

In the meantime Edward's heart panted to visit the North. But he could not with propriety leave his uncle in his present precarious situation. He, however, in almost daily letters, poured forth the ardour of his soul to his beloved, and received from her regular replies, which formed his only consolation during his present afflictions.

One day his uncle called him to his bed-side. "Edward," said he, "on you will soon devolve the duty of supporting, in the world, the name, rank, and respectability of our family, which I am proud to say has never yet been tarnished by a mean or an unprincipled act. There is nothing in the world I value so highly, as this family reputation. I received it pure from my ancestors, and neither your father nor I, have, thank God! Done anything to sully it. To you it shall soon be committed as a sacred trust. You will guard, therefore, with solicitude, and transmit it to your posterity as pure as you found it; and may heaven grant you a virtuous offspring to know its value, and perpetuate its purity!

"There is one thing in which, if you can indulge me, you will afford me great gratification. I understand that your father, on his death-bed, gave his assent to your marriage with a lady in the county of Antrim, to whom you are attached. I should be glad before I die to see that lady, whose conduct is to have such influence on the future reputation of the name of Barrymore; for, on the mother of a family, the transmission of its character depends more than

on any other individual. You may deem such a desire as this whimsical; and,
perhaps, with respect to the lady, not altogether delicate. But it is surely natural
that I should be desirous to see the mother of the future Barrymores.

"From the lady my desire may be kept concealed; consequently no wound
will be given to her delicacy. Her father, without any impropriety, may introduce her to your mother and sister, as a friend; and I am sure he would not
object to do so if he knew how ardently I wish it."

Edward conceived that it would be fruitless as well as cruel to oppose this
strange fancy of his uncle. Besides he was secretly pleased with the opportunity
it afforded of soliciting Sir Francis to bring his daughter to this part of the
country.

"To the North," said he to himself, "my thoughts every day, every hour,
every minute, direct themselves. But, if Ellen were here, I should not think of
the North."

The next day he rode into the city; and stated simply to Sir Francis, his
uncle's request, together with its motives. Sir Francis made no hesitation in
soliciting his daughter and O'Halloran to visit the metropolis, which they did
in little more than a week afterwards. In a few days, he drove them to Barrymount, on a visit to the old Earl's, with whom he had of late became intimate.

Edward had received intelligence of the day on which they were to arrive.
How did his heart beat with joyful impatience! He rose that morning earlier
than usual; for he could not sleep. The day which he had thus rendered longer
than ordinary, appeared to him preternaturally so. Many an anxious look he
cast at his watch. "The deuce take it, it will never be the afternoon," thought
he.

He was almost tempted to move the hands of the watch forward, but he
reflected that such a measure would add no velocity to the wheels of Sir Francis's coach. He then tried to read, but it would not do. He then tried to walk,
but it was equally vain. He next had recourse to writing a letter to Martin, but
he dated it wrong; took another sheet of paper, wrote 'my dear Sir,' twice; and,
in the first line, instead of the word 'pleasure,' wrote 'perplexity' and, in the
second, for the words, 'I learn you are still at home', he substituted, 'I think
she will surely soon come'. He dashed the pen across the lines, execrated his
stupidity, and gave it up as an impracticable task.

He then threw himself on a sofa; and bravely determined, since he could
not get rid of his impatience, to bear it like a man. He lay for about five minutes
quiet enough; and then looked around.

"Charlotte," said he to his sister, who was present. "Charlotte, my dear,
what o'clock is it?"

"Why, Edward, you have asked me that question, I believe, ten times since breakfast."

"Is it two, my dear?"

"No, I believe it is scarcely one. But consult your watch."

"I have consulted it twenty times today, but I cannot think it right. It goes very slow. Well, well, if it were two, and it wants but an hour and twenty minutes of it, it would then be only three hours till five. But, Charlotte, won't you take a ride? I shall order the chaise."

"I shall go with you in an hour, Edward."

In short they took their ride, met Sir Francis's coach, returned in company with it to the Earl's; and Edward's time for about ten days, the duration of Ellen's visit, flew with the rapidity of a delicious dream.

It is needless to say that the Earl was well pleased, when he beheld the lovely mother of the future Barrymores.

"Upon my honour," said he to Edward, the evening after Ellen had left them, "you are a happy young man. No wonder you spent so much time in the North, where you discovered such a beauteous flower ripening into perfection. If Providence would only spare me to behold your eldest son, I think that there might yet be attractions for me even in this world. But no, I must hasten to your father and my brother, to my God, his God, and your God."

Accordingly in less than three weeks afterwards, he resigned his spirit into the hands of him who made it, and his earthly remains were deposited amidst his kindred dust, alongside of his brother.

CHAP. XXIV.

Enough of this. To deal in wordy compliment Is much against the plainness of my nature; I judge you by myself, a clear true spirit, And as such join you to my bosom — Farewell, and be my friend.
Rowe.

The deceased Earl had never possessed any children. His title, therefore, together with his immense property, devolved on Edward, who in a very short period, took occasion, in company with his mother and sister, to visit the North, and lay them at the feet of Ellen.

"My lord!" said she, as he warmly pressed for an immediate union, "it would be mere affectation in me to deny what you already know, that my heart pleads in your favour. But I am at my father's disposal, and must request you to wait till his consent be obtained in form."

"Then, my love, you may name the happy day," he replied, "for before I left Dublin, I obtained Sir Francis's promise that he would follow me here, in a few days, to be present at our nuptials."

"Then, my lord," she answered, "when he comes we may permit him to name it."

When she had said this, her countenance changed, she blushed deeply, and looking to the ground, almost burst into tears.

"What is the matter, my Ellen?" enquired the young Earl, who was himself considerably agitated.

"Oh!" said she, "the word has passed my lips. I have committed my liberty into your hands. I cannot now recall it. The change is awful!"

"Surely, sweetest Ellen, you do not wish to recall it."

"No, my lord, otherwise I should not have said it. I have said it deliberately, willingly, and without scruple. But it brings to my mind the recollection of the freedom I have hitherto enjoyed, in parting with which I cannot help shedding a few natural tears. Besides, I cannot without concern, contemplate the high responsibility of the station I am about to fill. Should I fail in any part of my duty—"

"My Ellen!" he interrupted her, "my treasure, be comforted. It is impossible that one of your goodness of heart and understanding, can fail in any duty. As to the station, you will adorn it. You will be an example to our peeresses of all that is virtuous, lovely, dignified, and wise. In the eyes of your Edward, station cannot exalt you. He found you among these rocks, on this romantic shore, a jewel of perfection, valuable beyond all price, and such a one as in his estimation, no change of scene or circumstance, neither humiliation nor exaltation, can alter. He will soon move you to a more busy and brilliant sphere, where, while every eye admires your lustre, and every heart acknowledges your value, you will still be to him, as you have been here, the pride, the delight of his soul, the dearest part of himself."

But it would be tedious to detail the whole of his love conversation, which lasted nearly three hours, as everyone in the Castle, who knew they were together, felt unwilling to disturb them; and Mrs. Brown had the good nature to postpone making tea for a whole hour after the usual time, rather than interrupt their agreeable tête-à-tête. Tea was, however, at length, got ready; and when the lovers were summoned to attend, they could scarcely be convinced that the old lady had not prepared it much earlier than usual. On their entering the parlour, Edward's sister maliciously consulted her watch.

"It is past seven o'clock," said she.

"Past seven o'clock!" cried his lordship. "Why, Charlotte, your watch must be wrong. I cannot suppose it to be more than five."

"That is owing to your having been in pleasant company," said she. "Time does not now lag with your lordship, as it did at Barrymount one day, when you insisted that it was two o'clock when it was hardly past twelve; and in sheer pity, I had to drive away in a chaise with you, to try to make it move faster."

"Ah! Charlotte, you may now laugh; — but, I hope, I shall yet have my revenge, by observing your little heart beating impatiently for the arrival of an esteemed friend."

"And a dearly beloved one too," added she, with emphasis.

"Yes, my sister," said he, "and may he who can excite similar emotions in your heart, be as worthy of love, as the object who occasioned that day's impatience in mine!"

"Amen," she replied.

The tea-table was scarcely removed, when Miss Barrymore, looking from a window, exclaimed, "Why, my lord, I declare, yonder is the old beggar woman you left an invalid on our hands, when you set off so hastily from Dublin in June last.

His lordship looked out, and beheld Peg Dornan advancing briskly up the avenue. She had become perfectly convalescent, and had returned from Dublin during the time that Edward was employed in Cornwallis's army; and was now a fund of great entertainment to the whole neighbourhood, for several miles round, by her inexhaustible descriptions of the great city, and the great folks in it.

She was soon heard addressing one of the servants. "I'm tauld he's come," said she, "an' I'll wait here till I see him, for I hae na cast an ee on him syne the day he left me in sic a hurry, in his father's hoose, a perfect cripple, wi' my twa shanks as thick as butter-firkins, an' my feet blistered like broiled herrin's. An' the bit lassie, his sister — Gude bless her bonnie face. She gied me baith wine an' plenty o' sweetmeats every day, whilk was a great comfort to a puir body in a muckle wild toon sae far frae hame."

"Old Peg has a good heart," said Edward. "I must go to speak with her."

O'Halloran went with him.

"Fare fa' you!" quoth she, making a low courtesy as soon as she saw them. "I may be owre bauld, but I wished to see his honour, wha, they tell me, is noo a young lord, yince mair."

"Well, Peg, how have you been, since we parted?" asked his lordship.

"Weel enough for a poor body like me, but I'm still better noo since I see you whare you oucht to be; an' since I hear you're sune gaun to get wha' I aye thoucht you should get."

"Peg!" replied Edward, "you have rendered us many and great services. I shall have a little cottage built for you, in which you can spend your old days in comfort."

"I thank you, kindly," she said, "but you need na be at the pains. His honour there, my auld master an' frien', has already gi'en me a snug yin; an' he lets me besides hae a hantel o' siller every week; indeed mair than I ken weel what to do wi', for I can neither wear it, nor eat it; an' ye ken it wad na be richt to drink it. But, gin it wad na be makin' owre free, I would like to see the bonny bairn your sister, wha was sae kind to me when I was a bedrill in Dublin."

At that instant Miss Barrymore made her appearance.

"My bonnie lady," said Peg, curtseying to her, "I was unco troublesome to you up the country, an' I just wanted to thank you, noo when I'm won back to my ain country."

"I'm glad to see you so stout, Peg!" said the young lady.

"If it would na affront you," returned Peg, abruptly, "to tak' a gift frae an auld beggar wife, I would fain gie you a pretty thing I fan' among the stanes near the Point Rock, yestreen, as I was saunterin' alang gathering limpits."

While saying this, she unfolded a piece of old rag, and presented to view a handsome gold broach, set with diamonds, of great value. Edward instantly recognised it as one that he had lost when struggling with the waves on the evening which had so nearly proved fatal to him. His sister also knew it to be his.

"Why, Peg, you have been fortunate yesterday," said his lordship. "That broach was once mine. It was valued at two hundred guineas, and you are entitled to that sum. How will you dispose of it?"

"Dispose of it! In trowth, I'll no dispose of it at all," she replied; "for I'll no hae't at all. Gin the breest-pin be yours, you maun get it. But I thoucht to pay the debt I owed to this bonnie lassie, wi' it."

"She shall have it since you desire it," said his lordship, "but you must also derive some benefit from your good fortune in finding it. Mention anything I can do for you."

"Weel, since I think o't, maybe you'll no' object to tak' Jock Dornan, my poor gomerill sin — but he's a sturdy chiel — into your service; an' try to mak' a man o' him, whilk is mair than ever his mither could."

"It shall be so," said his lordship; "and he shall be amply provided for. And now, Charlotte, you may take the broach, as a present, from Peg."

"I shall," she said, "but Peg must receive from me in return, a new bonnet and a new cloak every year."

"Whate'er you like!" replied Peg. "I'll refuse naething o' that sort. But I'll awa an' sen' Jock Dornan to you in the mornin'. Guid een, an' the blessing o' an auld woman be wi' you a'."

When she was gone, O'Halloran informed his lordship that after her return from Dublin, in consequence of her active instrumentality in saving his life, he felt himself bound to provide for her future comfort; and had bestowed her a cottage, and settled on her a weekly allowance during her life, which, considering her careless and wandering disposition, he observed was a more effectual way of rewarding her, than by the actual donation of a more considerable sum of money, or a larger piece of property.

Edward being desirous to see M'Nelvin, O'Halloran and he walked to Jemmy Hunter's with the expectation of finding him there. It was a fine moonlight evening, about the middle of October. The grain harvest was all gathered in; and the country people had been busied during the day in raising and securing the potatoes, and as our friends went along, they passed many car-loads of this wholesome and agreeable root, so precious to the Irish, on their way to the farm-houses. The peasantry were cheerful and civil, and seemed to have completely recovered their spirits after the late disastrous events.

On arriving at Jemmy Hunter's, all was quiet around the dwelling house, for it was now dark, and candles were lighted within. After the capture of the French, Jemmy, whose habits of life were not formed for dependence on the great, and whose domestic attachments were too strong to permit his long continuance from his family, relinquished his situation under Sir Francis Hamilton and returned home.

On Barrymore and O'Halloran approaching close to the house, the cheering sounds of rustic mirth and happiness saluted their ears.

"Come here," said O'Halloran, who had advanced to the unscreened window of the apartment in which the contented group were sitting round a large blazing turf fire, "Come here, my lord, and behold a true specimen of the winter-night enjoyments of our Northern peasantry."

Barrymore looked, and his heart swelled with joy to behold a number of as healthy, honest and happy human countenances, as any family group in Christendom could exhibit. Between the window and the fireplace, sat four women, busily employed at the spinning wheel, the chief engine of the Northern Irish industry and prosperity. These were Jemmy Hunter's mother, his two sisters, and his wife. On the other side of the hearth, in a large arm chair, sat William Caldwell, who, from the staff in his hand, and the great coat that hung loosely on his shoulders, appeared to have just come on an evening visit to his son-in-law.

M'Nelvin, Jemmy Hunter, and a decent looking young man whom Barrymore did not know, but who, it will be no harm to suppose, was a suitor to one of the Miss Hunters, sat in front of the hearth; while on a long bench between the hearth and a stone wall, which ran across the apartment, sat two ruddy faced youths, younger brothers to Jemmy, one of whom had the housedog, which was of the large black species, called in that part of the country, the 'Collie', between his knees.

To some remark of M'Nelvin, which Edward did not hear, old Caldwell replied, "I'm very happy at the turn things hae ta'en; an' I'm sure a' the country will be rejoiced at it, for he's a guid youth."

"Father," said Jemmy, "Peggy can sing you yin o' the best sangs ye hae heard this lang time; an' its a new yin. She gat it frae M'Nelvin here. I listened to her singing it last nicht, till I amaist grat, it touched me sae much. Come, Peggy, let your father hear it; it will do his heart guid."

After some little hesitation, Peggy complied, and sang as follows:

Oh! thousands shall mourn, and thousands shall fall,
And ruin shall light upon castle and hall;
And our chieftain shall forfeit his bonnie estate,
And be sentenced to die at his own castle gate;
And the Flower of the North, her sire shall wail,
And the Pride of the South shall hear the tale,
And, with speed, shall hasten our chief to free,
For the sake of the Flower of the North country.
"I fear not death," our brave chieftain said,
"But my daughter is fair, and I fear for the maid:
To be friendless and lovely, are evils in store,
To work her misfortune, when I am no more."
Then burst from her bosom the heart-breaking sighs,
And the tears fall fast from her lovely black eyes;
As she said to her father, "O grieve not for me,
For, to peace, in the grave, I shall soon follow thee!"
The guards move slow, for their errand is death,
While the foes of our chieftain are foaming with wrath,
but the noble youth follows on mercy's swift wings,
And life and estate to our chieftain he brings.
Now the land rejoices, our bosoms beat high,
And maids and their lovers sing songs of joy;
For the Pride of the South soon married shall be,
To Ellen, the Flower of the North country.

"Why, M'Nelvin!" said Jemmy, clapping the poet on the knee, when the song was ended, "you deserve a fairin' for making it. I wonder man hoo you can gar the words clink sae?"

But before the poet could reply, a rapping at the door drew the attention of the party.

"Come in, frien's!" cried Jemmy, rising at the same time, to open the door. The next moment Edward and O'Halloran advanced, and saluted the company. They all rose. The women made courtesies, and the men bows.

"Ah! how are you, M'Nelvin!" cried Edward, ardently shaking the poet by the hand. "Your friend, Sir Francis, sent his kind respects to you. I expect him to follow me here in a few days."

"My lord, I am really rejoiced to see you," replied the bard. "I need not say that the present prospects of both you and that best of my friends, afford me much happiness."

Edward now turned to salute William Caldwell and the rest of the company. "Mr. Caldwell," said he, "it gives me true pleasure to witness your good fortune, in being surrounded by such an amiable and happy group of relatives."

"We maun thank your lordship for some o' our happiness," replied the old man. "What you did for his honour there, will no' sune be forgotten amang us."

By this time Peggy had her neat little parlour lighted; and, with all the winning sweetness of rural modesty, invited her guests to step ben to it, as she said, "it was a decenter place for the like o' them than the kitchen," the apartment in which they had met.

A pitcher of warm whiskey punch soon diffused its inspiring fumes through the room.

"How did you like the city, Jemmy?" asked Lord Barrymore. "You seemed very anxious to leave it."

"I liked it weel enough; an' had it no' been for twa folk, an' there is yin o' them," said he, pointing to his blushing Peggy, "an' the ither is in the craddle yonder, I wadna hae left Sir Francis sae sune.

"Peggy, bring here the wean, till his lordship sees it. It's a bonnie bit thing, an' I hae ca'd it for you, my lord."

His spouse, now, with an almost trembling fondness, produced the young Hunter to view. "Eddy, Eddy!" cried its father, catching its little hand, "Look up, my boy, an' see your namesake."

His lordship took the child in his arms. "It is a fine boy, Jemmy," said he; "its features are extremely like your own. I do not wonder that you were impatient to return to objects so attractive as such a wife and such a son. I thought, my friend, to add to your happiness for the many great services you have rendered me, but I find it impossible; for these treasures make you happier than man can make you. Yet you will permit me to make my little namesake a present, in token of my esteem for his parents, and my affection for himself."

He then returned the child to its mother, and requested some writing materials, with which being supplied, he drew forth a valuable gold watch, and cutting a piece of paper into a circular form, so as to fit the inside of the watch, he wrote on it as follows:

"Oct. 17, 1798. The gift of Edward, earl of Barrymore, to Edward Hunter. The earl hereby binds himself and his heirs forever, to pay annually fifty pounds sterling to the said Edward Hunter and his heirs."

He enclosed the paper within the watch, and handing it to Peggy, "Receive this in trust for your child," said he; "it is but a small recompense for the numerous and important services his father has rendered to me, and those dear to me."

When Jemmy understood the nature of the gift, "Na, na," said he, "we'll no' hae't: it is owre muckle, my lord. It was na for ony such thing that I helped you in your pinches. It was for mere frien'ship; an' I would hae done the same for ony frien' in the country."

"This disinterestedness," observed his lordship, "makes you still the more entitled to recompense. But if you will not receive this gift, as a reward, you will gratify me by receiving it as a token of friendship, for I am proud of being capable of exciting such friendship as you have shown for me.

"Besides, Jemmy, it is scarcely in your power to refuse it, for it is not to you, but to your son, my young namesake here, that I give it."

"Weel, weel, gin it maun be sae, let it be sae," replied Jemmy. "But I think the young rascal has got owre mony presents already; for Miss O'Halloran has gien him hale trunkfu's o' cleas an' ither things, mair, I believe, than we ken weel hoo to use. An' I'll no' hide it, though it is a secret she does na hersel' ken; it was mair to please her than to compliment ony body else, that we ca'd him Edward."

"Candidly confessed!" cried Lord Barrymore, much pleased with Jemmy's simplicity, but, at the same time, more delighted with the idea that Ellen had displayed such attention to a child that was named after himself.

"I canna weel tell what to think o' ye, gentlemen," remarked Jemmy. "Ye seem to care naething o' the warld's gear. His honour, there, Mr. O'Halloran, has gien me the farm rent free forever; an' would insist on me that it was paying a debt he owed me, whereas I only did for either o' you, what yae neighbour should be aye ready to do for anither.

"But let us hae anither glass. Wi' your leave, I'll drink lang life to you, Mr. O'Halloran; an' lang life to your lordship, an' may ye sune be married to her ye like best!"

Having thanked Jemmy for his good wishes, and emptied their glasses to a toast expressive of theirs for him and his interesting family, O'Halloran and Lord Barrymore arose, and, accompanied by M'Nelvin and Jemmy, proceeded towards the castle.

On their way, the poet and his lordship having fallen somewhat behind their companions, "Mr. M'Nelvin," said the latter, "the obligations I lie under to you, for your ardent and effective services in the behalf of me, and those I love, demand my sincere acknowledgments, and embolden me to make a request, your compliance with which will afford me much satisfaction, as it will give me an opportunity of making some return for the numerous favours you have conferred on me."

"Any service I have rendered your lordship," replied M'Nelvin, "brought with it its own reward, in the gratification I experienced in the performance; and if there be any I can yet render you, let me know it, and, with the same zeal and pleasure, it shall be done."

"In the county of Cavan," said his lordship, "I have an estate, the manager of which died a few months ago. I should like you to fill his place, for I want it filled with a man in whose honesty to myself, and attention to the comforts and happiness of my tenantry, I can confide. The compensation of the late agent was £500 per annum; yours shall be £800."

"I see, my lord, your motive for this generous offer," returned M'Nelvin. "You wish to make me independent as to worldly matters; and your friendship and delicacy have suggested this method. I thank you, sincerely do I thank you. But, my lord, my affections are rooted to this part of the country. The neighbourhood for about ten miles round us, is all the world to me. It is all I ever enjoyed or ever wish to enjoy. In an adjoining valley I had my birth; amidst these hills I was educated; everything that has interested me from the days of childhood to this very hour, has appeared within these limits; and, if I were to remove from them, I should remove from that portion of the world, which could alone yield me enjoyment by interesting my affections.

"On your estate, I should feel as if I were exiled from my native land; and although it would yield me pleasure to afford you any assistance in my power in managing your affairs, yet, as I know that your lordship can sustain no injury by my present refusal, there being numerous individuals who would be thankful for such an employment, better qualified both from experience and disposition to fulfil its duties than I am, I decline your friendly offer, with the less reluctance.

"My lord, while I refuse your kindness in this instance, I trust that you are too fully aware of the nature of my motives for so doing, to take them amiss. Indeed, I assure your lordship, that the governorship of the richest of His Majesty's colonies, would not tempt me to forego the pleasure of every day beholding my native hills and valleys; the pleasure of wandering, in my hours of meditation, along those streamlets, or concealing myself amidst those well-known groves and glens; or of enjoying in my hours of sociability, the cheerful hospitality, and kindly, though rustic conversation, of those beloved friends and neighbours, to whom I have been long accustomed and endeared."

"Is there no other way, my romantic friend," inquired his lordship, "by which I can manifest my gratitude for what you have done for me?"

"There is no other way," replied the poet, "than by continuing to favour me with your good opinion. As to pecuniary matters, they are of little or no consideration with me. I need but little, and that little I can easily earn. To possess more, might only produce cares and perplexities with which I wish not to be encumbered. My days may be few or many, as Providence shall please to order, but they shall be spent in the indulgence of affections which wealth cannot excite, and in the enjoyment of those luxuries of mind it cannot purchase."

"Happy M'Nelvin," exclaimed his lordship, "since you have thus the making of your own happiness, independent of the frowns or the smiles of a fickle world! I shall not urge you further on this subject. But assure yourself of my lasting friendship and gratitude; and of my sincere wish that you may long live to enjoy the intellectual blessings of which you are enamoured, amidst the interesting scenery of your native vales, and in possession of the esteem and admiration of their honest inhabitants." Having now arrived at the avenue to the Castle, they separated, and the poet returned with Hunter to the rural dwelling of the latter, which had of late become his favourite place of residence.

CHAP. XXV.

The most delightful lot beneath the sun,
Is when two faithful hearts that fondly love,
By sacred rites are made for ever one,
While bounteous fortune smiles, and friends approve.
Their's are the exalted joys of saints above,
Each word, each look, imparting mutual bliss:
On rapturous wings their golden moments move;
Nor can they wish a happier world than this,
For holy wedded love, turns earth to Paradise.
Irish Soothsayer.

As this history is drawing to a close, it may not be amiss to take notice of the great lesson for the inculcation of which, it has been written; namely, that intimidation and vengeance are, and ever will be, unsuccessful in preserving the peace of a country; whereas conciliation and kindness will scarcely ever fail.

The blood of martyrs has been truly said to be like seed to the cause for which they suffer; and perhaps, in no portion of the history of nations, has this truth been more clearly illustrated, than in that we have just recited. The unnecessary, unjust, impolitic, and cruel execution of William Orr, almost instantaneously resulted in thousands of William Orrs, or rather of characters such as he was accused of being, starting into existence, and vowing revenge upon his persecutors.

While Camden governed in Ireland, the system which occasioned that irritating execution, was continued until it involved the country into all the horrors of which we have in the preceding pages, given a faint sketch.

How long these horrors would have continued, had he continued to govern, is happily now only matter of conjecture. The realization of the evils, which the most enlightened statesmen of both England and Ireland, predicted would be the consequence of his coercive measures, brought at length conviction of their impropriety home to the minds of the British ministers and he was suddenly, and fortunately, superseded in his office, by a man of a more enlightened understanding and a more humane temper.

The almost immediate consequence of this happy change we have seen. In the course of a few months, rebellion was converted into submission, and disaffection into loyalty. With the restoration of the ordinary laws, confidence in the government, tranquillity, industry, and national prosperity were also restored.

It is true that the flames of the civil war had been too extensive for its dying embers to be all at once extinguished; and amidst a numerous population, it could not be expected, but that some would fanatically continue to urge the prosecution of desperate measures, even after their abandonment by the general mass Besides the government, comparatively mild and merciful, as it was still, displayed, in some instances, a harshness towards several proscribed individuals, which kept alive, for a considerable time, a soreness in the minds of many, who would otherwise have returned at once to their former habits and feelings of loyalty.

But as these unfortunate individuals, against whom the national authority continued to direct its vengeance with unabated rigour, were all, in the course of some months, either taken and executed, or died in their coverts from the hardships they endured, or else found means to fly from the country, this source of irritation and danger, became also, before the expiration of the year, removed.

Indeed, about that period, so evidently had the majority of the people of the North became loyal, that it seemed, by their conduct and expressions, as if a species of re-action had taken place in their feelings; and the government appeared so much convinced that these professions were sincere, that it scrupled not to entrust arms into the hands of thousands who had been active in the rebellion.

A species of military force, denominated 'Yeomanry', the members of which could not be taken out of their own county, were not liable to military law, and had the privilege of withdrawing whenever they pleased, from the service, had been projected sometime previous to the insurrection, but, on account of the general disaffection, had been joined but by few. Its ranks, however, were now swelled by multitudes, eager to evince their reawakened fidelity to the government, which was therefore soon enabled to withdraw the regular troops from the country, and despatch them against the foreign enemy.

It is true that, previous to the arrival of Cornwallis, and the adoption of healing measures, although the insurrection had been nearly suppressed, the minds of the people were still much agitated; and there existed in the country such causes of irritation, as would, in all probability, have occasioned it to become once more a scene of bloodshed and terror; and, on the first favourable opportunity, there is scarcely a doubt that another rising would have taken place, if a period had not been put to Camden's coercive system of government. They know very little of the temper and feelings of men, especially of Irishmen, who suppose that the mere danger of losing life will compel them to look quietly on, while their friends are suffering, and they themselves are in the daily danger of suffering, all the evils of a needless and relentless persecution. The persecutors may, it is true, by an overwhelming military power, enforce an occasional and temporary submission, but human fears commonly yield to resentment and exasperation; and, although disunion, or want of warlike means, may deprive the persecuted of all hopes of success, their very despair, which will be thus excited, may become dreadful, perhaps fatal, to their adversaries.

But to proceed with our story.

On the day following the occurrences related in the last chapter, Ellen's favourite and faithful friend, Miss Agnew, arrived at the castle. Ellen had sent for this young lady shortly after consenting that her father should name the wedding-day, in order that she, who had shared so sensibly in her afflictions, should now have an opportunity of sharing in her joys. Into her bosom she poured all her feelings, her hopes, her joys, her wishes, her anxieties, the intensity of her love and admiration for the generous youth who had done so much for her, who already possessed her heart, and into whose keeping she, with so much fondness and delight, was so soon to commit her destiny.

Then, with a species of transient fear, she would revert to the awful change that was about to take place in her situation, and the high responsibility as a wife, as a peeress, and, perhaps, as a mother, she was about to incur. Then reflecting on her removal from the scenes, and the friends of her youth, she would say, "And when I am married, I must also reside at a distance from these haunts, so endeared to me by a thousand recollections; and from my youthful friends; and from thee too, Maria, the earliest and best beloved of them all, I must separate. But," she would add, "without my Edward, the enjoyment of friends, country, and everything else I have hitherto prized, could not make me happy. Ah! I feel that the possession of such a husband is worth every sacrifice. Oh, Maria! rejoice with your friend, for I am indeed happy! Heaven, in giving me him, gives me the highest boon earth can afford."

Miss Agnew would often rally her on these bursts of love and joy, but with such visible satisfaction in her looks, as showed that in her heart she rejoiced in her friend's happiness, and consequently contributed to increase it. It is not

to be supposed that in these confidential conversations, the gallant, gay
Charles Martin was altogether forgotten. Miss Agnew delighted to talk of him.

"I confess I love him," she would say. "He is so sweet in his looks, so
tender in his manner, that, during the day, I can scarcely ever withdraw my
thoughts from him; and, during the night, I can do nothing but dream of him.
But I hope I shall yet get the better of such folly. He wrote to my father lately,
requesting permission to visit me, and the old man was silly enough to ask my
opinion on the subject. I told him to act as he thought proper, for I would not
have him, on my account, to forbid the coming of any respectable person to
our house."

"We expect him here every day," said Ellen. "Lord Barrymore has written
him an invitation to attend our marriage. I wish we could have a double wedding. What say you, Maria?"

"Hush!" cried Maria. "One uproar of the kind is enough at one time."

Thus passed several days, which, to our heroine, flew on the wings of love
and friendship, when her father arrived, accompanied with Sir Philip Martin
and his son Charles. It would be wrong to stop at present to describe the joyful
welcome they received at the Castle, for the reader must be impatient to come
to the grand conclusion of the whole affair, the making our hero and heroine
husband and wife.

The important day arrived sometime in the middle of November. The wedding garments were prepared, the wedding guests were invited, and the
wedding feast was provided. But hold! We must have no formal descriptions
of such trifles. They are unfashionable, and in these days, anything unfashionable, is as intolerable in a novel as in a drawing room.

But it ought to be known that, on this occasion, O'Halloran regulated the
proceedings according to his own fancy, which was somewhat old fashioned.
He accordingly managed it so that the whole scene was almost a repetition of
what took place when he himself was married to Ellen's grandmother.

The party consisted of about twenty four persons, comprising a tolerably
well-proportioned assortment of males and females. Among the former, as a
most essential personage on the occasion, was the Rev. Mr. Nichols, who was
O'Halloran's spiritual teacher, and with whose character the reader has already
had some acquaintance.

At about five in the afternoon the company sat down to a very comfortable
dinner, after partaking of which, at the usual time, the ladies withdrew, and
the gentlemen remained behind, perhaps so long that each had a reasonable
time to drink two glasses of port, and one goblet of Jamaica rum punch. Some

them betook themselves to backgammon, some to the library, and some to the ladies for amusement.

"Why, this was only an ordinary dinner! What appearance of a wedding is there in all this?" Have patience, dear reader, we are not yet come to the wedding. But I trust we soon shall, although O'Halloran must have his own old jog-trot way.

Great people do things of this kind far more dashingly now-a-days — that is, when their fathers and mothers, or guardians happen to give their consent. They roll to church and back again, with a long splendid train of carriages behind them, driving with as much velocity as if they had lost their senses, or were running for a wager, causing the streets and highways to tremble, and the gaping multitude to stare with astonishment, as they pass along. But O'Halloran was none of those dashing people; and as to Lord Barrymore, provided the knot was made firm and legal, he cared not how small a degree of pomp and pageantry attended the tying of it. He wanted his Ellen to be his wife, and if the forms that made her so, were agreeable to both divine and human laws, the mere embellishing accompaniments were to him matters of indifference. But let us, 'haste to the wedding'.

At about seven o'clock the whole party assembled to tea in the usual sitting room. The task of presiding at this repast was assigned to Miss Agnew, as Ellen's thoughts were supposed to be too much occupied with more important concerns, to undertake it. She sat at Miss Agnew's right hand. Her lover sat beside her; and attended to all her wants with punctilious delicacy and solicitude. Ah! Is there a youth in Christendom, who would not have envied his situation?

After the tea table was removed, and the company promiscuously seated around the room, while all, except the lovers who engrossed in mutual fondness sat beside each other on a sofa, were engaged in a lively desultory conversation, O'Halloran whispered something to Sir Francis, who immediately rising, advanced to his daughter. The clergymen perceiving what was intended, rose also, and standing behind a large arm chair on which he had been sitting, pronounced the words, "Let us proceed."

At once, the whole company stood up.

Sir Francis then led his blushing daughter, accompanied by her lover, forward, saying, "I here bestow you, my Ellen, to a man, whom I think, in every respect, worthy of such a gift. Receive her, my lord, and may God bless you both!"

With a graceful bow, and an exulting heart, the young lord received possession of the long-loved maid thus presented to him; and the two stood before the clergyman.

That holy man then proceeded with the ceremony according to the form observed by the reverend ministers of the Synod of Ulster, being nearly the same as that prescribed by the Church of Scotland. After some appropriate observations on the nature and design of the institution of marriage, and the duties and obligations which it imposes on the parties who engage in it, he administered to our lovers those solemn vows, whose miraculous power can form two into one; and having declared them to be husband and wife, he addressed heaven in a short prayer suited to the occasion, and concluded by desiring Lord Barrymore to embrace his wife.

"My wife! O blessed sound!" thought the young bridegroom, as, with an enraptured heart, he imprinted the ardent embrace on her glowing lips.

After spending a reasonable time in courtship, Charles Martin followed the example of his friend Barrymore, and, in due form, exchanged matrimonial vows with the sprightly and laughter-loving Miss Agnew.

It is unnecessary to pursue the history of these personages further. It may be mentioned, however, that the Insurgent Chief, lived to see several of his great grand-children; and then calmly withdrew to his fathers, leaving behind him a memory which will be long honoured by the warm-hearted people of the romantic country, for whose independence he had, in vain, contended so bravely, and suffered so much.

THE END

About the Author

James McHenry[2]

Author of "O'Halloran," "Hearts of Steel," etc., etc.
Bv DR. W. CLARKE-ROBINSON.
Reproduced by kind permission of the *Ulster Journal of Archaeology*

James M'HENRY was born in Lame in 1785, as he tells us in a note to "O'Halloran" that he witnessed the fight in Lame streets between the Insurgents and the troops during the Insurrection of 1798, when he was a boy of 12 years old. He was the son of George M'Henry and Mary Smiley.

Few, if any, of his father's race and name remain about Lame. They are scattered over different parts of Ireland and America, but his mother's people still flourish in the neighbourhood. She had for parents, Sam Smiley of Larne, and Christiana Robinson of Cairncastle, and her brother, John Smiley was grandfather of the present Sir Hugh Smiley, Baronet.

James M'Henry also tells us in his novels that he was educated as a resident pupil in the house of Rev. J. Nicholson, of the seceding congregation in Lame, who removed, in the year 1801, to Berry Street Congregation in Belfast. This Rev. Nicholson is affectionately pictured in [McHenry's novel] *The Hearts of Steel* under the name of Rev. M'Culloch and at the end of *O'Halloran* the author appends a beautiful poem in honour of this same teacher, who, he says, first made him a poet; a poem which reminds us in its style of Goldsmith's picture of his own reverend father in *The Deserted Village*.

I have not been able to find out where James M'Henry obtained his medical degree, and I am informed authoritatively that his name does not appear in Trinity College, Dublin, nor in the Royal College of Surgeons, Ireland; nor yet in Glasgow, nor Edinburgh. Possibly he may have taken his MD after he went to America.

---

[2] Initially published as James MacHenry

He practiced medicine for a time in Belfast, about North Street, and always seems to have been fond of letters and of intellectual society. He had also a vast love for the country, for he knew every glen, and wood, and burn, and cave, and mountain for miles and miles round Larne, most of his excursions being on foot or horseback. On some of his tours round Cairncastle he seems to have met and married a beautiful young girl of 16, a second cousin of his own, named Jane Robinson, of Fox Hall, who displaced his, "first love, Anna, of the Inver's shore." In a poem on *A Scene on the Coast of Co. Antrim*, he gives a picture of her woodland home at Fox Hall, built by my great grandfather, James Robinson, in 1771:

" 'Midst pendant rocks o'erhung with wood,
Far from the busy haunts of men,
Yon briar-entangled trackless road
Leads to the wily Fox's den !
There, in the early morn of life,
Along the wildly pleasing shore,
I passed the sweetest of my days
In harmless mirth and joys of yore !"

The wedding, which took place about 1816, was long remembered as a famous event in the country, the bridegroom being just double the age of the fair young bride!

About 1820 Dr. M'Henry published *O'Halloran, or the Insurgent Chief*, his most successful novel, describing some of the chief characters and events about Lame during the Insurrection of 1798. In *O'Halloran* the author tries to steer an even keel between the Insurgents and the Loyalists. He leans to neither side, but he shows the injustice and oppression to which the people were subjected by unjust laws, and by selfish and unsympathetic magistrates and landlords and rulers. He shows the causes that made the Insurrection righteous in the eyes of an oppressed people and he also shows the hopelessness of their attempts to wrest justice by force of arms from the Powers that were. He would doubtless have agreed with Goethe, who said, "There never yet has been a revolution but what was produced by the government and not by the people" — .*i.e,* by the government refusing to deal fairly, or to make just concessions in the right time and spirit. Eighteen years after the first appearance of *O'Halloran*, that is, in 1838, we find the book has been published by six different London firms — five of them without the author's sanction! And five years later, in 1843, we find it re published by a John Henderson, of Belfast — with corrections, a complete revision, and. a valuable appendix explaining the characters and scenes, by the author. This John Henderson was a Scotchman, settled in Belfast, and is still remembered by many of our citizens; he had a large family, and one of his daughters has long kept a book shop in Ann Street, near Church Lane. *O'Halloran, or the Insurgent Chief*, is really a work of art and genius; the story is fascinating from the very first; the interest never flags; the characters are kept well in hand, and are all perfectly natural and human; the author's knowledge of human nature, of the Ulster peasantry and dialect, and of the surrounding localities, is unsurpassed. After nearly ninety years the novel is still alive with pictures of reality, as well as with the history and life of the most interesting times through which our country has passed. O'Halloran, the chief character in the novel, was really Farrell, who is represented as occupying the tall castle on the inland side of the Shore Road at Ballygally — a structure built by a Scottish laird named John Shaw in 1624, and always known as "Shaw's Castle" until the fame of M'Henry's novel gradually changed the name to "O'Halloran's Castle" — another proof that fiction is stronger than fact!

About 1824 Dr. M'Henry went to America, but returned to Lame in 1825, to take out his wife and two sons, Alexander and James — James being only six weeks old. They had a fearful passage of over six weeks, and were subjected to all sorts of privations. The "cabouse" or cooking-house, was washed overboard off the coast of Donegal, and my aunt, Mrs. M'Henry, besides her own violent sickness, had to nurse her sick baby night and day, till her arms bore the marks for many months.

James M'Henry seems to have had the same passion for exploring America as he had for exploring the glens and hills around Lame, for we find him singing, "Oft as by fair Ohio's side," etc. But his wife preferred a more domestic life and settled in Philadelphia, where she lived at 32 South Second Street, supervising the education of her four children: Alexander, James, George, and Mary (Mrs. Cox) — all of whom became famous in after life. Their father practiced medicine also in Philadelphia, but seemed to have a greater fondness of literature; and he became noted in America for the vigour with which he employed his pen as poet, novelist, playwright, and as the literary champion of his native land.

This feeling is strongly expressed in *The Hearts of Steel*, his second great novel. Its sub-title — *The Saxon and the Celt* — indicates its nature; for it tells of the English spoliation of Irish chiefs during the various English invasions. Colonel Rosendale is represented as an officer in the army of William III, who, by his seizure of the estate of MacManus in Meath, became Lord Rosendale; while MacManus fled to Glenariff, to nurse vengeance on the English, and founded the secret society, *The Hearts of Steel*. But after much blood and torture the tale ends with Isabella, niece and heiress of MacManus, marrying a Rosendale, and thus bringing back the blood of MacManus to their native home in Meath.

The Hearts of Steel is full of moving incidents and hair-breadth escapes, and though less artistic than *O'Halloran*, both novels should be read and re-read again by all Ulstermen and women of today, for the reading of them again would help all creeds and classes now to understand and sympathise with each other's difficulties better than any other books I know of. The spirit that produced *The Hearts of Steel* is not yet dead; nor is the spirit of intolerant oppression that caused it dead either! But the sooner they play fair and then join hands, like Rosendale and MacManus, the better for all parties — as the author has well shown!

M'Henry generally spoke his mind without mincing words, and was thought to be "flighty" and too much of an idealist; he regarded Andrew Jackson as the foremost American patriot? He delighted to have men of letters at his board, and usually assumed the leadership. In Philadelphia he edited for some years *The American Monthly Magazine*; and he thus came in contact with the poet Longfellow, whose poems, during his student years, M'Henry published in this magazine, which was then the first of its kind in America.

Dr. M'Henry also wrote numerous other works, including such prose Tales as: "*The Wilderness or Braddock's Times;*", "*A Spectre of the Forest, or Annals of the Housatonic;*" "*The Betrothed of Wyoming;*" "*Meredith, or the Mystery of the Mischianza,*" a tale of the American Revolution; his longer poems include: "*Waltham,*" a Revolutionary Tale in 3 Cantos; "*The Antideluvians, or the World Destroyed,*" a narrative poem in 10 Books. And this heavy list is exclusive of his extant volume of 31 Poems, dedicated to Sir James Mackintosh, M.P., which I received from his daughter, Mrs Mary M'Henry Cox, a few months before her recent death. [3 Nov 1906 at Wayne, Philadelphia].

This volume contains *The Blessing of Friendship*, which is probably the best of his longer pieces; there are also some well-known local songs, such as *The Maid of Tobergill*. M'Henry's poems are often after the manner of Moore's and deal more with outside nature than with internal character.

The poet's muse also drew him to the tragic stage: his principal tragedy, called *The Usurper*, was acted in Philadelphia by the best cast in the city for some two nights before an enthusiastic Irish-American audience; and the Mayor of Philadelphia, quite a literary man, wrote the prologue to the play. This was about the year 1829, when O'Connell's campaigns and the Catholic Emancipation Act made Ireland the universal theme, but the manager of the theatre, F. C. Wemyss, being English, and not relishing the tone of *The Usurper*, prevented its further performance in his theatre. He was then accused of slighting "native talent," and of being an unpatriotic American, and had to defend himself against an angry crowd, and M'Henry transferred his drama to the theatre in Arch Street.

On the 18 October, 1842, Dr. M'Henry was appointed American Consul at Derry, by President Tyler, and held the office till his death. His wife did not return with him to Ireland; she and her four children, in Philadelphia, grew and flourished with the growth of the city. M'Henry is said to have managed most of his consular business in Belfast, where his genial enthusiasm made him always welcome in literary circles and where his son, James M'Henry, jun., found his wife, Lydia Gardner, whose brother, James Gardner, still conducts a business in Belfast. Riding in from Maxwellswalls, near Connor, to Larne, on a wet day, Dr. M'Henry contracted an illness which developed rapidly. All the physicians about Lame called to offer their services to the distinguished doctor and author and consul, where he lay in Stewart's hotel, but all in vain; and the little maid in the hotel, 'tis said, seeing the blank faces of the retiring physicians, ran into the author's bedroom, saying, "Oh! Doctor, Doctor, I know you are going to die! And I am fearful, fearful for your immortal soul. Oh, Doctor, what about your soul?"

"My dear girl," said he, quietly, "I am in great bodily pain, and every word costs me a pang, but my mind is at perfect ease; I know whom I have trusted. He who has led me in all my wanderings over sea and land will not now desert me at the last."

And there, "The Bard of Larne" died in his native town, on 21 July, 1845, at the age of 59 years. He was buried beside his mother, Mary Smiley, in the grounds of the old church, at Inver.

The following inscription is on his grave: [where his birth date is incorrect by 10 years]

IN MEMORY OF
MARY SMILEY,
WIFE OF GEORGE M'HENRY.

Born 1765. Died June 21 1827.

AND OF HER SON,
JAMES MCHENRY, M.D.
Born Dec. 20, 1795.   Died July 21, 1845.

Some dozen years ago his distinguished daughter, Mary M'Henry Cox (widow of J. Belangee Cox), of Philadelphia, gave his painting to her cousin, Sir Hugh Smiley, who very thoughtfully presented it to the local corporation, and it is now "skied" in the Larne Town Hall.

His most celebrated son was James M'Henry, who learned business in Philadelphia, then went to England, where he was one of the first importers of American produce. In Liverpool he was made the victim of a gigantic failure, but afterwards retrieving his position, he invited all his creditors to a dinner and there in every man's napkin was a cheque for all his money and interest. This dramatic coup gave great confidence in young M'Henry's probity. He became financial agent to the Queen of Spain; he floated the bonds for the American Great Western and Atlantic Railway; his reputation was extended by his lordly hospitality in his London mansion beside Holland House in Kensington. He was also agent for the empress Eugenie of France; and it was to his Kensington mansion that Napoleon III first went on coming to England after his defeat at Sedan in 1870, and in that Kensington mansion the French royalists often met; and there schemes were laid for the restoration of the young prince Imperial to the throne of France. But the Zulu assegai, by piercing the prince, frustrated the plans and saved the French Republic.

Source: Ulster Journal of Archaeology, Second Series, Vol. 14, No. 2/3 (May - Aug., 1908), pp. 127-132, James MacHenry, Author of "O'Halloran," "Hearts of Steel," etc., etc.
Author(s): W. Clarke-Robinson
Published with the kind permission of: Ulster Archaeological Society

Bibliography and Suggested Reading

Beiner, Guy (2018) *Forgetful Remembrance: Social Forgetting and Vernacular Historiography of a Rebellion in Ulster.* [Kindle Edition]. Oxford: Oxford University Press.

Clarke-Robinson, W (1908) 'James MacHenry, Author of "O'Halloran", "Hearts of Steel," etc., etc.', in *Ulster Journal of Archaeology: Second Series, Vol. 14, No. 2/3*, pp. 127-132. (Note: reproduced in full within this edition of O'Halloran).

Dornan, Stephen (2009) 'Irish and American Frontiers in the Novels of James McHenry', *Journal of Irish and Scottish Studies*, pp. 139-156.

LLAJ (1839) *Larne Literary and Agricultural Journal, no. 9.* This article, part of a local history series, was probably written by Rev. Classon Porter of Larne.

Mitchell, Claire (2022) *The Ghost Limb: Alternative Protestants and the Spirit of 1798.* Belfast: Beyond The Pale.

O'Connor Morris, William (1898) *Ireland 1494-1868.* Cambridge: The University Press.

Young, Robert M. (1893) *Ulster in '98, Episodes and Anecdotes.* Belfast: Marcus Ward & Co. Ltd Available online:
https://books.google.com.au/books/about/Ulster_in_98.html

Latharna Press

Latharna Press is an imprint of Leschenault Press, a small, independent publisher and publishing assistance service. We aim to give a platform for local authors to tell local stories that might otherwise be overlooked by mainstream, traditional publishing houses.

And what is our idea of local?

Well, our name probably best illustrates that.

We are based on the shores of a small inlet in Western Australia, but we are named for a part of the minor-kingdom of Dalriada[3].

Latharna means 'descendants of Lathar', he was the son of King Úgaine Mór (or so the legend goes). The town that sprang up where the River Inver flows into the lough is now called, Larne. Strangely, that lough and our Aussie inlet are quite similar.

So we are named for a Northern Irish town, yet based half a world away, and that's the answer – we take local stories by local writers from across the world and make them available on the global stage.

This book, *O'Halloran; or, The Insurgent Chief* is based mostly in and around Larne and was written by Dr James McHenry, a son of Larne; so we thought it would be a very suitable first title in the Latharna imprint.

---

[3] Latharna was a territory, or túath, that was part of the Ulaid (Ulster) minor-kingdom of Dál nAraidi (written and pronounced variously as Dál Riata, Dál Riada or Dalriada).